⟨UAUHTÉMO⟩

DESCENT OF THE SUN PRIESTS

DL DAVIES

BOOKSIDE Press

BOOKSIDE Press

BookSide Press
877-741-8091
www.booksidepress.com
orders@booksidepress.com

CONTENTS

CHAPTER 1

He circled the soldier's camp, climbing ever higher and the world slowly fell away. Down below he saw the Commander, his Sergeant and others looking upwards at him; as he watched, all of them bowed in the way of bidding him good journey, and he waggled his wings dipping first left and then right in recognition. The Commander, having done what he came for began to limp off, leaning on his cane as he walked. A moment later he was followed by his Sergeant and Lieutenant but Qualaktec and Twuondan—his own two Sergeants—stood and stared upwards as long as they could see him.

He climbed the uplift as high as he could reach, being carried well inland by the winds. Below him the soldier's camp and near-by town lay stretched out across the land and the town's main center gave way to farmlands and other outlying businesses that all such towns and cities need for support. The mountain range drew ever closer and with it came cooler air.

Only after he felt he could climb no higher did he head out towards the south and the great city where the Mayan Emperor lived. He saw the size of the message package his Commander gave him and felt the weight so he knew without question a great many things were covered by these messages; which increased his desire to obey.

The prevailing winds today swept down from the northeast, swinging across the land and being forced up by the lofty mountains, creating the uplifts that all birdmen

need to carry out their duties. When he was before his Commander and had stared off towards the south, he felt the breeze against the back of his neck and watched the movement of scattered clouds as they glided on by. This helped him think he would be able to deliver the messages before Father Inti settled himself down into the west for the night; this, among other things, drove him on.

He flew well inland; closer to the great mountain range that formed the backbone of the land. Looking off to his left he could clearly see the great waters where Inti first showed his face every morning. Even from the distance he flew he could see tiny waves forming and flowing inland towards the shore.

He flew on and slowly, fist by fist, the sun moved ever westward. He was watching for the outlines of a large bay that reached well inland from the vast waters that lay to the east. He had never been this far south before and knew little of what to expect but he was very intelligent and his memory infallible and he recalled hearing descriptions of what to look for. It never occurred to him he might miss the city: it was much too large for that.

He flew over vast areas of jungle. The canopy below him was a solid green for as far as the eye could see much of the time. He saw hundreds of brightly-colored birds flitting from limb to limb, while other, larger birds soared nearby at times. In each and every case the bird in view was either looking for food or trying to keep from becoming food. A great eagle soared nearby. He screed his wild sweet cry and the raptor replied and came in closer for a better look, not he had to get close, considering how good an eagle's eyesight is. Perhaps he just wondered what kind of eagle Cuauhtémoc was and thought maybe he was the grandfather of all eagles everywhere.

The two soared on, nearly wingtip to wingtip for awhile and then the raptor veered off and went back to its search for food. It was now late enough in the spring it would have long since taken a mate and there would be eaglets in the nest and the young of any species are always hungry.

He grew very thirsty. There were no practical means of carrying water, nor was that much of a problem for it was rare any birdman would fly more than two fists of the sun—about two hours—without landing in some village along the route, and while there were a great many villages and towns below he could land in, doing so would delay him, and he was not willing to risk it.

He also grew hungry. This, at least, was something he could work on since he had some limited supplies of dried fruit and meat that he carried along with his other survival supplies. He reached his right hand down into the pouch under him, located a strip of dried meat and began biting off pieces of it, chewing it up and swallowing. While the food helped fill him it made him even thirstier; he decided the trade-off was not worth it and from then on he ignored both needs.

Inti was heeled well into the west before he finally spotted the city of the Mayan Emperor. Below, the landscape was steadily changing. Where there had been vast stretches of jungle beneath his wings; there were now numerous villages and larger towns strewn across the countryside. Below him he could see farmers working in their fields. The crops were starting to ripen and that meant raids by birds and other animals intent on an easy, tasty meal. The farmers, of course, were not about to put up with this and he could see small boys ranging throughout their fields, throwing stones at birds, and one particularly persistent band of monkeys was keeping several young boys busy until the shadow of his wings passed over them. Then ancient instinct kicked in; to them, the shadow meant a great eagle or hawk was in the sky, both were deadly enemies to the monkey folk. The entire band headed towards the safety of the trees, giving the children below a break before the primeval warfare would break out again.

Several eagles joined him as they had been doing since he had left early in the day. As was his habit, he greeted them with the cries they made and they responded in kind.

By the time he came up on the city it had grown very late. Off to the west the sun hung little more than a thumb's thickness above the distant mountain. He could see a great body of water stretching inland and two curving fingers of land reached out into the sea from the bay like a finger and thumb pinching off the water from the ocean. A large river flowed into the bay and everywhere he looked he saw houses and roads and people moving about, busy with the life they led.

By now three eagles followed along at his side. These were young ones, full-sized, but wearing the plumage of the immature. It was impossible for him to tell if they were all males or females or mixed, but they were too young yet to have nests and nestlings of their own, and perhaps he was one of the more interesting things to fly through their skies this day. He screed welcoming cries at them and they answered him with wild cries of their own.

The favorable winds that carried him all day and provided the uplifts he needed to gain altitude to continue on, were rapidly dying out, as the sun hung over the distant mountains. He swung around once he located the palace where the Emperor lived. It was not hard to find since great gold suns were inlaid on the faces of the buildings and there were a great many paintings done everywhere and the palace was surrounded by many gardens and trees and was beautifully kept up. The three eagles that were following him moved in closer; at times it almost seemed to him he could reach out and touch their wingtips. He watched them as much as he could, because except for the one time when his Mother Eagle landed and had captured the rat he had put out for her, he had never been this close. He could see individual feathers and how the passing air ruffled them about and he saw the movement of the raptor's eyes as they looked first at him and then around and then back again.

One of the juveniles changed position and flew over his head. He glanced upward and laughed aloud. "Brother Eagle, I do hope you do not need the *toidi* right now; it would be a sad thing to show up before the Emperor covered with eagle droppings . . . not that I wouldn't be honored; of course. He laughed at the thought and then focused his mind on where to land.

His orders were quite clear: bring the messages to the Emperor and see they were put directly into his hands. Exactly how he was supposed to do this was left entirely up to him. The palace was drawing nearer. Most buildings everywhere had flat roofs; landing on any one of them would be easy. This was especially so of the palace; this building was much larger than any other in the city; with the exception of the great pyramid of the Sun Priests, which was not too far away, more towards the south.

He located a very large rooftop and aimed himself at it. His honor guard, as he had come to think of them, followed him as he made his final descent. He saw perhaps ten or so people on the roof he chose; even as he watched, they all faced him and bowed deeply, which astonished him: they couldn't know that he was coming; could they? Even if they did, why would they bow so respectfully before him? He was only a birdman; and a very young one at that. No sooner had that unlikely thought entered his mind than he saw the shadow of his wings moving steadily up the side of the building. Of course! They were worshiping Father Inti, and since he was flying directly from the west, the Sun was at his back and he was between them and their deity.

He was much closer now. He could make out different individuals and the way they were dressed. The Lieutenant headdress he wore for some days before he returned it to its rightful owner had a few fairly short feathers to mark his rank. The feather headdress of the Commander had more feathers and the feathers were much longer and more beautiful; but the headdresses some of the people below wore were the largest and longest and most beautifully crafted he had ever seen. This was surely the Emperor himself and probably members of his Royal Court.

He was very close now and for reasons he could not guess, the three eagles that had been with him for over a fist of the sun were still with him. He made his final approach and gave forth his wild cry to warn the people below he was coming down; as he screed, the three raptors with him also joined in, and the people below stopped their bowing, stood up, and shaded their eyes with their hands; trying to see against the blinding brilliance of their god.

There was a generous gap in the group somewhat to his left and he leaned that way and headed for it. In a very few more heartbeats he would be down. Father Inti was just now kissing the mountain peaks; he had fulfilled his promise to his Commander. This day the Emperor, who was just to his right, would have the messages in his hands. He had completed his promise and he felt pleased.

Then almost in the last moment an old man stepped out from the small crowd and with his eyes shaded by his right hand, he seemed to stare directly at the incoming birdman. Someone's grandfather had just stepped into his landing area! In the same instant he saw that the old man wore a feathered cloak around his shoulders and the hand he shaded his eyes with held the most beautifully crafted headdress of all. This old man was his Emperor and he was about to fly directly into him.

He was too close to veer off and moving too slow to even hope to be able to fly over the Emperor. Trained reflexes kicked in and he leaned hard to his left in an effort to avoid what would be an absolute disaster. His left wingtip made contact with the stone rooftop and friction spun him around like a top; an instant later the beak of his wings also scraped across the stone and for just an eye blink or so the tail of his wings was higher than his head and he was flying backwards. Then all movement ceased; he stuck his feet out and they made contact with the stone rooftop—and he felt nothing.

Wings were not made for long flights. The cross bar he sat on was not very comfortable and the foot rest even less so and there was nothing to protect his body from the air as he flew through it. With all factors working against him, his body—and his legs especially—had grown very cold and with the cold he lost most of his feeling.

He dismounted his wings, or at least made every effort to do so, as he looked he could see the damage his unorthodox landing made to the beak and left wingtip of Xymatoc's wings: it was not good but it was repairable. He bent down to untie the message packet, and toppled forward, only barely catching himself before his face hit the stone. He looked up and the sun was now just touching the horizon.

Being on his knees, even though he couldn't feel them, seemed to be a good idea. He bowed deeply before the setting sun; he placed his right hand over his left shoulder, his fingers splayed widely and did the same with his other hand to the opposite side. "I thank you Father Inti for giving me safe flight this day, that I might obey your commands, and deliver your messages as I promised." He struggled erect. As he did, the three eagles circled overhead, flying quite low and they screed out their calls to him. He lifted his head and responded. "K-e-e-e-r," he cried to them and then spoke; "Thank you for seeing me safely here, my brothers; now go and fly to Father Inti and tell him I have obeyed His will and have done as He commanded."

The three eagles circled once more, gave their wild cries one last time and since whatever curiosity they had was satisfied, they headed back toward their home range and the nests that awaited them. This lay directly west, and as they flew into the setting sun, it seemed to the observers this strange youth could both talk to, and understand what the eagles said, and that the great raptors obeyed his commands. The people stared, round-eyed, and said nothing.

Cuauhtémoc turned to his Emperor, who now stood directly in front of him. He bowed deeply before him and as he did, he realized he had no idea of the proper way of addressing him. "Greatest Mayan," he began, "this day the Commander of the northern soldier's camp ordered me to bring this message packet to you and to tell you your Empire is being invaded by strangers from a far land who come in great boats. The Commander, however, did not order me to fly into you and knock you down: please forgive me for that was never my intent;" and he bowed deeply once again.

The Emperor nodded to him and then asked; "Child, why do you tremble so, is there something wrong?"

"No, Greatest Mayan, I am just cold. From the time Inti was a fist or so above the great waters until just now, I was in the air, bringing these messages to you as I have been commanded. For reasons I do not understand, the higher I climb, the colder the air. This seems wrong to me as it is logical the closer one gets to Inti, the warmer it should be, but a thousand tall trees above the ground the air can be quite cold." As he spoke he began to shiver more and he fought to keep his teeth from chattering.

"A thousand tall trees?" one of the men asked politely.

"Yes; that is how we birdmen speak it. If I were to climb to the topmost branches of a tall tree I would be one tall tree above the ground. If I could somehow put a second tall tree on top of that and climb up into its topmost branches I would be two tall trees above the ground. While no birdman knows exactly how many tall trees he is above the ground; we use such phrases to describe things. A hundred tall trees are about average for most birdmen. A thousand tall trees mean we are as high as we can climb and we can go no higher." One of the men who wore the headdress of higher rank turned slightly green and backed quickly away, moving toward the wall of the entryway to the roof.

His hands were shaking badly by now. Only by concentrating could he make himself untie the knots that held the message packet onto his wings and having done this difficult task, he handed the package to the Emperor who stood before him. He in turn handed the package to the one who Cuauhtémoc thought on approach was the Emperor; "We shall look this over later," he told the man, "for now, we will see to the needs of this child." The Emperor turned back to him. "Do you hunger, child? Do you thirst; do you have needs that must be attended to?"

"Yes, Greatest Mayan, thank you for asking; I am both hungry and thirsty but the other needs I have taken care of as I flew here." He stopped and thought for a single heartbeat and an impish idea formed in his mind: "Yes," he said, feigning sadness, "even as we speak, two of your townsmen stand on the edge of this very city. One is saying – and he pretended to brush himself off, a disgusted expression on his face – 'What manner of bird was that?' And the second one replies – again he pretended to wipe himself down – 'Never mind that, what manner of betel leaf does he chew?'"

He stared his Emperor in the eyes and his own eyes twinkled merrily. The Emperor stared at him for just a moment and then his wizen face split into a broad smile. "How terrible for them," the old man said and began to laugh very softly.

"This is why we birdmen say, 'never look up.' And if you do anyway—'" he stared at the sky with his mouth agape, then reaching up with his right hand he carefully pushed up on his chin, shutting his mouth.

"That's very wise; under the conditions. You look exhausted; we will have you put in our map-maker's room; he is out chasing after some map-drawer he has been raving about these last few months."

"Thank you, Greatest Mayan, it will be nice to get warm again even though I will have to live through the prickles to get there;" he said with a deep bow.

"Prickles;" the Emperor asked, surprised, "what are you talking about; child?"

"Have you ever slept wrong on your arm or sat on a leg for awhile, only to find that you have no feeling in it and that the flesh feels cold, Greatest Mayan? My grandfather is a Healer up in one of your north-most villages and he says there are hollow reeds of sorts that our blood runs through. He also says there are tiny roadways that carry messages from our brains. It is these messages that allow us to move about and walk and talk. When one has sat or laid on the arm or leg, the pressure prevents the flow of these things. As the feeling comes back there will be a strong tingling sensation that is disagreeable. It will be the same when my body warms back, up but instead of just one arm or leg, it will be all of me; I am not looking forward to that."

"Yes; I understand, child, and I have done exactly that; slept on an arm wrong but I never knew why it was so." The Emperor turned to the same man he handed the message package to: "See that this young birdman is taken care of, Quoholocet, see he is properly fed; and a good warming bath should help him regain feeling. I do not like how cold this child's body is; that can't be good. Once that is done I want to look into these messages; perhaps they are part of the answers we have prayed for. They must be important to send a child half-way across my Empire to deliver them."

"Yes, father," Prince Quoholocet said and bowed to the old man before him. He turned to Cuauhtémoc: "Follow me, birdman; are you able to walk? I will have some guards escort you if you feel unsteady."

"Yes, Great Prince, I can walk if I do not move too fast. I can't feel my feet at all and I thank you for asking," he replied courteously.

The Prince eyed the birdman before him with an odd expression on his face. Things were happening very suddenly, and at the present there were many gaps in his understanding, and he was wary he didn't jump to conclusions too quickly. He turned; off to his right two women stood, an older, mature woman and a young girl not much older than the birdman; if any. "You will see to the needs of this child and see he is properly cared for.

We will speak more on this sometime tomorrow morning." This last was directed at Cuauhtémoc; who bowed again.

The two women came and took him one by each arm and led him off. "Birdman; your flesh is cold!" the older of the two said to him; he nodded.

"Your hands feel like fire to me, but in a good way," he admitted. By now he was starting to shake badly and he only barely controlled the chattering of his teeth. The two females led him into the entry way, down stone stairs, and into a corridor and turned right. By the time they reached the place they were going to his trembling reached near-violence. The older woman, now very concerned, immediately led him over to an ornate bath that was filled with water that flowed into the bath and then out again in a never-ending stream: she stuck her hand in the water for a moment.

"The water only feels barely warm to my hand, but in the state that you are in, I doubt you would want it warmer anyway;" she said. He nodded his head as best he could because his lower jaw was bouncing up and down uncontrollably. He stripped off what little he wore and let them drop to the floor.

He stepped into the water and inhaled through his teeth. "You are right; it feels like I am being boiled alive; I am sure I would not want it warmer than this."

"Watch him, Eilei, while I go and get him some food;" the older woman said. The young girl nodded her head. She watched the adult as she left the room. The moment she vanished around the corner she slipped out of her clothing and into the water with him. She was easily the most beautiful girl he had ever seen. Her features were very even and she had gorgeous eyes and long dark hair that hung down to her waist. Her body was trim and she had not yet started to bud: from the evidence of his eyes he thought she was younger than he had first believed and was probably even younger than his own tender years. She smiled at him and he smiled in return although under the circumstances it was more of a grimace for his body, and his legs in particular, felt like they were on fire.

"Oh; you must hurt so much," she said concernedly, "what can I do to help?"

"Very little I'm afraid," he admitted, "my body must warm up. Until it does I will be like this. It will only take a thumb of the sun to do it, or perhaps less, but until it does it will feel like forever to me."

"I can help," she insisted. She moved close to him and began to rub the calves of his legs between her hands. This did hurt; but he swallowed and nodded his head.

"I've never had anything hurt so much and feel so good at the same time," he admitted between clenched and chattering teeth. She kept kneading his legs, first one and then the other, keeping her hands under the water at all times. After a bit the older woman returned with two other women; between them they had enough food to feed a small crowd.

"Eilei; what do you think you are doing?" the older woman gasped, scandalized.

"The birdman's legs are paining him, Mother, this is the only way I knew to help;" she said very calmly—she kept rubbing his legs and they were not hurting nearly as bad as they had only a short while ago. The woman shook her head and the three of them brought in trays of food.

Cuauhtémoc did not know food could taste so good. Even the corn soup that was the staple of the Mayan people had other things in with it; maybe meat and fish, he really couldn't tell. It had also been seasoned with herbs and some salt had been added. He thanked the women profusely and sitting nearly chest deep in water he dug in and made a pig of himself.

The three women watched him eat and nodded to themselves. There is, in the female psyche, that which enjoys seeing the males around her appreciating a good meal. Preparing food is a thing a woman does every day and it gives her a sense of accomplishment to see the men and children of her world pleasuring in her handiwork.

Once he was done he bowed politely and thanked the women. The older woman looked at the girl who was making no effort to leave the water. "Take care, Eilei, and make sure your father does not catch you in here." The corners of the girl's mouth turned upwards in a sly smile and she nodded. The three women headed towards the door, trays with uneaten food in their hands. They stopped just short of the door, turned around and looked again, and then they shook their heads and left.

As the three women left; Cuauhtémoc permitted his eyes to travel around the room. It was built of stone that had been quarried out of the distant mountain and brought down through brute strength and gravity. Once carefully placed according to detailed plans, the craftsmen had carefully rubbed the walls smooth, and then probably over many succeeding generations of craftsmen, painted the walls with colorful scenes taken out of different Mayan legends, tales that depicted different gods and goddesses doing improbable things. It was very bright and beautiful and there was more on the walls than he could see with only a short, single glance. He climbed out of the bath and carefully dried himself off. His hands were not shaking as much as they were a short while ago; by morning's light he would undoubtedly be back to his usual self.

Cuauhtémoc had put in a very long day and had traveled further and faster than any man had ever gone before: he was exhausted. Eilei guided him over to where the bed was and helped him lay down. Neither put their clothes back on, which was normal, since most people slept in the nude. "You are still cold, birdman; I will lay behind you and help you get warmed up." Having said this, she climbed in behind him and pulled the cover over them both. It was wool and very soft; probably alpaca, he thought.

He lay on his side with her body firmly against his back; she felt very warm and soft against him and he laid his head on a pillow and closed his eyes; he felt fatigue sweep through him and he began to relax and let the day's activities run through his mind. After awhile she started rubbing his chest and belly; gently; it was very nice. Then her hand moved gradually lower and lower and he heard her soft giggle. He thought if he was not quite so tired he'd show her what happened to beautiful young girls who did things like this.

CHAPTER 2

He slept. He found himself standing on a high bluff overlooking the ocean. The waters were calm and beautiful and a white sandy beach stretched out along the shore as far as the eye could see. There were birds there, birds with long legs and long curved bills and they ran up and down the beach, digging in the sand with their beaks, looking for insects. How he knew this he didn't know and he had no idea he was dreaming.

The tides lapped against the sand; stirring the whiteness around. Some of the sand was pulled away by the restless waters but what the ocean took it also replaced, so the beach stayed as it had been, incredibly beautiful and peaceful.

While he watched, he saw a small splash of water reach deeper into the sand. Only this time when the tide retreated it left a red gash in the beach. Not much of a gash, it is true, but a gash none the less. As he watched; the tide did it again and yet again. The waters grew stronger, more violent, and the red tides reached further into the white sands and each time they pulled back they left a bloody red streak in the whiteness.

The sea formed hands with ugly claws on them. They were the claws of some hideous beast, and where they raked the beach, only bare rock remained. A face shaped in the ocean's depths and came close to shore. The claw-like hands belonged to the foul creature whose face was twisted in unnatural ways and its thin lips lie at an angle across its face like a gash made with a dull knife; more torn than cut.

By now large sections of the beach was ripped out, and nothing remained except blood-stained rocks that were jagged and sharp, and not smoothly worn; with only a few scattered patches of sand that was no longer pristine. What had been a scene of incredible beauty was now ugly and decayed and there was a stench of rotting flesh in the air.

He understood, without knowing how, that a very long time passed; centuries rather than years or decades and the beach was now defiled beyond recognition. He looked up at the sun, hanging like a golden balloon in an azure sky. "No, Father Inti, this must not be. Please, I beg of you, make it back as it was." In the blink of an eye it was so. Well, no, not exactly the same. There were still some fingers of the red tide eroding the sand away and the face in the water was yet still there, but it was much better.

Cuauhtémoc looked at the sun in a bemused manner and saw it seemed to be coming closer to him. He could make out the outline of a man. There were arms and legs and a body, but the face could not be discerned, because of a white light that filled the earth with its beauty.

"Please, Father Inti, make the shore as it was before" he pleaded.

"I cannot;" a gentle, quiet voice said to him. "That which you first saw is past and the past cannot be changed. The second thing you saw yet lies in the future and this part *can* be changed; what you see now and what you saw then are two different fates. The white sands are the Mayan people, the children I have made. The Mayan people now stand upon the brink of a great change that is taking place all over the world. If the second scene prevails; many great nations will fall and become shadows of their former selves. If the scene you now look upon prevails, then the countries shall flourish and in the end, the scene you saw first will be the final fate of all nations."

"Then make it so, Father Inti; you are mighty and there is nothing you cannot do." As he spoke he could feel tears run down his cheeks to fall on the ground at his feet.

"I can do anything except break my own vow. Any promise I make I will not break. It doesn't matter to whom that vow is made or what that one does afterward; a promise is a promise and I cannot and will not do otherwise."

"Then *I* shall, Father Inti; tell me what to do and I will do it, this I swear on Xymatoc's wings; this evil must not be allowed to take place," he vowed.

"I cannot tell you that Cuauhtémoc. The future is in a fluid state and must change as circumstances change. This much I *can* say; you have within you the ability to bring about your heart's desires. If you persevere, if you work at it with the same single-minded intent you have shown on all else you do, then you will succeed. And if you do this, then I will give you any reward that you ask, if it is within my power."

"I wish no reward Father Inti; only that I may continue to serve you first, the Greatest Mayan second, and these your many children; look into my heart see it is so."

Cuauhtémoc knew his words pleased Inti, and even though he could only see the great god's eyes, he knew He smiled down upon him. "You will now go back to sleep, my child. When you awake you will not remember this dream until you have need of it. It is not good for mortals to know too much of the future, because such knowledge confuses, and confusion begets mistakes."

He found himself on his knees, face-first on the sand and his arms were out-stretched toward the sun which had returned to its former position. Then he awoke.

For just a flicker he remembered he had dreamed, and remembered the dream was very important, but even as the memory floated to the surface of his mind the oily thoughts slipped through his mental fingers and were gone . . . and in another heartbeat even that vanished.

He lay on his side as he had lain when he fell asleep. He became aware of a hand on his shoulder and the pressure of a young girl's body up against his back and with these things the memory of the girl's activities just as he was falling asleep sprang into his mind. He smiled to himself. That was an interesting thing she had done, but for the moment, internal pressures took precedence over all other matters.

He eased himself quietly out from under Eilei's arm; trying not to waken her. The call of nature now controlled his immediate future; he needed the toidi in the worst way.

In the palace of the Emperor, at least, a toidi was not a simple trench dug into the ground or a pot that needed to be carried out in the morning. Instead, there was water flowing constantly through a place for such, much like the bath that he'd taken earlier. He used the facility for the intended purpose and then started looking around. The Emperor said to put him in the map-maker's room and from what he could see; that was exactly where he was. Some of the walls were covered with maps of every size and description, from small sketches not much larger than his hand on up to giant-sized stretches of paper that covered large sections that were otherwise covered with artwork depicting fanciful scenes. There were many rolls of parchment laid out in neat stacks; it was logical to think these too were yet more maps.

Up against one wall were several three-legged supports of a kind he had never seen before; one held yet another map. This one was better-drawn and more detailed than any of the other maps in the room. As he looked; familiarity took hold. Not only had he seen this map before; he had drawn it. Memory flooded his mind. It was a year and a half earlier and the rainy weather was upon them. He sat in Dispatcher's hut over several days, drawing this particular map, a map that covered an area he had flown over on one of his message runs.

Cuauhtémoc began to laugh softly to himself, trying to keep the noise down so he wouldn't waken the girl sleeping peacefully not far away. The Emperor said he was to be put into the map-maker's room because the man was out chasing after some map-drawer he'd been raving about. The conclusion was inevitable. The map-maker was out in the jungles, looking for the boy who spent the night in his bed, sleeping with the most beautiful girl in the world.

This thought brought him back to the present; he turned and walked silently over to where the girl lay asleep. It was much warmer down near the ocean than the high camps where he had lived all of his life; as such, blankets and other covers could be too warm at night. Either she had pushed the blanket down or his getting out of bed had done so but now only her lower half was covered. She now laid half on her side and half on her back. Her dark hair lay swirled around her head loosely and her eyes were closed in peaceful slumber. As he looked down upon this scene of innocence; a tender, protective feeling washed over him, a feeling he had never felt before. It was an attraction—not of the body but of the spirit—and it pulled powerfully upon his soul.

He leaned over and smelled her hair, just over her right ear, and breathed in deeply. She smelled of youth and innocence: how a scent could elicit such information was beyond him; but it did anyway. He brushed her cheek gently with the back of his right fingers and she stirred in her sleep and a sweet smile played at the corners of her mouth.

He backed up a step and stared at her, memorizing every detail effortlessly. To him; she seemed more like a sleeping goddess than anyone of flesh and blood. He glanced around the room. All of his senses were uncommonly sharp; he could see quite well in the moon-lit room. His eyes fell on one of the three-legged stands the map-maker used; this one had a large blank piece of paper on it as if the man was going to draw something and then left suddenly. He glanced around. Everything he needed was right before him and the qualities of the supplies were far better than anything he'd ever used before. Which was a given since he was in the palace of the Greatest Mayan and the Emperor would only stock the very best.

He carried the three-legged stand out onto the patio next to a private garden and set it down. Another two short trips and he had all of the inks and drawing sticks he needed. With the image of the young girl fresh in his mind he touched one of the sticks to the ink and lifted it up to draw, and instead of a blank sheet, he found a pair of eyes staring out at him in calm wisdom. It took him less than a heartbeat to understand the sheet was still blank and the eyes were in his mind and not on paper. He stood transfixed as images began to flow through his mind. It was his grandfather when he was three years old and the old man was watching him as he struggled to understand the things he had just been told. Again; it was his grandfather as he watched him prepare a complicated potion for a sick child—he was seven at the time. Next; it was the Greatest Mayan as he looked upon him as he stood shivering upon the rooftops; and it stayed the Greatest Mayan and did not change. He pondered the expression, thinking how much the Emperor and his grandfather looked alike; not as twin brothers might look alike—but how?

He came to understand both men had wisdom within their eyes; wisdom born of many years and then, deep within he saw yet another pair of eyes, eyes he had seen quite recently, eyes infinitely more wise; and even deeper within a voice said softly; "Not yet, child; the time to remember is not yet." Then that impression was gone before it fully reached his conscious mind. He began to draw.

This was the most complicated depiction he had ever attempted; nothing he had ever tried before could come close. He wasn't even sure anyone had ever done such a thing; but the image of the Greatest Mayan was now as clear in his mind as if the Emperor was standing in front of him. He started with the eyes, working with both hands, dipping the sticks into the ink as needed. His left held a drawing stick with a very fine edge, the right held a second stick with a much broader edge.

He moved about, looking at the picture growing before him from different angles. He worked on the eyes awhile and then moved down to the nose and mouth; back to the eyes and then up to the forehead. Next came the ears and then back to the eyes again. All the while the waning moon moved slowly across the night sky, sending her silvery light down onto the earth below, and the paper he was filling in. Time telescoped in on him. He looked up at the sky and the moon-goddess was far to the east. What seemed no more than a few slow breaths later he looked up and the moon was directly overhead. Not much more time than that and the moon hung over the mountain tops, ready to bid the Mayan world goodbye for yet another night.

The moon-goddess dipped below the western mountains but the available light stayed the same. This seemed odd to him until he looked towards the east and saw false dawn was upon them. He had no idea how long he slept but he had spent most of the night on the drawing before him: he looked upon it and saw it was good. He had managed to capture the essence of the Mayan Emperor and the drawing seemed to blur the lines between life and art; he stared at it for a long time and wondered if anyone had ever managed to do such a thing or if he was the only one to have ever succeeded. This did not seem likely to him, but at the same time, he didn't know for sure.

Last night's meal had long since left him and his stomach grumbled over the lack. When the three women left they tool all the food with them, but there was plenty of water to drink, and that too was a need. He gave the drawing a last glance and decided he had done better than he'd thought; he went inside, found a stone cup and dipped water out of the fountain and drank deeply.

He heard a soft whimper off to his left. He turned and saw that Eilei was starting to stir; she had rolled over onto her back and her left hand was now up next to her face. He walked over and stared down at her. She was incredibly beautiful lying there and again he felt an unfamiliar pull deep within his soul. He was falling in love, and having never experienced this particular variation of that emotion, he was no better prepared for it than any other boy anywhere near his age.

"Good morning, beautiful one, did you sleep well this night?" he asked softly. She smiled and nodded and then her eyes popped open wide.

"What are you doing in the women's quarters?" she demanded, and then stopped and stared wildly around as her memory caught up with facts. "Oh no!" she wailed, "I fell asleep! I didn't mean to fall asleep. Oh; if I get caught here I will be in so much trouble." She jumped out of the bed and headed towards the door, her lithe body moving in ways that attracts the male mind; attracts and thus beguiles. He watched her go. Just as she reached for the door he called out—

"Eilei!" She stopped; one hand on the door latch and stared at him. He pointed at her clothes lying on the floor. He pointed in the Inca fashion, with a jut of his chin, the act confused her for just a moment. "If you get caught running through the palace with no clothes on, someone is going to start asking questions," he said with a smile.

"Oh, right, yes; of course; thank you birdman," she said. She crossed the distance, and with an incredibly supple movement, bent down, and scooped her clothing up in her hand. She gave him a shy, tremulous smile and headed back towards the door. Just as she touched the door release he said—

"Eilei!" She turned and stared, her eyes were wide and her lips slightly parted. At that moment Cuauhtémoc thought he had never seen a more beautiful sight. "Clothes should be worn, not carried," he said and smiled at her in good humor: she glanced down.

"Oh, yes; right. Thank you again, birdman." She started to put her clothes on, looked at him and said, "Turn your head, birdman."

"No, I don't believe that I shall—why should I? I have seen you walking towards me and walking away and walking past me in both directions. I have already seen everything you have to show, and in truth, what I have seen I like very much. Why *should* I turn my head?" He looked her over; his eyes started with her eyes, slowly dropped to her feet and then back again.

Eilei missed his theatrics; while she was staring at him; she was not looking at his face.

"My eyes are up here, Eilei," he said.

She flinched and her dark eyes jerked upwards and a confused expression came over her. "So; did you enjoy yourself last night; that thing that you were doing with your hand?" he asked, staring at her, his expression soft and gentle.

"Well, yes, I suppose so;" she said. "After all, you were in so much pain, and I know that rubbing sore muscles helps, so naturally I thought that rubbing would also help muscles that are cold."

"Not then; later; after you thought I had fallen asleep." He stared at her; an amused expression on his face. He saw the instant understanding took her.

"*You were awake?*" she demanded, aghast, and then her eyes opened wide as she realized she had just convicted herself. "I mean—you were asleep. Of course! You were asleep, and it was just a dream you had, birdman." She lifted her chin and a self-satisfied smirk came into her eyes and face; this seemed very logical, she obviously believed.

"Ah; a dream, of course," he said. "But isn't it unusual we both should have the same dream at the same time; even though neither of us were asleep? After all; why else would you be blushing so prettily?"

"I am not blushing," she sniffed and in the same moment, did so. He reached out and pulled her into his arms. She resisted for less than a heartbeat and then she hugged him in return with frantic strength. "I must not feel this way, birdman, don't you know anything?"

"Most likely not," he admitted. "As you may recall, I only came here late last night and there are a great many things I do not know. But if you wish to tell me I shall be pleased to listen." She snuggled down against him, the top of her head came to just below his chin and from the way she settled in it seemed she intended to spend the rest of her life right there in his arms; a thought that did not displease him.

It was too soon she pushed him away. "My name is Eilei, and I am the favorite daughter of Prince Quoholocet, and the youngest daughter of his favorite wife; ask around, anyone will tell you this is so. In Maya; only the oldest son of the Emperor has any guarantees. While everyone else is usually set up in a good position, there are no promises. It is even less so for daughters. We all hope to marry into wealthy families so we may be taken care of properly. When I was nine my father arraigned with our Lord Herdsman for me to be married to his oldest son when we are both old enough. They are quite wealthy and it will be a good position; Father did well by me for setting this thing up as he did."

"He is a very lucky man; how is he, is he nice, do you like him?

"How would I know? I've never met him! As I just told you; Father and Lord Herdsman set the whole thing up." Eilei wore a very impatient, irritated expression on her face, one that quickly gave way to remorse. "I'm sorry, birdman, I shouldn't have snapped at you that way."

"I think that I understand; Eilei. So tell me; do you want to marry this boy you have never seen and know nothing about?"

"Well; yes! He will inherit his father's holdings when his father grows old and he will be able to take care of me; and, ah, that is— No! I do *not* want to marry him. Since I first saw you land on the roof I can think of no one else. You are the most beautifully perfect boy I have ever seen. Are you a god; are you Inti in human form?"

He shook his head; a gentle expression on his face. "No, Eilei, I am not a god. Nor am I Inti in human form. But I understand how you feel. Very early this morning, long before you awoke, I saw you asleep; your hair all tossed about and I thought then you were the most perfect girl I had ever seen. To me, at that time and place, you looked more like a goddess than anything human. I think what we must do is to talk to Father Inti and ask him to direct us to each other, if that is his will. Otherwise, we must go our different ways. But we are both still children, and as such, we still have time to grow up. Before that, you must get dressed and get back to the women's quarters and pretend none of this happened. It is not what I wish but it is how it must be for now."

He took her clothing from her hand and helped her put it on. There really wasn't much and it didn't take very long and then, holding her hand in his, he cracked the door and looked outside into the hallway; checking for people. There were none.

"Go quickly, Eilei, and do not look back. It is still very early and if we do not hesitate you will be able to get back to where you belong without anyone being the wiser."

She gave his hand a quick squeeze and darted down the hallway and vanished around a corner. He went back into the room and gently shut the door.

The map-maker's room was large by his measure of things but it was so filled with maps, both rolled and hung from the walls that it seemed crowded. He walked through the room and out onto the patio. The sun was just now starting to peek over the ocean's waters. He placed his hands on opposite shoulders; his spread fingers formed the rays of the sun and he bowed deeply before the Sun God. "I thank you Father Inti for giving me yet another day. I vow to use this day as wisely as I can. I ask you to consider Eilei. It is my wish you give her to me and not to another, but no matter what your will may be, I shall obey you in this as I have tried to do in everything else." He again bowed deeply and then turned and re-entered the room.

The bath beckoned and he stepped into it. Last night it was like being boiled alive; today it felt just right. He took his bath in more beautiful surroundings than he could have ever imagined.

He climbed out and rubbed himself down with a coarse cloth that Eilei had shown him how to use and then put his clothes on. They would soon need to be laundered, but before he could do that, he wanted to find out exactly what was expected of him.

A sharp rap came from the door; the sound startled him. He remembered there was a knocker of some sort on the door, but since no one he had ever known had such, he had no idea of what its use was. A moment later the door opened and the older woman and two younger serving girls came in with trays filled with fresh fruit and thinly sliced meats and freshly baked bread. The aroma hit his twitching nostrils and his stomach growled in anticipation.

The serving woman and her two assistants entered the room and set the trays they carried on tables that served that purpose; all the while the woman's eyes darted about the room, looking into corners and out into the small garden just outside the other door.

"Eilei is not here, Mother serving-woman," he said politely; "she has returned to her own place."

Relief flooded the woman's face and she nodded and smiled. "Ah, good, then she returned to the women's quarters' right after I left."

Cuauhtémoc rarely ever lied about anything; ever. He did not consider things said in humor to be lies, as long as everyone understood he spoke in jest, and did not intend to deceive. "No, Mother serving-woman," he said calmly; "she left here less than a thumb ago. Last night, after I got out of the water, I was still cold and she was very concerned about me. She crawled into bed behind me and laid up close to help me get warm. Somewhere along the way we both fell asleep. When she awoke a short time ago she was very upset and fearful she would get in trouble. I looked out the door to make sure that no one would see her leaving and get the wrong impression, for we are both still children, and we slept together as children usually do." He bowed before the woman, not as he would have bowed to another male, but politely none the less.

In a few short words he neatly summed up all of the important information without showing he left much out. The woman nodded her head and sighed in relief for she didn't want Eilei to get into trouble either.

Eilei was having better luck than any young girl deserved. She made her way through the twists and turns of the palace without meeting anyone; for the day was very young yet. Even the guard who was supposed to be at the door was missing; she could see him down the hallway, chatting with one of the serving girls. Over the distance she could hear them talking softly but could not make out what they were saying. She tried to slip through the door and found it latched.

At that moment the serving girl gave a soft gasp and nudged the guard. He swung around and came over to her. "What are you doing out in the hall at this time of the morning, Eilei; your father will not be pleased when he learns of this!" The guard spoke very sternly and stared at her in a manner intended to intimidate her.

"What do you speak of, guardsman?" she asked, feigning innocence; "I thought I heard a noise as I walked past the door. I stepped out to see what it was but there was no one here; not even you. But when I tried to get back inside I found the door latched. Perhaps one of my sisters walked by and saw the door open and pushed it closed, latching it in the process."

"Ah, yes, about that—maybe I should just let you back in and say no more."

"Well; if that is your wish, guardsman," she said demurely. He operated the mechanism that opened the door and she slipped inside; both gave a sigh of relief, each for their own reasons.

⟨HAPTER 3

⟨uauhtémoc smiled at the serving women and moved politely out of their way as they placed trays of food before him. "I thank you for the food you have brought me," he said, "it smells wonderful and I am very hungry this morning. Are you three going to eat with me? I see there is enough food for many people and I enjoy having someone to talk with as I eat."

In the palace of the Emperor, as was true throughout his kingdom, the men ate before the women and children; it was not often the two would eat together. It was not consciously a sexist way of doing things, but merely a tradition that dated back many centuries, a tradition no one even questioned. But when a male did invite a female or females to join in a meal with him it was considered rude of her not to accept: the three women promptly nodded their heads and moved in closer.

"My name is Cuauhtémoc," he began, "this means 'descending eagle' in the Incan language. My name can be hard to pronounce to the Mayan tongue, so many just call me Temmo or Temoc, but most who know me just call me Inca because that is what I am. What are your names if I may ask?"

"My name is Trifalitix, Great One," the older woman said "but I like it very much when you call me 'Mother serving-woman'" and a shy expression came over her face and just for a moment he could see the young girl she once was.

He smiled back at her and nodded; "Well; you are a serving-woman, and as lovely as you are, you must surely be a mother."

Trifalitix blushed and ducked her head coyly. "You are a rascal, Great One, and no child to speak this way."

Cuauhtémoc looked at her and chuckled softly. "I am twelve years old the day after this last full moon, Mother serving-woman. Anything else you see in me comes from my grandfather, who is the wisest man I have ever known . . . and the greatest rascal as well, no doubt."

The three women burst into laughter. The unexpected answer, coupled with the mischievous twinkle in his eyes was too much for them, and they were all filled with giggles. He added one of his best smiles and laughed along with them.

Now that the ice was broken, the four ate the food the women brought, and talked throughout the entire meal. As for him, he told of his early life up in the High Reaches village, without going into too many specifics; and how the eagles and his big brother Xymatoc had come to get him and take him down to the Northern Birdman's training camp where he was trained to become a birdman. He glossed over the parts where the enemy was attacking, mentioning it only enough to explain why he came from the west and seemingly from out of the sun, to deliver what were obviously important messages for the Emperor.

The women in turn filled him in on many of the happenings that took place on a daily basis within the palace. Much of this was gossip—who was doing what and with whom—but even this taught him much about palace life. To wit, it wasn't all that different than any life he had already known, it was just being done in far wealthier surroundings. This made sense to him since all humans are flesh by definition, and because of this, the things the wealthy and privileged do is not so different from the goings-on of the common folk.

He also learned Prince Quoholocet had ordered the Mother serving-woman to take care of him, a thing he already knew, and only now discovered this order had turned into a sort of triumph for her. From her description; a great many others such as she were deeply envious.

And his arrival had become *the* hot topic throughout the entire palace staff. He also learned the two young girls with Mother serving-woman were her daughters and were named Zypolitc and Kymeninie and that a sort of power struggle had taken place among the servants as to exactly who would be taking this meal to him. Obviously, she had won, and had chosen her own daughters to come with her; much to the displeasure of many other young girls.

Time passed on fleeting wings and he was explaining again for the second and third time he was not a Great One, nor was he a god or Father Inti in human form, but only a mere birdman; when there was a sharp rap on the outer door. All four were sitting cross-legged on mats, their meal long since eaten. He stood up, seeming to float upwards in defiance of gravity as he usually did, and thus destroyed almost a fist's worth of denials; from the women's viewpoints only a god could rise up like that.

When he had been led to this room last night he watched the soldier who come with him operate the mechanism that opened the door. Then again; he saw Eilei use it just that morning. It was child's play for him to work it now. He opened the door, which swung inward, and stared up into calm brown eyes that stared back at him.

"Greatest Mayan!" he gasped in astonishment and he immediately placed his hands on opposite shoulders and bowed deeply. "Please, Greatest Mayan, won't you come in? You should not have come to me, Greatest Mayan, you should have sent for me and I would have come to you."

"I am Emperor. As such; I do as I please. For now; what pleases me is to come here and see for myself you are properly taken care of. Does this room suit you? The map-maker who usually occupies this room is off on some errand. He is seeking some map-drawer he has been pestering me about for months now. I let him go mostly to get some rest from his tongue." The Emperor smiled down on Cuauhtémoc, who smiled broadly, giving his Emperor the full benefit of that smile.

"Yes, Greatest Mayan, I remember you saying that last night; right after I handed you the messages. And look at what I have discovered." He led the Emperor the few steps needed, and the men who surrounded the great monarch moved along as well, for they too were very interested in what was taking place. He pointed to the map still sitting on the three-legged stand.

"Yes," the Greatest Mayan admitted, "that is the drawing our map-maker has been raving about; do you know who made this?"

"Yes, Greatest Mayan, and now; so do you."

"I do?" the Emperor asked, startled, and looked into Cuauhtémoc's eyes. The Emperor stared into the face of the youth before him. The child radiated joy and laughter as the sun radiates light and heat and then understanding came to the old man: "You? You are the one who drew this map?" he demanded in astonishment.

"Yes!" Cuauhtémoc exclaimed, all but doubling up in merriment. "While your map-maker is out in the jungles looking for me, I spent the night sleeping in his bed."

"So you say;" one of the men standing next to the Emperor said with a sniff.

"My name is on the map," Cuauhtémoc said quietly; "if you look down onto the lower right area you can see a drawing of the head of a descending eagle, complete with a feather falling below her. This is the eagle that chose me at birth, and marked me as her own, a mark that I will bear for the rest of my life. It is this eagle that I am named for. My name is Cuauhtémoc; which in the Incan language means 'descending eagle.'" He touched the spot in the center of his chest with tender fondness since it was his favorite story of all.

"A doodle, nothing more," the same man announced; "it doesn't mean—"

The Emperor turned and stared at the man before him. "It means 'descending eagle;' it means this birdman's name. Further;" and he raised his right hand in an imperious manner, "when it is like this it means this child, and when it is in a word-box it means 'birdman.' We have needed a good symbol for birdman for some time; and now we have one. I have decided and it is so."

The man stared back at the Emperor with a surly expression on his face. "My father served your throne as did my fathers before and this is all the thanks I get."

Cuauhtémoc stared at the man in growing disbelief. Ever since he remembered who his great-grandfather was, he made a point of learning all he could about a man who had been dead for many decades, and the one thing he was sure of was Texaquahotyl would not have put up with something like that for even a heartbeat. Evidently the Emperor also reached his limits for he stared at his servant with implacable resolve: "I have spoken!" he said and the servant bowed his head.

"Yes, Emperor Cuz—"

"Greatest Mayan," the Emperor snapped, interrupting. "Must I remind you every other thumb of the sun? I am now called Greatest . . . Mayan!"

The servant realized he had gone too far. He bowed very deeply and said, "Yes, Greatest Mayan."

That was the end of it.

The moment the Emperor and the rest entered the room, the three women gathered up all of the food and trays, and bowing deeply before everyone who entered; left. This was now men's work and a wise woman knew when to get out of the line of fire. Besides; the three picked up enough information to guarantee they would be the center of gossip the moment they got back to where they worked and they couldn't wait to start adding grist to the rumor mill.

Cuauhtémoc looked up at the Emperor and then reached out and took the monarch's right hand and sandwiched it between his own. "My grandfather told me when I was very young that those who stand upon the deeds of their fathers; do so because they have done no deeds of their own. I never understood his words, how could I, I was only six at the time; what did I know? Sometimes I think grandfathers say things like this to their grandsons just to see if they are paying attention."

He pressed the Emperor's hand gently against his face. Cuauhtémoc was nearly a free spirit locked in flesh. He knew nothing about hate or greed or lust or any of the other deadly vices of men—but he understood love and gave love as unconditionally as he was able. It would have taken a harder heart than the Emperor possessed to have not been touched by the outpouring of respect the child gave so freely.

In the background, the two youngest Princes looked at each other and grinned. No one liked this particular servant and to see him get his ears pinned back so neatly by such a young source was a treat. The two were fraternal twins, but growing up so closely, had given them almost the ability to read each other's minds. As one, both formed their right hands into fists. The first tapped the bottom of his fist onto the top of the second's; a moment later the second returned the gesture and then both gently banged their knuckles together twice. This was a little routine they had been doing almost since they could walk. Cuauhtémoc saw the pair doing their thing and remembered the sequence.

"Please, Greatest Mayan," he begged respectfully; "come out into the garden just over here; I have a gift for you, a thing I made last night to thank you for the kindness you have shown me. My grandfather is the wisest man I have ever known, and when I look into your eyes, I see the same wisdom I saw in his. It is not quite done, because I didn't get to see you with your headdress on, but I can take care of that whenever you wish."

The Emperor allowed himself to be led by a child, out onto a patio that opened into the private garden that was part of the map-maker's perks. Behind him, Quoholocet stood; staring at his two brothers in a bemused manner and the chastised servant had backed away from the group, leaving the Captain of the Palace guards and several of his subordinates to bring up the rear. The Emperor stopped and gaped in astonishment. "Quoholocet, Imhoquotep, H'ratli; come out here please," he said after he regained his poise. Summoned by their father, the twins ceased their antics, and all three sons walked out onto the patio and as a single man, stopped and stared.

Cuauhtémoc spent much of the night on this drawing, moving the three-legged stand repeatedly to catch the moon goddess's light. At the moment it was facing the group, showing the Emperor very much as he had first seen him. A calm serenity seemed to form around the face; and the eyes stared out at the group with an almost eerie wisdom. As he looked at his work for the first time in what was becoming full daylight he realized his drawing had somehow grown far greater than he thought possible. He said nothing but stood off to one side and looked at the drawing the same as everyone else.

Well; not quite everyone. The Emperor, his three sons, the Captain of the Palace Guards and the soldiers that were with him, all stared at the drawing with growing wonder. The servant, on the other hand, took one look at the picture. His eyes dropped to the lower-right and he clearly saw the sketch of a descending eagle, complete with feather dropping away. He promptly turned his head and looked at anything and everything else. The birdman's mark proved beyond doubt he had indeed drawn the map in the map-maker's room, and thus, his snide comments about 'doodles' were revealed for what they were. He began to make plans to extract his vengeance on the youth . . . but how?

The Emperor turned to Cuauhtémoc with tears forming in his eyes. "How is it you can do such a thing, child? I have seen many drawings of many things and I have never seen anything like this."

"I do not know, Greatest Mayan," he said softly. "It seems I can do anything I put my mind to but I don't always know how I do them. I must believe when Father Inti made me, he must have created me for a special job, and that he gave me greater abilities so I am able to do this job well. But I don't know what that job is. I am still very young yet; perhaps my job waits until I am old enough. I do know being a birdman gives me the greatest joy of all. Perhaps my special job has something to do with flying. That would make me happiest; and it is said that a man who is happy in his work has found the job Inti made him for.

"As you can see, the drawing I made for you is not complete. I need only to see you in your headdress for a short time and then I will know how to finish it. When ever you wish it done I shall do it." He bowed deeply before his Emperor and gave honor that was due him.

The Emperor turned to the servant who was staring out into the garden as if fascinated by a flower or leaf; he clapped his hands together twice, bringing the servant around to face him.

"You will go and get my best ceremonial headdress and bring it to me. You will go directly there without any side trips. You will pick the headdress I have named and no other and you will bring it directly here. You shall not stop to talk to anyone or do anything needless. Do I make myself clear?"

"Yes, Emp . . . yes, Greatest Mayan," he said. He wore the expression of a man who was eating an apple and had just discovered half a worm. His face twisted in dislike and the servant turned and left the garden without a backwards glance.

"Even with the clearest instructions it will take him twice as long as it should," the Emperor said softly. "While we wait for his return, let us go over here and sit awhile; I have many questions I would ask of you if I may."

Cuauhtémoc followed the elderly Emperor over to where a series of low stone benches were lined up along the edge of the garden; where he sat down. The birdman in turn folded his legs under him and settled down in front his Ruler with effortless ease. "I am your child to command, Greatest Mayan, say what you will and I shall answer to the best of my ability." He stared up at his Monarch and waited.

"I am not convinced that I *can* command you my child. After you were led away to be taken care of; I summoned the commander of our local birdmen and had him look at your wings. He tells me your wings are very well built, and even though they have taken minor damage in landing, they are repairable and still safe to fly as they are. He pointed out there are three rods that extend from the tail piece he does not know the use of. He also informs me quite bluntly it is impossible for a birdman, any birdman, to fly half-way across my Empire in a single days' time, even though the messages in your pouch prove this is so.

He further states a rooftop is too small to land on and it is impossible for any birdman to flip his wings around and fly backwards, even if it is to avoid hitting his Emperor who foolishly allowed himself to wander into the birdman's landing zone. He also says that he has no idea how you intend to get your wings off the rooftop and out to the flight area.

"He cannot explain how it is ten adult males, including his Emperor, saw you do these things, nor can he explain how you can talk to eagles. He does admit all birdmen take one of the bird groups as their own and always make the calls of that group, but he cannot explain the fact we ten both saw and heard you talking with the eagles in their own language as well as ours and saw the birds obey your commands. So, my child, I must again admit I am not convinced I can command you to do anything."

The Emperor reached his left hand out and ran his fingers through Cuauhtémoc's hair: "You need a trim, child; perhaps that is something that I can have done for you."

The birdman looked up at his Emperor and smiled a brilliant smile. He took his sovereign's hand and cupped it in his own then, raised it to his face and pressed his cheek into the palm of the old man's hand. The look he gave was purest love and respect, and the Greatest Mayan thought until this moment, he had never been truly appreciated in his entire life.

"That's quite all right; I can just stand here with this as long as it takes," a snide voice said off from the birdman's left. The servant had returned with the Emperor's headdress. Cuauhtémoc saw the man walk up a few scant heartbeats before but from the aggrieved expression on the servant's face, one would think he had been standing there, ignored for hours on end.

"That is so," he said, turning his head just enough to make eye contact with the servant. "Frankly, I wasn't sure you were aware of that; perhaps there is hope for you yet." He released the Greatest Mayan's hand and stood up with the graceful ease he affected so effortlessly. The manner in which he rose sometimes smacked of magic but the reality was much easier to understand. He was still young and quite slender and his muscles were very strong for his body weight. It for this reason the great cats can move and jump with such incredible grace; they are exceedingly muscular for their size and that strength makes the difficult seem ridiculously easy.

"My fathers . . . ." the servant began hotly.

"Are not here," Cuauhtémoc injected, interrupting the servant's spiel before he even began. "A thing you should be very grateful for as they would no doubt rise up as a single man and give you a beating you would never forget. Then they would likely disown you. They might even hunt down your mother and demand to know exactly what she was doing on all of those 'ladies night's out' she used to go to. 'The deeds of a good servant lives on after him in the heart's of those he serves; but the mewling of a bad servant cease the moment his head and neck part company.' I suggest you keep that in mind."

He turned his back on the astonished servant and placing his right hand on his left shoulder and the left on his right he bowed deeply before his Emperor. "If you wish it to be, Greatest Mayan, you can have the headdress placed upon you. It may seem a foolish thing but I will only have to see it on you for a few moments and then I can begin to finish your picture. While I draw the headdress in, perhaps I can explain away most of your concerns, if not all of them."

He extended his hand and the Emperor took it. Not because he was unable to get up by himself but because the child was unfailingly polite in all things and it never occurred to the great ruler not to take the hand so freely given.

The servant put the headdress on his monarch with uncharacteristic silence. The look the birdman gave him was the unwinking stare of a carnivore and the comment about his head and neck parting company was entirely too graphic for his tastes. At least for the moment; he was subdued.

As the servant fitted the headdress to his Emperor's head, Cuauhtémoc turned and headed back inside the map-maker's room to get the inks and sticks that he would need to complete the drawing, closely followed by the three Princes. "We also have many questions we would like to ask, if you are willing;" Prince Quoholocet said politely.

"I will gladly answer all questions I am able, Great Prince," he said with a respectful bow. "In fact, you will soon discover getting me to talk about anything shall be the easiest thing that you have ever done; getting me to *stop* talking—now *that* might prove to be a challenge." He looked up at the three and smiled slyly and an impish expression came into his face. They stared at him for a single heartbeat and then exploded in laughter.

He sorted his supplies as he talked. He now had both hands full of drawing sticks and ink supplies and there was yet more needed to be taken outside. "Allow me, birdman," Prince Quoholocet said and reached out to take some of the items from the birdman's hand.

"Thank you, Great Prince," he said with a courteous bow. "I am coming to understand the truly great are always the most gracious in their dealings with those of lesser position." Prince Quoholocet inclined his head in recognition of the compliment.

"I would apologize to the three of you if I may," he said politely. "I know you are Prince Quoholocet, because last night I heard the Greatest Mayan so name you, and just a bit ago I heard him call you two Imhoquotep and H'ratli, but I don't know which of you is which: please forgive me."

"There is nothing to forgive," the eldest said. "As you have already learned, I am Quoholocet and am thought to be the next Emperor. The Palace Guards as well as all of the armed forces of the Mayan Empire are before my eyes."

"I am Imhoquotep and am thought to be second in line for the Throne;" the second one said. "I am the overseer of all plants that are grown for food as well as all of the animals. It is my job to make sure these supplies flow in the proper directions and amounts."

"I am H'ratli and thought to be third in line for the Throne. Which is to say; no chance at all;" he looked at his two brothers who laughed softly and shook their heads. Cuauhtémoc watched them with glee; the three had a sense of humor about things and laughter was something he loved greatly. "I am the overseer of all merchants and merchandise; it is my responsibility to make sure all supplies of such move in an orderly manner; and ensure none of the merchants get overly greedy."

"I am Cuauhtémoc and I am a birdman and carry messages to wherever I am told to go. Evidently; I also berate mouthy servants and kill the enemies that rise up and attack the children of the Greatest Mayan in my spare time."

"Evidently, you are gifted in all of these things," Prince Quoholocet said in an impressed voice. Cuauhtémoc bowed before the Prince to thank him for the compliment.

By this time Cuauhtémoc had gathered all of the supplies he would need and he and the three Princes carried the inks and drawing sticks out onto the patio where the unfinished drawing sat. As they stepped out of the room, the servant finished setting the headdress onto the Emperor and was fussing over the last placement of the feathers: their timing was perfect.

Cuauhtémoc put the sticks in his hand down, took the things the three Princes held and laid them in their proper places and then turned to his Emperor and stared at him. He circled first left and then right and then bowed before the Greatest Mayan. "As I already said; it may seem silly, perhaps, but I need only just this long to know what to do."

"You didn't even look at him;" the servant protested petulantly.

Cuauhtémoc turned to the man. "You bore me;" he said quietly. "At first I thought you to be simple of mind; but now I see that you have an obstructive spirit. Such spirits are always destructive; take care it doesn't destroy you as well."

"I discover I am also bored with you," the Emperor said. "Take my headdress and put it back where it belongs. Do not bother returning when you are done; I find I am done with you for today." The servant, with a sour look on his face, moved to obey.

Cuauhtémoc stood and watched the servant as he went about the task he was given. His eyes were the unwinking stare of the great carnivores that inhabit the jungle's dank depths and there was a thoughtful expression on his face as he observed the servant as he eased through the doorway and out of sight. The Emperor, his three sons and the Captain of the Guards and his men saw the look on the child's face. They, in their own hearts, wondered exactly what was going through the youth's mind. And each was pleased the child was looking at the servant like that; and not them.

CHAPTER 4

The Emperor watched the birdman with great interest. Cuauhtémoc picked up two sticks, the finer in his left hand and the broader in his right. He paused, focusing the picture he saw in his mind with the drawing that was already on the parchment before him.

His hands floated above the picture like two hummingbirds, the sticks being their beaks. He paused just for a single heartbeat and then his right hand dipped and the stick seemed to taste the ink daintily and he began to draw.

At first he concentrated on the banding of the headdress and how it sat upon the Emperor's head. His right hand filled in the outlines with broad, firm strokes, and his left put in the finer details and added shading and depth. Next he started in on the quills of the feathers as they reached upwards.

"As you can see, Greatest Mayan, I did not leave quite enough room at the top of the picture to complete your feathers. I admit this is an oversight on my part because I didn't know how long your feathers were. As it turns out I think that it will be for the good: the main thrust of the picture is, and must be, the wisdom in your eyes; anything that detracts from this should be avoided."

Once he had the main details in; he started in on the bulk of the feathers. He put the drawing sticks in hands down and went through the rest of the sticks, looking for one that would work for him. He couldn't find a stick wide enough on the shaped end so he chose one of the regular sticks at random and switched it around, holding it by the point. He moved his waist pouch around, rummaged through it for just a moment, and pulled out his knife. He pulled the knife from the wooden sheath and with a few precise strokes he shaped it the way he wished. He returned the blade to its scabbard because the edge was too dangerous to have around otherwise.

"What kind of knife is that, birdman?" Prince Quoholocet asked politely. Rather than explain, he simply handed the sheathed blade to the Prince, who stood immediately to his left.

"Take care if you pull it from its case," he warned, "those blades come out of the furnace wickedly sharp and they don't care what they cut . . . or who." He took the shaped drawing stick and stuck it into his mouth and began chewing on it thoughtfully. He pulled it out after a few bites, stared at it closely, stuck it back into his mouth and bit it several times more. Once he was satisfied, he dipped it into the ink and began drawing the leading and trailing edges of the feathers, but instead of a single broad stroke, the shattered stick traced the paper leaving many tiny lines. With incredible ease and speed he began to fill in the softer parts of the feathers and the headdress took form very quickly.

He experimented with the chewed stick, twisting it slightly between his fingers, and discovered he could add interesting swirls as well as the upward sweep that feathers normally have. As he drew, the Emperor who was on his right and the three Princes, just to his left, moved closer and watched in rapt fascination as his hands glided across the picture, flitting about like well-trained hummingbirds and the details flowed from his mind, through the sticks in his hand, and onto the paper.

He finished the top-part of the first feather, or at least as far as he intended to draw it. It was as he had told the Emperor; the paper really wasn't quite high enough to get all of the feathers in. So he deliberately left them well short of the paper's edge. It was his intent to simply fade the drawing out as he got near the top. He experimented with the chewed-up stick and discovered he could not only draw with it along its broad edge but he could also swirl it around until he created a thin but very dark line. At the upper edge he did so, swirling the stick around until the ends of the feather formed a graceful arc above the feather's shaft. The next feather over he did the same but this time he moved the direction of the swirl so that the ends moved outwards. As he stared at the developing picture, it seemed tiny arms had formed with even smaller hands on the ends, and both were uplifted as if in prayer.

This produced an entire sequence of thought that flashed through his mind at warp speed. He leaned forward slightly, took a careful look and then leaned back to where he was, and continued on until all feathers ended in a similar way. He stepped back and studied what he had done. He was vaguely aware of the Emperor on his right and the three Crown Princes on his left, but at the moment, most of his attention was on the picture before him. The ends of the feathers now all swooped gracefully up; as if reaching for the edge of the paper and beyond.

He turned to Prince Quoholocet and bowed respectfully. "May I have use of that knife for just a moment, Great Prince?" he asked politely. The Prince was studying the developing picture with rapt fascination and it took a blink of an eye for his mind to refocus. He forgot the birdman had handed the knife to him, or that he was still holding it, and had not as yet given it a glance.

"Yes; yes birdman, here it is," the Prince said and handed the knife back to him.

Cuauhtémoc turned and re-entered the map-maker's room. The Mayan people as a whole were great admirers of birds, and few rooms did not have at least some feathers floating around somewhere, and the map-maker's room was no exception. Some of the feathers were very large and looked to come from a condor. Yet others were much smaller and perhaps came from the wings of sparrows. He chose a number of feathers of different sizes and went back outside. The Greatest Mayan, his three sons and the palace guards had not moved from where they stood and all were looking at the picture with overt wonder on their faces.

He held several of the larger feathers up to the drawing; close to, but not touching. He found one that he liked, set the other feathers down, drew the knife from its sheath and surgically cut the nib off exactly where he wished. He laid the knife down, used a piece of straw to knock out the small hairs that had grown within the feather and then he used the end to create almost perfect circles, slightly smaller than his least fingernail, just above each feather's shaft. He then took one of the smallest feathers, and did the same thing, creating a much smaller circle inside the larger one. He took the finest drawing stick he could find, cut the edge even smaller, and with deft strokes, created small slashes within the circle, making eyes, as well as inwardly curving strokes that joined the greater circle with the feather's shafts as if they were necks. He stepped back, eyed the result and saw it was good.

He carefully put the knife back into its wooden sheath, handed it back to Prince Quoholocet and then turned to his Emperor and bowed deeply. "The drawing is now complete," he said. "At first; I intended to just leave the feathers of your headdress unfinished towards the top because I didn't know to leave more room, and at that time I believed that it would be best to draw it that way. But as I was finishing up, Father Inti opened my eyes and I discovered a picture can also have a picture within it; even as a story can hold another story inside.

"If you should look at the upper ends of your feathers you will see there seems to be a small head atop of each feather with a mouth and eyes and that each feather forms arms that look to be lifted upwards. In my mind's eye these represent your children. Not just your sons here with us but all Mayan people who look to you for guidance and protection. Your reign has been for more than fifty years and this has been a time of endless peace and prosperity. And so I see we who are your children, springing from your head with our arms uplifted to Father Inti above, while we praise you and thank our Great God for giving us such a wondrous Ruler; and we pray He will spare you to rule over us for many more years to come."

The Greatest Mayan's face puckered up and tears began to course down his aged cheeks. "My child," he said with trembling lips and held his arms out. Cuauhtémoc never in his life missed a chance at getting a hug from anyone and he wasn't about to start now: he cleared his hands of tools and moved forward.

"Grandfather," he said and put his arms around his Emperor and hugged him in the manner of grandsons everywhere.

"My child," the Emperor said and held him close. Cuauhtémoc stood like this for long moments and when the Greatest Mayan released him he moved on to Prince Quoholocet and gave him a quick hug and then on to his two brothers, the Captain of the Royal Guard and the guardsmen that were there; it was not in him to leave anyone out.

"I would like to explain your concerns now Greatest Mayan and answer whatever questions you might have. The questions you wish to ask as well as any questions that you may have, Great Prince;" and he bowed respectfully at the three brothers, "but I do not wish to take up any more of your valuable time than I have already."

"I am Emperor. I am the Greatest Mayan and my time is to use as I will. For now, my will is to be here in the place with you, and to listen to whatever words you wish to speak."

"Then I shall speak all that is in my heart and explain away your concerns to the best of my ability. As I recently told your son, Prince Quoholocet, it is easy to get me to talk on any subject; getting me to stop talking—that at times can be a challenge.

"Yesterday morning, when Inti was about a fist above the great waters, the Sergeant who serves the Commander came to me and told me I was wanted. He led me down to the landing area where your Commander and others were waiting. Your Commander handed me the message package and told me it needed to be taken to you as quickly as possible. I read the winds by the way the clouds floated by and I saw it was from the northeast and blowing steady: this is the best wind possible when one wishes to fly south. Strictly speaking; no birdman can fly, we fall, but at a slower speed because of our wings. Much of a birdman's flight time is spent in uplifts that carry us high enough we can quit them and move in the wished-for direction. Because the winds were perfect for my needs I spent very little time in uplifts and all of my time being carried south by the winds. It is for this reason I was able to make the flight in a single day. Otherwise; your Birdman-Commander would be correct in saying it can't be done.

"The winds that carried me south also blew me towards the great mountains that lay to the west of us, which is where I wished to go. The winds in the mountains can be tricky at times, but the uplifts are the strongest there, so I climbed as high as I could, which is why my body was so cold by the time that I got here."

"A thousand tall trees in the air?" Prince H'ratli asked politely; there was a greenish tinge to his face and he looked very uncomfortable.

"The thought of great heights bothers you, does it not, Great Prince?" he asked politely.

"Yes, birdman, I have always had a morbid fear of high places."

"This is not a thing to be ashamed of; Great Prince. My grandfather is the Great Healer of the High Reaches village where I was born. He told me when I was five that fear of falling is the only fear humans are born with and all other fears are learned. He also said when you find a new mother with a cranky baby, many times it is because she does not yet know how to properly hold her infant, and the newly born is experiencing this fear.

"While most people learn to control the fear of falling; not everyone does. This may be something that will help ease your dread; Great Prince. There is no such thing as up or down, left or right, forward or back; there is only distance. Some distances are small," and he held his hand up, finger and thumb a short space apart. "And some distances are large; look towards the mountains and you can see what I mean. What we think of as up or down, left or right, are only our personal interpretations of distance; our way of seeing things. If one stands on a rooftop and looks down at the ground, the distance is the same if that one stands on the roof looking down, or if he is on the ground looking up. It only seems up or down because that is how our minds interpret such and each interpretation of what we see is unique to us for that time and place. No one else can see it the same way as we do since no one else can see through our eyes: it is how we look at life and nothing more. Since these things are so, it makes no more sense to fear falling 'down,' than to fear falling 'up.' Using caution in dangerous situations is another thing entirely; that is not fear, it is common sense."

Prince H'ratli stared at the birdman with unwinking eyes the entire time he was talking; he didn't move a muscle and perhaps stopped breathing as well. He inhaled suddenly, exhaled and then he put his right hand on his left shoulder, his left on his right, his fingers and thumb splayed widely as the rays of the sun and he bowed deeply before him. "Thank you Birdman; your words are logical and I find truth within them. And they have indeed eased the fears within my soul. I can never repay you your kindness," and he bowed deeply again.

"It is my greatest joy and pleasure to serve. Father Inti first, the Greatest Mayan second and then all the children of the Greatest Mayan in any way I can; if my words give you solace then I am pleased.

"So, Greatest Mayan," he said, turning back to his Emperor, "I followed the mountains south, always keeping the great waters within sight for I knew from words of others that your great city lay within a great bay with a large river flowing into it and your palace was up on the hillside overlooking that bay. By the time I rode Inti's Breath all the way here, He was near the mountains, getting ready to set. I turned away from the mountains and headed directly towards your palace; this put the mountains and Father Inti directly behind me.

"I have always loved the eagles above all other birds, and while I do not believe eagles have a language as such, I believe they are attracted to me because I can make their sounds so accurately. We humans can often tell when someone around us does not like us, or hates us, as well as when we are greatly loved. I believe the eagles may also understand the feeling of love when it is directed at them and that could also be part of the reason why they often come when I call them and why they will many times follow me in my flights. I think they respond to these things. I also believe Father Inti sometimes sends them to me for reasons of His own. It was the eagles that came for me just over a month before my tenth birthday and it was the eagles that flew escort for my big brother Xymatoc and me when we left my village and flew to where the Northern Birdman's training camp is.

"No one had ever flown two-to-a-wing before Xymatoc and I did. He later admitted he never understood how I managed to talk him into it and further spoke I could talk a jaguar away from a fresh kill. In any case, he took me from my village and the eagles, which are the servants of Inti, came along with us. Xymatoc gave me lessons on flight as we were flying and by the time we got to the Birdman's camp I'd been doing all of the flying for over a fist of the sun.

"When we made our approach; Xymatoc was still letting me guide the wings. Because I didn't know better, I waited until the last moment, then leaned backwards, lifting the beak up sharply which made the tail drag on the ground, bringing us to a stop more quickly than normal. It was only afterwards I learned the way birdmen have landed for centuries is to keep the wings level and run along the ground as fast as they can until the whole thing comes to a stop. Xymatoc told Flightmaster what I had done and what the results were. In the end, three 'drag-sticks' were stuck onto the tail piece to protect the tail and now all of our wings are built that way and all of our birdmen are taught to drag-tail on landing. This makes the landing much quicker and safer and is also the reason why your Birdman-Commander did not know what the sticks were for and why he thought no one could land on a roof. We are dealing with two entirely different techniques that yield similar results but in different ways."

Cuauhtémoc was watching Prince Quoholocet out of the corner of his eyes and he saw the moment when the Great Prince decided to pull the knife from its sheath and take a closer look at it. "As long as you take care, it will be well with you, but I suggest you do not test the edge on the ball of your thumb. At the least you will draw blood and at the worst you will lose part of your thumb."

This was exactly what Prince Quoholocet intended to do and the birdman's words stopped him in the act of pulling the knife out of its sheath. "Is it really that sharp?" he demanded.

Cuauhtémoc turned to his Ruler and bowed politely: "May I; Greatest Mayan?"

"Of course, my child," the Monarch replied.

He turned to the Prince and held out his hand. Before he could ask, Quoholocet gave the knife to him. He turned and went back into the map-maker's room. No more than a few heartbeats later he stepped out with a sheet of paper in his hand. This was the same kind of paper the drawing was on; as well as most of the maps in the room. He looked about quickly, positioned himself so that his Emperor could see clearly as well as this three sons. The Captain of the Guards and his men promptly jockeyed for position.

He held the piece of paper about arm's length and nearly shoulder-high, holding it at the top of the page between finger and thumb and very nearly in the center. He put the knife sheath between his first and middle finger and curled the other fingers around the sheath. He was careful to grip it well away from where the blade came out. He pulled the knife out and three smooth strokes along the paper's right side gave him three slender strips of paper falling towards the ground. In the next eye-blink he cut from the upper right-hand corner towards the lower left and half the paper dropped away. In the following blink he cut from the upper left towards the center of the paper and that too fell. Now the only thing that he held was a much smaller, roughly triangular-shaped piece of paper. He opened his finger and thumb and the paper dropped away. Before the fragment could descend more than a hand's width his right hand shot out like a snake striking and the single remaining piece became two. He carefully put the knife back into the sheath and offered to return it. "Yes, Prince Quoholocet, it really is that sharp;" he said calmly. The Prince took one horrified look at the pieces of paper littering the ground, shook his head, and moved back a step; he would not take the knife.

"I would give a hundred in gold for such a knife," the Guard Captain said in awe.

Cuauhtémoc turned to the Captain and stared thoughtfully. "I find it fascinating you would say that, Captain, for it brings up something that I wished to speak to Prince H'ratli about." He turned towards his Emperor. "On my wings and tied to the main-shaft right next to the message net is yet another pouch; in it is a sack with most of my possessions. If I may, Greatest Mayan, I would like to go and get it because there are things in it there I would like to show you and your sons."

"It is my wish you stay here, my child," the Greatest Mayan said promptly; he turned towards one of the guardsmen and gestured gracefully. "You shall go to the birdman's wings and bring him the item he needs."

"Yes, Greatest Mayan." The guard started to turn, then and stopped and stared at the birdman. "Um . . ." he said.

Cuauhtémoc understood what was going through the guard's mind. Like every one else, he was watching and listening very carefully, and he was afraid he would miss something interesting. "It will be all right, guardsman," he said politely, "I shall take care to not say or do anything remarkable until you return. And if I do anyway; one of your brothers can catch you up after you come back."

"Yes; thank you birdman," he said and turned and left.

While the guardsman was about his task the Greatest Mayan walked over to where his picture sat and stared at it for long moments. "Tell me, my sons, what do you make of this drawing our birdman made for us?"

The three Princes stood and stared at the drawing without comment and then after awhile Prince Quoholocet turned to his father and bowed politely. "I find the symbolism of the heads on the feathers to be astonishing. How this child could come up with such a thing is more than I can understand. The more I look into the picture; the more things my eyes discover."

"Your thoughts are the same as mine, Quoholocet; it is my wish all of my headdresses be altered to look like the one in this drawing. If my headdress makers do not understand, then we will have them look at this picture. If they still cannot figure it out, I shall tell them to talk to our birdman; I do not doubt he can properly instruct them."

While the Greatest Mayan was talking to his oldest son, Imhoquotep walked from one side to the other, staring at the picture as he did so. "It is your eyes that are the most powerful, Father;" he said. "I have moved over here and your eyes look directly at me, but when I move to another place, your eyes also look at me and as I walk back and forth I find your eyes follow me no matter where I go. This is powerfully done and I cannot begin to understand how this can be."

This started a small investigation where everyone tried what Imhoquotep said, walking back and forth and looking at the drawing from different viewpoints, all with identical results.

They were now gathered in the small garden that was part of the map maker's perks and the garden was filled with tropical ferns, flowers and other assorted plants and as all such gardens were, surrounded by a tall stone wall that kept people out unless they entered from the main room of whoever lived in this particular place; this was both to insure some privacy within the palace as well as to protect those who lived within.

"Had I been only told of this and had not seen it I would have not believed," Prince H'ratli admitted ruefully to his father. "But since I have seen it; and since I have even seen it being finished, I must believe, but admit I do not understand. I look upon this sketch and I can see your spirit, your soul, captured within the lines, but when I look upon your face I see your essences as they have always been. Only a god can take a soul from a human body and put it back again so I must believe you are correct, Father: we cannot command this child but we must in turn be commanded by him."

The Emperor, his three sons and all of the guardsmen turned and stared at Cuauhtémoc. "I am not a god," he insisted; "I am only a child, a kid. True, Flightmaster told me I am the youngest birdman that has ever flown, and I have invented a number of things in the last two years, and I have managed to destroy a number of your enemies, but that doesn't make me a god; I've just been lucky. Also, I've had some very good help along the way . . . but I am not a god."

"Did I miss anything?" the guardsman asked, looking around, he just this moment stepped out of the map-maker's room and he held the birdman's pouch in his hand.

"Not really," his fellow-guardsman said, "although there was that one thing." He turned to the man next to him; "Was that before or after all the rest? I keep getting it all mixed up."

"I have no idea," his friend said dolefully, "the birdman lost me when he started talking about stars: what they are, where they came from, how they're made; that stuff."

The guardsman swiveled his head around and stared at Cuauhtémoc in horror: "*What have I missed?*" The comment, combined with the expression on the man's face, was too much for him and Cuauhtémoc collapsed into peals of giggles. At first he wrapped his arms around his slim waist, and then his knees buckled. He fell forward in slow motion, his forehead touched the ground and he rolled over onto his left side and from there onto his back. His knees were up against his chest and his feet kicked feebly in the air and his head was thrown back as far as he could get it. Giggles are the domain of children and young females; anyone else who engages in it usually comes out looking vapid. Which is a shame; because there is no happier sound on Earth.

None of the adults could resist laughing with him, and in truth, no one even tried. In time even Cuauhtémoc got his merriment under control and was again on his feet, brushing himself off while his Emperor and Prince Quoholocet helped him. "I need another bath, Greatest Mayan," he said, "and my clothes need laundering as well."

"Another bath, yes, and a hair trim as well; but not those clothes laundered. You are now my child and you are in my house and you shall be dressed as all of my children are dressed.

"I understand you have many more things to tell me and more things to show but for now my heart has taken all that it can hold. I shall rest awhile and let my heart ponder the things I have seen and heard. Perhaps tomorrow, if you wish, we can cover yet more of your wonders." And it was so.

CHAPTER 5

The Emperor was as good as his word; no sooner had the birdman finished his bath and gotten himself dried off when the first batch of servants entered his room, armed with cloth and knives and other tools of their trade. They held fabrics against his body and fitted him from his shoulders down to his legs. Yet another man slipped in and started putting sandals on his feet, trying all the while to do as he had been instructed without actually getting in the way of other craftsmen. The man who trimmed the hair of the Royal family came in next. He took a look and turned to Prince H'ratli and demanded indignantly; "How am I to trim this child's hair with all of these others in my way?"

Prince H'ratli stared at the man coldly. "You shall obey the will of your Emperor as these other do; you shall wait your turn as they have." The craftsman realized he had stepped onto shaky ground; he bowed respectfully to the Prince and backed off and waited.

It was not long. Both the men who fitted the clothes as well as the man who was fitting the sandals came fully prepared; it was a common thing where one child or another needed yet new clothes or sandals for it is the way of children to grow taller; almost daily it sometimes seems. The men, having done their jobs, backed off, bowed deeply before Prince H'ratli and left.

"Please, young birdman, do try and hold still as possible while I give your hair a trim," the craftsman said. "While I do not expect you to understand, the knives I use for my work are very sharp and I have no wish to nick you or do you harm in any way." Truer words were never spoken. The pay and the perks of being a haircutter to the Royal family were many, but as it often is in such cases, the downside was dire indeed. His instructions were made crystal clear the day he accepted this position: if one of his customers lost an ear, he would lose his head.

"I shall not move," Cuauhtémoc said, and seemed to freeze where he stood. The haircutter disliked trimming children, but the Greatest Mayan commanded him here, so he approached the birdman with his obsidian knife in his hand and began his work.

He started on the back of the birdman's head. There were no barber's chairs or anything else to sit on unless the customer was quite tall. With the boy standing before him, his head was ideally placed. He ran the fingers of his left hand through the youth's hair and as he moved his hand away he dragged the edge of the knife along with it; rather than slicing or sawing at the strands. As he progressed, an increasing amount of hair dropped to the ground. He worked around to the birdman's left, using the identical method to trim the sides, for the hair hung long enough to cover the child's ears completely, and this looked very wrong to his practiced eyes.

He trimmed the left side first and then the right and then evened both sides up with the back. "Now I must do the area over your eyes, birdman. Please close them and do not open them again until I say so." He barely began talking when the child's eyes closed and stayed that way. Except for the pulse in the youth's throat, and the regular rise and fall of his chest in breathing, he might well have been a statue cut from flesh and blood instead of stone.

He trimmed the hair over the birdman's eyes and blended it in with the shape of his sides. "There is some hair on your face, birdman; don't be alarmed, I just mean to blow it away from your eyes." He leaned forward and blew a small puff of air at the boy's face and then once again. He stood back and looked at his work. He walked around, repeatedly fluffing the youth's hair, checking it for evenness. Even by his standards of perfection the result was very good. "You may move and speak as you like, Birdman, and I thank you for being so still. I think you must be the best young customer I have ever had, and this is very good, because you would not believe how sharp my knives are."

"The Birdman understands 'sharp' better than you do Haircutter;" Prince H'ratli said quietly. "Go on, Birdman; if you don't mind, show him what sharp is all about."

Cuauhtémoc bowed deeply, only he wasn't bowing to anyone: he shook his head like a dog shakes to shed water. He stood erect and gave his head another vigorous shake and he was done.

"I could have run my fingers through your hair for a fist of the sun and still not get it to hang that naturally," the haircutter said in open admiration.

"Thank you, Haircutter," he said politely and then turned and bowed respectfully to his prince. "As for the subject of sharpness, please watch carefully."

He walked not back into the map-maker's room but towards the garden area where all kinds of greenery grew. He used a piece of paper earlier to demonstrate the knife he carried. It wasn't until after he turned an expensive piece of paper into confetti he realized the large leaves growing nearby would work as well, and since they could grow anew, there was no cost at all. He pulled the knife out of his pouch, slipped the blade out of the sheath and proceeded to do to a large leaf what he had done to the paper.

"Father Inti; what manner of knife is that?" the haircutter gasped in surprise.

"Technically, it is not a knife at all, it is a Temmo: all arrowheads are called Temocs, all knives are called Temmos and all spearheads are called Tem-tems. My name is Cuauhtémoc, which in the Incan language means 'descending eagle.' Many people have trouble saying my name so at times they call me Tem, Temmo or Temoc, but for the most part, those who are my friends call me Inca because that is what I am. The hunt-leader named these things after me because I am the one who discovered how this thing is done. He said he and his people decided to call them such in order to keep them separate from obsidian weapons. We went to these things because obsidian has gotten so terribly expensive over the last few years that too much of our trade-goods and coinage was going to the obsidian merchant when he came through."

"Obsidian? Expensive? Where did you ever hear that? There's a huge deposit; what, four or five days travel north of us?" The speaker was the same guardsman who had gone and gotten the birdman's sack for him earlier.

"Something like that," the second guard said; "four days for sure."

"The thing is,' the first one continued, "this outcropping is enormous and since it is on land owned by the Greatest Mayan, anyone can go there and just take whatever he wants. For all intents, if you can pick it up and walk off with it, it is yours."

"Now that is interesting, and from what I found out later, it doesn't surprise me at all. Tell me Great Prince; what is a normal mark-up for trade goods?"

"That would depend on the item involved," Prince H'ratli said thoughtfully. "But as a general rule, for every finger one pays for an item, they will ask two or three fingers in returns. If the item is truly scarce, or if it has to come from a great distance, it might be as much as four or five fingers. In other words, if I can buy a thing for a single piece of silver, I will want three or four pieces of silver for it in returns. And if it is rare, or comes from a great distance, it could be as high as six pieces of silver. The difference is what the transportation costs; 'carrying-charges' it is called."

Cuauhtémoc nodded his head and rummaged around in his sack for a few moments. He pulled several items out, each wrapped in pieces of leather and tied with leather thongs. He untied them and laid them on the ground for everyone to see. "This is a Temoc, he said, picking up one of the arrowheads. "This is what we started making at first because these are what were needed most."

"The end is broken off," one of the guards said.

"It seems to be but if you look at it closely you will see it is as sharp as the other edges; this Temoc will cut deeper than an obsidian arrowhead. Prince H'ratli; our Dispatcher sells five rows of five stuck into a piece of cork bark because it is the safest way to transport them; he is paid five pieces of silver for the twenty-five Temocs: does this sound about right?"

"No," Prince H'ratli said thoughtfully, "from what I see here I would think perhaps ten pieces of silver for a block and as many as fifteen. It would depend upon how much I could get in returns."

"The obsidian merchant who covers our route has been buying Temocs ever since he learned of them. He pays five silvers for a block of twenty-five. Several times I heard him trying to buy them for less; he says he can only barely make a profit on them as it is, and yet the last time he was through, he ordered a hundred blocks; he claims he can only make money in volume sales. When I flew into the Northern soldier's camp there was a fight going on; our soldiers were being attacked by the black-flag people. I have since learned they are called pirates by their own people and they are feared and hated by all. As I flew in, I put an arrow into the right ear of the one who looked to be the leader, because it is always best to kill the leader first."

"You shot a bow from your wings?" one of the guardsmen demanded.

"Yes," Cuauhtémoc said quietly.

"While you were in the air?" the same one asked.

"Yes; that is so," the birdman said.

"While you were flying?" the same one asked yet again.

"I would certainly hope so, guardsman. If I am in the air and am in my wings I had better be flying or I am in a great deal of trouble." He spoke not in anger but in humor and his eyes twinkled merrily. The guardsman flinched, grinned guiltily, and nodded his head.

"So that *is* what the Commander was trying to say in his messages;" Prince H'ratli said, almost to himself. He stared at the birdman before him. "Only it looked as if he said that you put an arrow into a man's eye. At times, writings can be vague at best. I often wish there was a better way of making messages but there doesn't seem to be."

"I also put an arrow into a man's eye; but that was earlier. Actually, Great Prince, there *is* a better way of writing messages; the Spaniard showed me how and taught me the way of it, But before we go down that road I would like very much to finish up my earlier thought." Prince H'ratli stared at the birdman and then nodded but he was starting to look confused.

"I put an arrow into one of the enemy's head, entering his right ear and going out the left; this was not an accident but was exactly what I wished. A great many people saw me do this thing; including your Commander. Later on, one of the soldiers who saw this pulled the arrow out of the enemy's head and brought it to me. He did so because he recognized the Temoc on the end of the arrow and believed it was quite valuable. As it turned out he had several Temocs he purchased with his own money; he paid five in silver for each, but kept calling them *Klamtdons*."

"I see," Prince H'ratli said; "he bought them with his own money and he . . . ah.

He paid **how much**?"

"Yes, Great Prince. Evidence shows the same obsidian merchant who has been telling the birdman camp for many years that obsidian is increasingly hard to get, is the same merchant who has been buying twenty-five Temocs for five in silver, and selling them for five in silver for each. I figured it out and the merchant is making twenty-four fingers profit for every one finger he pays out. Then to throw salt into everyone's eyes, he changed the name and presumably named them after himself. Does this sound like the way an honorable merchant operates to you?"

"It does not!" Prince H'ratli snapped. "I would love to get that one in front of me in my court. Once he faced me he would regret the day he let his greed rule his common sense."

"There is a very good chance you will get your wish, Great Prince. I made it my duty to report everything I had seen and learned each day to the Commander at the end of the day and when I explained this to him he was beyond angry and well into livid. He told me he placed an order with that same merchant for one hundred blocks of twenty-five each; which is exactly what the merchant ordered from Dispatcher the last time he swung by. The Commander ordered his Sergeant to seize the merchant the next time he comes through. I feel that it will be an easy thing to have that merchant sent here, bound and under armed guard, to await your judgment. I also wrote to the Dispatcher of the birdman's camp and told him not to sell anything else to the obsidian merchant. One of my sergeants flew the message to him and I had Sergeant Twuondan explain the prices to him. Sergeant Twuondan later said that Dispatcher was very displeased when he heard of it."

"He shall not be happy to see me; I can tell you this. But you spoke of a better method of writing messages. One of the greatest problems in communications is trying to interpret the exact meanings. If one does not have a good idea of what to look for, some messages cannot be interpreted at all. Quoholocet knows the Commander very well; they used to hunt together. In fact, that is how the Commander got his leg injured. He, Quoholocet and some others were hunting boar and somehow the Commander got tusked up pretty seriously. Even with that in our favor we are having trouble understanding some of the things he wrote."

"When the Commander sent me here yesterday he told me the reason he was sending me was because I was the first to see the pirates and witness their atrocities. I am sure it was also his wish I explain these things to the Greatest Mayan, as well as to you, his sons. If it is your desire and the will of your father, show me these writings and I will read them to you and explain what they mean.

"As far as the rest; yes, there is a better system of writing. The Spaniard showed me the way of it and taught it to me, and while he wrote his words in Spanish, there is no reason why this same system cannot be applied to the Mayan language. It shall be a vastly superior way of communicating once people learn the way of it."

"The Spaniard?" Prince H'ratli asked; a perplexed expression on his face.

"Yes; Great Prince. He was one of the men taken off of the two ships that were in the harbor when I flew into the soldier's camp."

"Ships? Harbor?" Prince H'ratli asked, drifting yet further out into the sea of confusion.

"Yes, Great Prince; when I flew into the soldier's camp they were being attacked by enemy soldiers, by the pirates; there were two great ships in the harbor, and—"

"Oh, please, Great One; forgive me. I know I have failed you and you are disappointed in me but my heart can hold no more for now. As my Father said, I must go and ponder these things and try and make sense of all you have told me."

"There is nothing to forgive, Prince H'ratli. And you have not failed me nor am I disappointed in you; you are my friend and I cannot be displeased with anything you do."

"I . . . you consider me a friend?"

"Of course, Great Prince," and he held his right hand out. The Prince looked down and did not understand. He looked up into H'ratli's eyes and then glanced back down. Prince H'ratli looked at the birdman's hand and then hesitantly stuck his own hand out. Cuauhtémoc reached out and clasped his Prince's wrist and he, without thinking, did the same. "As you can see, what we have here is the hand-clasp of friendship. Each of us holds the other's wrist. Such a grip cannot be broken unless both of us let go and what I am offering with my hand I am also offering with my heart. And my heart does not know how to let go; it only knows how to hold fast forever."

Tears formed in H'ratli's eyes and he covered the birdman's right hand with his left. "Now it is doubly so," he said. Cuauhtémoc nodded his head and placed his left hand over the Prince's right.

The Prince bowed to him as if he were a god, turned and left. Now only two guardsmen and the hair-cutter remained; Cuauhtémoc faced the craftsman. "You wish to speak to me further?" he asked politely.

"Well, yes Great One," he replied hesitantly; "I do have one question if I may."

"You would like to get a Temmo, I presume," he said.

"Well, yes Great One, I've never seen anything that will cut like that; I would very much like to have one of my own."

"I prefer to not be called 'Great One.' My proper name is Cuauhtémoc. If you find that you cannot pronounce it to your satisfaction you may call me Tem or Temmo. Most of my friends just call me Inca because that is what I am, and while I am aware there are those who look down on anyone of Incan heritage, those who do are ignorant and I disregard the ignorant because I can learn nothing worthwhile from them. Or you can call me birdman if you wish because that is also what I am.

"As for the Temmo: try to understand that greater power brings greater responsibility. A servant who cleans up after his master has little power but his responsibilities are also small. A dull knife is more forgiving of mistakes than a sharp knife but a dull knife is not very useful. The Captain of the Royal Guard recently said he would pay a hundred in gold for a knife like I have, but I suspect before too long, anyone who wishes a Temmo will be able to buy one, and at a far cheaper price than what the Captain said. But until this is so, you must wait like everyone else."

"Yes . . . Birdman, I understand; I shall wait like the others." The craftsman bowed before him, turned and left. He did not need to pick anything up because except for the knife he held securely in its leather sheath, he brought nothing.

He turned to the two guardsmen who were still with him. "Do you also have questions to ask, guardsmen, or has the Greatest Mayan assigned you here to keep me out of mischief?"

"Both, I think," one of the guards said. "The Greatest Mayan directed us to stay with you but I don't think it was to keep you out of mischief. More likely it was to make sure if you should leave your room you won't get lost or go into one of the forbidden parts of the palace, although in your case, I'm not sure any part of the palace is forbidden to you."

"I, for one, have questions as well, but I'm not sure I am permitted to ask any," the second guard said cautiously.

"If you have questions and seek answers, then we are brothers, because I am eaten up with curiosity from the top of my head, to the soles of my feet. It is by asking questions I have learned much of what I know. So if you look for answers, ask and I will answer to the best of my ability."

"How many enemy have you killed so far?" the guardsman blurted out. An instant later he looked like he had not asked that question at all.

"I'm not sure what you mean by 'so far.' There was only the one day I fought the enemy, and 'how many' would depend upon what you mean by 'killed.' As far as killing by direct action, I have killed three. The first was the pirate who killed the child; the second was—"

"The pirate killed a child?" the guardsman exclaimed in horror.

"Yes; a small one. The small one could not have been over four and he or she had not done the pirate any harm. In fact, the little one was only trying to flee but the pirate killed the child with his cutlass like he was swatting an insect and then I killed him."

"While you were in flight?" the same guard asked.

"Yes, that is so," the birdman admitted.

"We guardsmen are not often told things, except orders we must obey, but we listen and hear much and we learn. My brother guardsman and I both heard the Greatest Mayan and his son talking to the Commander of the local birdmen and the Commander told the

Greatest Mayan such a thing is impossible, even though the Soldier's Camp Commander evidently wrote he saw you do this thing with his own eyes."

"I have discovered when people want to do something strongly enough; they can, at times, surprise even themselves. Before I saw the child killed, I would have not believed a bow could be shot from wings when one is in flight, but the murder of an innocent made me so angry I did it anyway; whether it is possible or not. It seems to me the Commander of the local birdmen doesn't believe in anything he doesn't see with his own eyes, or that he does not do himself. But he is wrong; and if he should wish to challenge my word I will gladly fly over his head and do to him what I did to the others. Perhaps as he lies dying he will understand."

The two guardsmen looked at each other in wide-eyed amazement. The youth had an implacably cold expression on his face and they did not doubt for an instant the birdman could and would do as he said.

"So; the first pirate received an arrow in his right eye. The second one took an arrow in his right ear; he was with a band of his brothers and they were killing the Mayan soldiers. The pirates are not better fighters and our soldiers are not lesser. The pirates wore a metal covering called 'armor,' from what the Spaniard said, and it was this protection that kept them safe from most of the arrows and spear attacks. Then our soldiers began to understand how to fight them and the battle changed.

"The third one I dropped a load of rock onto. Again; I think people just don't know what they can do until they try.

"Those are the three that I killed directly. When I dropped the load of rock on the third man, the rocks flew all over the place, once they hit. I also hit a man directly behind the ship's commander. I now know he was using a swivel-gun and he was doing great damage to our soldiers. I saw two rocks strike him, one behind the head and the other at waist-high, and he was knocked overboard and into the water. If the rocks had not already killed him then he drowned. So that would make four."

The Greatest Mayan was concerned with the running of his Empire, and Prince H'ratli concerned himself with merchandizing, and so neither was directly interested in battles. But soldiers know at any time they might have to take up arms in defense of their Emperor and their land, and as such, the guardsmen were captivated with what the birdman was telling them. At the time and place a great many soldiers lived long and full lives without ever once raising up arms other than in practice, but here was a child whose head did not quite come up to their chins, a youth who had already seen more actual combat than they had ever heard of, and they were fascinated.

"I heard Prince Quoholocet say you so frightened the enemy that five of them jumped off a ravine to their deaths rather than face your wrath. Our Birdman-Commander doesn't believe this either."

Cuauhtémoc chuckled softly. "Our Birdman-Commander can't always be wrong; this time he is correct. The five men were standing with their backs to a deep ravine that leads out towards the sea. I flew directly towards them because by this time I was completely out of arrows and I had nothing to drop. It was my intent to fly into the leader of the group and knock him into the ravine, and I believed that my right wing would carry one or two more to their deaths as well. I would have been killed or injured at the same time but it was a price I was willing to pay, for the ground was littered with our soldiers, and if I could save even two or three lives I felt it was worth it.

"Just as I was ready to hit the leader, a very powerful uplift caught me and raised me over the leader's head. I kicked at him as I passed over him but I missed because I was just too high and still climbing. As I flew past I looked under my arm and I saw the leader step backward onto air and he tumbled off the lip. Here, give me a hand for a moment, and I will show you exactly how this thing came to be."

The garden was surrounded by stone blocks. He led the two guards to where rock and soil met and stood them side by side with their backs to the plants. "As I flew towards the leader, I was lifted above his head like so," and he gestured with his right hand. "The first soldier stepped backward, but his foot was on air and not ground." He gently led the guard to do so and then lifted the man's arms up by his wrists. "As he started to fall his arms flailed and he struck the man next to him in the face with his shield," he gently guided the guard's hand into the face of his friend. "This one was also knocked backwards and he too threw his arms out and hit the third in the face with his shield," he said, demonstrating by gently moving the second guard's hands properly, "who struck the fourth and who knocked the fifth over and they all went tumbling down into the ravine below. As they fell, they knocked many large rocks free, and once they hit the bottom, they were buried by a landslide of rocks and dirt they loosened on their way down. If you should wish to include these five, it would then make nine enemies I killed."

By this time both guardsmen were grinning broadly and they bowed politely to Cuauhtémoc. "Thank you for your explanation, Birdman, your words are clear and logical and we understand; your version makes far more sense than anything else we have heard so far." Again they bowed before him and he returned the same.

CHAPTER 6

The next few days slipped by quietly. He was a handsome child by any measure, but by the time the haircutter and the rest were done with him, he looked the part of a young god who had come to earth to dwell among man for reasons of his own. It seemed he could not turn a corner or walk down a hallway without a gaggle of giggling girls following him, or laying in wait, and Eilei was as bad as the rest. In her case at least, he was always glad to see her, although he was careful not to give either of them away.

The Emperor was not satisfied with the room he'd been given, and before long the Greatest Mayan, his three sons and members of the Royal Guard took him to several other rooms that were much larger, more beautifully appointed and grander in every way and he was offered his choice of which he wanted. He turned to his Emperor and bowed deeply; "I am pleased with the room you gave me, and would willingly stay there, except I know the map-maker will return in time and need his room back. All of these you have shown me are very nice, and I will be satisfied with any of them, but it is my desire to serve you however I can. So I ask you to put me in a room that is the most convenient for you so I may always be at hand should you need me."

His words pleased the aged Emperor and he put the birdman in a room not far from where he and his sons and families lived. This seemed to make everyone involved happy. However; there seems to be an unwritten law of nature that no matter how pleased some people are with the status quo; there is at least one other someone, somewhere, who is not satisfied at all.

He met with the Birdman-Commander early the next day. It was not an arranged meeting but more by chance. At least he didn't think it was planned. In truth, the Birdman-Commander had been laying in wait for the youth, trying to catch him when he was not with the Emperor or his sons. He finally sensed he had his chance and he and two of his people walked up to Cuauhtémoc and he stared insolently into Inca's eyes.

"You really think you're something, don't you, Birdman? Well; in my eyes you are nothing but a young suck-up whose time is done. You are a birdman and as such you are under my command and not the Emperor's; you will obey my orders and not his. You will go and get what little you own and you will report to the barracks to be with the other birdmen. And understand this: I know the ways of flight, as the Emperor does not, and I know your lies for what they are. Any such in front of me and you will get a beating such as never been. Have I made myself clear, *Birdman?*"

The last word was delivered in sneering scorn. As Cuauhtémoc stared into the eyes of the Birdman-Commander he saw much of what he had seen in the eyes of the Wingmaster some years back and like the Wingmaster in days of yore, the Birdman-Commander had not truly looked around. Or more specifically, behind him, which was unfortunate; because Prince H'ratli and several of the palace guards chose the exact moment the Birdman-Commander began his tirade to walk around the corner and they both saw and heard everything.

"Well; answer me birdman!" the Commander snarled.

"No, Inca, allow me;" Prince H'ratli said coldly.

The Birdman-Commander and his people turned as one, just as their Prince walked up: he was not pleased. "Oh; Great Prince," the Commander said smarmily, "how good to see you. Your birdman and I were having a friendly little chat here; nothing important, actually."

"Friendly? Nothing important? Really? Now let me see. I heard you call Inca a 'little suck-up'; that doesn't sound very friendly to me. I also seem to remember you calling him a liar: that most definitely does not sound friendly. And wasn't there something in there concerning your authority being higher than the Greatest Mayan's?"

"Well; I can see that you're going to take his side of things. I might as well go back to my own place; I have more important things to take care of anyway."

"More important than explaining yourself to your Emperor? I think not! Arrest and bind him," Prince H'ratli snapped, and his guards all but fell over each other in their eagerness to obey.

Two guards grabbed the commander's arms and bent them behind him. The third took a leather thong out of his carrying pouch and slipped the noose on one end over the commander's right wrist and pulled it tight. The strap went around his neck from his left side, across his throat and back down and then the other end was tied tightly around his left wrist. This left the man with both arms twisted behind him and gave the guardsman full control over his prisoner. By holding the thong where the X was formed, he could pull up on it which twisted the shoulders in their sockets, causing extreme pain. Or he could pull down which choked the prisoner; and pulling back, sharply, did both. It was a simple, yet elegant, method of prisoner control.

The Greatest Mayan usually knew fairly closely where his birdman was and Cuauhtémoc almost always knew where his Emperor was. There was a kind of rapport between the two that sometimes verged on the eerie, but both were content with the arrangement, and that was all that mattered.

The guards frog-walked their prisoner down different hallways while their prisoner tried in vain to first vindicate himself, and lacking that, accuse Inca of starting the whole thing. But each time he started in, the guard guiding him pulled down on the X, choking him. It gradually came to him exactly how much trouble he had gotten himself into, and with this understanding, came a dawning realization he might not get out of his predicament alive. Then they were there.

The guards outside the door saw Inca coming and they started to grin because the child was the nicest boy on the planet and he had made friends with all of them. He knew them, knew their names, the names of their wives and often the names of their children, for he was the one who never forgets. Then the guards saw their Prince loom around the corner, followed by guards, a prisoner, yet more guards and people from the Birdman-Commander's group and then they realized the prisoner was the Commander. The guards stood stiffly erect, banged the doorknocker twice and opened the door. The group walked in unannounced.

The Greatest Mayan and a select number of his scholars were gathered around a table, a stack of papers on one side with some writing sticks and ink. Five days earlier Inca introduced the Emperor and his sons to the concept of the alphabetic method of writing messages. To the absolute delight of the old monarch, he grasped the idea well ahead of anyone else, including those who wrote and read messages every day; which was perhaps odd since the Greatest Mayan had never learned to read or write his own form of writing. Or perhaps it was because of it. In any case he was currently bent over a piece of parchment, demonstrating the upper and lower case letters and explaining yet again, patiently, that A was for anteater; B was for banana. There was a sharp double-rap on the door and then the door swung open and the birdman walked in.

Seeing his birdman was always a happy thing for the elderly Monarch and he started to smile but before he was well begun the rest filed in. He stared at the group, analyzing what he saw and who, and then looked at his son. "H'ratli; what seems to be going on here?" he asked softly.

"These guards and I were walking through the palace when we turned a corner and witnessed the Birdman-Commander talking to Inca. Since the Commander was speaking to Inca, and because Inca's memory is infallible, I think that it would be best if he should tell you what was said." Ever since Prince H'ratli heard the birdman say most of his friends called him 'Inca' the Prince would rarely call him anything else. The Emperor knew the rhyme and the reason for it and approved completely.

"Thank you; H'ratli. My child; would you please explain exactly what happened and what was said?" the Emperor asked politely. From the first, the Greatest Mayan insisted he could not command the birdman. Cuauhtémoc got around that small detail by treating any request given him by his Emperor as a command, which he obeyed immediately and fully; he bowed deeply and began his report.

He started from the moment the Birdman-Commander accosted him in the hallway, and repeated the commander's exact words, including gestures, facial expressions and inflections. As he often said, it is easier to get him to start talking than to get him to stop, so he continued on, repeating the words and deeds of Prince H'ratli as well as the guardsmen and he brought them forward until the guard outside knocked on the door and let them in. By the time he was done the Emperor understood things as clearly as if he had witnessed the entire fiasco.

"Gurk!" The prisoner tried to speak, no doubt in his own defense, but the Greatest Mayan would have nothing to do with him.

"Turn him around, guardsman, I do not wish to look upon his face, I do not wish hear his feeble excuses, I do not wish to speak to him, I do not wish to . . . um."

"To smell him, Greatest Mayan?" Cuauhtémoc asked, trying to be helpful.

"Yes, child," the Emperor said with a smile, "thank you; that was exactly the words I was looking for: I don't wish to smell him either. Tell me, child, has this one done any harm to you?"

"No, Greatest Mayan, he did not. What his plans were for later, I of course can not know, but he had no time to do anything."

"If I may, Father," Prince H'ratli said; "it occurs to me no only did this one call Inca a liar, he has been doing so all along. He said it was impossible for any birdmen to land on the roof, in spite that Inca's wings are there. He also stated it is impossible for any birdman to cross half your Empire in a single day, even though there are messages from the Commander proving this was so. He said it is impossible for a birdman to flip his wings around and fly backwards even though his Emperor, three Crown Princes, the Captain of the palace guards and other guardsmen saw it happen and have attested to it. And now I think of it; he was calling us liars as well. I do not believe such a one deserves the post that he holds, and at minimum, this post should be stripped from him."

"I agree my son;" the Greatest Mayan said. He raised his hands up about shoulder high and clapped his hands together three times; Clap! . . . Clap! . . . Clap! This was the Emperor's way of finalizing any decision. The post of Birdman-Commander was permanently and irrevocably stripped from the prisoner. He turned and looked at Cuauhtémoc; a gentle, doting expression came over his face as grandfathers will often do when watching a favored grandchild.

"It seems to me, my child, you are the one most insulted by this one's ill manners. What do you think should be done with him?"

Cuauhtémoc bowed before his Emperor and then calmly looked up in his eyes. "I have told you about my life in the village where I was raised and about my grandfather, the Great Healer, and how the eagles chose me on the day I was born. I have also spoken how the eagles and my big brother, Xymatoc, came and got me and how we flew two-to-a-wing to the birdman's camp and how Temmos and Temocs came to be. What I have not yet told you is I have an enemy in the birdman's camp. Why this one hates me and wants me dead I cannot understand; but he does. I mention this only because the look I saw in his eyes then is the same look I see in the eyes of this one here, as well as in the eyes of your servant—the one who is so proud of his fathers. We Mayan believe we live in a world of flesh, but there is also a world of spirits that lay beyond us, and that this world of spirits has both good and evil spirits in it, as our world of flesh has good and evil people.

"I now understand all three of these people have obstructive spirits in them and all such spirits are always destructive as well, for they are founded in false pride and selfishness, and they roil the waters around them, creating turmoil and confusion wherever they are. No one has ever explained these things to me, Greatest Mayan, or I would remember who they were and the circumstances behind it; but I know these things are so none the less.

"Because such spirits cannot be reasoned with by human interventions, I would say that this one should be executed, as one will kill a rabid animal and for the same reason; to protect the innocent around them. I have, however, heard the Mine Masters are always in need of workers. It seems to me should this one be sent to the mines, then you will at least get some worthwhile labors out of him, and who knows, in perhaps a year or two the evil spirit will be worked out of him and he can return to polite society and live again among free men."

"Um; Inca? You do know the reason the Mine Masters are always in need of new men is the lifespan of most workers is about six months," Prince H'ratli said quietly.

Cuauhtémoc turned and looked up at his Prince; his face wreathed in absolute delight. "You heard that as well!" he exclaimed joyously; "maybe there is some truth in it after all." He turned back to the Greatest Mayan; "Perhaps that should be three years in the mines; just to be sure."

The guardsmen in the room sucked their lips over their teeth and tried to look elsewhere to keep from laughing but the Emperor and his son had no such restraints and both laughed softly and nodded their heads. "Your words and reasoning are rational as always," the Emperor said. "This one shall be sent to the mines to spend no less than three years in hard labor. Unless, of course, the obstructive spirit spoils things by making him die first. Since we seem to be clearing driftwood from our shores; go and get my servant—the one who is so proud of his fathers—and send him to the mines as well. Do not bother explaining why this is being done. And since I have come to notice his voice is nasal and whiney and irritating at times, you have my permission to stuff whatever you wish into his mouth should his voice grate upon your nerves; there is no reason you should have to suffer."

The Emperor turned his attention on the two men who accompanied the one-time Birdman-Commander; who was at that moment being hustled through the doorway. "What of these two here, my child, what do you think should be done with them?" The men in question flinched; from the moment their Prince entered the scene they knew their own future was in doubt.

"I clearly saw the eyes and faces of all three of them, Greatest Mayan, and nothing I saw in either of these two led me to believe they were aware of what was coming. If anything, I saw dismay when that one said I was to obey him and not you, and that I would get a beating for speaking the truth. I would willingly forgive them except I am not convinced they have done wrong. I suggest they be permitted to return to their usual duties."

"As you say; my child." The Emperor turned his attention from his birdman to the two men who awaited their fates. "Inca has spoken in your behalf and I can see you should not suffer the punishment of your one-time superior; you have my permission to return to your regular tasks."

"Thank you Greatest Mayan . . . um, may we speak with . . . ah, Inca . . . for a moment only?"

"Say what you wish and I shall listen;" the birdman said willingly.

"Well, it has to do with that one; the one who was just taken away."

"Please go on," Cuauhtémoc said quietly, "and do not fear you will be held accountable for him. I believe you obeyed orders to the best of your ability and that is not a thing to be punished for."

"Thank you, Birdman," the spokesman said; relief clear on his face. "The thing is: that one started abusing the power of his post almost as soon as he was given it; not much at first but his abuses increased over time. More recently, in the last few moon-cycles, he started reading all outgoing messages, a thing that he definitely does not have authority for because that is the responsibility of our Dispatcher. Very recently, he started throwing out any message he didn't approve of. He never explained why, he just threw the message in the fire. What I'm trying to say is, three days ago he was given an outgoing message with some strange writings on it. I saw a bit of it and it was like nothing I have ever seen. Evidently; that one could not read it either because it made him mad and he got up and threw it into the flames. The reason I wished to tell you this, is because I saw your 'descending eagle' at the bottom, and I knew it had to have come from your hand. I wish to let you know whatever the message was and whoever it was to be sent to - was destroyed - and I truly regret being the one to inform you of this; Birdman."

"Thank you for telling me; if you had not explained it I would be waiting endlessly for a response, not knowing why it never came. Now I understand, it will be a small thing to write another message, and send it on. In fact, if you can spare a short time, I will write it now and you can take it back to the message center and get it on the way for me."

"This will be a glad thing we can do for you, Birdman," the man said; the second nodded agreement and both bowed deeply before him.

"May I, Greatest Mayan?" he asked politely. The Emperor nodded his head and moved over, making room at the table for him.

He selected a clean sheet of paper, picked up a writing stick and eyed it closely; it looked like it would do. On the upper parts of the paper he wrote Mayan glyphs, writing down the directions and steps that would send the message to the Commander at the Northern soldier's camp, and once that was done, he wrote a letter to the Spaniard in his own tongue and writings, telling him where he was and what he was doing and offering him a position within the palace as a teacher. He ended the note with his 'descending eagle' signature and then gently sprinkled fine dust over the manuscript to be absorbed by the ink to aid drying.

"As long as you hold it carefully while you return, birdmen, the ink should not smear and the message can go out on the next flight that direction."

"Yes, Birdman . . . but we are not birdmen; we are assigned . . . *were* assigned to that one."

"You never flew? I supposed you did fly at one time," he said politely.

"At one time, yes, but no more;" the spokesman for the pair said; a sad expression on his face.

"You miss it very much then?" Inca asked in sympathy.

"With every beat of my heart; with every breath I take. Yes, I miss it," the same one replied. "I remember how it was to soar above the green jungles, to see the animals moving about and the birds flying below me. Can you believe it? I could look down upon birds in flight instead of having to look up as I do now. Those days are gone for good and I must find other things to do but I swear before Father Inti there are times when I wish I had flown out to meet Him while I could still fly."

"Those days are not gone forever, birdman, and once one has been a birdman and has flown, that one is a birdman forever, even when they must put their wings down."

"I dream of flying sometimes," the second one said softly. "I can feel the wind on my face and see the world spread out below but then I awake and realize that it is only a dream. I would give all of my tomorrows if I could just be a birdman again for today."

"Would you be willing to give your today that you might be a birdman again for all your tomorrows?" he asked the second man, a gentle expression on his face.

"I don't understand," the second man wailed, and he looked miserable.

"Are you willing to go around and talk to people and get things started, that will in time, give you a set of wings you can take up and fly; perhaps even higher and further than you have ever flown before?"

"Father Inti; **yes**! I am willing to do anything if it means someday I might fly again; tell me what I must do and it shall be done."

"Do you recall your first actual flight, the very first time you went down the fledgling slope and caught enough air you could swing around and land where you had started, without having to carry your wings back up by hand? I ask this as an idle question because I know you do: all birdmen remember this time." The man stared at him, his eyes aglow at the memory, and nodded.

"Do you remember how heavy your wings were and how difficult it was to carry them and run with them? And as you got older, how much lighter they seemed to be?"

"Yes!" the second one said, his eyes getting misty over the thought, "when I first picked up my wings they felt so heavy I didn't think I would ever be able to fly with them. And the first flight is also a thing no birdman can ever forget. It took me so many tries I thought for sure I would wash out of flight and be a groundsman forever after. I will also never forget how it felt the first time I actually caught air; it was a feeling like none I had ever felt before, I felt like I was at last one with the birds. Even after all of these years I still get chills when I remember that day and how it felt. What of you, how many times did you try, how old were you when you made your first flight; do you remember?"

"I remember everything because I cannot forget. I made my first flight on my first attempt and I was not quite yet ten years of age when I first flew alone."

"You remember everything?" the first demanded incredulously.

"Yes. I remember being born and I remember the eagle that marked me as her own. If I am careful I can even remember before my birth. It wasn't bad; actually. I had my own little room and no one to bother me. I even had a kick-ball to play with when I got bored. It wasn't until some years later I learned it wasn't a kick-ball at all but my mother's bladder. How was I supposed to know? I hadn't been born yet."

There was a brief instant while everyone analyzed what they heard and then the room erupted in laughter. The Greatest Mayan moved over to where a stone bench was nearby and sat down, doubled over; the rest of the people in the room were not doing any better. Cuauhtémoc smiled and nodded his head. In years past, some people got upset when he told them he could remember everything and never forget. Along the way he learned if he could make them laugh, it seemed to give their minds a few moments to adjust to the thought, and it could save some hurt feelings.

He waited until everyone once again contained their mirth and he bowed to them very politely, "I admit I was lying about the kick-ball, but it seemed a funny thing to say, and I have always enjoyed making people laugh." He turned his focus on the two birdmen before him. "I wish you to remember when you first flew, that your wings were about all that you could handle, and then over time they seemed to grow lighter until it was no challenge at all for you to run with them and catch air and fly. I wish you to also remember the time when you understood that the same wings that had served you so well for so long would no longer lift your weight. Your wings did not slowly get smaller over the years; you grew, and the muscles that made it easy for to carry your wings, were the reason that you could no longer fly. Suppose for a moment your wings could grow with you. If this were so; no birdman would ever outgrow his wings. Such a birdman would never quit flying unless he wished, and he could still be flying when he was in his thirties or forties and even beyond if he chose. We know wings cannot grow but people do not realize all is needed is for us to build yet larger wings.

"I have heard some say the larger wings would be too large and heavy, and no fledgling could possibly lift them, but why would a fledgling wish to? He has wings of his own. I tell you, brothers, the only thing needed to get you back into the air, you and all of our older brothers, is to design and build yet larger wings; wings that are longer and wider to catch more air. And if we as birdmen do this thing and do it well, no birdman need ever quit flying unless he wishes. This can be done and must be done because we now have an enemy without heart or soul, an enemy who kills without mercy. We must do this, not only to regain air that has been lost to us, but also to fly in defense of the Greatest Mayan and all of his children.

"I have fought this enemy from the air and have fought well and I have seen the enemy does not know how to fight birdmen because we are small and moving and their accuracy with their weapons does not impress me. I will help you in any way I can to make this so and when the enemy comes here again—as he surely will—we shall have a nasty surprise awaiting him; a surprise he will not survive." He stared at the men who stood in the room with him with a wolfish expression on his face.

The two men bowed deeply before him and then with his message in their hands they turned and left for their hearts were full of his words and there was much to think about and much that needed to be done.

⟨HAPTER 7

uauhtémoc sat at his desk, a drawing stick in hand, some papers and ink to his left and right and a set of wings gradually taking shape on a piece of paper in front of him. Ever since he had spoken to the two older birdmen yesterday; his mind was churning with ideas of different wings. Back when he was at the birdman's camp, he'd taken balsawood and carefully carved different models over many months in an effort to find a set of wings that flew further, and were also more stable. While it was true a drawing could not be lightly tossed across the room, it was equally true he could make many such drawings in a single day, and at the moment, concepts were what he was after. He just laid his latest effort up on a shelf to dry when there came a sharp double-rap at his door and in the same moment the door swung open and a servant came rushing in.

"Birdman, the Emperor commands you to come to him immediately," the servant said breathlessly. He stared thoughtfully. At no time had the Greatest Mayan ever commanded him to do anything. Quite the opposite in fact; the Emperor always insisted he could not command him at all. He pulled his waist pouch around where he could reach into it and he pulled his Temmo out and started playing with it, still kept carefully in its sheath. He had come to understand there were those who envied him, and hated him because of it, and at least a few of them would willingly send him to his death.

"What were the Greatest Mayan's exact words; Servingman?" he asked politely.

The servant stared at him, drew a breath and then released it. The expression on his face showed he would rather eat a bug than obey; but in the end he accepted the inevitable. "The words of the Greatest Mayan were, I was to come and find you, and then I was to 'request' you come as soon as it is convenient for you. But the Greatest Mayan is Emperor; he shouldn't have to 'ask' your permission; he should command and you should obey."

This sounded more reasonable to the birdman and he put the Temmo back into the pouch where it was still accessible. "Take me to him, please," he told the servant.

"Yes, but first I must explain what is happening," the man began.

"I will understand once I get there," he injected, "please, just take me to him."

"You don't understand; there are certain things . . . ."

"Less talking and more walking," Cuauhtémoc insisted, "now take me to him."

"I really need to explain things so you will be prepared . . . ."

"Where is the Greatest Mayan at this exact moment?" he said, interrupting again.

"Well; he's up on the roof where your wings are. But first I must explain . . . ."

"Most excellent! You stand here and explain things to yourself; be sure to repeat them at least three times until you understand them perfectly; but I must go to the Greatest Mayan because he needs me." He turned and left; leaving the servant muttering to himself.

"Young people nowadays; what is this world coming to? With my luck that young one will go and get himself lost and I'll get blamed for it. I'll go up on the roof and make it clear to the Emperor I tried to get the birdman to come up but he went charging off before I could explain anything. Yes, that's what I'll do. That will absolve me of error and hopefully I won't get hauled off like that poor man yesterday. There was no explanation or reason given, he was just whisked away; he didn't even have time to finish his meal." The servant was younger than his Emperor but his mind was less resilient and it took him far longer to understand things—if he ever did.

Cuauhtémoc did not get lost. He had been upon the roof that same morning as he was every morning since he arrived; checking on Xymatoc's wings to make sure all was well. It was not because he questioned the abilities of the guards who keep watch over such things, but because he was a birdman, and this is what birdmen do. He made the twists and turns needed and raced up the stairs leading to the roof, taking the steps two and three at a time with a speed and grace that would have gotten approving looks from a gazelle, if one had been around . . . and then he was there.

As he stepped out onto the roof a dull, distant blast thudded, echoing off of the surrounding mountains and buildings.

He knew that sound; that was cannon-fire.

The Emperor, his three sons, the Captain of the Palace Guards and a number of guardsmen were standing just to his right; he immediately went over and bowed before his Ruler. "I am here, Greatest Mayan; how may I serve you today?"

"Oh, thank you for coming so quickly my child; please look out into the bay and tell me what you think is taking place." He took a few steps forward and stared out across the blue waters.

From the air, as he was flying in, he had seen the bay formed an almost perfect circle, the center of which would have been found somewhat inland. The great circle was probably the caldera of a volcano which had blown its top endless ages in the past. Or it could have even been the product of an ancient meteor strike eons earlier. In either case the result must have been cataclysmic because the bay was very wide and deep. Fingers of land reached out into the ocean, and were heavily covered with jungle growth, right up to shortly before the break on either side. If one were able to put themselves directly into the center of the bay and if they used true east for the twelve o'clock position, the gap would then lay between one and two. The gap was large enough that perhaps four or five sailing ships could enter the space, sailing abreast of each other and still have some room on either side. He thought this because at the moment two such ships were just entering the bay, their sails carrying them against the current created by the great river which flowed down the mountains and out into the ocean.

"What do you make of it, my child?" his Emperor asked softly; "these great boats seem to be fighting but they do not seem to be fighting each other."

"I agree, Greatest Mayan; look at how wide they seem compared to their height. From what the Spaniard told me back at the soldier's camp, these would be merchant vessels. They are spoken of, as 'wide abeam,' and are built this way that they may carry as much trade goods as the merchants can get aboard, and it would be very unlikely two merchant vessels would attack one another.

"Look, Greatest Mayan! The ship that lies to our left is swerving. The Captain of the vessel is sailing his ship to his right. Onboard these vessels they speak of the right side of the ship as 'starboard' and the left side as 'port;' why they don't just say 'right' and 'left' I can't imagine, but that one is turning 'starboard' . . . and now the other ship is doing the same. Ah! I think I understand; they are fighting a common enemy. Yes! See how they are now one after another? Now the first ship has fired her cannons all at once. This is called a 'barrage' but why the Captain would order such is . . . oh ho! Now I see! Look just to the edge of the trees, Greatest Mayan, there to the left, you can see the prow of another ship coming into view. I wonder why the Captain of the first ship didn't hold his fire for a bit longer. Look! The Captain of the first ship is turning away! Why would he . . . ahh! I understand now." As he spoke the enemy ship let loose with a barrage of its own. Even to the uninitiated it was obvious the enemy ship was far more powerful for the thunder of her guns dwarfed what had been happening so far. By turning his ship immediately after firing he was putting his ships' stern to the enemy, offering a much smaller target as well as moving his ship away from the attacker.

A heartbeat after the enemy ship fired her guns; the second merchant ship fired hers. Perhaps this Captain knew better what he was about or perhaps his luck was greater but in any case the attacker's ship was within range and the broadside caught the attacker in places that were damaging, and even from the distance they watched and not knowing such things, everyone on the rooftop could tell the attacker was injured by the cannon fire.

The second merchant ship also veered and headed toward the distant palace where the Mayan Emperor and his people watched. No more than a few heartbeats later a second enemy ship pulled into view. This one was further out to sea, and the first enemy was in the way, so the second ship did not fire her cannons but both ships sailed towards the opening that led into the great bay. For the first time since spotting the enemy ships Cuauhtémoc looked for national flags and within a blink he found what he was looking for.

Greatest Mayan, Great Princes; look at the top part of the mainsail, do you see the black flag with the white skull and crossed bones? These are the pirates I spoke of earlier; these are the brothers of those I fought fifteen days ago. The Spaniard told me of them; he said pirates have operated on the high seas for over a hundred years but it's only been recently they've banded together and started cooperating with each other. The Spaniard said perhaps twenty years back a young pirate captain called Greenbeard started getting other pirates to work with each other instead of against. They now travel the seas in what the Spaniard called 'wolf packs' and they prey on anyone weaker than they. He said the only ships the wolf packs will consistently avoid are the British Man o'Wars and only then because these ships are heavily armed with the greatest of all cannons and because they have double-decks that both carry the 'Long Toms,' and . . ." His voice trailed off.

A third ship now glided out from behind dense jungle growth. This, like her sisters, flew the black flag called the Jolly Rogers by many and her foredeck carried a long rope that led from her upper rigging, out to the front of the deck, and this rope was lined with triangular-shaped pennants of different colors—and in that instant he understood.

"It's them!" he exclaimed in disbelief. "These are the same ships I spoke of earlier. Remember when I told you of the three ships in the inlet and how they were attacking your children? This is not the brothers of those murderers; this is them in person!" He turned to his Emperor and his face blazed with fury. He pointed with his left forefinger, his hand shook with rage; "*those ships are **mine!***" There was a deep growl in his voice, and fangs and claws and teeth, and his dark eyes promised death.

The Emperor, his three sons and the guardsmen stared at the birdman in astonishment. It was like adopting a half-grown cat, feeding it and petting it and being used to its purrs of contentment, only to have an enemy show up at the front door and seeing the cat suddenly morph into a raging tiger—or more appropriately for the time and place, a raging jaguar—right before their eyes He became energized. His eyes roamed about the rooftop in quick glances. His mind raced. He could see mental pictures inside his head of rocks falling away from between his knees as well as the net-load of rocks that Twuondan dropped, bisecting the main mast to carom crazily about the ship, wreaking havoc everywhere. But there were no rock around and deep within he knew rocks were not what he needed.

He looked about; frantic for a weapon that would work. As his eyes roved around they passed one of the torch-bowls that were filled with oil every night and kept burning for the light they give. His eyes passed the torch and then jerked back again of their own volition. Yes! This was what he needed; he turned. The servant who had been sent to get him stood very near by; his mind immediately dismissed him. He did not hold the servant responsible for being what he was; some people just can't think quickly, especially under stress, and it was not his fault for being what he was born. At the same time he was useless.

He turned his attention to the nearest guard; who happened to be one of the guards initially assigned to him.

"The oil that is used in the torches at night, how is it brought in, in clay pots or in skins?" he asked quickly.

"In skins, Inca," the guard promptly answered.

"What sizes are they, how large and heavy are they?"

"There are three general sizes, Inca; a smaller size for the torches that are high to reach; a medium size for general usage, and the largest size used to refill the others. The first two are not very heavy but the largest size usually takes two men to carry it: not because of its great weight but because we have to be careful not to rip any stitches."

"I require several each of the two smaller sizes, please; as quickly as possible."

"Yes, Lieutenant Inca," the guardsman said; saluting smartly as to a superior officer. There was in the child's expression, that which demanded instant obedience; a look that left no room for delays or discussions. The guardsman didn't even glance at his Emperor to see if it was to be. He just nudged the two men next to him and all three put their spears and other gear down where it would be out of the way and turned to obey their orders.

Cuauhtémoc was by nature, a friendly, outgoing child, and was more than willing to share his life's experiences with anyone who cared to listen. He had long since told almost everyone about his days in his home village as well as the time he had spent in the birdman's camp and the soldier's camp. The guards knew the Commander made him a Lieutenant and in their minds he still carried that rank.

While the three guardsmen were leaving to do their task he turned and walked briskly over to the edge of the roof and looked down. There was a small wall of sorts around all roofs but none of them were more than shin-high on him. He looked down, moved a few paces to his left, looked down and then moved yet again. He nodded to himself; satisfied. He turned directly about and took several quick paces away from the short wall; looked back and then took several more. Again;

he nodded to himself. He walked over and picked up his wings and carried them over to the exact spot he had stood at just a few heartbeats before. He set the wings down, keeping his left wing out of his way and made a quick sprint at the roof's edge, stopping a single pace from the rim. He stared back at his wings, looked over the edge and walked back to where his wings were. He moved them back slightly and then turned them until the beak of the wings pointed in the direction he wanted to go.

Because of the way the city of the Emperor was situated, there was almost always a good breeze blowing inland, and today it was especially so. He bent down and loosened his message net and quietly waited. It wasn't long and the first guard came back up with two small skins of oil in his hands; he brought them over to the birdman and gently set them down. Before he was finished, the second and then the third guardsmen came back; each carefully carried a much larger skin that bulged generously. They set these down next to the smaller skins and stepped back and waited further orders.

"I believe that the lesser two will be too small," he admitted, "I apologize you had to bring them up but I had never seen them before and I didn't know." He lifted one of the two medium-sized skins of oil and smiled wolfishly. "Yes," he said, "this size is perfect; thank you."

The skin started out life as a young goat. Once the animal reached the proper size for eating it was slaughtered for food. The Mayan people tried to not waste any parts of animals and almost everything on it was either eaten or used for other things; such as sewing the skins tightly with a thread that swelled when wet with oil and once all seams were properly done the skin was fitted with a wooden spout where the neck once was and filled with oil and a cork-wood stopper shoved into the hole to keep leakage to a minimum.

He took the sack of oil and carefully placed it into his message net, drawing the leading part up snug against the spine of his wings and then tied it off with the slipknot a soldier had taught him some fifteen days earlier. But this time he changed it slightly because the first knot yanked the leather thong out of his hands, stinging his fingers. This knot was only slightly different and required a somewhat longer pull but the strap would stay in his hand until he wished to release it.

A thudding sound echoed up from the shoreline down below. Prince Quoholocet walked over to the edge of the roof, looked down and then turned around to face the birdman. "Forgive me for interrupting, Inca, but my war-kaks are ready to be launched and the kaks-leaders are waiting orders."

"Tell them to hold on; Great Prince. With the enemy they now face they can only get themselves killed and they are far too valuable to waste like that;" he said.

Prince Quoholocet bowed politely and then he turned to the distant leaders and held his fists high, slightly more than shoulder width. It looked as if he was holding on to an invisible branch, and 'hold on,' was exactly what the signal meant. The leaders bowed, turned and held their own fists high, keeping the war-kaks safely on shore.

Cuauhtémoc turned and faced the rising sun for it was still fairly early in the day; he raised his hands, palms up towards the sun. "Look down upon me Father Inti and see what I am doing. This enemy is not the brothers of those who destroyed your children far to the north but the same ones. Give them to me, Great One, and I shall avenge the deaths of your innocents. It will not bring them back to life, but it will make it so, their deaths were not in vain." He placed his hands on the opposite shoulders and bowed deeply, bringing his right knee down to touch the stone flooring at his feet.

He stood up and kicked his sandals off. He worn them faithfully since the day the Greatest Mayan gave them to him but they always felt strange because he wasn't used to wearing them. Now, in flight, he wasn't about to leave them on. He picked his wings up, paused as he gathered strength and focus and then ran as fast as he could, jumped onto the small wall and leaped off and in the blink of an eye he was gone.

Prince H'ratli ran to the edge of the roof, horrified, afraid of what he would see. Instead of the broken body of the child down at the base of the palace he saw Inca, safely seated in his wings, gradually leaning back. As he did, the rushing air leveled him off and then began to lift him powerfully. The oncoming wind was being funneled between the walls of man-made cliffs, intensifying the uplift so much Cuauhtémoc felt himself being blown aloft at an amazing rate. This was height he would soon desperately need because the same wind that lifted him so strongly, also tried to blow him towards the mountains, in the opposite direction he wanted to go. He got around this by leaning his wings down as in a sort of dive; this lessened his climb but permitted him to move slowly out into the bay and towards the area where the pirates were gathering.

The first two pirate ships were now well into the bay and were sailing directly at the merchant ships. Both of these swerved and presented their sides to the oncoming pirates and each ship fired a broadside at the fronts of the pirates. Cuauhtémoc knew from talking to the Spaniard that bow shots were among the most difficult to make because not only was the front of the ship the smallest part to shoot at, it was also built the strongest since it had to take the pounding of heavy waves over its entire lifetime. The two merchant captains were not firing *at* the bows of the oncoming ships as much as *over* them and the cannon balls flew above the prow and created paths of destruction.

The merchant Captains were making the best of a very bad situation but it was a battle they could not win. Even with the painful blows they inflicted, the two pirate ships were still fully functional and both ships were starting to come about, presenting their own sides for a barrage, and that didn't include the third ship that was now entering the main current and headed—not directly towards the doomed merchants—but ahead of them. This would make a very neat scissors play and would catch the hapless ships in a crossfire that would unquestionably sink them both.

Cuauhtémoc had another plan.

Prince H'ratli turned and looked at his father and brothers in wonder. He was the closest to the edge and had seen what the others had not yet discovered for themselves. "He did it!" he exclaimed in growing delight, "Inca actually, factually caught air and not only is he flying, he's all but shooting up into the sky. He did it!" He turned and looked about and then he began jumping up and down like a puppet on strings: "He did it! He did it! He did it!" he yelled. He grabbed his brother Imhoquotep by the forearms and began dancing around him in a berserk manner, yelling "He did it, he did it, he did it," over and over, acting more like a loon than a dignified Prince of the realm. Next he grabbed one of the guards by the forearms and did the exact same thing.

For a few moments it looked as if H'ratli intended to 'dance' with every single person on the rooftop but Prince Quoholocet caught Imhoquotep's eye and silently mouthed the words, "Watch this." He turned to face Inca's departing form and exclaimed, "Oh look; look what Inca's doing now."

"He did it, he di— what? What is Inca doing now; what, what, what?" He rushed back over to the edge of the roof and stared at Inca, who was climbing swiftly but moving forward slowly. "O-o-o-h, look at that birdman fly," he sighed rapturously, his face aglow like a hajji looking upon Mecca for the first time. The City of Emperors spread out before those who were up on the palace roof, and the surrounding buildings as well, and the great pyramid where the Sun Priest stood was also filled with observers.

The Greatest Mayan watched the antics of his youngest legitimate son with an odd expression on his face. He walked up to H'ratli and stood slightly behind him and off to his right: "My son?" he asked softly.

"Yes Father," H'ratli answered, turning his head so he could see his father.

"Do you understand you are now at the edge of the roof, looking down, and have no fear?" the Greatest Mayan asked quietly.

"Well; yes, Father, there is no such thing as 'down' or 'up,' there is only distance. And it makes no more sense to fear falling 'down' than to fear falling 'up.' Using caution in times of danger is different; that's just common sense."

"Yes;" the Emperor said softly, "I heard someone say that not long ago." The Greatest Mayan and the rest watched as Cuauhtémoc swung about and began his attack.

From the moment Inca laid eyes on the torches he envisioned his assault. He would come from upwind of his target and drop the sack of oil. This would splash all over the enemy ship; creating fires everywhere. And he knew from his discussions with the Spaniard that fire was one of the greatest fears of all, because such ships carried many barrels of gunpowder, and fire and gunpowder are not a good combination.

He climbed as high as the uplift could carry him and spent the rest of the time in a glide, dropping down in height as he swung by. The first two pirate ships were well into the bay and were moving towards the merchant ships, veering to intercept; or lacking that, to fire more broadsides at the hapless ships, a thing that would soon doom them. The third and final pirate was now in the middle of the bay and sailing directly against the current, obviously intending to move as far upstream as needed and then swerve into the merchants. The river that moved past the Emperor's palace and flowed into the great bay was fairly large, but not a giant, and the swiftly moving waters were greatly slowed by the much greater mass of the water within the cove;. By the time it reached where the last pirate ship sailed it was a slow but relentless tide moving eternally towards the sea.

He came in from the ship's stern, perhaps twelve tall trees in the air. This was higher than he liked, but he was far from shore, and there would be no uplifts any closer. He timed his speed by counting the beats of his heart, watching objects in the water and seeing how many heartbeats it took from the time the beak of his wings passed over it, until it was directly below his knees. This was a technique taught by the Flightmaster back at the training grounds and was most useful. By the time he had a good idea of how many beats he needed he was properly lined up on the ship and closing fast for the winds he fought on the way out were now carrying him very quickly towards the ship. He lined up on the rear mast and concentrated his utmost. When everything felt right he yanked the strap in a long pull and the goatskin of oil tumbled free. In the blink of an eye he shot up and forward for he now had less mass to move through the air. In his mind he saw the goatskin tumble through the air to strike the rear mast up high and splatter all over. Reality was not exactly that but it was close enough he did not feel cheated. As his knees passed over the rear mast, the skin of oil struck the mast just above the spar. The skin did not quite hit dead center but slightly off to one side, perhaps one-third to the left and the rest to the right. The skin split as if cut by a knife and the two pieces spun off, slinging oil in circles, not unlike sprinklers watering a lawn.

What he did not know - and could not anticipate - was the volatility of oil. As the spray was whipped about by the wind, the sheets of oil became drops and the drops became smaller drops which were quickly being turned into a vapor, all of which was falling through the oxygen-rich air of the equatorial jungle. By the time the vapor found a lit torch, or someone shooting one of the muskets that the attackers used, the formula was set for a disaster that turned the upper ship into a massive fireball blossoming outward in a sphere of red and yellow flames and the shockwave spread out and hit Cuauhtémoc in the tail section of his wings; rocking him about.

"Well that was fun," he muttered to himself; "for me, I mean, of course."

CHAPTER 8

Inca looked under his right arm as he swung around and gazed upon a scene that might have been lifted directly out of the Spaniard's idea of hell. The Spaniard spent some time expounding to him about the demons that sprang out of the 'rift,' wherever that was thought to be. These creatures were believed to be evil, incarnate, and they would shriek and cackle insanely as they flew about. The man believed in these creatures as devoutly as he believed in the existence of sea-dragons, mermaids, giant squid and sailing off the edge of the world if one wasn't careful. The Spaniard was a happy, cheerful fellow, and Cuauhtémoc was pleased to spend as much time with him as possible, both learning the man's language as well as just in idle chatter. In was in one of the latter times they discussed demons in general and the man was eager to demonstrate what he thought these foul creatures sounded like. He shrieked and cackled and Inca joined in, creating some very strange looks from the Mayan soldiers around them. But in the end, the man admitted Cuauhtémoc sounded exactly like the demons. How he was supposed to know this, Inca never learned, for the man swore he never personally saw or heard such.

None of which mattered at the moment; except for the insane shrieking. Seamen as such tend to be even more superstitious than their land-bound cousins and that should prove true even among pirates. It is a matter of record bullies rule through fear and there is no man on earth more scared than a bully who has just discovered that his own sweet self is now in trouble. Cuauhtémoc swung about and flew directly to the pirate ship to his right, the ship closest to shore. He made a determined run on the ship just as if he were going to drop yet another goatskin of oil. He had no such thing but the pirates below did not know that, nor did they know what he had done to the first ship, filling those below with horror.

As he passed over the first ship, the pirates aboard completely forgot they were fighting merchants. Everyone on both ships who could lay their hands on one of the muskets started shooting at him and those who didn't have shoulder arms were trying other things. One petrified pirate threw belaying pins up into the air at Cuauhtémoc, oblivious to the fact he was well out of range and the pins had to come back to earth somewhere. Even as the thought came to Temmo he saw one of the heavy pins rise up, spin briefly in the air, only to land squarely in the face of the man who threw it. The man was so terrified he didn't seem to realize his nose was broken and blood was now pouring down his face. And with that; it all came into focus for him.

He shrieked insanely and cackled and gibbered and made all the weird noises he could think of and it was like tossing oil onto a fire and people below went insane with terror. Pirates are well aware what they do is evil and they have no business plundering and murdering the innocent. This, of course, creates a guilty conscience and to many of the men below it seemed their worst nightmares had just come true and that one of the demons from the Pit had been summoned to drag each and every one of them back down into the burning hells with him.

He began his run on the ships, passing from the rear to the front. As he flew ahead of them he banked sharply left, losing precious altitude in the process and began a second run. The two ships were directly side-by-side and perhaps forty or fifty long steps apart; more than enough for a birdman and a set of wings. Cackling and shrieking maniacally he began his next pass. This pass was lower for he traded yet more precious height for speed and he all but shot between the two ships. This was very good thinking on his part because the moment he passed, everyone on both ships who had any kind of weapon at all started trying to knock him out of the sky. The two things that saved his life was the speed of his passing and the fact that the panicked pirates were shooting at where he was and not where he would be when their shots arrived. This was true of those with shoulder arms as well as the cannoneers. What none of the people on either ship realized until it was much too late, was their sister ship lay directly opposite, and both ships delivered point-blank cannonades upon each other, effectively ending this particular part of the war.

The enemy had taken all that they could endure. First one black flag went down to be replaced by a white flag, and then the other. The merchants witnessed the entire show and while they weren't sure but what this strange creature was trying to help them, they weren't going to take any chances either, and they very quickly sprouted the white 'I surrender' flags as well.

Cuauhtémoc now had problems of his own for he was far out over the waters and lower than he liked. He was almost in the center of the great bay and much too far from any shore to hope to make it to land. His options were very limited. He could splash down in the water and hope one of the war-kaks would see and respond and get to him before he drowned—a hope that was dim at best because he didn't know how to swim. The thing that bothered him the most about this choice was it would destroy Xymatoc's wings and he was not going to permit that if he had anything to say about it.

His only other chance lay directly before him and he was closing in fast. Almost from the moment the fireball exploded, various kegs of gunpowder cooked off with thunderous blasts, but that finally died down for the time being. The center mast was now shattered and lay at an angle off its portside and pointed aft. At the moment, various parts of the ship were burning but the wooden mid-deck had yet to fully ignite. This produced a fairly brisk fire both fore and aft, leaving the middle afire, but not nearly as much. He could see sparks and smoke swirling briskly up into the air and he knew a fire could easily produce a localized but powerful uplift: he aimed his wings toward the ship's midsection and waited.

A moment before he hit he threw both arms up over his eyes, took a deep breath and held it, covering his ears with his hands as best he could because he knew from talks with his grandfather in days of yore, that the ears, eyes and nose of a person are the most delicate parts of their faces and neither will heal as readily as the other parts of the body, if at all. It was unbearably hot but in the instant before he felt the heat he experienced an incredibly powerful uplift and felt himself shoot up into the sky like toast out of an over-sprung toaster. He was in, and then out of the heat, before he could actually be harmed. He dropped his arms and looked around. He was well over a tall tree higher than he'd been just moments before. "Wow; that was fun," he said and then added as an afterthought, "but not the heat, of course." He looked around; the southern part of the bay lay before him and the palace and the main part of the city lay to his right. Behind him and out of his view were the merchant ships as well as the pirates. He glanced briefly at the water below, and decided that unless he wanted to end up there, he'd better do something about it.

This worked out so well he swung about in the air and headed back in the same direction he had just come from and once again flew above the flames, covering his eyes and ears as before; it was hot, but not quite as much. The important thing from his point of view was he was gaining much-needed height each and every time he did this, so he swung through it time and time again and with each pass he climbed ever higher; this was height he would soon need desperately.

It seemed to be somewhat cooler now when he flew through the flames that erupted on either side of him and below. He was concentrating on getting out of the fix he was in and so was unaware that virtually every eye in the city, as well as those on the four ships that still lived, were watching his every move, mesmerized, unable to take their eyes off of him for a minute; many even seemed unwilling to blink, afraid that they might miss something of interest.

The burning ship had long since lost her sails to the consuming flames and without that to push her on, her forward momentum slowed and then ceased and she began to slowly be carried back towards the distant sea by the relentless flow of the river. He could not continue his tactics forever, because even though he was in and out so quickly, the great heat would in time take its toll upon him. He swung around and instead of passing from side to side as he had been, he flew over the doomed ship from stern to bow. This was very nearly too much of a good thing because even though he reclaimed a lot more of the height he had lost, the two hottest parts were directly over the fore and aft of the ship and by the time he ended the final pass, the ship was drifting further from where he wanted to be and the last blast of heat was all that he wanted for as far into the future as he could see.

The winds that had fought him on the way out were now favorable; and he moved over the water's surface faster than he had ever covered distance before. The soldiers in the waiting war-kaks waved at him and pointed in his direction and at least two of the kaks-leaders made eye contact with him and raised their hands aloft and shrugged: "What do we do now?" was the obvious question in their minds. He swung his right hand over his head twice in a wide circle and then pointed at the distant ships with his forefinger. 'Sic 'em' was the meaning. This was exactly what the kaks-leaders wanted to see and almost as a single man they ordered their boats out into the bay and into action.

As he glided further into the city the people on the streets and rooftops pointed and waved at him; they obviously saw his attacks on the pirates, and were wishing him well, but he had no time to respond. He was becoming increasingly aware that when he left the burning ship he didn't have quite enough altitude, and from what he could now see, he would be too low to land on the palace rooftop. This was a minor nuisance; he would swing around and catch the uplift and make a few circles until he was high enough. But as he approached the palace, several of the guardsmen raised their right arms up and down frantically, and pointed at him.

For a moment he didn't understand. He glanced over at his right wing but there was nothing wrong there. As he stared, he realized the arm-wavers were pointing more towards his left. He glanced that way and was astonished to find his left wingtip was on fire. That wingtip had become badly frayed when he made his unorthodox landing eight days back; and it looked as if the heat of going through the flames so many times had caught some of the ragged areas on fire. By now his flight managed to start a nifty little blaze. It wasn't enough to roast meat over but it wouldn't be long before it was. He glared at the offending wing. "What's with you; why can't you be good like your brother over there?" he demanded, pointing at his right wingtip with a chin-jut.

Any visions of him making another few leisurely laps to gain height evaporated before his eyes. It seemed to him - just off-hand - that the Lord of Darkness was going through a lot of trouble to get him killed. Obviously; the foul Lord did not like his servants slaughtered in wholesale numbers. But he believed when one door was closed to mortal man, then Inti opened another door, but He left it up to people to figure out where that door was and how they were supposed to slip through it.

He could land on one of the lower rooftops but that is not where he wanted to be: there had to be a way; there just had to. As he approached the palace walls he could see he was not going to make it, he would slam into the wall perhaps the height of one tall man below the edge. And in that moment he understood where his other door was.

People were rushing towards the wall where he was going to hit; he waved them off with gestures, trying to get them out of his landing zone and then in a blink his downward angle hid them from view. He remembered when he jumped; there had been a very strong uplift where the wind was forced upward by the wall. He also understood; as a birdman could exchange height for forward speed by leaning downward, he could also exchange forward speed for height by leaning back, and at the moment, height was what he needed more than anything. He waited until he felt the time was right and then he leaned back. The beak of his wings promptly lifted and the uplift from earlier caught him at the same moment and he shot upwards: not as powerfully as when he flew through the fire but strongly none the less. He popped up without warning and all those who were rushing towards the edge to see him do his imitation of a bug hitting a windshield, turned and did their imitation of a covey of frightened quail and they scattered in an ever-widening ring.

He only barely made it over the roof's edge; he felt at least one of his tail-drag sticks scrape as he passed over—much too close for comfort—he immediately leaned to his left and the wingtip dragged against the rough stone roof leaving a long streak of charred wood, sparks and smoke behind and in the same instant friction spun him around as it had some eight days before. The wing's beak bit the roof next and just for a heartbeat or two he was again flying backwards, his tail higher than his head and then all movement ceased and he stuck his feet onto the roof and he was landed. Several servants rushed forward with watering pots used for plants and they extinguished the flames on his wingtip, preventing further damage.

He stepped away from his wings and lifted his hands, palm upwards, towards the sun above. The sun had not moved a half-fist in the time he had been gone. He bowed deeply, placing his hand, fingers widely splayed on this opposite shoulders. "Thank you Father Inti for keeping me safe and bringing me back again; and thank you for delivering these others into my hands, that I may avenge your innocent children, and make sure these will never again harm another child of yours." He dropped to his right knee, held his position for a moment and then stood up and turned around and stared up into the eyes of his Emperor.

"My child; are you well? We saw you fly into the flames and come out again repeatedly; what possessed you to do such a thing; you could have been killed."

"I was out of height, Greatest Mayan, and had no other place to go. Had I flown into the water I would have drowned before your war-kaks reach me because I don't know how to swim. The burning ship was directly before me, and while I don't think you could see it from here, the middle section was not burning as much as the ends and I flew between the worst parts. It was the only chance I had to come out alive. True, I may be a bit smoked up and singed around the edges but I am alive and well and that is enough to make my heart glad."

"My heart as well; my child. I cannot say how afraid I was for you and I can not thank you enough for your deeds. Speak what you wish for a reward and it shall be yours, up to half my kingdom; the north half or the south, whichever you desire. Do you like this palace? If you want it you can have it; I will have my people build another palace for me somewhere else."

"I wish no reward, Greatest Mayan for I fought a common foe. These here are the same ones who murdered your innocent children far to the north, and if they murdered innocents here in Maya, they have murdered innocents in other places as well. People like this are not humans, but vermin in human form, and they must be exterminated as quickly as they are found if the rest of us are to live in peace."

"It is my wish that you be rewarded, Birdman," the Greatest Mayan said and his dark eyes glinted dangerously. From the very first, the Emperor said he did not feel he could command the youth, and instead always phrased his words as polite requests, which Cuauhtémoc always accepted and obeyed as commands. Both parties understood the rules and both stuck to these rules without fail, but now the great monarch felt strongly, and he was not about to permit disobedience; not even from his birdman.

"It shall be as you wish, Greatest Mayan," he said and bowed deeply before his ruler. "I know what reward I want. I wish to obey Father Inti in all things and do my best to serve Him. I wish to be permitted to serve you and your children, both here and to the far extents of your kingdom and be allowed to do all that I can to give you and all of your children as long and happy lives as I am able. I now understand this is the job Inti has made me for because it the job that makes me the most happy. I can think of no greater reward and I will accept nothing less."

His emperor stared at him for long moments and then nodded his head slowly as understanding came to him; "It shall be as you say, my child," he said. He lifted his hands up and clapped once, twice and then again and it was so. Cuauhtémoc stared the aged ruler in his eyes and then in an exceedingly graceful flow of motion he dropped to his knees and then down onto his face. He cradled his monarch's left foot between his hands and pressed his cheek against his instep. This is the ultimate expression of love and devotion and the Greatest Mayan looked down upon his child and tears began to trickle down his weathered cheeks to drop unnoticed onto the back of Inca's head.

The two held this pose for long moments and then Inca stood up in the fluid flow he affected so well and then turned and stared off into the bay where the war-kaks were just now starting to surround all four ships. Neither the pirates nor the merchants offered even token resistance for they had experienced the demon's attacks, and since none of them understood it was only a child and not a demon, none of them wished to risk another such assault. No; it was far better to face any sort of death than to be hauled off into the burning hells by one of the Fallen. He stood quietly and watched the distant ships and a sad expression came into his face. What he did, he did very well, but that did not mean he enjoyed it.

"I think I must be tired, Greatest Mayan," he said, turning to his monarch, "perhaps I should go to my room and take a bath and lie down awhile and maybe have some of my tea."

"Just a moment young man, I have somewhat to say to you," Prince H'ratli said. He saw the expression on Inca's face and the look bothered him. "Do you understand your Grandfather went to a great deal of trouble and expense to bring these toys for you to play with? Do you see what you have done with them?" Inca looked out into the bay and then turned back to Prince H'ratli and nodded. "What of that ship floating out of the bay? You didn't even have that for a fist of the sun and look at what you did to it. What do you have to say for yourself?"

Cuauhtémoc took another look at the ship now in full blaze as it drifted slowly towards the mouth of the bay; he turned back and faced his prince. "Oops? he asked softly.

"Oops?" Prince H'ratli demanded and then turned his head, trying vainly to fight off laughter. "'Oops' doesn't begin to cover it. And what about those other ships over there?"

Inca looked at the four ships which were now being swarmed over by Mayan warriors and then turned his attention back to his prince. "They were damaged when I got them," he said defensively, but he was starting to smile.

"Scratched up a bit I'll admit, but still— and I don't suppose you even thought to thank your Grandfather for buying all these toys for you to play with."

He turned to the Greatest Mayan who was watching his youngest son with an odd expression on his face; "Thank you Grandfather," he said in a somewhat nasal monotone. The emperor gave the child a small bow in recognition. The birdman turned his attention back to Prince H'ratli.

"Well; I can only hope that you have learned your lesson here, Birdman, and the next time your grandfather buys you more ships to play with—"

"I shall smash them up even faster," Cuauhtémoc said, and peals of giggles escaped him as he spoke, and an impudent look came into his face and eyes.

"What? What-what? Just for that; you go straight to your room right now . . . and do take a bath while you're there. Don't forget to give your grandfather a hug before you leave; grandfathers require things like that on a regular basis."

"Yes Uncle H'ratli;" he said. He went over to the emperor and gave him a hug; "Thank you, Grandfather," he said and moved over to the next person in line, giving him a hug; "thank you Uncle Quoholocet" he said and moved over to the next and hugged him as well; "thank you Uncle Imhoquotep" and then he came back to Prince H'ratli; "thank you, friend," he said and gave him the longest hug of all. He walked off and peals of giggles followed him through the doorway and down the steps and as long as they could hear him he was still giggling.

"Um;" one of the guardsmen who had been originally assigned to watch out for Inca was looking at his prince and then where the child had just gone.

"Yes, I agree," Prince H'ratli said. "Please go and keep an eye on him and make sure he is all right. And see if you can't get the woman who serves him to bring some food and hot water for that drink that he likes. Please don't forget to take his sandals with you as you go; he honestly tries to remember to wear them but he is more used to going barefoot and I suppose it feels more natural for him that way." The guard, with a relieved look on his face, bent down and picked the up sandals and left on his task.

Prince H'ratli turned and found his father, brothers and the guards and servants all looking at him. "It was in his eyes," he said, "he wasn't tired; he was sad. Do you remember him telling us about when he was in the Northern Soldier's camp and the Commander was getting the butcher's bill for the dead and injured? Remember how he told the Commander that silly thing about the new salute that he thought of?" And he tucked his thumbs under his armpits and began to flap his elbows. "Do you remember how he said he could only take so much sadness and then he has to either laugh or cry and he prefers to laugh? Remember how he said it made the Commander and everyone else laugh? Accusing him of breaking his toys was the silliest thing I could come up with; because I didn't want to see him cry."

Everyone bowed politely to him in recognition of his words. "Thank you, my Son," the emperor said softly, "I would not wish to see him cry either."

Far up on the side of the mountain, somewhat southwest of the City of Emperors stood a long line of men: these men were the latest recruits for the mines and they were halfway up a very long trail when the first cannon blast echoed off of the mountains; through some acoustical twist of the terrain they heard the cannon discharge very clearly and everyone stopped and stared. The prisoners stopped because the guards wanted to watch and all stood spellbound as the entire scenario play out before them.

Among the prisoners was the one-time Birdman-Commander. He stood with a stick of wood jammed crossways in his mouth and held in place with a leather thong that reached around the back of his head. His arms were twisted behind him and strapped at the wrists and the leather thong ran up and around his neck; like everyone else in line; and like everyone else he was tied by the neck to a long rope that kept everybody in a tight, easily controlled group. He had an almost ideal spot to watch things and with the guards and other prisoners he saw Cuauhtémoc jump from the top of the palace; for he alone of all present knew who it was. He felt a surge of joy for he knew the child would be killed and it would almost make his fate bearable. But no, the child lived, only to fly far out into the bay, seeming to ignore a number of laws of physics in the process, only to torch one ship completely and fly between yet other ships, and somehow escaped the deadly gunfire the ships exchanged. The boy flew through the flames repeatedly and then flew all the way back to the palace with one wingtip on fire and somehow, again defying other physical laws, managed to land once again on top of the palace roof. He clearly saw the birdman spin around and fly backwards for a very short distance before he came to a stop. None of which was even remotely possible for a birdman to do.

That one's heart was filled with hate and plans. He would bide his time and when things were right he would escape with as much gold as he could carry. He would make it back to the city with the gold, find and buy the right people and before he was done the broken body of the birdman would lie at his feet and he would be avenged.

Unfortunately for him; the worlds of fantasy and reality rarely ever meet. If the average lifespan of a mine worker was about six months; that meant while some lived longer, yet others lived considerably less.

He was not quite a full month into his sentence when he managed to do something stupid and stubborn, as was typical of him, and he brought part of one of the supporting walls down upon himself. The other prisoners carried him up to the mouth of the mine where soldiers took over. These called the healer in; another prisoner who, to his good fortune, knew about the healing arts and was thus spared labor deep in the mines. The healer looked his broken body over and pronounced him good as dead. Two of the burliest guards packed his broken body down to the river and on the count of three they launched him out into the water where he floated no more than two or three heartbeats before he was surrounded by hundreds of flashing fins and razor-sharp teeth for this particular river was the home of the piranha and in much less than a thumb of the sun he was reduced to a pile of fresh bones that lay among the many who proceeded him there, and even as he died, he blamed all of his troubles on . . .

CHAPTER 9

uauhtémoc. He was laying in his bath while the water poured around and over him. He managed to scrub most of the smoke and stink off and even his hair didn't smell as singed as it had a short while ago. There came a sharp double-rap at his door and a moment later one of the guards poked his head through. "Um; Inca? Prince H'ratli said for me to go and get the serving woman and have her bring you some food and some hot water, and I've got your sandals with me."

"Thank you Guardsman, please come in; I'm in the bath trying to get the last of the smells off me."

The guardsman, the mother serving-woman and her two daughters came in, laden with food from the kitchens as well as some hot water. He climbed out of the bath and quickly rubbed himself down with the cloth used for such and slipped into some fresh clothes. He was anxious to get at the hot water; he preferred his tea to be hot as possible, because cooler water couldn't get all the nutrients out, what he thought of as 'flavors.' He much preferred the water boiling when his leaves went in and then he liked to let them soak awhile and let the water cool at the same time.

The women watched him with their hands over their mouths. They were obviously concerned about something and then he saw what he thought to be a guilty look on the guard's face and understood he must have been filling them in on the details. This made sense because he knew this particular guardsman and Zypolitc, one of the mother serving-woman's daughters, had something going between them.

"Birdman, what has happened to you, you've been burned;" the mother serving-woman said concernedly as she moved forward. She touched his arm in a motherly way and then ran her hand gently down his cheek; a look of deep worry on her face.

"Yes; I had to fly through fire repeatedly in order to get enough height to return back to the palace roof, and if you don't mind, I prefer not to discuss it further. You can say whatever you wish on the subject in my presence and I shall not mind, I just don't wish to speak of it myself."

"You should see the healer; you're burned in places and your hair is singed," mother serving-woman said anxiously as she stared at him; her eyes raked him from hair-line to foot and back again and concern was clear upon her features.

"I do not need to see the healer," he replied, "my grandfather is the Great Healer, and he taught me most of what he knows. I remember it all and I know I am not hurt badly and I will heal up soon and be none the worse for it."

"Well; you're going to see the healer whether you wish it or not," the guardsman said. "Just as I was leaving I heard the Greatest Mayan tell his servant to go and get the healer and send him to you; the Emperor is very concerned."

"If it is the Greatest Mayan's wish then I will obey . . . but I am not seriously hurt. In a few days some of my skin may peel, and I may well be tender for awhile, but in time I will heal up and my hair will grow back out and before the next full moon I shall be as I was before."

Cuauhtémoc managed to get the leaves into the hot water to soak; the water was not as hot as he liked but it was hotter than expected and he thanked the woman who brought it.

He was just about to take his first sip when a double rap sounded on his door and an instant later an older man entered the room, followed by a much younger man. "Are you the birdman?" the Healer demanded.

Inca nodded his head.

"You don't look damaged to me. From what I was led to believe you were badly burned all over your body. Whatever made you do such a crazy thing anyway; jump into a fire like that?"

"In the first, I didn't jump, I flew. In the second; I didn't just fly in and out again; I did it a total of nine times. And for the third; it was my only chance to live. Had I landed in the water I would have drowned before anyone could get to me because I don't know how to swim."

"How could you be near enough to a fire to fly through it and still be surrounded by water?" the healer demanded indignantly.

"I was out in the middle of the bay, fighting pirates, and I set one of their ships on fire. If you wish to hear more you will have to speak to someone else because I don't wish to discuss it."

The healer glanced around and saw the guardsman with both hands over his mouth and he was shaking his head vigorously. He lowered his hands just long enough to say "Greatest Mayan," and immediately clamped his hands back over his mouth and shook his head once again. The Healer gave the guardsman a single long look and then nodded his head as understanding came to him.

The healer started to speak and then stopped. He raised his nose slightly and began sniffing the air. He did this several times and then looked again at Inca. "What's that scent? It smells herbal. I don't recall ever smelling that particular herb though."

"That is my drink. My grandfather is the Great Healer up in the northern High Reaches village and he sends them to me regularly," he answered.

"He is not; he does not," the healer snapped, "the Great Healer is right here in our city. I know because I have met with him many times. I even have one of his drawings: it is one of a flower and it is exquisitely done. You wouldn't want to know how much gold I had to give him for it. He didn't want to sell it but I kept offering him more and more until he finally gave in and sold it to me. This is quite a feather in my headdress I can tell you; all of the other healers in the city are insanely jealous."

"The Great Healer is here in this city?" he asked in sudden interest. "This healer, does look like me, is he tall and slender; is he Incan as I am?" Now Inca stared at the Healer and his full attention was upon him and the one who followed him, learning healing at his master's feet.

"He is not," the healer sniffed, "he's Mayan as I am and slightly shorter than me; I can certainly see you've never met him."

"A moment please," Cuauhtémoc said and crossed the room; he picked up a drawing of a set of wings he was working on earlier; he returned and handed the sketch to the older healer. "Please take care in handling it, the ink may not be quite dry yet and I'd prefer not to have it smeared."

The oldest of the pair took the paper in hand and looked it over. "Oh look," he said, "a pair of wings . . . and very nicely done as well. I presume this is some of your work; you being a birdman and all."

"It is," he admitted, "please look down into the lower right corner and say what you see."

"Well, it looks to be the head of some bird or other . . . now that's strange; I've seen that somewhere . . . and fairly recently too."

"Have you seen the sketch of the Greatest Mayan that he has in his throne room?"

"Why yes! The eyes give me the crawlies; they follow me everywhere I go. I wouldn't want that up in my office I can tell you that, I'd feel the Greatest Mayan was always watching me . . . not that I'm doing anything wrong, of course."

"Did you notice the lower right corner?" Inca asked politely.

"Well; no, like I said, the eyes follow me and I guess that's all I ever looked at. Do you know who drew it? It's incredible."

"I think I might know," the youngest said thoughtfully, "I saw that drawing as well and the symbol on this sketch of wings is also on that drawing of the Emperor. You drew them both, didn't you, birdman?"

"Yes I did," Inca said softly. "And did you happen to notice the lower-right hand corner of the drawing you paid so much gold for?"

"Well, no, I . . . uh, yes; that's where I saw that bird's head before: now I remember." The healer looked absolutely sick. He hung his head and an expression of resentment slowly filled his face.

"Tell me; what bothers you most; that you paid out all that gold for a drawing intended to go to all healers, free, or that this one lied to you and claimed he was the Great Healer?"

"The deceit, without question," the healer said with a look of growing anger.

"You are wiser than many," Cuauhtémoc said softly, "gold can always be replaced but when trust is lost it can never be regained. Now then; how would you like to get this false healer shut down for good and perhaps even get some of your gold back; if not all of it?"

"I would like that very much;" the healer admitted.

The three women were watching things with rapt attention; their heads moved back and forth between the two so much they were starting to look like people watching a tennis match.

"This is what I suggest. Go ahead and examine me to your liking and even give me some burn salve if you think I need it; and then, when you report your findings to the Greatest Mayan, you can tell him I am not seriously harmed; which will please him. While you're making your report you can mention you said the Great Healer is here in this city and when we discussed it I learned this man is impersonating my grandfather and I was upset. Not only is this one stealing my grandfather's good name, he is also stealing papers I have written and is claiming them as his own, and selling these papers for large amounts of gold. If you tell the Greatest Mayan these things I believe you will soon find you will get some sort of satisfaction . . . but before you do that, there is a favor I would ask of you."

He went over to one wall where some of his drawings were and selected one and brought it over to the healer: it was a very detailed sketch of a leaf. "The herbal drink you asked about when you came in comes from this kind of leaf. Before; all leaves I have ever gotten have been crushed but this leaf was entire. Here; I can show you the dried leaf as well as the drawing. You are welcome to keep the sketch and show it around to your brother healers and whoever supplies you with your medicines but I do not have very many leaves left and I will not let you take the leaf with you."

"Thank you for showing me this, Birdman," the healer said. "I admit I've never seen the like; is this something that your grandfather, the Great Healer, has given you? What are its properties, do you know?"

"I will be pleased to answer your question, Healer, but before I can I must speak of other things first. Do you have some time to spare; a thumb of the sun or so?"

"I have as much time as it takes. My orders from the Greatest Mayan are very clear. I am to do whatever it takes to make sure you are well and comfortable; even if it takes the rest of today and all of tomorrow;" the healer said. But he spoke with a smile and Cuauhtémoc knew this was not displeasing to him.

"Then the first thing that I must say is I remember everything. I remember being born, I remember my grandfather's face, and I remember both the eagle's cry as well as the feather hitting me right over my heart. I can remember these things *with* my mind today but at that time I could only remember things *to* my mind; I could not recall anything. If I felt hungry; it was as if I was always hungry and never knew of a time when I was not. And when I was full; I could not know there were times when I was hungry."

Everyone in the room was fascinated by Inca's words and at times it appeared no one was breathing. "When I was about three I started following my grandfather everywhere. I suppose most grandsons are this way with their grandfathers. Or perhaps it was because his was the first face I saw; as I already said. From that time onward, until I left the village, my grandfather taught me everything he could about the healing arts for he intended I follow in his footsteps, and everything that he ever told me, I still recall. We villagers all speak the Incan tongue and it is the Incan language I learned first. It was not until later when I heard my grandfather speaking to one of the birdmen in Mayan I even knew there was another language other than the one we spoke. I remember how curious it made me and how I pestered my grandfather until he started teaching me Mayan as well as all of the rest.

"The thing I wish to stress is; grandfather always told me the names of every plant: the leaves, the roots, the stems, the berries and everything else and always told me the proper time and way of harvesting these plants and how to best store and use them. He, of course, always spoke in Incan when he did this. But the one plant he never told me about; where to find it, what its proper name was, how to harvest and store it; is this drink." He reached over and picked the cup up and took a sip. "Cold again, I hate it when it gets cold." He shrugged his shoulders and finished the cup off in a few quick swallows.

"What I would like to ask of you is for you to show this drawing to all of your brother-healers as well as the ones you buy your herbs and powders from and see if you hear of anyone who has knowledge of it. I can perhaps tell you two things about this herb; the first is everyone who has ever tasted it has told me that it is very bitter—I have never had anyone ask for a second taste. As for the second thing; maybe we should all go over to my bed while I lay down; I'm not sure I can stand up for this."

They all followed him over to where his bed was and he lay down upon it. "As I have already told you, I can remember everything I have ever seen, heard or tasted; if I go deep enough it is as if I am reliving it again. This memory I am about to expose is one of my very earliest, perhaps from the day I was born. I certainly do not recall anything before this; after my birth. I am laying on my back—he rolled into position—and my grandfather is giving me a drink from a hollow straw by dipping it into the liquid and sealing it with his finger and letting me have a few drops at a time. My mother is speaking: 'Father, why must my son drink this; wasn't it enough I had to drink it all the time I was pregnant with him?' His voice sounded very feminine.

"'No daughter, it is not enough. Do not forget it was you who first showed me the markings on the Great Calendar and explained the meanings of them.'" Now his voice was deeper, definitely masculine.

"Please try and understand," he said, speaking in his normal voice, "that we all speak Incan in my village, so I must also translate while I'm remembering." His voice changed once again; "'this drink must be given him all of his life, certainly until he is fully grown. This plant only grows in one place I know of; and all efforts I have made over the years to make it grow elsewhere have ended in failure. The drink itself is a cathartic, a purifier of the blood and body, but where most cathartics stop there, I have reason to believe this herb goes much farther and helps strengthen not only the body, but also the mind, the spirit and the soul. Our little boy will grow up to be one of a kind and he shall be a child who knows no fear.'"

His eyes were unfocused as he was speaking; but now he returned to his normal self. "I rarely sleep very long at nights and many times I will just lie abed and think and remember things from years past because from time to time I recall something that is useful for here and now . . . much like what I've just said; but I had not bothered to recall everything until just now. From what I now understand, I doubt any of the healers or suppliers will be able to identify that leaf, but try anyway if you don't mind."

Inca got up and faced the people before him.

"You're never afraid?" the guardsman asked; impressed.

"No. At least I've never experienced anything that sounds like fear. In truth, I don't understand fear anymore than I understand forgetting things, because I do neither. I understand when people say they have forgotten something; I just don't understand how. In fact, I'm not convinced there really is such a thing as fear, anymore than there is up or down, left or right, front or back. In either case it is our minds interpreting things happening around us."

"I would very much like you to explain that statement, if you can," the oldest healer said.

"I shall try," he said, "Zypolitc, would you help me please," he asked politely.

"Yes, Birdman," she said and immediately came over to him.

"Please stand just here in front of me with your back to me," he said; she did so. "Thank you. Now would you please walk ten steps directly away from me, stop and turn towards me." Again she obeyed his requests.

"Zypolitc now stands ten steps away from me, as we all see. From her viewpoint, I am directly in front of her and from my viewpoint she is in front of me. Each of you sees this is so; but each of you see it from a different perspective; it is not the same for any of us. In fact, the only thing consistent for all of us is the fact we two are ten paces apart. I must believe anything other than distance is a perception of the individual, and therefore is not real, and that the only thing is real is distance. Zypolitc; would you please hold your right arm out like so;" and he extended his arm to show her: she obeyed. "Do you see the direction that your hand points? Please turn in that direction but do not move otherwise." She again did as she was asked.

"Our perceptions have again changed for each of us but the distance has not; I insist distance is the only thing here that can be proven. Zypolitc, would you again point your right arm and then turn in that direction," he asked politely; she did as she was asked.

"I now stand behind her even though I have not moved nor has the distance changed. From my viewpoint, she stands the same distance apart from me but now her back is to me. This perception is shared by all, each from our own specific time and place; but having ones back to others can cause other problems. For one, Zypolitc can't tell if I am still where I am or if I have a knife in my hand and am approaching her with intent to do bodily harm."

Zypolitc gave a startled gasp and whirled around but the birdman had not moved from where he was. She stood with her right hand to her chest and her eyes were wide with alarm.

"She has now experienced fear; but why? I believe she felt this way because she lacks both trust and understanding: trust in me, and understanding, that under no conditions would I harm her or any other innocent. I say that both fear, and front and back, are perceptions of the mind, each stemming from something else."

"That doesn't even make sense, Birdman;" the guardsman said, confused.

Cuauhtémoc slowly turned towards the guardsman and his face changed. He lifted his chin slightly and turned his head away; looking at the man out of the corner of his eyes. His face darkened and his head began to shake as if consumed with rage. "Are you saying I am wrong, guardsman?" he growled menacingly, "because if you are—"

"No, no, Birdman; please . . ." the guardsman said in a panicky voice as he backed away, his hands held to fend off an attack.

"—because if you are, you may be right," he admitted calmly. He stared at the guardsman quietly while the man regained his composure. "What you just experienced was fear . . . but was it? I say fear is brought about by a lack of trust and understanding. You do not yet fully trust me or you wouldn't have reacted that way, and you do not yet understand, or you would have realized the expression on my face just now is not how I look when I am truly angry. You, of all people here, should know this because you are the only one here who has ever seen me when I *am* angry.

The guardsman looked at Cuauhtémoc and then nodded. "You're right; I should have known. And you're also right; I have seen you angry and the thing you did just doesn't look anything like the other. So; what did you just do? I've never seen anything like it; I thought you had become insane."

"Your words are not far from the truth; Guardsman. All birdmen consider them-selves to be brothers; the brotherhood of birdmen so to say; I presume this to be so among guardsmen as well as others?" the guardsman nodded his head.

"Every birdman starts out as a nestling; this is the lowest level of being a birdman and is where we all start when we learn how to fly. I expect there are as many reasons to become birdmen as there are boys in any given class. One of my classmates, a brother named Bitumen, wanted to become a birdman mostly to get away from an abusive father. I will say this as an aside; if I should ever meet his father and know for sure he is indeed the father of Bitumen I will spare no effort at putting an arrow directly into that one's eye for I saw and heard the results of his cruelty to his son. At any rate, after we became good friends, he explained to me what 'crazy eyes' were, a thing his father would do just before he gave him a beating. He showed me how it looked and being still young, I had to see if I could make that look as well. I must have done too well because when I showed him my latest effort he started to cry. Which is why I would kill his father; no child should ever have to feel like that.

"It is not a difficult thing to do; if you wish to learn the way of it I shall be pleased to show it to you. First; you start out by staring directly at the other's eyes, like this," and he did so. "Now, do as I do. Without breaking eye contact, lift your chin slightly and turn your head somewhat away; this exposes more of the eye's whites and increases the effect. Now you shake your head slightly, this gives the effect of great fury and at the same time, bear down; this will push more blood up inside your face, making you look darker."

"'Bear down; what do you mean, Inca?" the guardsman asked. While he was showing the guardsman what to do, both healers were watching with rapt attention and both were following instructions as best they could. The three women watched the men and shook their heads—it must be a 'guy' thing; they seemed to think.

"Think of sitting on a 'toidi' or maybe it's called a 'needed' here. Your insides are somewhat bound up so you 'bear down' harder. If you've ever seen someone else in a similar position you may have noticed how darker their face became."

"Yes to both of those," the guardsman said, "I have seen others in that position and I remember their faces did get dark; now let me try again:" and he did.

"Not bad," Cuauhtémoc said thoughtfully, watching the guardsman's effort, "but you need to work on your sequences. First; you give me a long, hard stare – this indicates displeasure. Then you lift your chin slowly and *then* start turning your head to one side or the other, still keeping an unwinking eye contact. As your eyes get to their corners, start shaking your head slightly and bear down to darken your face. I should warn you not to 'bear down' too hard though; I'm sure I needn't elaborate."

That was the end of the 'crazy eyes' lesson. No sooner had the words left Inca's mouth, when all three men dissolved into near-hysterical laughter, because none of them saw it coming.

The three women looked at each other and shook their heads: *definitely* a 'guy' thing. They picked up their trays and other utensils and headed for the door. Just as mother serving-woman opened the door the Emperor's servant stood at the entrance with his hand raised, caught in the act of reaching for the knocker. "Please come in;" Mother serving-woman said. "Inca, the two healers and the guardsman are all inside, making faces at each other." She shook her head in disbelief and she and her daughters stepped around the servant and headed back to where they normally worked.

The servant entered the room, a confused expression on his face; he saw Inca standing, facing him, and he stopped and stared. "You look none the worse for your burns, Birdman. I thought you were hurt far more than you seem."

"I think much of that was just smoke; that would make it look much worse no doubt. All that I knew was I did not feel bad, other than some singed hair and some smoke up my nose," he admitted.

"The Greatest Mayan sent me here to see how you are," the servant explained, "if I go back and tell him what I have seen he will not believe me."

"I think that you are right; Serving man. I feel if I do not go up to him, then he will come down to me, and you were correct earlier; he should command and I should obey, but for whatever reasoning he possesses, he doesn't wish to do it that way. So I try to get around it by obeying his polite requests."

"Forgive me, Birdman, I should never have said that. Had I seen what you did out in the bay beforehand I would never have been so foolish."

"That is not a problem but I think we should go up on top of the roof to make our reports and to show the Greatest Mayan I am well and content; this should please him and in turn will make my heart glad."

The roof was further from Cuauhtémoc's new room than the map-maker's room and it took awhile for the five of them to reach the rooftop. As they walked out of the entryway and onto the roof he could see the Emperor talking with his three sons and the Captain of the Royal guards, with the Emperor's back to him. The moment he came into view, Prince Quoholocet spoke to his father, and all turned to face him.

CHAPTER 10

"**M**y child," the Emperor said and immediately headed towards him. The two met somewhere in between and he put his arms around his Ruler and hugged him and burrowed his face into the Monarch's chest. The Greatest Mayan gave Cuauhtémoc as good as he got and then held the boy at arm's length and stared at him. "My child," he said, marveling, "you have taken no damage whatsoever! How can this be? When I saw you last you looked to be badly burned."

"It was more smoke than anything else, Greatest Mayan. My flights through the flames were not as dangerous as it must have looked from here; but there was a lot of smoke as well as heat. The Healers have obeyed your will and have examined me. I will gladly let them deliver their findings to you in person." He bowed deeply before his Ruler and backed off just enough that the two healers could approach; which both did.

"As you can see for yourself, Greatest Mayan, this child is in very good health considering what he must have gone through. May I presume the fire he flew through nine times is the ship which burns just on the edge of our bay?"

"Yes," the Emperor said as a doting expression came into his face. "But I did not know he flew through it nine times. Is this so my child?" he asked.

"Yes; Greatest Mayan. My grandfather told me when I was not yet four that the greatest problem that faces healers everywhere is not just healing the sick and injured but simply getting the entire story out of them. He said it is sometimes difficult for a healer to properly help his patients when the individual does not, or will not, tell them all the particulars; and a healer can make an error in judgment because of this lack. This being so; I was careful to give your healers all the facts that seemed to apply.

"Since we are on this subject; while the healers were examining me, that one (he indicated the oldest healer with a chin-jut,) spoke that the Great Healer is here in your city and he had bought a drawing from him for a great deal of gold. I was excited to hear this; because I thought somehow my grandfather was in this same city as I. As we spoke, I came to understand the one this healer spoke of is not my grandfather, but one who is passing himself off as my grandfather, and the drawing this healer bought for so much gold is one of the drawings I made while I was still in the birdman's camp; a drawing both I and the healer there intended to go out to all healers that they might study it and learn. When I came to fully understand the truth I was very displeased that this false Great Healer would steal both my grandfather's good name, as well as the drawings that were to be given freely to all healers, and sell them for profit. It is my wish this person be punished for his misdeeds and the gold he took from others returned to the rightful owners."

By the time he was done speaking the Greatest Mayan's face was dark with fury. He turned to the Captain of the Royal Guards and said: "You will have your Underling and some of your men accompany these two healers who will take them to the place of this false Healer and you will have that one arrested. Be sure to bring back all belongings of that one as well."

The Captain turned to the nearest man and gave him his orders, a thing was mostly for appearance because the soldier heard the Greatest Mayan the same as everyone else. The Underling, soldiers and two healers headed out to the place where the false Great Healer was known to be.

Unfortunately for many, the false Great Healer gathered others who thought as he did, and by the time the dust settled there was a scene of carnage such as has been seldom seen by mortal eyes. And so we shall turn our attention towards vast fields of flowers blooming beneath beautiful blue skies and butterflies flitting about while songbirds fill the air with their sweet trills: this is for the best; trust me.

The Greatest Mayan turned to Cuauhtémoc and smiled; "My three sons and I have been talking about how to best use this magnificent gift that you have given us;" he said.

"Gift, Greatest Mayan;" he asked with a perplexed expression on his face, "what gift was that?"

"Why; the gift of yourself; you said what you wanted for a reward was to serve Father Inti first, the Royal family second and the Mayan people third. Unless, of course, you have changed your mind;" the Emperor said with a sly smile on his face.

Cuauhtémoc looked up at his ruler with the unwinking stare he did so well. "No, Greatest Mayan, I have not changed my mind nor will I ever. I do not easily make a promise to anyone, but when I do, I intend to keep it even if it costs my life. I believe a promise is sacred to Inti, and should never be broken once it is given, no matter what the other may do or say afterwards."

"Please forgive me, child, I meant my words in jest but I now see I should have not said them;" the aged Emperor said, his face full of regret.

"There is nothing to forgive, Greatest Mayan, and even if there were I could never be angry with you; you have show me such kindness I would be ashamed of myself if I were anything else. Have you thought of a way to best use me? All you need to do is speak your desires and I shall do my best to make your wishes come true."

"We've been remembering the things you said you told my friend, the Commander at the Northern Soldier's camp," Prince Quoholocet said; starting the conversation; "the part where you said that the birdmen are now an arm of the military. This not only pleased the Commander, it also pleases me, for you have introduced an entirely different kind of warfare; a kind that has never been known."

"The thing is, we think that the birdmen of Maya can play a much greater part in our lives than just delivering messages," Prince Imhoquotep injected, "we can see birdmen can be far more useful than we once thought."

"We now believe the Birdmen of Maya can be trained to fight the enemies that seem to be springing up out of the ground like toadstools," Prince H'ratli added.

Cuauhtémoc stood, watching the three Princes, his head swiveling from one to another in turn. They were up to something, and while he had an idea what, he didn't want to speak and interrupt what was obviously a well-rehearsed conversation.

"What we need, then, is someone who can teach birdmen to be more than mere messengers," Prince Quoholocet said. From all appearances the three Princes were now talking among themselves, and ignoring everyone else, except for quick glances out of the corners of their eyes at Inca.

"Where could we find such a one; though?" Prince Imhoquotep asked seriously.

"We could write help-wanted ads and post them about town;" Prince Quoholocet suggested brightly.

"Not bad; not bad at all: except I don't believe many of our people can actually read;" Prince Imhoquotep pointed out.

"A good thought; I'd missed that completely," Prince Quoholocet admitted.

"What about a town crier? We could have him run around and ask about someone like this;" Prince Imhoquotep said musingly.

"A town what;" Prince Quoholocet demanded. "Who would pay attention to anyone who ran throughout the town, bawling his eyes out?"

"No, no, not that kind of crier: I'm talking about one who goes throughout the city, crying the news . . . you know, things like . . . Who's on first, What's on second; that sort of thing."

"Who's what?" Prince Quoholocet asked; puzzled.

"What's where?" Prince H'ratli demanded; baffled.

"Never mind, it was a bad suggestion, probably centuries ahead of its time;" Prince Imhoquotep admitted.

"Well; the way I see it, we need someone who has been there and done that," Prince H'ratli said seriously; "someone who has actually fought the enemy."

"And won; don't forget that; we need someone who knows how to win;" Prince Imhoquotep injected quickly.

"That is so," Prince H'ratli admitted, "but where are we going to *find* someone like that?" All three brothers turned on Cuauhtémoc and stared at him.

By now; Cuauhtémoc was giggling non-stop. His hands were up against his mouth with his elbows tucked into his waist. He was slightly bent over and taking very small steps backwards—and bumped into his Emperor: he turned. "They're picking on me Grandfather," he said between giggles.

"Yes they are; and they're doing a very nice job of it, considering how little time they had to rehearse," the aged Emperor said with a gentle smile.

He looked up at his Ruler and moved in close for a hug. "If this is the thing you wish of me, Greatest Mayan, then it is a thing that I will do gladly. I have come to understand we humans can do far more than we think we can if we will just give ourselves a chance.

"It seems to me what we could do is create an elite group among the birdmen. We would not wish to interrupt the flow of messages because that is a critical part of the Mayan communications. But if we were to test all birdmen for accuracy in dropping message arrows, among other things, and then select only those who excel in their tasks, it will give them bragging rights and give the others a reason to try harder, because I must admit I have known birdmen who could not reliably hit the ground with a message arrow. Most of this, I think, is they just don't care.

"What we could do is create a special marker or feathers only birdman-soldiers can wear. This is bound to make the slackers work harder; out of envy if nothing else. This also will show birdmen there is a way to gain honor and recognition and still be a birdman. One of the greatest problems facing birdman training-camps is lack of volunteers. Many children are not suited for the task but there are many other children who *are* suitable but whose parents will not permit them to become birdmen because they are afraid or because they think it is a lesser job. If we can present at least some of the birdmen in a more heroic way; I believe that many of these same parents will start urging their sons to at least think of becoming a birdman.

"This might mean many will come in to be trained who are unsuitable for one reason or another, but our Flightmaster is skilled in separating the fit and the unfit, and I do not doubt other camps will be the same. I can see the day will come, when instead of a single birdman flying out to defend your shores, there will be many tens of birdmen, all of whom shall be better trained and better prepared than I was. And this can only be the better for you, Greatest Mayan, and for all of your children. If enough pirate ships vanish on our shores, and if enough pirates are killed, then the rest will learn caution; and will in time learn to not come to Maya at all. I think this shall be a very good thing for everyone concerned."

"My child; you have again exceeded my hopes and expectations and I can see no one else will be able to do this job as well as you; it shall be as you say." The Greatest Mayan clapped his hands together three times slowly and it was so. He held his arms out and Inca darted in for more hugs because he was a very affectionate child at heart and getting hugs from his Emperor was much the same as getting hugs from his grandfather; and that was very good.

Prince H'ratli watched the birdman with a half-smile playing across his face. "You know, Inca, you have an interesting sense of humor and I usually understand your jokes but you just told one I can't figure out at all." Cuauhtémoc looked his Prince in the eyes and gave a slight shake of his head. "You just said you know of birdmen who can't reliably hit the ground with a message arrow. If they can't hit the ground, what do they hit?"

"Oh, that; the reason you don't understand, is because it is not a joke, but the truth. This one I spoke of tended to put message arrows into the tops of trees and people's roofs. He once dropped a message arrow into a small stream that ran through a village, and by the time they got the arrow out, the message was ruined and could not be read. He got so bad some of the villages sent runners to the birdman's camp to complain. When Dispatcher heard of it he grounded the birdman and had the Whipmaster give him ten strokes, hard enough to hurt, but not enough to break skin or leave scars. Later on that same one snuck his wings out of the wings shed and flew off and was never seen again. And right after that, Dispatcher discovered several blocks of Temocs were missing as well as a number of Temmos and Tem-tems. While Dispatcher could never prove one way or another, we all suspect the birdman flew off to join another camp somewhere else, and took the items along to sell for coin; our Dispatcher was not amused."

"We shall have to give you enough authority you can make all these things happen," Prince Quoholocet said. You explained how the Commander made you a Lieutenant, but that will not be enough rank. Otherwise; every petty Lord you cross will try and force his will upon you

"We could make him a 'pettier' Lord?" Prince H'ratli asked; puzzled.

"No! I forbid it! It shall not be;" the Emperor snapped. "This is for the good of all Mayan people; I will not permit some minor Lord somewhere on my lands to interfere. H'ratli, you are the smallest of you three, lend me your headdress for a short time."

"Yes, Father," he said and promptly removed his headdress and gave it to the Emperor.

"Please hold still, my child," he said and started placing the feathered band upon Cuauhtémoc's head. The Emperor was not present when the haircutter made a similar request; so this was the old Ruler's first experience with this facet of the child. Inca seemed to freeze and except for his breathing and the pulse in his throat he didn't appear to still be alive. "I must say, my child, when you decide to hold still, you hold still," his Emperor said in quiet admiration. "There; I believe that does it. Please turn around and face my sons; I wish to hear what they think."

Cuauhtémoc looked up into his Emperor's face. "Have you found a way to give me yet another reward Greatest Mayan?" he asked softly.

"No, my child, I have given you the reward you asked for; the right to serve the Greatest Mayan and his people. And I will never again make the mistake of asking if you have changed your mind: not even in jest. What I am doing now, is giving you the tools you will need, to accomplish the task you set for yourself. This is a thing that would crush many grown men but I believe you will do the impossible and do it in an astonishingly short period of time, and once you are done, you will be unaware you have done anything remarkable at all. Exactly the same as you have done everything else since the day you flew into our lives. Now then; please turn around and let my sons see you that I may get their opinions."

"Yes, Greatest Mayan," he said, and did as he was told.

"Very nice;" Prince Quoholocet said.

"You sure look like a Prince to me;" Prince Imhoquotep declared.

"Walk around a bit," Prince Quoholocet added. He did as he was commanded and he walked away from the group, towards the east. He looked out over the bay and watched for a moment as tens of war-kaks busied themselves transporting prisoners and goods from the four ships back to shore. He turned to his right, intending to return to the Emperor and his sons, but his eyes raked the temple of the Sun Priests, swung past them and then snapped back. The top of the roof was crowded with many priests and he could see one in particular the rest appeared to be bowing to; this was likely the High Priest. Without actually thinking of it, he walked away from the group and headed south, almost to the edge of the rooftop to get a better look.

The Emperor, his three sons and the rest watched the birdman as he walked to the southern edge of the roof. Then, without any of them consulting the others, all moved en bloc to where he stood, staring off towards the Sun Temple.

"What is it my child; what do you see; what are your thoughts?" the Emperor asked quietly.

Cuauhtémoc stared off to the south and without turning his head, spoke. "It has just now occurred to me, Greatest Mayan, there is absolutely no difference between a pirate murdering a child with his sword; just because he can, and a Sun Priest murdering a child with his sacrificial knife, just because he can. The pirate might say the child was in his way, which is a lie, and the Sun Priest might say it is a sacrifice to Inti; which is also a lie. Father Inti is the giver of life. It is the Lord of Darkness, Death and Decay who pleasures in the death of the innocent." He turned his head and stared up at his Monarch. "It is my intent to destroy the Sun Priests, Greatest Mayan; it is my wish to destroy them all. It seems to me I made this promise to Inti, but if I did, I can't remember when or where; which seems very odd. But I shall destroy them in any case."

"Of course you shall, my child," the old Monarch said gently. "That *was* the rest of our prayer; after all."

While he had been staring at the Sun Priests, Inca's expression was not the blazing fury he had shown earlier, but more of a calculating look. If he was a cat, instead of human, the expression might have taken place shortly after he spotted a mouse and not long before he decided to pounce. But now; he had a puzzled look on his face. "Your prayer; Greatest Mayan?" he asked politely.

"Yes; my child. You have been so kind in sharing your knowledge; we never got around to explaining what we were doing up on the roof just before you landed."

Cuauhtémoc glanced over at Prince Quoholocet and his eyes twinkled in mischief. "Translation: I never stopped talking and the Greatest Mayan is too polite to interrupt."

Everyone started to laugh. "There is enough truth to your words, my child, that your comment is amusing. Never-the-less, I wish to explain these things so you may understand; because you have taken on a great task and I wish no stone be left unturned to make sure you have all the help I and my sons can give."

Inca turned his attention upward, into the calm, dark eyes of his Emperor and bowed respectfully and waited.

"You are a very handsome child, Cuauhtémoc, and you have a graceful way of moving as you walk and go about. I have noticed this from the first day you arrived, but it is only now while I see you with feathers I realize you have an undeniably regal air about you as well. Tell me, do you know anything about your ancestry, do you know about your fathers before your grandfather?"

He looked up at the old monarch before him and bowed respectfully. That the Emperor had used his proper name was interesting, that he had pronounced it correctly was more so because many of the Mayan people had trouble speaking it at all. "Yes Greatest Mayan; my grandfather told me when I was about eleven months old, I am a direct descendant of Texaquahotyl, who was the last true emperor of the Incan people."

There was a prolonged silence as people digested this thought and then Prince H'ratli exclaimed; "Yes! Yes, yes, yes, yes, *yes*!" He jumped into the air, punched his fist upward and did his best to spin completely around before his feet once again touched the roof top. "Yes; it makes perfect sense—and it explains so much! Oh; um, sorry, Father; I got carried away."

"That's quite all right my son. If I were younger and more agile I would, no doubt, be jumping up into the air with you. And you are correct; it does make perfect sense."

The Emperor reached out and removed the headdress from Cuauhtémoc and handed it back to H'ratli, who put it back on his own head. The monarch caressed Inca's face gently. "You are a remarkable child in many ways. The fact you are a descendant of one of the greatest Emperors to rule anywhere does not surprise me. And yes, I know quite a bit about your ancestor: it is the way of wise rulers everywhere, to study other rulers who have gone before them, both of their own nations and the nations around them; that they may learn from the successes and failures of others. You have told us you remember everything: may I presume you also recall the exact words your grandfather spoke to you when you were so small?"

"Yes, Greatest Mayan. I had not yet learned to walk. My mother dropped me off with my grandfather. My grandfather was sitting cross-legged and he had me between his knees; I was holding on to his fingers, trying to walk. I remember how hard it was for me because my legs would not do what I wished.

"As I stood so, my hands raised up, holding onto his fingers because I could not yet stay erect, he looked down upon me and said; 'Ah, my little Cuauhtémoc. You must stand straight and tall for you are the descendant of the great Emperor Texaquahotyl. Yes; I know you do not understand, but I am the youngest of his seven legitimate sons, and I know this to be true; you must grow up to be a man and become the greatest healer of all for you must cure—' At this point my mother returned for me and my grandfather picked me up and handed me to her. I was much too young to understand any of this, but as I have already said, I remember everything. It was not until my big brother Xymatoc asked if I had an Incan lord in my linage that I realized I knew the answer to his question. I have asked many people what they think I must 'cure' but so far; no one has been able to give me even a guess that sounds right. I must hope at some time when I am older, I will understand, because I believe somehow it is tied to the job Father Inti has made me for."

There were always a number of people who followed the Emperor no matter where he went; there were guards to protect him and servants to run and fetch things he might want or need. Cuauhtémoc looked at these and said; "I prefer what I have just told the Greatest Mayan and the Crown Princes is not spread throughout the palace and beyond. Those who are successful always have enemies among the lesser folk and these are often not content until they have caused trouble and strife. I do not wish to give this information to anyone who can cause more grief than already is. I shall be very displeased if I learn anyone here has been indiscreet with this."

Clap . . . clap . . . clap. The sound came from behind him. As he turned; he found his emperor standing there. The monarch stared at the group Inca was talking to: "Cuauhtémoc's words are my words. Further; if I hear so much as a hint of such floating through the palace you will all lose your lives. And remember; this child does not forget." Everyone bowed very deeply before the Greatest Mayan and each knew within their hearts it would not be they who had loose lips.

"I have reached a decision;" the Emperor said. "Quoholocet is my first Crown Prince and has rule over the palace guards and soldiers as well as all soldiers and soldier-camps throughout all of Maya. Imhoquotep is my second Crown Prince and he is in charge of all herdsmen and farmers and governs the proper flow of such throughout Maya. H'ratli is my third Crown Prince and has rule over all merchants and the materials they buy and sell. Cuauhtémoc shall become my fourth Crown Prince and he shall have dominion over all birdmen everywhere, whether they carry messages or whether they are birdmen-soldiers, and he shall have rule over all birdmen-camps. By giving him Crown Prince Status, he will be superior in authority to anyone else within my Realm, with the exception of me and my three sons. I can see the importance of what he is doing and I believe if my empire is to survive this new danger, among so many others, the steps he shall implement cannot be interfered with: I have spoken and it is so." He clapped his hands three times and Inca was suddenly promoted.

Cuauhtémoc looked around; a stunned look on his face.

"What are your thoughts, my child, what are you feeling right now?" the Emperor asked softly.

He looked up at his monarch and an incredibly shy expression came over him. "If I am a Crown Prince, and they are Crown Princes, does that mean we are brothers? I've never had a brother before; not a *real* brother. The brotherhood of birdmen is nice, but it's not the same as a *real* brother. If that is so, it would make me very happy. And if we are brothers, does that make you my father? Because if it does; that will make me the happiest of all." And he smiled wistfully up at his monarch.

"Yes, my ch . . . yes, my Son; that is exactly what it means, and not because I say it, but because you say it." Cuauhtémoc's face seemed to catch fire with joy. He rushed forward and hugged his Emperor frantically, and then turning as quickly, he started in on his new brothers. The Greatest Mayan looked upwards towards the sun and bowed deeply; "If this child you sent us has done no other thing, he has taught us how to love . . . and that is huge."

CHAPTER 11

Prince Inca was surrounded by his newest brothers, hugging and being hugged in return, all the while being congratulated on his sudden rise in authority, a thing that did not impress him at all: he was still who he had always been, But three new brothers where there had only been sisters; that was special. He was perhaps the happiest child on earth; not even his very first flight had given him this kind of joy; although it had come very close. The Greatest Mayan watched the child radiate joy as the sun radiates light, and his own heart felt uplifted; he knew without doubt this was the right thing to do and he was pleased.

It was not long before Cuauhtémoc returned to his ruler's side; he hugged him once again and wiped tears of joy from his face with the heels of his hands. He looked up into the old man's face and then bowed deeply. "Thank you, Greatest Mayan, thank you Father; I swear I will do all within my power to make you pleased with me."

"You have already done that, my son, and so much more. If I may; I would like to take time now to explain to you what we were doing on the roof the evening you flew into our lives." Cuauhtémoc bowed politely and nodded; he focused himself and listened.

"We have been aware of this menace from the seas for some years now; but it was you who gave us the proper name for them. These pirates have been raiding up and down the coast, killing villagers and looting and sometimes taking people off to be used as slaves, and so on. They had not raided the Mayan lands much, until just recently, but we heard of their predations from other Monarchs.

"We appealed to the Sun Priests to do what they could, to find us deliverance, but all they could come up with was yet more sacrifices to Inti to appease what we came to think of as His Displeasure with us, who are his children. The Sun Priests have, in the last few months, demanded weekly sacrifices and yet the scourge was not getting better; it was getting worse. I finally told the High Priest I would not permit any more sacrifices. He swore Inti demanded more sacrifices before He would lift the curse upon us, and when I denied him that, the High Priest told me the enemy would come into our bay within ten days and destroy us all. He swore he could only lift this curse with tens of sacrifices and then he and his priests left my throne room.

"That same day, my sons and I decided the Sun Priests were not doing a very good job of things, so we came up on this roof to appeal to Father Inti in person, to beg Him to have mercy upon we who are his children. Our prayers were in two parts: for one, we asked Him to deliver us from the pirates who are getting bolder with every passing year. For the second, we begged him for an answer to the Sun Priests for they clamor for still more blood. We just finished our prayers and were bowing to the Greatest One when I heard your cry. I looked up and you seemed to be coming out of the sun; your wings were on either side of the sun and your head was in line with it and there was a fiery light surrounding your head, your body and your wings. I thought Inti Himself was coming for me and my heart knew joy as it has never felt before. You came to us and did that amazing flip to avoid hitting me and then you landed. We did not know if you were a god, or a child as you looked to be, and now eight days have passed and we have seen glimpses of what you are capable of, we still are not sure. Of this much I am convinced; you mean well for me and for my people and I would be the greatest fool to have lived not to give you every help I can. So do what you have come to do and speak your needs and it will be given you if it is within my power."

"I will do all that I can to be worthy of the trust you have placed in me, Greatest Mayan," he said humbly.

He looked towards the east where his new brothers had moved to, all were staring out over the bay, watching the great ships bobbing in the waters. Without either speaking to the other, both Inca and his Ruler walked over and joined the three men.

"Hey, Inca . . . I mean Prince Inca; we were just standing here, wondering what your plans are for your ships and the people and materials on them," Prince H'ratli said with a mischievous twinkle in his eyes.

"My ships?" he asked, astonished, "how did they come to be my ships?"

"You told us that they were yours;" H'ratli replied.

"I did? When did I do that? I don't remember saying those ships belong to me," he said, puzzled.

"I thought you were the one who never forgets," H'ratli declared, teasing. "I remember it like it was only today. You were standing very much as you now stand and you pointed at them with your left forefinger—I remember this part especially well because you usually do that chin-thing of yours. You pointed right at them and told us that those ships were yours! Now; I **saw** the expression on your face, and I'm thinking if *you* say those ships are yours, then *I* say those ships are yours."

By now; Cuauhtémoc was giggling. When he said that, he was talking about the pirates and not all the ships, and everyone knew that, but it is the way of brothers to tease one another and he knew that was exactly what was going on and this pleased him greatly because he had never had brothers to talk to and argue with and do all of the things that brothers do . . . and he had always missed that very much.

"So . . . what do you plan on doing with your ships, people and materials?"

He stared up at H'ratli and shook his head. "I will not know what to do with anything until I know more about them. I will say this: the pirates will have to be killed and the bodies disposed of. Perhaps the dead can be taken by war-kaks, out beyond the entrance to the bay, and be permitted to float out to sea; sharks need to eat the same as everything else. Even their own people do not trust them or want them and I cannot see we would fare any better.

"The rest; we will have to handle as we face them. I would very much like to try and speak with them to see if any of them understand Spanish. While I speak the language fairly well, there are many words I do not yet know, and there are other languages I would also like to learn to speak and understand. The more we know of these people the better prepared we shall be when the next group comes. We need to make sure we recognize who is friend and who is foe, that we do not embrace the enemy by mistake, and kill the friend in error."

The three princes looked at each other; a somewhat embarrassed expression on their faces.

"That didn't turn out quite as you expected; did it my Son?" the emperor asked gently.

"No, Father, it did not. And I should have known better by now. What's more discomforting is he is absolutely correct;" H'ratli admitted.

They stood and quietly watched as war-kaks brought in load after load and even the long boats such ships use were lowered and rowed in by the sailors on the ships while Maya guardsmen watched with bows and arrows ready in case of treachery. Even the pirates who were widely known for their blood-thirsty ways seemed strangely subdued. Or perhaps not so strange after all, for they seemed to spend an inordinate amount of time searching the skies, lest another demon should come and attack them.

The Emperor and his retinue were the first to leave since he had other matters needing his attention. The next to leave was Prince Quoholocet: as absolute commander of all the armed forces he had citizens down on the beach who needed to be told what to do with all of the peoples and supplies that were flowing in a steady stream from the four damaged ships. That left Cuauhtémoc, H'ratli and Imhoquotep and their assorted guards, still on the roof. The birdman's interest now lay in Xymatoc's wings. He needed to know exactly how much damage had been done to them, and being a birdman, few things if any, were more important to him than the condition of his wings. He walked over to where the wings lay; closely followed by his two new brothers and a small collection of guards.

He carefully examined the wing-end and the beak of the wings; it was not good but it was repairable, providing he could get the wings to a proper place for such. What seemed almost incredible to him was the wings looked like they could still be flown as they were, without any real danger. He mentally bowed to his big brother back at the birdman's camp for making, what was in fact, a superbly-built set of wings.

Once he was convinced Xymatoc's wings were basically sound he started to head back to his own room. There seemed to be no demands upon him at the moment; and the morning's activities had given fruit to a number of ideas for modifications of not only existing wings but future wings as well. These changes would not only improve their usefulness for carrying messages, they would also greatly enhance their efficiency for defending against future attacks, a thing he believed to be as inevitable as dawn.

He turned to leave and found Prince H'ratli and his brother standing before him. "Um, Inca . . . that is, I mean Prince Inca. If you don't mind, I and my brother would like to be with you for awhile . . . that is, if we're not in your way or anything."

He smiled up at the two. "I would like that very much," he said. "I've never had brothers before and the thought I now do makes my heart happy. When I was young I once asked my mother if I couldn't have a brother of my own and she told me mothers and fathers have no control over things like that and only Inti can say if it will be a boy or a girl. I always felt left out because other boys had brothers, and I never did, but now I have three. In many ways I feel this is my home now and that the other place I had up in the northern mountains was only temporary.

"The day that Xymatoc came and took me to the birdman's camp my mother would not even come out of her hut to bid me good journey. That hurt for a long time until I came to understand I am her only son and seeing me leave was probably too painful for her and so she went into her hut so I wouldn't see her cry."

"You gave up much to become a birdman;" H'ratli said gently.

"Truth; but I gained even more in return. I feel that my place is here, that the job the Father Inti created me for is to be found here, and I am determined do all I can to make sure I do this job well, that Father Inti, the Greatest Mayan, you who are my brothers and all of the children of the Greatest Mayan will not be disappointed in me."

"This you have already achieved, my brother, far beyond our wildest hopes and dreams;" Prince Imhoquotep vowed.

Cuauhtémoc, closely followed by his two brothers and their guards, walked down the stairs, to where his room awaited, talking happily the whole time. They reached his room and entered. It seemed to the two Princes and guards nearly every shelf and nook had drawings of wings on it, with a partially-drafted picture of a raven done much larger than life-size fastened to one of the drawing tripods. Almost as a group, they walked up to the sketch, drawn like iron filings to a magnet.

"I killed that raven out in our corn field when I was eight years old," he said in way of explanation, "that bird was after some of our corn and I wasn't about to let him have any. After I left the field I laid him out on the ground and studied him for the better part of a fist and then I laid his carcass out on an anthill, intending to let the ants strip him down to bones so I could study them as well, but some passing animal took him that night, and that was the end of it. I've always been interested in birds and in flight. As I already told you, an eagle chose me at birth, and I've been fascinated by them ever since. From that time on I've studied every bird I've ever gotten my hands on and all those that I could get close enough to see the details of their wings and feathers. If you're interested, I have several sketches of different wings, comparing one kind of wing with another.

"What I'm trying to do is come up with the ideal design for birdmen's wings, a shape that will give all birdmen the greatest speed through the air, combined with the best stability and soaring time. Unfortunately; the wings that are the fastest—like gulls and terns and some of the faster hawks—are the poorest for staying aloft for the greatest length of time."

For perhaps the next two thumbs of the sun Cuauhtémoc took his new brothers and the guardsmen through his room, showing them many drawings he had done over the last few days. Some of them were wing designs; the rest of them were outlines of bird wings of every imaginable size and shape, from tiny hummingbird wings on up to the great condors and even well-executed examples of the wings of different bats because anything that flew caught his eye and got his undivided attention.

Two sharp raps on the door, followed by two more and then two after that brought everything to a halt. He started for the door but his guardsman held up his hand and shook his head no. He was the guard, and it was his duty to keep the birdman safe, and having three sets of knocks that close together set off some sort of alarm inside his head. Just as he was reaching for the door release the door swung inwards and the two men who had fitted the birdman with clothes a week earlier came in, closely followed by the same pair who had fitted him with sandals, tailed by the hair-cutter and another two men Cuauhtémoc had never seen.

"We are here at the command of the Greatest Mayan," the clothes men announced as they swept into the room.

"No, we have to fit the young Prince with Royal Sandals," the second pair avowed as they tried to elbow the first two aside.

"Stop!" Inca snapped, "you shall not compete against each other; I will tell you who waits and who does not. Haircutter, you waited patiently last time, I will permit you to take care of me first. Not only that, I expect your requirements can be met the quickest, and I see no reason to delay you needlessly." Behind him the two Crown Princes looked at each other and both grinned. As if born of a single mind they formed their hands into fists, the first tapped his fist on top of the second, a eye blink later the second did it to the first and then both rapped their knuckles against each other twice; it was their way of saying 'Right on!'

"Thank you, Great Prince," the haircutter said politely. "I've been told you got singed up fighting enemy ships out in our harbor. May I thank you for myself and the rest of the palace staff; it was an incredibly brave and selfless thing for you to do."

"I am pleased to have been of service, but if you don't mind, I would prefer not to talk about it further. I feel about pirates the same as I feel about rats and roaches: all are vermin and all must be eliminated or we shall be overrun with them . . . but I don't see the gain from discussing it endlessly."

"Yes; of course, Great Prince."

"I would prefer not to be called 'Great Prince.' You may call me Inca if you wish, or even Prince Inca—whichever you prefer."

"Yes, Prince Inca; now if I may, I would like to examine your hair . . . hm; not bad, not as bad as I had feared. From all I have heard, you are a very lucky and skillful young lad, if I'm not discussing things endlessly. Yes; I believe this can easily be repaired. It will require my cutting your hair much closer than I usually do; the choice is up to you, say what you want, and I will do my best to obey."

"I do not doubt you have cut many hundreds of heads of hair, if not thousands, while I have never cut even one. Do what ever you think is best, and I will not criticize, nor will I permit anyone else to criticize."

"Thank you, Inca," the haircutter said very softly. He drew his knife from its sheath and began to work. The hair was singed mostly on the left side, the area most exposed to the flames, because he covered his eyes, face and ears repeatedly with his arms and hands to protect them. The haircutter worked his way around his head quietly, trimming everything as neatly as he could and within a short period of time he once again stood back and looked at his handiwork. "May I be permitted to say again what a pleasure it is to cut your hair Prince Inca; I've never had a customer, including adults, who can hold so still."

"The only ones who can hold stiller than our little brother are the dead;" Prince H'ratli said proudly. "Say; that haircut looks really good on you Inca; give your head a shake like you do and let's see what you look like."

Cuauhtémoc stepped away from the group, bent himself about 45 degrees and shook his head like a dog shaking water; then he stood back up, gave his head a single shake again and looked at H'ratli.

Both H'ratli and Imhoquotep walked around Inca, looking and sometimes touching the Birdman's hair. "I like it, Haircutter, you know I really do. If you're not busy right now I'd like you to do the same for me."

"Make that both of us," Imhoquotep added.

"Of course, Great Princes," the haircutter said with a deep bow.

"Um; maybe you'd better forget that 'Great' part for now; at least until I've managed to destroy *four* enemy ships." Prince H'ratli glanced at Inca and gave him a sly grin: Inca started to giggle. "You don't mind if I mention it do you?" he asked.

The crown of Inca's head came up to no more than the top of H'ratli's chest and he stared up at H'ratli and cocked his head; birdlike. "No," he admitted, "I don't care what you say as long as it is accurate. I guess I just feel like I'm being big-chested if I say it."

"Modest to a fault; that's our little brother;" Imhoquotep said slyly.

"Please wait until I am finished with the haircuts, before you start your tale, Princes. I very much want to hear what happened and I don't want to take someone's ear off because I'm not paying full attention;" the hair-cutter said.

"Speaking as one whose ears may be in jeopardy, I'll wait until you're working on Imhoquotep," H'ratli said with a slow smile.

"Yeah; right! Do you actually think I'm going to keep quiet after a comment like that?" Both men laughed; then they stopped talking and let the haircutter do his work while Cuauhtémoc submitted himself to the ministrations of first the sandal-maker and then the ones who had fitted him with new clothes earlier . . . and in each case, no one left the room once they were done. Other than rumors that had been circulating for a fist or so, no one knew for sure exactly what had happened and no one wanted to miss out on what was sure to be an interesting story.

By the time the Headdress Maker had finished with his measurements of Inca's head, the haircutter was done with Imhoquotep. Both he and H'ratli tried their best to shake their heads like Cuauhtémoc did, with varying degrees of success.

Once all of the servants were finished with their assigned tasks, all turned to the two Princes and gave them their full attention. H'ratli and Imhoquotep looked at each other; H'ratli shrugged his shoulders, opened his mouth and took a breath. There was a double knock on the door and a moment later Mother serving-woman and her two daughters entered the room, their arms filled with trays of steaming meats, fruits, breads, various roots, nuts and the usual array of corn products. The three stopped and stared at the people inside.

"Oh, please forgive us, Inca; we didn't know that you were busy," Mother serving-woman said quickly.

"Please come in, Mother serving-woman, you and your daughters; I am very hungry and the food that you hold smells delicious." He turned to the others in the room. "What about the rest of you, have you eaten yet? If not; I will have more food brought to us."

"I could eat," H'ratli admitted, what about you?" he asked; turning to his brother.

"Like brother Inca said, the food smells delicious," Imhoquotep answered.

"Kymeninie; would you please return to the kitchens and have another seven trays of food brought up for everyone;" Inca said, "be sure that there is enough food for you, your mother and sister as well. And Kymeninie," he leaned close and whispered conspiratorially, "be sure and pick your personal friends to help you bring the trays back." She laughed merrily and headed for the door.

"Inca, your hair, what happened?" Mother serving-woman asked, moving closer. Kymeninie stopped with one hand on the door and turned around and stared.

"I got it singed in the fire as I told you earlier; our haircutter did a very nice job of making it even again" . . . and an entire chain of thoughts flowed through his mind.

"Fire? I had forgotten about the fire." Mother serving-woman said anxiously. At that moment his stomach grumbled. His nose was smelling food, but his mouth was not eating, and his stomach could not understand why.

"Yes; when I was fighting the enemy ships out in the harbor and I got singed up;" he said in way of explanation.

"There are enemy ships in our harbor?" Zypolitc asked anxiously; "we down in the kitchens are the last to hear anything."

"Please; Kymeninie, Zypolitc, both of you go and get us some food. Once you have returned, everything will be explained, and then you will understand. Just go," and he made motions with his hands to emphasize. The two young women bowed before him and immediately left.

He turned to his two brothers who were watching him with unwinking eyes. "You do recall a short time since, when we were speaking to our father, the Greatest Mayan? We were talking about creating a group of birdmen-soldiers and giving them a special marker or feathers to set them apart from the other birdmen. What, if instead of a marker or feathers, we give them a special haircut; one that only a birdman-soldier can wear?"

He turned slightly; "Haircutter, if you would, please tell me if what I have to say is possible. I presume that all three of our haircuts are very close to the same." The hair-cutter nodded his head. "Look and tell me if what I describe here can be done—forgive me brother Imhoquotep, but may I use the back of your head for an example?" His brother bowed as an equal and immediately turned around.

"Once a birdman has graduated from fledgling class he will adopt one of the types of birds for his clan. A birdman may call himself an owl or a hawk or as is in my case, an eagle, and we imitate the call of that type of bird the best we can. It is how we identify ourselves in the air as we fly over villages when we drop messages or land or whatever the need. It just now occurs to me that perhaps it would be possible to have a haircut done to make the hair look like feathers, instead of smooth as you do now: is this possible?" he asked, tracing his finger on the back of his brother's head.

The Haircutter looked at Inca, deeply intrigued. "I don't actually know," he admitted. "It would be a challenge, but if you are asking me to do such, I would be glad to try. For one thing, I might be able to cut the hair at angles, leaving sections of long and short; this might look like feathers. I would be interested in following this if you wish."

"I would like that very much," Inca admitted. "There is another thing you may want to try. My grandfather is the Great Healer in the High Reaches village far to the north. He is the greatest expert on plant life I have ever met. Since he is a healer, he is more interested in plants that can be used for curing, but in the study of such, he has examined every plant he has ever seen.

"There is a plant, a relative of the milkweed, when the stalks are cut, the plant seeps white colored foam. If this foam comes in contact with the skin it can stain, but grandfather showed me that the plants juices can also make things much lighter in color. We used it to make designs on our clothing. Once the item is washed, the juices are gone but the lighter color stays. I mention this because I once saw one of the village women get some in her hair and her hair became a light yellow in that place. The effect was different than anything any of us had ever seen, and several other women tried to do similar things to their hair, before they got tired of it.

"I'm wondering if you could use that plant to make feather-looking outlines in the hair. Once the plant has lightened the hair, one can wash the saps out and the hair will stay that way until it grows out and must be cut again, which is what happened to that woman in our village. Or perhaps you could even use a combination of haircutting and yellowing to create designs. What are your thoughts on this; Haircutter?"

"From words I've heard you speak, I think I must love cutting hair as you love flying, Prince Inca;" he admitted. "I would be very interested in trying this thing. From your description of the women in your village it would different from anything I've ever done.

"In that case; I wish for you to do your very best. If it works out as well as I expect, I will ask the Greatest Mayan if you can be Haircutter to the birdmen-soldiers; you and any others you might wish to train under you." The Haircutter bowed deeply and looked immensely pleased.

CHAPTER 12

A double knock echoed briefly and the door opened; Zypolitc and Kymeninie entered the room, followed by five other girls, all of whom were carrying trays . . . and one of the girls was Eilei.

Mother serving-woman looked as surprised as Cuauhtémoc felt. She looked at the birdman and then at Eilei and then back at the birdman, but in the time she did this, he turned away. "I think my room may be too small to hold this many," he admitted, "let's all go out into the garden area. Not only is it larger, it is far more pleasant, with all of the flowers and plants around." He walked in that direction and everyone followed without questions or second thoughts.

He proved to the most gracious of hosts, making sure that everyone— Prince and servant alike—were served before he took food for himself. He didn't ignore a custom that dated back to the dawn of the Mayan Empire, where men ate first, as much as he politely danced around it. It was only after everyone had food and were eating that he glanced at his two brothers and nodded his head; the two Princes were watching him carefully, waiting for their signal.

It turned out that H'ratli was a gifted orator, or perhaps he just got caught up in his story, but in any case he did most of the talking. Inca found himself as interested in the Prince's words as everyone else since he had experienced everything firsthand and was now hearing it from the viewpoint of an observer.

Prince H'ratli started his story with Cuauhtémoc discovering the three pirate ships attacking the merchants were the same ships that had murdered innocent villagers far to the north. He accurately described him jumping off the roof with a goatskin of oil beneath his wings, and brought everyone forward to when he came limping back, his left wingtip on fire, and just when everyone had thought he had surely flown into the wall, popped up scattering soldiers and Princes alike and landed, smoked up but otherwise no worse for the wear. Once Prince H'ratli was done, Inca had to admit from the point of view of an observer, it was an intense and sometimes unnerving event. He glanced at Eilei several times during the telling, and for most of that time she was staring at him, her eyes huge and both fists shoved up against her mouth; which for some unknown reason made her look even more appealing.

"Weren't you afraid?"

"You could have been killed!"

Both Kymeninie and Zypolitc said, speaking at the same time.

"No," he said calmly, "I've never been afraid of anything in my life. Even then; there was no time to do anything except fight. And I could not have been killed, because dying would mean I lost the battle, and I do not consider losing to be an option."

By this time everyone had eaten their fill: the serving women picked up the trays and the food that was left and bowing respectfully to their new Prince, departed, headed back to the kitchens where they would quickly be surrounded by kitchen staff and the tale would be told yet again. The clothing makers and the man who fitted him with yet newer and much nicer sandals bowed deeply and left without comment. The Haircutter stayed behind because he had further questions to ask about the new hair designs; which perhaps interested him as much at new wing designs interested Inca.

He was a people-person at heart and was always happiest when surrounded by friends, which usually meant anyone who was willing, provided their hearts were good. He and the hair-cutter talked for a long time, trying to come up with an idea that would be a unique look and at the same time be something that could be put into a birdman's hair in a reasonable amount of time. Cuauhtémoc explained about the plant he'd been talking about, and in the end, made a reasonably quick drawing of the plant and gave the still-wet sketch to the haircutter. This gave him a goal; he could use the picture to show to different suppliers and explain the plants must be gathered up roots and all, and better yet, with clumps of dirt clinging on and still growing. Armed with his new knowledge the Haircutter bowed deeply before his three Princes and left.

Inca was in his idea of Heaven. He was now with two of his new brothers and each of the three were teasing and harassing the other two. Instead of hurt feelings there was non-stop laughter, and it was in the middle of one of these outbursts when a double-knock sounded on the door, and an instant later Prince Quoholocet entered and looked around.

"So there you are," he said, looking at H'ratli and Imhoquotep. "I was wondering where you two had gotten off to."

"We have been sharing wisdom;" Cuauhtémoc said, "I've been waiting patiently, but nothing yet."

"What!" his two brothers exclaimed, feigning indignation, "now you've gone too far; let's get him for that." 'Getting him for that' was easier said than done, for the Birdman was slender, quick and very strong and before long, all three brothers were trying to pin him down with little success. After awhile, H'ratli stopped, panting, and stared at Cuauhtémoc. "You know; that comment wasn't *that* bad; I think we should let him off; just this once."

"Forgive and forget, that's my motto," Imhoquotep added; gasping for air.

"I've just remembered why I came here in the first place," Quoholocet injected, "we've been doing as you said, Inca, separating the pirates from the rest, killing them and taking them by war-kaks out to beyond the bay. But my men found something; or rather someone - I think that you should see for yourself; we are all in the throne room where our father waits." Inca bowed to his brothers as equals and the four of them, followed by their various guards, walked out of his room and headed to where the Greatest Mayan was.

The Palace of the Emperor was not a finished structure. It had been started many centuries earlier and was still being added to as time went on. As such, it was a vast building and a person could easily get lost amid the labyrinth that was its hallways and rooms; lost, that is, if one didn't have the memory Inca had. In any case the throne room was not far off and it didn't take long to get there.

They entered from a back door. From where they came in, the throne of the Greatest Mayan was to their right, and the cavernous interior stretched out before them. The walls were covered with artwork depicting colorful scenes taken from Mayan legends and myths and all of the supporting columns that were not otherwise covered with artwork were onlaid with pure gold. The Mayan nation spread across some of the richest gold and emerald mines known and the makers of the palace were generous with both. As Cuauhtémoc entered the room he saw a motley crew scattered about in front of the throne, all surrounded by Mayan guards, and all of them looked utterly disreputable amid such lavish wealth. He walked around to the front of the throne and bowed deeply to his father: "How may I serve you this day, Greatest Mayan?" he asked politely.

The Emperor sat upon a golden throne. His clothing was adorned with gold and silver and the richest fabrics; his fingers had gold tips with long gold fingernails crafted into them and he held a gold scepter in his right hand and a gold scythe in his left and his face was completely covered with a mask of hammered gold. There were holes to see through and to breathe through and a hole so he could talk and be understood. The mask was of the sun; and fingers of golden rays radiated out in a circle.

"Thank you for coming so quickly, my Son," he said. "As you can see, we have been following your words. The pirates are being killed and taken out beyond the bay and the merchants and sailors have been brought before me. Not all of them, obviously, but at least those who look to be the high-ranking.

"In the process of cleaning the pirate ships of vermin, as you so aptly put it, my men found someone who does not seem to belong. Since I trust your judgment, I thought I would turn her over to you, and let you decide what you want done with her."

Cuauhtémoc turned his attention back to the people gathered before the throne at a safe distance. Almost directly before the great monarch, a young girl stood with her hands by her side, and she was watching everything with lively interest. She was strangely dressed to the Mayan eye, but then, that could be said of everyone. He bowed respectfully to the Greatest Mayan, and then walked out to where she was, surrounded by the Mayan soldiers who brought her in.

"What is her story?" he asked the soldier in charge of the small group.

"We found her locked in a room down in the belly of one of the pirate ships. We know nothing about her, except she looks to be a prisoner and not likely to be one of the pirates, so we spared her life that you might decide what to do with her; Great Prince."

"Thank you, soldier," he said; "one such as this could not possibly be anything other than a prisoner; I will try and see if I can talk to her.

"Tell me, do you speak and understand Spanish?" he asked politely.

"Mon Dieu; quel magnifique," she murmured softly to herself; only his keen hearing caught her words. He had no idea what she'd said, but even in her disheveled shape, she was looking him over like a slab of fresh meat and her eyes showed distinct interest. She looked to be no more than perhaps ten or eleven and her hair and eyes were black as coal and her face, throat and arms were like alabaster, not he'd ever seen such or heard it so-named. *"Oui, Monsieur, I speak Spanish; 'ow else can one tell the servants what to do?"*

"You, boy, you speak our language. I want you to tell this King or whatever he is that it is our property his men are taking off of our ships. Well; turn about and do what you're told."

Cuauhtémoc turned his head slightly and stared at the man who spoke to him with the icy glare he did so well. *"I am not a servant you may order about,"* he said coldly, *"I am the youngest son of our Emperor and fourth in line for the throne of Maya. I am not speaking to you just yet; wait and I will get to you when I am ready."*

Instead of respecting the youth's words, the man grew more indignant. *"You heard me boy; do as I told you. And don't give me any nonsense of you being a Prince because I can see for myself you are only a lowly servant: now obey!"*

He turned to several of the nearby guards who were staring at the man with bad intent. They might not understand his words but his expression made things reasonably clear. "Take the one with the mouth and feed him to the sharks. Whether he is dead or alive when he hits the water is entirely up to you."

"Yes, Prince Inca," the guards murmured respectfully. Then they seized the one with the mouth and hustled him out the door and down the hallway, and in due course, into one of the war-kaks where he was rowed out beyond the bay and pitched overboard to fend for himself.

"My name is Cuauhtémoc; or call me Inca," he said, turning his attention back to the young girl before him, *"I am the youngest of the Emperor's sons and am thought to be fourth in line for the crown of Maya. I speak some Spanish, but I only had seven days to learn in, so there are many words I do not know yet; for one, I don't know the proper Spanish word for the son of a King or Emperor. Any help you can give me in better understanding would be welcome,"* he said, speaking in Spanish

"The word you want is 'Crown Prince,'" she said, pronouncing the word very carefully; *"I am mademoiselle Yvette Marie de la Coeur and my parents were of the de la Coeur of France before the barbarians overcame us and we had to flee France. On the way to the New World we were attacked by pirates. The captains of the ships we were on were gallant and brave but were no match for the pirates for they were badly out-gunned. My mother and father were killed as were many others and the only reason I was permitted to live is because the name of de la Coeur is widely known and*

they thought to get a great ransom from my grandpapa and grandmamma. I was kept down in that filthy hole, never knowing if I would be killed, or worse, and then I heard much cannon fire and the sounds of fighting and then all was quiet until your soldiers came and knocked my door down and brought me out into the sunshine again. I am most grateful for my rescue."

"It was not a problem; mademoiselle. I will have you taken to my room where you will be fed and cleaned by serving women. And so you will know, we do not harm innocents here, anymore than we tolerate evil. I wish to speak with you later; the language you speak is unknown to me and I would like very much if you would teach it to me; both the speaking and the writing of it, if you understand such." She nodded her head and then curtsied politely, a thing that intrigued him as he had never seen such an unfamiliar, yet elegant movement. A few words to one of the nearby servants and the young French girl was on her way. Inca watched the French girl until she was out of sight. There were many things he did not yet understand, and his mind actively probed every avenue, in an effort to get everything into focus.

He was translating to the Greatest Mayan all through his discussion with the young girl so the Emperor would understand what was going on. He bowed respectfully to the Greatest Mayan and then turned briefly to H'ratli. "I think I will need your help with these merchants, if we are to get things off to a proper beginning, but please let me get started first. When I am ready; I will wave with my fingers behind my back. When I do that; you will know to come and interfere with what I'm saying." The puzzled Prince bowed as equals and agreed.

"I am now ready to speak with you," he told the group of merchants, *"what are your complaints or comments?"*

"Our comrade . . ." one of the men began.

"Now sleeps with the fish," Cuauhtémoc said calmly. *"We do not tolerate rude behavior among our own people and we certainly are not going to put up with it from a group of strangers."*

"We . . . ah, we're very concerned about what is happening to our wares, the supplies your soldiers insist on stealing off our ships."

"I would advise you not to use the term 'stealing' in the presence of my father and the rest of my brothers; all are very sensitive to such accusations. Besides; you surrendered to us. That means you, your ships, and all of the materials on your ships now belong to the Mayan Empire."

"We were being attacked by pirates!" the man protested weakly.

"That is another thing. We were quietly minding our own business and your two merchant ships led three pirate ships into our bay, disturbing our peace. What do you have to say about this?"

"We were fighting for our lives," the spokesperson declared.

"You were fighting for your lives, so you sailed your ships into our bay, enticing enemies to follow you; causing further disruption. Then you surrendered when the enemy surrendered and yet you believe the ships and belongings are still yours?"

"That demon was in the air, killing everyone, we had to surrender; we had no choice," the man exclaimed, growing more agitated with every passing moment.

"Demon?" Inca demanded, puzzled, *"demon? We have no demons here. Oh, wait; you mean our birdman! That was just one of our birdmen. When the Greatest Mayan saw enemy ships come into our harbor, shooting off their cannons and making a disturbance, he sent one of his birdmen out to quiet things down. A very young birdman at that; I'm quite sure he is no more than twelve years of age. Our Greatest Mayan often gives the young ones little jobs like that; it makes them feel useful and a part of things and that's very important to the young. It also gives the other young birdmen heart, because they know the next time there is a disturbance, perhaps it will be they who are sent out. Yes, that's what you must be talking about, because we have no demons here. They're all afraid of our birdmen; I suppose."*

"Are you saying that a twelve year-old did all of that?" the Spaniard demanded weakly, wiping his brow as he spoke.

"Well, yes; of course—who else? What! Did you think the Greatest Mayan would disturb an adult birdman for only three ships? What are you thinking; was your head with you all day? The Cock Birdman would be no more than a few wing-flaps off the nest and the chicks would have

the hen's throat out. The chicks aren't vicious; they're just mindless at that age and have way too much energy for their own good. No; the Greatest Mayan, our Emperor, would never dispatch an adult birdman for only three ships. Maybe if there were eight or ten he might risk it. But more likely he would just send several young ones; it would be safer for everyone that way."

As Cuauhtémoc spoke to the merchants he stood at an angle to them. This way he could turn slightly to his right and speak to them; turning to his left he could talk to the Emperor. His voice had not yet changed and he was still a light, sweet tenor, a voice that carried well. He spoke louder than he would have normally; to make sure the Greatest Mayan and others in the throne room could hear him. As he translated his comments about birdmen—and the Cock Birdman in particular—many of the men sucked their lips between their teeth to keep from laughing and Prince Quoholocet turned his back on everyone because he could barely contain himself.

"There; you see?" he said to the merchants, *"the one who turned his back is Crown Prince Quoholocet, thought to be the next Emperor, and even he shakes in fear and turns away at the thought of releasing a Cock Birdman. No; it is not a thing the Emperor would do lightly. Perhaps if an armada of sorts approached our shores he would send The Birdman out, but in that case, I would not wish to be on any of those ships. No; it is much better to not attack Maya at all."*

This, then, was the message he wanted to impress upon the minds of the merchants and ship's captains who stood before him. It is never safe to attack Maya, or to attack the citizens of Maya, no matter where they may be. As he translated his latest comments, Prince Quoholocet's trembling approached critical mass, and he knew he would have to change the subject or the Great Prince risked rolling around on the floor, laughing hysterically, which would be very difficult to explain as quaking in fear.

"You, your ships and all things aboard these ships are now the property of Maya," he said. *"You must understand this is Maya and not Spain; this is the throne of the Greatest Mayan, our Emperor, and not the throne of*

King Ferdinand and Queen Isabella and you live and die by the rules of Maya." As he spoke he put his right hand behind his back where the Spaniards could not see and waved H'ratli to him as he said he would. The Prince was watching for the signal and even though he did not know what the birdman was up to, the moment he saw it he walked away from the throne and came up to Inca.

"This is Crown Prince H'ratli and is thought to be third in line for the crown of Maya. He is our Prince over all merchants, and all merchants and their wares are before his eyes, I will listen to what he has to say;" he told the Spaniards. He turned at Prince H'ratli's approach and bowed very deeply before him.

"I am here as you asked, little brother, but I admit I don't know what you require of me;" he said.

"You understand I have claimed all in the name of Maya but this is not for the good of all. You must speak to me sternly, and gesture at the merchants, so they may understand they are being discussed. You will tell me we cannot just keep these things for ourselves, but we must pay an honorable price, because they are merchants and if merchants cannot make an honest profit they will not be able to operate and that would be bad for the entire world. You will then inform me because we pay an honest price you insist, even demand, we be given Favored Nation Status on all future transactions."

"I like the way you think, little brother," H'ratli said in admiration; and then raised his voice so that not only the merchants could hear but also his father and the rest of the people. He harangued Inca, gesturing broadly, and repeated if not the exact words then at least the precise meanings of Inca's words and as he spoke his eyes raked not only the Spanish Merchants but also all who were in the throne room and when he was done the birdman bowed deeply before his brother and then turned to the strangers before him.

"This man here is our merchant Prince and he informs me we may not just take your wares but we must pay an honorable price for them because if merchants cannot make a profit, marketing will collapse, and the entire

world will suffer. I do not understand much of this, but because he says it is so, then I must agree. He further insists, even demands, that because he has required we extend this courtesy to you that you must give us Favored Nation Status on all future trades. What means 'Favored Nation Status' anyway?"

How much of this got through to the merchants Inca was not sure; but in an instant all of the men were talking at once. His limited experience with the Spaniard back in the Northern soldier's camp showed him at least some Spaniards were very excitable. If this batch was any indication; they all were. *"Stop!"* he yelled in Spanish, stopping the forward surge of humanity. At least his yelling 'stop' helped; mostly, it was a large number of spears that suddenly appeared, that halted the flow.

"What do you people think you are doing? Did your brains stop working the moment you heard the word 'profit?' This one is a Crown . . . Prince!" he said, stressing the last two words. *"I don't know if you are permitted to go running up to Philip, son of your King Ferdinand like that, but this is Maya! Watch me carefully; you must take your right hand and put it on your left shoulder . . . your right hand . . . your other right hand! Don't you know which of your hands is right and which is left? Yes, that's better; the right hand on the left shoulder and the left hand on the right shoulder; the arms should form an 'X' over your heart. Yes; that is much better. Now watch me as I greet my brother as you must greet him."*

He explained what was happening in a voice loud enough his Emperor could clearly hear him and then he turned to H'ratli. "Please do not acknowledge me the first time," he said politely. He stepped back a few paces and then approached his brother to within a few steps where he stopped, placed his hands as he was supposed to and bowed deeply before Prince H'ratli. *"Once you have stood back up, wait to see if he recognizes you . . . and he does not."* H'ratli ignored Inca with a disdainful expression on his face. *"I must now bow again and without standing up, back up three paces because he does not notice I am alive. He is a Prince and this is his right."*

"Let's try again, but this time acknowledge me please," he said to his brother. He walked away, turned and again approached H'ratli. This time when he bowed deeply and stood back up, H'ratli looked at him for a moment, and then made a single nod of his head.

He turned to the Spaniards; *We Mayans are very polite and we require politeness from others; whether they are our own people or strangers such as you. You may now respectfully approach our Merchant Prince, bow properly, and wait to see if he notices you are alive. Remember this; he does not speak or understand Spanish and I seriously doubt any of you speak Mayan.*

"What does Cuauhtémoc do now?" the Emperor asked Imhoquotep.

"He seems to be giving the unwashed, lessons in courtesy," Imhoquotep said. He stood directly to the right of the Emperor and at the moment his sole function was to listen carefully to what was going on and then explain to his father anything the old man missed, because he was no longer young, and his hearing wasn't as good as it once was. So far, his duties were light, because Inca spoke very clearly and he used hand gestures a great deal which also helped his Emperor understand.

The Greatest Mayan nodded his head; "Who better? Cuauhtémoc is the most polite child I have ever known. Ever since he flew into our lives he has only shown courtesy and respect to those around him; and this is not only towards his Emperor and Princes but to everyone."

The Spaniards were learning; they approached Prince H'ratli at a careful pace, stopped at a respectful distance, and bowed before him as they were instructed. He looked at them for a moment and then nodded once. "What must I do now, Inca?" he asked softly.

"Choose whomever you wish to speak to and ignore the rest," he said, and then turning slightly he explained the terms to the Spaniards. Prince H'ratli selected the one who had been speaking all along. He nodded briefly at the one who stood before him and looked him in the eyes; he turned slightly towards Inca.

"You must look directly at our Prince when you speak to him; do not look at me. I am only your voice so you must keep your attention on him." Things were off to a shaky but satisfactory start and there have been many successful alliances that didn't even have this much for a beginning.

CHAPTER 13

Once the dust settled, and things were as organized as they were going to get for the present, Inca returned to his own room. He sent the French girl there with orders to have Mother serving-woman and her daughters get her comfortable and clean. As he walked through his door there was an accented shriek. The girl was in the bath and was vainly trying to cover herself up. Mother serving-woman and her two daughters were there, as was Eilei, against all odds; that girl could get herself in the darnedest places at times. As he entered the room he could see Eilei giving Yvette the evil eye and she was muttering imprecations that were most definitely not under her breath.

"Eilei, that is enough," he snapped. "This girl is no older than you. She had to flee her home because of barbarians—whatever they are— and after she and her parents fled she saw her mother and father killed by pirates. Then she was stuck down in a dark hole and kept there for days on end with very little to eat or drink, and no place to clean up, not knowing from day to day if she would be killed; or worse. Now she has been rescued, and desperately needs a friend close to her age, you stand there saying evil things about her. I am exceedingly disappointed in you, Eilei; I thought you had a kinder heart than that. I still intend to marry you when we are old enough but the question you should be asking yourself is this; do you want a husband who will hold you and love you the way you wish, or a husband who turns you upside-down across your bed, and beats your backside with a switch?

"Now take off all of your clothes, climb into the water and help her get clean again, using whatever it is young girls use to make themselves look and smell so pretty. I mean now; Eilei!"

"Yes, Birdman, yes;" she said and with a frightened look on her face she slipped out of her clothes in a blink of an eye and not long after she was in the water next to the French girl, looking at Inca with wide eyes. Yvette understood no Mayan but she didn't have to know any to see the girl was in trouble with the young boy who talked to her earlier. She was very kind-hearted and her own problems seemed far away compared to what was going on now. Without thought, she put her arms around Eilei and hugged her, and the two children stood wrapped in each other's arms, cheek to cheek, staring at him with large eyes.

"Be a friend now, when she needs it most, and she will love you for it for the rest of her life." He stood for a moment and watched the two girls and he felt something moving deep with him. For a moment he wondered if he was at last getting old enough to actually be interested in girls. Then he thought perhaps he just needed to go to the 'toidi.' Ultimately, he decided he was just hungry again, and he started looking around for the trays of food he was sure Mother serving-woman and her daughters brought for the girl . . . then he saw Quoholocet leaning against the door frame, just out of his daughter's line of sight, but in a position he could see her. The Prince stared Inca in the eyes; he pointed his finger at him and then curled it, summoning the birdman.

He walked toward his oldest brother, who backed out of the doorway and into the hall. "How in thunder did you do that Inca?" he demanded. His face held no anger but seemed to be a mixture of curiosity and disbelief.

Cuauhtémoc looked up at his brother with a puzzled expression.

"That thing you did in there. You gave Eilei an order and she obeyed without hesitation. I am her father and I have known her since she was born and I can tell you with great authority she has never obeyed anyone that quickly; or obeyed without argument."

He stared up and shrugged his shoulders; "Phase of the moon perhaps?" he asked.

Quoholocet looked down at him for long moments, then said, "You don't know how you did it either; is that what you mean?"

"I'm not sure what I mean . . . give me your headdress," he said, and held out his hand. Quoholocet looked at Inca for no more than a single, quick blink of the eye, and immediately obeyed.

"Why did you do that?" Inca asked.

"You told me to," the Prince said in disbelief, "you ordered me to hand you my headdress and I, uh, I . . . I've no idea why; that is not something I would normally do."

Prince Quoholocet stared at Inca, a confused expression on his face.

Cuauhtémoc handed his eldest brother his headdress back and bowed politely. "This is a thing I do not understand, but there are times when I have told someone to do something in this manner, and so far I have always been obeyed. I must presume this is a gift Father Inti put into me; or perhaps it is something I have inherited from my great-grandfather. I will say this; it is a thing I use carefully because I would not wish to make Father Inti sad he trusted me with a blessing and I would then abuse it."

"You are the most honorable person I have ever known, Inca, and I am proud to have you for my brother;" Prince Quoholocet said gently.

"It is good to be your brother, my brother," he said with a polite bow.

The two stood together quietly, each lost in their own thoughts, and then Quoholocet spoke. "I came after you to make sure that all was well with you; instead I find you handling things better than I have ever been able. I did hear you say to my daughter you still intend to marry her when she is old enough did I not?"

"Yes, my brother, that is what I said;" he replied.

"Just how well do you know Eilei? You do know she is given to the oldest son of our Lord Herdsman when he becomes of age do you not?"

"Yes, I understand all of this, and as for how well I know her—" He started a very accurate description of everything that had been said and done the evening he landed: he began with the Prince's orders to the serving woman and to Eilei who was beside her.

"I was not speaking to my daughter," the Prince said, interrupting. "In truth, I didn't even notice she was there. As I have already said, she pretty much does what she wishes, and her mother and I have given her too much freedom at times."

"She spoke she is your favorite daughter and is the youngest child of your favorite wife," Inca said quietly.

"True; every bit of it. She is so very much like her mother in so many ways I have somewhat spoiled her. I gave her to the son of the Lord Herdsman because I hoped it would keep her out of mischief and because the Lord Herdsman has long hinted he would like one of my daughters for his son; sort of a feather in his headdress so to speak." Prince Quoholocet looked at Cuauhtémoc for a long moment; "I heard you tell her you still intend to marry her. I am sorry my brother but this cannot be; I have given my promise and I will not break my oath." He looked at Inca with true regret in his eyes.

"Of course not, my brother, I would not want you to break your oath. Which is why I intend your Lord Herdsman to break *his* oath; I don't know him at all so I don't care if I lose respect or not. Of course, I understand from your perspective, having the son of a llama-herder for a son-in-law is much more desirable than a mere birdman: none the less —"Quoholocet stared at Inca for a single, disbelieving heartbeat, and then exploded in laughter. "Llama herder," he gasped, "mere birdman! Come here, Inca, I'm going to give your head a knuckling such as never been." He reached for Inca, but the youth easily ducked his reach and moved out range, only to move back in to give his oldest brother a hug. The Prince gave as good as he got and then held Inca by both shoulders at arm's length and stared down into his eyes. "I swear; if any other than you told me such I would not believe them, but from what I have seen this day, I am prepared to believe anything you say.

In fact, if you don't mind too much, the next time I see Eilei's mother I will tell her your words. She, like everyone else in the palace, knows your name and to have you for her daughter will be a real feather in her headdress; so to say. In fact it will be a great feather in mine as well."

"I would prefer it goes not further than that, except you may tell our Father and brothers, of course. If it becomes common gossip, the Lord Herdsman may hear of it, and I rather he walk in on that date believing the marriage will take place on schedule. I believe it will be best he doesn't hear it in advance; we can leave it as an unhappy surprise for him."

"Agreed," Prince Quoholocet said, "and now I would like to hear the rest of 'how well do you know my daughter?'"

Cuauhtémoc took up exactly where he left off, describing his journey into the depths of the palace and the pain of warming up in the bath. He told of how Mother serving-woman told Eilei to keep an eye on him and how the instant the serving-woman left the room, Eilei stripped off her clothes and climbed into the bath with him and how she rubbed his legs and how good it felt.

"She did what?" Quoholocet said, interrupting again, "that little minx deserves a spanking. I would be delighted to do so but it seems to me you have things well in hand so I will leave it up to you; please continue."

Inca continued on through where Mother serving-woman and her daughters caught Eilei in the bath with him and that she showed no sign of remorse and how the serving-woman's parting words were to 'not let her father catch her there' and he accurately described the sly smile she wore. He then said how cold he was and how concerned Eilei was and how she cuddled up against his back to help warm him up and then when she thought him asleep, the thing she did with her hand.

"She did what?" Quoholocet exclaimed, interrupting yet again. "Any girl who did that to me would get herself raped: young or not, daughter or not."

"Truth;" Inca admitted, "and had I not been so exhausted, that is exactly what would have happened."

"So you are not so young that you don't know what to do in such a case?" the Prince asked cautiously.

"I had my first experience in such not long after my eighth birthday," he admitted, "I was seduced by an older woman in our village, a woman with a storied past—she was eleven at the time, I believe."

"Go away;" his older brother said, "go on, beat it; you're plucking my feathers."

"Truth, all of it," Inca insisted; "she was pregnant before she was twelve and had a healthy baby boy not long after. I don't believe she ever did take any one man for a husband; she liked all men equally, I suppose."

"You villagers have all the luck. I was older than you when I, ah, never mind. What else did my daughter do that night?"

"We slept together as children usually do. I awoke and had to go to the 'toidi' and then I spent some time looking around the map-drawer's room. My night vision has always been excellent; probably because of the drink my grandfather has given me all of my life. I saw her lying on the bed with the blanket half-off and thought then I had never seen a more beautiful sight. I noticed one of the stands used for drawing; with a fresh sheet of paper on it. I thought to draw her as I had seen her and took the stand outside in the moonlight, intending to do so, but when I started to draw I saw our father's eyes staring out at me. It took a moment but I understood it was in my mind and not on paper. So I drew him instead. I never did get around to drawing her; perhaps I will do so one day and give it to you and your favorite wife as a gift for your kindness. If I should do so I want it understood that under no conditions am I going to spend the rest of my time here drawing pictures of middle-aged wives because they want to look twenty years younger."

"Understood. And I thank you for the thought as well as the deed if you decide to do so and I will not mention it to anyone. And

I understand what you mean about 'middle-aged women.' After your drawing was first set up in the throne room our Father had his hands filled with 'middle-aged women' requesting and even demanding he make you do one for them. Father refused them all, and when some would not take no for an answer, he threatened to have their husbands beaten because they had not properly trained their wives. The husbands got wind of things and for a few days afterwards some of the worst offenders moved somewhat stiffly and there has been no further discussion of such."

Cuauhtémoc's stomach gurgled: "I think I must be hungry;" he admitted.

"Of course you're hungry. You're a kid, you're awake, and you're standing up; naturally you're hungry. Come to think of it, so am I. I think I saw some trays of food in your room, let's go and see if any of it is left."

The two walked back into the room and headed toward the food. Mother serving-woman saw Prince Quoholocet for the first time and her eyes opened in alarm. He put his left hand over his mouth and shook his head no. Two young girls were standing waist-deep in the water, looking at each other; both were soaked, with water still running down their hair. "My name is Eilei," Eilei said slowly, carefully enunciating each word; "your name is Yah-vette." As she spoke she put her hands first on her chest and then on Yvette's chest.

"Oui, bon;" Yvette said; "my name is Yvette; your name is Eely-eye." At that, Yvette's accent wasn't as bad as Eilei's, but neither girl seemed to care.

Both males headed directly to where the food was. They barely started heaping food on the metal plates the palace used when Eilei saw her father in the room for the first time: "Yeep!" she squealed and dropped down into the water where only her head showed. She wasn't afraid of her father seeing her nude because he had seen her that way from the day she was born. No; it was simply she hadn't known until that exact moment he was anywhere near and her first impression was she was in a lot of trouble. He looked at his daughter, shook his head sadly, and gave her a dismissive wave of his hand and went back to the business of loading his own plate with fruit, nuts, corn cake and other edibles. She slowly stood up and faced the puzzled look on Yvette's face. "He is my father;" Eilei said in way of explanation and made motions of rocking a baby as well as putting one over her shoulder and burping it. Yvette looked at the Prince and nodded her head.

Cuauhtémoc loaded his plate up and walked over to the edge of the bathing pool. The facility in this room was much larger than the one in the room of the map-maker and it was flush with floor. With the plate loaded to overflowing he walked up to the edge of the bath. He stood at the very edge for a moment and then turned around, putting his back to the bath and the two girls. In the next heartbeat he spun smoothly on the balls of his feet and lowered himself gracefully onto the floor where he sat cross-legged.

"*Mon Dieu*;" Yvette said as she placed her hand over her mouth.

"How do you do things like that?" Prince Quoholocet asked in admiration.

"I don't know; I just do it. I guess it's because it's the easiest and most efficient way of getting seated on the ground . . . or in this case the floor."

He put his plate on the floor just to his right, picked up a banana and broke its stem and half-way peeled it; he took a bite. "Mmm, good," he said in Mayan, looking Yvette directly in her eyes; "*how do you say 'good' in French*?" he continued in Spanish.

"Bon," she said.

He beckoned her closer, and when she obeyed, he offered her a bite of the banana in his hand. He pointed at his mouth; "Bon," he said, and then pointed at her; "now you say it in Mayan."

He had spoken the last in Mayan but by his gestures as well as what was happening she understood clearly, "Good," she said, moving slightly closer. He turned to Eilei and offered her a bite of the fruit in his hand, she hesitated even less than Yvette and promptly moved over and also took a bite; "Bon . . . good," she said, looking at the girl beside her.

"Bon . . . good," Prince Quoholocet said; then moved over beside Inca and sat down cross-legged on the floor next to him. Inca turned towards his brother and bowed slightly. For the next thumb of the sun and more the two sat there, alternately feeding the girls and speaking the names of the food they were eating as well as other items near at hand. These were all everyday objects, things that would be spoken of often, and were thus a very good place to start language lessons.

Inca looked at the two girls who were immediately before him. All the food had been eaten and they were saying and repeating words they had learned; he looked both in the eyes. "You two must get out of the bath now or you'll be all wrinkly," he said.

"No; I'll get out when . . . yes Inca, yes Inca, I'll get out now;" Eilei said and started wading through the water, headed towards one of the serving women stood with a towel in hand, waiting to dry her off.

"I say if I live to be twice my age I'll never understand how you do that," Prince Quoholocet said very softly; "you are definitely the husband for her."

"Yes; I believe she shall be wife number one," Cuauhtémoc admitted with a sly smile, "providing she behaves: Yvette shall be number two. When I'm old enough to be interested in such; of course." He glanced down at his lap and then up at his brother: "no, nothing yet," he admitted with pure mischief in his eyes.

Quoholocet gave a bark of laughter and said; "You're taking a bath, clothes and all." He reached for the Birdman but Cuauhtémoc rolled backwards. He put his hands about ear level and as he continued over he pushed sharply up and flexed his muscles and in a blink he was standing several steps away from Quoholocet, who sat frozen, his hand still reaching out to where Inca no longer was: there was a stunned silence.

"Quel magnifique, monsieur, quel magnifique;" Yvette said, clapping her hands together very quickly and then lost to enthusiasm, she waded directly to the edge of the bath and pulled herself out. She rushed up to him and pressed her lips to his face; first his right cheek and then his left and then she backed away and curtseyed elegantly before him. The fact she was nude and dripping water did not stop her from taking hold of an imaginary skirt and she bowed deeply before him without taking her eyes off his.

He looked her over: he actually didn't have much choice under the circumstances. She was very beautiful with incredibly clear skin but painfully thin because of her long confinement. Obviously, the pirates didn't take good care of anyone but themselves; this was a thing plentiful food would cure in time. He held his arms out to her; she hesitated no more than a blink and then she came into his arms. Not far away, Eilei stared, the green-eyed demon of jealousy just now peeking over her shoulder. Before the imp could cause trouble he held his right arm out. She abandoned the serving woman and towel and rushed forward. He cuddled both up against him for long moments and then, regretfully, released them.

He gently caressed their faces with his hands. Both were very beautiful and they pulled powerfully upon his spirit because he really was too young for anything else. "Yvette and I will have to be together much of the time over the next few weeks and months, between my other duties," he told Eilei. "She knows much about her world and her language and I intend to learn all I can. It occurs to me it would be a very good thing if she had a girl more her age to be with, to help her feel comfortable, if nothing else . . . perhaps you would like to be that girl. For one, she will need other clothes, because she will suffocate in what she now wears."

"Oh, she can have some of mine," Eilei quickly exclaimed; "we're about the same size and I have plenty to spare." She turned in a blink and headed towards the door, her bottom moving enchantingly as she went. She reached the doorway, which was still open.

"Eilei," Cuauhtémoc said softly; she stopped and turned and stared at him. "Beautiful young girls should not be running through the palace with no clothes on. It would create all kinds of gossip . . . especially if that girl is the favorite daughter of Prince Quoholocet."

"Oh, yes, of course; thank you, Birdman," she said. With lithe movements she returned to her clothes laying on the floor and scooped them up and with clothes in hand she headed back toward the door; just as she reached it, Inca said—

"Eilei; clothes are supposed to be worn; not carried." He shook his head and walked over to her and took her clothes out of her hand; as he helped her get dressed he noticed a sly smile on her face. It was obvious, now he'd thought it over, he had helped her get dressed the last time and she was deliberately twisting things around to make him do it again. "You think you're pretty cute; don't you?" he asked very softly. "As a matter of fact, so do I." He got her clothed and then took her by the shoulders and turned her around. "Now go and get Yvette something to wear;" he said and gave her a gentle push, and when she didn't move fast enough, he swatted her lightly on her bottom. She stopped, turned around, and gaped at him.

"*No, no, my sister;*" Yvette said in liquid French, "*one must do this at times like these,*" and stuck her tongue out at Cuauhtémoc. Eilei knew very few words of French and none of those words were located anywhere in Yvette's sentence but she knew in a blink what the French girl meant and she also stuck her tongue out at Inca.

He stood between two young girls, two tongues sticking out at him at the same time; "You," he said, pointing at Yvette with his left forefinger and Eilei with his right, "are teaching her," and he switched hands so that his right hand forefinger pointed at Yvette and his left at Eilei, "bad habits. Now go before I find a switch and use it on both of you." Eilei stuck her tongue out once more, and before he could possibly make good on his threat, she whisked herself out the door and down the hallway and he could tell her progress by peals of giggles that followed her.

He turned and found many pairs of eyes staring at him. Mother serving-woman and her two daughters stood in near-identical poses, left arms across their stomachs with their right hands covering their mouths. The guards watched, and while they were more controlled, they were also laughing. Prince Quoholocet sat where he was sitting all along; shaking his head.

"There was a point where I intended to come to you and share my life's experiences with you on the best way to handle a woman. But now, I think I'll follow you around and see how you do it. Not only do I like your way better, the females seem to like it better too." Inca walked up to his brother who was still sitting and offered his hand; Quoholocet reached out and in a grip of friendship Inca easily pulled him to his feet: Quoholocet stared at the Birdman and marveled.

The next three days passed quietly. Cuauhtémoc did as he threatened and spent every spare moment with Yvette Marie and Eilei, learning everything about her world he could, and in turn, making sure she understood the things she would have to know in the months and years ahead. This was not nearly as much time as the two girls would have liked because by now both were utterly smitten with him. The two had much in common; both came from wealthy, influential families and both were used to servants waiting on them; but neither had ever encountered anyone like Inca. He was both elegant and unfailingly polite to everyone; servant and Prince, male and female, young and old and he seemed to genuinely care for every person he met.

Inca also spent a lot of this time talking to other birdmen, both the rank and file, as well as the top brass; so to speak. Not all of these were pleased to be ordered about by a twelve year old child. But when the Greatest Mayan explained the alternative—obey or die—they too fell into line and most of them discovered for themselves the child talked sense in everything, and once they understood, everything he said was within reach.

The merchants met at least daily with Prince H'ratli and every time this took place Inca was in the middle of things, because at least for the time being he was the only one in the palace who spoke Spanish, while none of the merchants understood more than a very few words of Mayan. One of the merchants insisted the wares taken off of the pirate's ships belonged to merchants and should be paid for as well. Yvette said the ships she and her parents were on were not merchant ships at all and that the belongings for the most part were owned by the dead. In the end; Inca had that one rowed out and fed to the sharks before things settled back down.

The headdress makers finished his feathered headdress, and in a small ceremony, the Greatest Mayan and his three sons, along with much of the higher staff, put it on Inca. It wasn't until then he discovered the Greatest Mayan had done yet another thing to make sure that all went well: on the banding of the headdress were the Mayan pictographs which read: 'Crown Prince Cuauhtémoc—Speaks for Emperor.'

CHAPTER 14

The Emperor's Voice sat between Yvette, who was to his left and Eilei, on his right. They were covering such foul things as verbs and adverbs; adjectives and proper nouns; this had come as an unhappy surprise to Cuauhtémoc. For him, words were a way of communicating, a manner of getting one's point across, and coming to understand the other person might also have a valid position to impart. Yvette, the picture of patience, led her two companions along the twisted pathways that form the French language. The nastiest surprise of all came with the spelling of these words. In the Spanish language, each and every vowel and consonant has a clear and defined sound, and each such sound is clearly spelled out in any message. It seemed to Inca the French written language had no such defined path and words were spelled and pronounced in what appeared to be an utterly random manner. Well; he had asked about writing after all. He knuckled down and put his memory to work; perhaps in the fullness of time some sense would come of it.

He was bent over, mentally tracing the flowing words Yvette had just written, when a double-rap came from the door and almost immediately the door swung open, and the servant that currently waited on the Greatest Mayan came in alone, and bowed deeply before him.

"Please forgive me Crown Prince Inca, but the Greatest Mayan sent me to you, and asks for your presence as soon as possible. I understand you dislike having things explained to you but there is something I believe you should know before you go to the Greatest Mayan."

"I do not dislike things being explained to me, Servingman; I just dislike wasting a lot of time in the telling. If this is something you can say quickly; I will listen."

"The Sun's High Priest is in the throne room with some of his followers. I think you should be aware he wants the girl that came off of the pirate ship. He states Inti claims the life of this child or all Maya shall suffer, and that you must bring her to him, and surrender her up. The Greatest Mayan says you may leave her here if you wish and the High Priest cannot command you to do anything because you are now Royalty and beyond his reach. The High Priest does not see it that way. Forgive me Great Prince; now I have come to know and admire you, I wish I did not have to deliver this message."

"There is nothing to forgive, because being warned in advance gives me greater strength, and I thank you." He turned to Eilei who stared at him; her eyes filled with horror. "That one shall not have your friend, Eilei, this I swear before Father Inti. I will die before I permit this to happen. But I want both of you to come; her, that she may be aware of events, and you; that you may comfort her and give her courage: is this a thing you can do?" Eilei swallowed and nodded her head and moved next to Yvette and cuddled her close. Yvette knew something was happening, and not knowing what, was worse than understanding.

They walked down the hallways that led to the Throne Room, he on one side of the French girl and Eilei on the other. They walked through the left-back door and Inca and the two girls moved up to the left of the Emperor. "Greatest Mayan; I am here as you have asked; speak your wishes and it shall be done."

"My Son; thank you for coming so quickly; was my servant able to explain why you have been disturbed at this time of day?"

"Yes, my Father, he gave me a quick peek at what lies before me; the rest I will no doubt figure out as things progress."

"You there, that girl is mine," the High Priest of the Sun said. He was smaller than most Mayans, and his body was strangely twisted, as was his face. Hezaraht looked at Inca's two companions and his face held a lust that was obscene in its nature. This was not the normal passion of a male for a female; but one that had been twisted into a thing that was diseased and ugly.

Cuauhtémoc stared at the grotesque character before him. "You are wrong. This girl belongs to me, and I shall not permit you to touch her," he said calmly.

"Do you not know who I am?" the creature shrilled, "I am Hezaraht, High Priest of the Sun god, and you shall obey my commands."

"Wrong again; Hezaraht. You do not serve Father Inti, our sun; you serve the Lord of Darkness. I shall never obey your words and you shall not have this girl; you will be best served by leaving this place now and never returning."

"Father Inti himself came to me today and told me this one must be sacrificed to Him or He will destroy the Mayan people; starting with the Emperor."

"Not only are you wrong, you are also a liar, a thief and a murderer. Under no circumstances would Father Inti give such a command. He wouldn't speak to you in any case, because you are allied with his most bitter enemy," Inca calmly said.

"Father Inti speaks only to me," the High Priest shrieked in impotent fury, "He says that this very day you shall lie dead at my feet."

"Wrong again and liar still; that is not what Father Inti told me; He told me—" For a few brief heartbeats the world seemed to go away and Inca once again stood upon a beautiful white beach, and words and deeds flowed faster than thought, and with these things Inca understood: the twisted, evil face had been in the red tide, was the same face before him. It was his hands killing the innocent that was creating the blood stains upon the white beach and it was he who was destroying the Mayan people; it all made sense and his comprehension was complete.

"It is you who lie," Hezaraht screeched in joy, "you stand there and cannot think of a lie good enough to cover yourself."

"Not at all," Inca said, "Father Inti just now told me you like to fondle the children repeatedly before you murder them. I only paused because I am surprised; I thought surely you'd given that filthy habit up long ago."

Hezaraht's face went ashen in shock. "I will have your heart out on my altar for that," he shrieked. His eyes rolled around inside his head and he looked to be one of the demented.

"Still wrong: at least you're consistent. It is I who shall have your head off on *my* altar—your head; because I have no desire to touch your putrid heart. It shall be your blood that flows down the steps of the great pyramid; followed by your grotesque head. Heed my words and be wise: leave this place and bother the children and the Greatest Mayan no more. Do these things and your life will be spared; disobey and you shall die. I have spoken and it is so." He raised his hands as he had seen his Emperor do and clapped slowly three times. He pointed with his left forefinger at the distant doors. "In the name of and for Father Inti I command you shall leave this place and never return. Now go!"

The High Priest wanted desperately to screech and rail at the birdman before him but another mind took over his body and his feet turned him about and headed him towards the great double doors that opened inward into the throne room. Each door was perhaps twice as wide as Hezaraht was tall and at least three times in height. For most uses; the left door, as seen from the throne, was open while the other remained closed. The giant doors were made from solid teak and had been hung so long ago no one alive could remember a time when they were not.

Cuauhtémoc watched the High Priest head for the great doors, closely followed by his followers. Without actually thinking things through he kicked his sandals off and then turning to his left he removed his headdress and handed it to Yvette, who was closest; *"Here, please hold this for me,"* he said in Spanish. He turned to the guardsmen who stood beside them: "Watch the girls; if any of the priests do manage to

DAVID DAVIES

approach them; kill the priests." He walked a few paces forward, and stood slightly behind and to the left of the Captain of the Royal Guard, who was watching the departing priests intently. He knew intuitively the twisted mind of the High Priest would not permit himself to be dismissed this easily and he wanted to be ready when things started to happen.

Hezaraht's mind was at war within. On the one hand, his abject cowardice commanded he leave, and quickly. On the other, his lust for fear in the eyes and faces of others was a true vice for him, and he knew on a deep basic level leaving so meekly was doing vast damage to his ability to create panic in the minds and hearts of his victims. He was just a single step short of the doors when pride overcame fear. He turned and glared venomously at the birdman. "This is not the end, birdman, it is not over yet;" he screeched in a shrill voice.

"Yes it is;" Cuauhtémoc said calmly. He took a short half-step. The Captain of the Guard stood just to his right. The man was right-handed and his sword was sheathed on his left side as was normal. He reached out and took the sword by the hilt and lifted it free of the scabbard in a single smooth motion. The sword was now in his right hand with his smallest finger to the hilt. He flipped the blade around and held it correctly and step by step he walked toward the Priests. He did not hurry; he did not dawdle; he moved with implacable resolve; his eyes fixed on the Priests like a carnivore, and like a force of nature that cannot be stopped or slowed or even diverted, he headed towards those who stood in a small clot of quaking humanity.

He was no more than halfway there when Hezaraht backed up and bumped into the right door. Inca could see the terrified man was on the verge of flight and he understood there was no practical way he could get to the High Priest before he scooted through the open left door and down the hallway, and not even his implacable resolve could rationalize him running through the palace, manically waving a sword around. He took the next best action.

He took two steps in quick succession. As his right foot hit the floor his right hand started the sword in an upper swing and when his left foot came down he flexed it at the knee. Now there was a line of force running from his right foot planted firmly on the solid stone floor of the throne room, up his right leg and torso and through his right arm. As his right leg flexed, his hips and abdominals, the largest and strongest muscles in the human body, flexed as well and a line of energy flowed downward to his right foot and in much less than a blink of an eye, back up through his body to his right arm which was now full back. He released all his energy in a single blinding flash of speed and power and the sword fled his hand, wind-milling across the room, exchanging hilt for point and point for hilt as it sped towards the High Priest's unprotected chest. In his mind's eye he saw the point of the sword buried deep into the wood of the great door with the High Priest nailed to the door, dead.

Hezaraht saw the sword coming toward him at incredible speed and his eyes bulged in terror. He no longer thought of people losing their fear of him; his only concern was flight; much less than a heartbeat before the blade skewered him front to back he turned to flee and in that instant the sword slammed into the door with such force the sound of impact echoed throughout the throne room and the door shuddered from top to bottom. For a moment, Inca thought instead of nailing the High Priest to the door, front to back, he had pinned him from side to side; but in an instant the grotesque little gnome tore himself free and squealing like a young pig stuck in a fence he and his followers fled through the open door and down the hall and all the way everyone could hear Hezaraht squealing and grunting like a terrified shoat as he and the rest ran away.

Cuauhtémoc felt energy ebb from his body; he looked at the ceiling and held his hands, palms upwards. "Forgive me Father Inti because I have failed you;" he said and dropped his head sadly in defeat.

The Emperor stared, transfixed, like everyone else in the room as the action unfolded. In the moment the sword struck the door and the priests rounded the corner he went into action himself. He handed the gold scepter to the nearest person to his right, the gold scythe to the one on the left and his gold mask to yet another; he had no idea who took what, nor did he care. The gold fingertips hit the floor as did the ornate robe that covered his shoulders. He shed everything because all they could do is slow him down and at the moment speed was his need. He crossed the throne room moving faster than he had in many years and he came up behind Cuauhtémoc just in time to hear the birdman's words.

"You have not failed Father Inti and you have not failed me. You have done as you always do; you have succeeded beyond my greatest hopes and dreams; I do not believe you even know how to fail."

"I had intended to kill him, Father, but I failed;" he said sadly.

"Yes, and you know why you didn't kill him, don't you?" the Emperor asked kindly as he pulled Inca up against him and hugged him gently.

"No, Father, I don't know why I failed;" he said, cuddling close.

"Stop saying that my Son; you have not failed. Stop and think: you just finished telling Hezaraht if he obeyed your commands, you would let him live, but if he did not obey; then you would cut his head off and his head and blood would flow down the steps of the great pyramid; you do remember that do you not?"

He looked up at his Emperor's face and nodded; "Yes, Father, I remember telling him that."

"Do you understand these words are not only words of intent but they are also a promise; a vow that is not only against Hezaraht, but also a vow to Father Inti, and to your Emperor as well as the peoples of Maya. If you had killed Hezaraht here; you would have been a vow-breaker. I now understand you well enough to know you would never knowingly break a promise you made to Inti or to anyone else."

"Thank you, Father, I had not thought of it that way. You are right; my words to Hezaraht is a vow, a promise that I fully intend to keep, and had I killed him here—no matter how pleasing it would have been to me—I would have broken my vow to Father Inti and to you and to your many people and I would never wish this."

Several guards were looking through the doorway. These were guards whose posts were on the outside and they were not permitted to leave their places until properly relieved by their Commander and their replacements. "Um, Great Prince Quoholocet, may one speak?" one of the guards asked hesitantly.

Prince Quoholocet was the Supreme Commander of all military forces; he gave the guard a glance and nodded his head once.

"What just happened? We heard a great thump and squealing like that of a pig and then the Sun's Priests came running out and we discovered that it was the High Priest who was squealing."

"Our Birdman happened; what else?" Prince Quoholocet said with a broad grin. He held the gold scythe in his left hand and he put his right hand possessively on Cuauhtémoc's shoulder.

"Truth," Cuauhtémoc admitted, "I tried to kill the High Priest with a thrown sword but I missed;" he said ruefully.

"Oh; you didn't miss, Prince Inca, perhaps you should come out and see for yourself." There were now four guards standing in the doorway and three of them were nodding their heads; the group moved as a single man and made their way through the doorway and out into the hall.

The first thing Inca saw was a small scrap of yellow cloth laying on the floor: only Hezaraht wore yellow. On closer look he saw blood on the scrap of cloth and drops of blood leading off towards the palace's exit. He turned to the Greatest Mayan, who was looking over his shoulders, along with everyone else who had been in the Throne Room at the time. "It would seem I didn't miss him by as much as I thought;" he admitted.

"That's not all," the same guard said, "look;" and he gestured at the door with a nod of his head because both hands were occupied with the spear he held. The wood was splintered about chest high on the nearly departed priest and perhaps a thumb's width of sword point stuck through.

Cuauhtémoc laughed in delight and darted around to the other side of the door. "Look, Greatest Mayan, my Father; there's more cloth and blood on this side as well."

People moved from one side of the door to the other, amazed at what they were seeing.

"I had no idea a sword could be thrown like a knife," the Captain of the Guards said in admiration, "where did you get a sword anyway? I swear you were not holding one when you came into the room."

"Um; actually, Captain, the sword is yours. I, ah, 'borrowed' it just as I headed out to attack Hezaraht;" Cuauhtémoc admitted sheepishly. The Captain looked down at his empty sheath in astonishment. "Forgive me Captain, I should have asked but there was no time so I just took it."

"You are a Crown Prince and you don't need my permission to do anything, including take my sword. But if I may ask, where was I when all this happened? I'm convinced no one could take a sword off my hip without my knowing it."

"You were watching Hezaraht shake his fist at me."

"Oh. I do not understand. But then, you are Inca, and much of what you do cannot be understood or explained; it can only be accepted." The Captain bowed deeply as he would to a god. "I have never been a very religious man," he admitted, "but since you have come into my life I find that I must look at these things in a different way;" and again he bowed.

"The least I can do is return your property to you, Captain," Cuauhtémoc said and started to reach for the sword: Clap . . . clap . . . clap. Everyone turned around and faced the Greatest Mayan.

"It is my wish the sword stay where it is," he said calmly. "I want to look upon it often while I am in this room and remember the look on that one's face." Cuauhtémoc and everyone else bowed before the Emperor and backed away from the sword in the door.

"You may go to the arms room, and take whichever sword you wish, Captain; this is my way of thanking you for the part you played in this."

Inca looked around for the girl whose presence started the entire thing. She was not far away and she was watching him with large eyes, his headdress still in her hands; he made eye contact with her and beckoned her over. She immediately came to him, sided by Eilei. *"What took place, Inca, what was that all about?"* she asked in concern.

He did not believe in sugar-coating things, he felt that it was better by far to tell the truth. *"The twisted little man who was here is the leader of the local priests;"* he told her in Spanish, *"he demanded I give you to him so he could sacrifice you upon his altar but I told him you belong to me and he could not have you. Most of the rest you saw for yourself. I would not under any circumstances allow an innocent to be killed by a twisted animal such as him. Please do not be afraid for you are safe here and you shall not be harmed."*

Her eyes and hair were black as midnight and her face as fair as dawn. She looked up at him, her eyes huge inside her face. She turned for a moment and wordlessly handed the headdress to Eilei and then turned and grabbed him by his shoulders and put her lips to his face. First the right cheek and next the left and then she put her mouth to his and held it there, moving her lips gently against his lips in ways that confused and bemused. For a moment he didn't have a clue what to do because the Mayan people did not do this, but as he stood as if in thrall, his arms moved of their own volition and he pulled her close and he gave as good as he got, to the best of his ability.

The two held this pose for long moments and then she regretfully removed her arms from around his neck and moved away. *"This is the way the women of my land thank a man for fighting for them and saving their lives . . . also to show a man she loves him with all her heart. Ooo-la-la, you are so very good at this, you have had much practice; yes?"*

"No, never, my people do not do this; I think we have missed a very good thing."

"You must be a natural; because you are very good."

He had never been embarrassed about anything in his life and he saw no reason to start now. He looked over her head at the people who were staring at him in interest. "This is a thing the women of her land do to thank a man for fighting for her and for saving her life: it is guaranteed to bring puberty on three months early in a boy my age." His Father, brothers, and others all laughed softly at his words; he turned his attention towards Eilei.

She stood wide-eyed, a look of utter dismay on her face. She was suffering from teen-age angst and since she was not yet twelve it was much too early. From her viewpoint she had clearly seen Inca preferred the French girl and so her young life was over for there was nothing left to live for. He reached out and gently took his headdress from her and handed it to Yvette; "Here, hold this please," he said in Mayan.

He took Eilei by her upper arms gently and pulled her up close to him. "Try to understand my experience in this is very limited; in fact you've seen it all, so if I'm somewhat clumsy in my attempt, please forgive me for my motives are pure." He ran his hands across her face, pushing her hair back and then leaned over and tenderly pressed his lips against her right cheek, then left, and then her mouth. He remembered with exquisite clarity what Yvette did to him and he did his best to do it to Eilei. For just a moment her body was stiff because she didn't know what was happening and then heartbeat by heartbeat she seemed to melt against him until he was sure if he suddenly stepped away she would fall because she no longer had any bones left in her entire body. In time this too came to an end and he looked at Yvette and the rest over the top of Eilei's head. "Make that six months early," he said thoughtfully, and then pressed his lips to Eilei's forehead.

"Father, brothers, I have just learned something; two somethings in fact. The first thing is; Mayan girls do not know how to properly say 'thank you.' The second thing is; she is very willing to learn if a boy will give her a chance."

He turned his attention to the Greatest Mayan; "How else may I serve you this evening; Father?" he asked politely.

"Your tasks are done for the day, my Son," the Greatest Mayan said serenely. "You have done as always; you have completed the impossible and made it look easy and in the end you seem unaware you have done anything remarkable at all. You have earned your rest; go back to whatever you were doing when my servant arrived or anything else you may choose."

"Thank you, Greatest Mayan," he said softly and then turned to the two girls beside him. "Shall we return and fight those wretched verbs some more or shall we do something else?"

"Let's wait until we get there to figure that out;" Eilei said.

"Oui;" Yvette echoed.

The three walked off, arms around each other, chatting happily away in a mixture of French, Spanish and Mayan no sane person could possibly hope to understand; but the children seemed content none the less.

A kind of calm existed after the storm and the adults singly and collectively took mental stock of what had just happened.

"I've just been looking at the door," one of the guards said. He was still on duty on the other side of the door so he had not ventured far, even with Prince Quoholocet to back him up. "From what I see, that sword point penetrated more than two fingers of solid teak . . . just how far away was Prince Inca when he threw it?"

"Perhaps half the length of the room," Prince Imhoquotep said.

"I would not care to face him in battle," the same guard said fervently.

"That's easy; just don't become a Sun Priest . . . or a pirate," another added.

"Y'know," H'ratli said pensively, still holding the golden mask; "I used to envy Inca; I really did. Just think; he's the handsomest boy in the entire city and he has the most brilliant mind anyone has ever seen. He's as quick and strong as the great cats and he seems able to solve the thorniest problems almost before they've been laid out before him. The girls all but faint when he walks by and don't even get me started on his flying ability; I swear the child could give lessons to the birds. I have moved on past envy though . . . I am now green-eyed, gut-twisting, soul-searing jealous."

"I feel your pain . . . serious!" Prince Imhoquotep said, laughing softly.

CHAPTER 15

Prince Inca spent most of the next few days dealing with the merchants, much to the displeasure of his two female friends, who decided between them he was not allowed to do anything that did not include them. The merchants certainly looked more presentable and smelled much better than on the day he had first met them. As he was quickly learning; there are very limited resources aboard ship for cleanliness.

Once Cuauhtémoc sent two of the merchants on one-way trips to shark-infested waters, the rest became far more reasonable in their demands, and in the process, learned Maya had a great many things of value that could be shipped back to Spain and sold for obscene prices to the wealthy; this made them very happy.

One of the more interesting finds on the pirate ships was several large rolls of sail cloth. Inca was still on his relentless pursuit of a better set of wings; as well as wings large enough to carry adult birdmen who had been forced to retire; years earlier in some cases. The sail cloth looked to be even better than the skins the birdmen currently used and it weighed less as well. This sent him on an extended discussion with the merchant who was the leader of the group. The leader of the Spanish merchants had learned from the fates of his two predecessors and knew better than to try and claim the sailcloth belonged to him. Instead, he started explaining silk to Prince Cuauhtémoc.

The man owned a single bolt of raw silk and he had it brought to the Birdman. Two men brought the bolt of silk over, carrying it carefully between them, and laid it at the feet of the merchant. Inca bent over, took the bolt by each end and stood up, hefting its weight, astounding both the merchant and the men who had carried it. Cuauhtémoc put the bolt down as easily as he picked it up then ran the cloth through his hands for a few brief moments and understood his search for wing-coverings was over.

"How much do you want for this cloth, merchant, and how many more of these can you bring on your next trip?" Cuauhtémoc asked in Spanish, staring the man directly in his eyes.

"I may speak openly?" the merchant asked politely.

"Speak the truth and you will go far towards making yourself trusted in the City of Emperors," the Birdman answered.

"I bought this cloth two years ago in the Far East for one-fourth its weight in gold. I have had many who want part of it but at rates that would lose me money. Because I have been unable to sell it for a profit I would be willing to let you have it for the same price I paid; one-fourth its weight in gold. And I must insist on gold, not trade goods in its place."

"This cloth is very light by itself, yet quite heavy as I pick it up. May I presume there is a great amount of silk here?" he asked.

"Uh, yes Great Prince," the merchant answered.

Inca turned to Prince H'ratli and the guards that followed the Princes everywhere. "This merchant speaks that he paid one finger in four of this one's weight in gold and says that it is called 'silk.' It is very fine and light but the amount is heavy. He further says because of the cost, no one wants all of it, but only pieces of it, and he would lose value. I believe this will be exactly what is needed for our wings because it is very light but seems far stronger and more durable than it looks. I would like to give him four fingers in four in payment and learn how many more such rolls of cloth can be bought for the same price; does this seem like a fair profit?"

"I spoke earlier I would want as much as six fingers of silver for one finger I paid for an object, the rest being 'carrying charges,'" H'ratli said. "This is so, only for small, fairly inexpensive things. For a greater thing that is worth large amounts I would expect much less than six fingers profit. If this cloth was mine and I was selling it to you I would feel two fingers for one would be a just and profitable price. What you actually agree to is up to you and our father will pay it willingly because I have been in the treasure room many times and I can tell you with great certainty there is enough gold in there alone, not counting silver and gems, to sink all four of the ships in the bay and still not use it all up."

Cuauhtémoc bowed to his brother as equals and turned to the merchant: *"This one is the Crown Prince of Merchants; as you already know. He speaks it would be a fair price to give you half of the cloth's weight in gold and not one-fourth. He further speaks I may ask you how many more such you can deliver for the same cost."*

The Merchant bowed deeply before the two Princes, giving them the respect due them. *"You have saved me, Prince Inca,"* the merchant admitted. *"It will be perhaps a little less than two years before I can return, but I can supply you with as many bolts as you wish, presuming we merchants can avoid the pirate's wolf packs."*

"I shall request ten such bolts at the same price, the gold to be paid upon delivery. As far as the pirates are concerned; why don't you paint your ships in such a way they are hard to see out over the deep waters?"

"What do you mean; Prince Inca?" the merchant asked as interest flared in his eyes.

"Turn and look out over the bay and into the ocean beyond. Do you not see how the blue of the water changes with the white caps of the waves? What if you painted your boats in a mottled pattern, one that is difficult to see at a distance? Do not forget to paint, or perhaps dye, your white sails in a pattern that is difficult to see as well. You merchants have told us the pirates spot you from afar and chase after you in ships which are much faster than yours. It seems logical if they can't see you easily you might well pass within sight of them undetected. It is a thought you might wish to consider."

"This is a very good thought, Great Prince, one we should have discovered for ourselves; you have my oath I will look into this as soon as I get back to Spain."

"We Mayan also have paint and dyes; and people who know how to apply these things. If you wish, you can hire some of these men at standard values, and when you leave our bay you may have a better chance of reaching Spain." The merchant held his left hand out, palm up, and slapped the bottom of his right fist into it; Inca looked at the hand interestedly and then glanced up at the man.

"My apologies Prince Inca; this is a gesture my people often use when we wish to agree to something. We have stamps we push onto inked pads and when we put this stamp onto paper it leaves a pattern; my movements only mean I am very pleased with your words and willingly agree to them."

Cuauhtémoc thought a moment and then duplicated the gesture; *"We are of the same mind then;"* he said with a smile.

Prince Cuauhtémoc had half of the sailcloth immediately sent to the nearby Birdman's Wingmaster with instructions to look into using the cloth as a replacement for the skins currently used on the wings. The rest of the sailcloth he sent to the Palace for safekeeping until he could get it to his home birdman's training camp, because he had many fond memories and good friends and brothers there, and they were never far from his mind.

The silk proved to be a thorny problem right from the start. The moment the women of the palace learned of it they singly and collectively requested and demanded they get the material for themselves, or if not all of it, at least the lion's share: this was a thing he was inflexible on. Perhaps when the next shipment came, and certainly the shipment after, but not this; in the end the Emperor had the silk put into one of the smaller, unused rooms in his own quarters and the room sealed until something could be decided.

The following morning he had his breakfast as he usually did and when he was ready he went up on the rooftop where Xymatoc's wings were. This was the day he would fly the wings over to the Wingmaster's domain where his people would take a long and careful look at the wings and decide the best way to repair them. His Father, two of his brothers, the new Birdman-Commander and the usual collection of guardsmen and servants were on the roof waiting for him when he arrived.

He bowed before his Father and hugged him and then turned and hugged Imhoquotep and H'ratli and greeted everyone else like long-lost relatives. The new Commander of the birdmen was one of the two who had been with the former Commander when he made his ill-advised approach to Cuauhtémoc. He had heard more about this particular set of wings than any other in immediate history, and he spent every spare moment he could, looking them over and examining them to see how they were built. Even though birdmen flew all over the Mayan Empire—and sometimes beyond—each and every birdman camp made their wings slightly different than any others.

"I very much like how your wings are built, Prince Birdman," the Commander said when he had a chance to speak without interrupting, "and I have heard about your tail drag-sticks; if you don't mind, please describe how they are used."

Talking was one of Inca's favorite pastimes and talking about flying was far above anything else. He immediately leaned down beside Xymatoc's wings and began describing how tail drag-sticks came to be; and how and why they were used. "I am told that in my camp before we went to these, it was not uncommon for a birdman to sprain an ankle, or something worse; once we started installing these and our birdmen came to understand how to properly use them, we had no further such, a thing that pleased Dispatcher and especially the birdmen. These wings before you are the very first wings to be so modified and they are the same wings Xymatoc and I flew two to a wing and the same wings I first leaned back and dragged tail. The fact that this is so, and that the wings belong to the brother who brought me to the birdman's camp in the first place, makes them very special to me and I wish no stone left unturned to return them to perfect condition. Xymatoc is forcibly retired, as you are, and he can no longer fly but they were in perfect shape when I took them from him and I am determined to return them in the same condition. Once I've returned them, I intend to create him an equally perfect set of greater wings, that he may fly again as you will soon do. Speaking of which; how goes the planning on such?"

"Confusion; as expected. There are those who insist in order for wings be made large enough to carry an adult, they will have to be twice as long and twice as wide, which will make them twice as heavy; and the wings will be too heavy to lift up and would not support an adult in any case."

"Idiots; all of them," Inca said in disgust. "For one; being twice as long and twice as wide would make them four times the weight, not twice, and even at your worst you are not four times as heavy as you were when you were flying;" and he gently poked the Birdman-Commander in the belly with his right forefinger.

His Commander laughed and rubbed his belly ruefully. "Truth," he said. "Ever since you told me I may fly again, I and my brother have once again been taking less food in an effort to drop as much weight as possible, We two, and all other like-minded brothers, are anxiously waiting for your words to come true and end the babblings of these 'idiots,' as you so accurately describe them."

It was the word 'idiots' that did it for Inca; his mind played back an exceedingly clear memory and he immediately told the tale about Toidi and what the name meant both forward and backwards as well as its meaning to the Inca people. "I swear, once brother Xymatoc understood, not even the shadow beneath his wings could keep up with him, he was so busy telling every man, woman and child in camp."

No one likes a bully, not even another such. By the time he told his tale, everyone on the rooftop were all but in tears they were laughing so hard, and there were few things in life he loved more than laughter.

In time the merriment died down and Inca picked up his wings and carried them over to the exact spot he stood when he attacked the enemy ships; now four days earlier. There really wasn't much mystery how he knew this was the same spot because the goatskins of oil left stains on the roof that would take many rains to finally wash away. The Commander of the local birdmen watched carefully. He was not here the day Inca attacked the ships, and even with the repeated telling of how Inca jumped from the roof, he was unsure it could be done. Cuauhtémoc gave his Emperor and brothers hugs goodbye, even though he would not be gone long, picked up his wings and ran as fleetly as a deer. His foot hit the small wall that surrounded the roof; he jumped and vanished from sight.

A moment later a wild k-e-e-e-r drifted up from beyond the wall and a few moments later he caught air and was rising fast. "Father Inti," the Birdman-Commander gasped, "did our Prince Birdman make that cry?"

"Yes; that was my Son, Cuauhtémoc," the Emperor said calmly.

"Look! Look over to the northeast; do you see those three eagles? They heard Inca and they're coming to investigate;" Prince H'ratli said excitedly.

"Yes, I see them, H'ratli. Now please be still as I wish to watch this and remember;" the Greatest Mayan serenely said.

Cuauhtémoc also saw the three eagles winging their way towards him and his heart took flight. He threw his head back and screed long and loud and the three eagles vented their wild cries back at him. The four met just over the water. Two of the eagles passed him on his left and the third went to his right. He banked sharply to his left and swung around and the three raptors also banked, swinging past each other and him, and for a few dizzying moments the four flew in intricate circles; passing above, below and to either side of each other, uttering their wild cries all the while. Cuauhtémoc was in his idea of heaven for he recognized the three as the same birds who escorted him to the palace nearly two weeks earlier. He was overjoyed to see the eagles again and they seemed equally delighted in finding him in their air space once more, for they uttered their wild cries again and again, and continued to circle him and finally flew beside him as he found a much-needed uplift and began to climb.

"Father Inti; our Prince Birdman can *fly!*" the Birdman-Commander said in hushed admiration.

By now, Prince Inca had gathered a large crowd of viewers scattered all over the city, and along the beaches. People stopped and stared and shaded their eyes against the glare of the sun and many dropped onto their knees to worship him, because they understood The Birdman was in their skies, and that meant all was well with the city and with the land. The Spanish merchants and sailors alike ceased their labors and also stared at the unfolding scene above them. They now knew this was not a demon as they'd first supposed but a birdman. But was it *a* birdman, or *the* Birdman, off his nest; because to the uninitiated below all the swirling about looked like some sort of intricate mating flight and they wondered if the Cock Birdman was going to do 'it' in the air or wait until he was in the privacy of his own nest with the curtains drawn.

Some of the Sun Priests also saw Prince Cuauhtémoc overhead. Their reaction was entirely different than the others. They immediately left the spacious rooftops they usually occupied and fled into the dark interior of the temple where there was a presumed measure of safety from attack. Hezaraht also saw the flight, and his heart burned with hate, and a lust for revenge. He would get the child down into his temple and place the youth on his altar and cut his living heart out of his body. This would show everyone he was stronger, and in his twisted logic, even the Emperor would see the error of his ways and he, Hezaraht, would once again savor the power that once was his. It never occurred to his warped mind if he succeeded, the Greatest Mayan would send every soldier he had into the temple, and would not quit until every priest within the city was dead.

Prince Birdman still needed to get his wings up to the aerie where the birdmen were, and where all of the tools and equipment lay, so he headed that way, once again flanked by his feathered friends. As he made his final approach to the landing area he saw Prince Quoholocet standing, waiting for him with his arms folded across his chest. Like everyone else in the aerie he saw Inca in flight and his pride in his little brother knew no bounds.

Inca came in, moving more quickly than most birdmen did when landing and he aimed his wings directly at his oldest brother. At first those standing next to Prince Quoholocet were nervous; then they were frightened, and then they scattered to the winds, but Quoholocet stood impassively waiting. No more than a few long steps from collision Inca leaned to his left—that wing needed repair anyway—and dragged it on the ground. He spun around and his beak bit dirt and his tail section was in the air for just a moment: he stuck his feet out and he was on the ground.

"Quick; everybody, anybody, get me something to feed my friends: anything; some small animals of some sort; they're not picky eaters."

People stared at each other.

"One of the sows farrowed six days ago and as usual there are more piglets than will survive; will they do?" one of the men asked anxiously.

"Yes! Bring three as quickly as you can," he commanded, and turned to the eagles that circled overhead. "K-e-e-e-r," he screed to the raptors above and the three cried back and began to circle above him.

The men had to distract the sow while two others darted in and grabbed three piglets up between them, and immediately escaped, for the sow heard the squeal of her young and the mother's instinct to protect rose within her.

The men came trotting up; one man held two piglets, one in each hand, and the other had just one. Cuauhtémoc reached out and took the two small animals from the first man and then turned and faced his feathered friends. "K-e-e-e-r; food, come and get it," he cried out to the eagles above. The three ceased their circling and lined up for the attack. He watched them carefully, timing his movements to their flight. He held one piglet in each hand, his index finger between two tiny hind legs, with the other fingers and thumbs providing grip. He swung the piglet in his right hand and the animal squealed non-stop. He waited until he felt the time was right and then swinging the doomed in a circle at his side he launched it skyward. The closest eagle beat its wings powerfully and plotted an intercept course. Just as the bird passed overhead its talons shot out and the small pig gave a final squeal and went limp. This act was duplicated with the piglet in his left hand, closely followed by the third animal. All three eagles screed one final time and flew off in search of limbs to land on so they could enjoy their meal; this was a very easy snack from their point of view.

Cuauhtémoc turned, and his oldest brother stood directly before him, a huge smile on his face. "Such a hug I would give you if you weren't all spattered with, ah, spatters," Quoholocet said.

He looked himself over. The piglets had anointed him with the only substance that piglets had on tap. "I need a bath," he admitted with a grin of his own.

Once he was clean and his clothes were laundered, he put them back on—still wet, it didn't matter—this was equatorial jungle and they would dry soon enough. The entire time he was getting himself and his clothing cleaned, the local experts were giving Xymatoc's wings a careful going-over, from beak to tail and wingtip to wingtip.

"Your wings are very well built, Prince Birdman. We now understand better how you were able to do some of the things that you did and still survive. We still do not understand how three sticks poking out the tail piece can make landing better; perhaps if you were to explain it to us."

"Explaining takes too long and is not efficient," he said, "it will be faster and better to show you; pay attention to what I do now." He picked up his wings and ran quickly into the wind and in a short time he was aloft and in an uplift that quickly carried him several trees high. He turned about and made a text-book approach exactly as he had done when he'd first flown with Xymatoc. He glided in just above stall speed as all birds and birdmen do, and just before others would put down their legs and start to run, he leaned back. The wing's beak came up, forcing the tail-section down, and the tail-rods scraped the ground leaving small furrows and some dust behind. This, combined with the increased angle of the wings into the wind, quickly slowed him down.

To the watchers it almost seemed to smack of magic he stopped so quick. "This is how it is used," he said, ending his explanation. "Once you have fitted your wings with tail drag-sticks and understand how to properly use them, and have practiced with them awhile, you will never wish to go back to the older way."

Inca spent most of the morning talking with the rank and file of the birdmen, stressing what had to be done and why. By the time he was ready to leave they believed almost to a man and were willing. This was another major victory, for many were overtly hostile when he'd first arrived, held in check only by the presence of Prince Quoholocet and members of the Royal Guards . . . which was why they were there in the first place.

There were two ways for Prince Inca to return to the palace. The first was obvious: borrow a spare set of wings from the aerie and fly. But no birdman worthy of the name would fly a set of wings he had not personally made; and this was as true of Inca as it was for others. The only exception lay at his feet, and only then because he trusted his brother Xymatoc as no other, when it came to wings if nothing else. The other way was on foot. This pleased him because all he had ever seen of the city was from the air; and seeing from the ground would give him an entirely different perspective.

The aerie lay on the top of a broad knoll that overlooked the city and a well-traveled path led downward. Prince Quoholocet brought Inca's feathers with him but it did not occur to him the Birdman would not fly with sandals on so he had to walk barefoot; a thing that he was more used to anyway.

The two Princes and their guardsmen walked downhill and into the city, headed back to the Palace where the Greatest Mayan waited for them. They walked between tall stone buildings and through many beautiful parks that were scattered throughout the city, and everywhere they went, people saw and recognized the feathers of royalty, and bowed deeply before them. Prince Quoholocet tended to ignore the commoners but Inca would look at them and nod and smile as he passed by them.

They were no more than halfway there when he heard a voice speaking indignantly in Spanish. *"I, Juan Carlos Sebastian Hernandez, the greatest bowyer to have lived; treated like a common mule."*

"A moment, please," he said to his brother and immediately headed toward the voice.

"You; you are Spanish are you not?" he asked the man as he walked up to him and the group he was with. One of the men looked to be very wealthy. He did not have the mark of a merchant but there were many other ways of being rich. The rest of the men seemed to be guards of sorts. All of them saw 'feathers' coming toward them and all bowed deeply.

"Yes; I am a son of Spain; who are you that speaks my language in this foreign land?" the Spaniard asked politely.

"I shall return to you in a moment," he told the man and then looked at the pack that was on the man's back; *"that looks to be heavy; put it down."*

He turned to the man who was the presumed leader of the group. "I have ordered this one to put the pack down;" he said. "How did you come by this one anyway?"

"I bought him legally;" the man replied. "The Great Emperor permits those such as me to have personal slaves."

He turned his attention back to the Spaniard who had gratefully dropped the load to the ground. *"How did you come to this land; Son of Spain?"* he asked.

"I was on one of the merchant ships down in the bay as a paying passenger. We were supposed to be headed to the new world, but we were assaulted by pirate, and then a demon of sorts flew overhead and destroyed the pirates and the Captain of the ship that I was on surrendered. I was brought ashore with all the others and then I was led aside and the first thing I knew, this one here purchased me, and I am a slave ever since." He made as to spit on the ground, thought better of it and swallowed his own saliva.

"You are wise to not have done that," Inca said softly, *"men have been killed for spitting in the presence of a Crown Prince; much less two."*

Inca turned to the one who was in charge of the group; "I am Prince Birdman; if you were outside awhile ago you saw me flying overhead. I am the Birdman who attacked the pirate ships four days back and the Greatest Mayan has given me all the ships and the materials and people on them: how came you by this man?"

CHAPTER 16

The man broke into a sweat and it was not just the heat of the day. "I bought him from a contact in the Palace," he said. "I have always had good contacts all over the city and I had no reason to question this one was any different."

"Do you know this contact by name; would you recognize him if you saw him again? Consider this before you answer; at the moment I do not suspect you of wrong-doing. I think you are an innocent who got caught in a web, unknowing evil was involved. Anything you say or do to help capture the true villains will go a long way towards proving your innocence."

"Yes, Great One, yes to everything you say. I know my contact's name, or rather I know the name he gave me, and I will most definitely recognize him if I ever see him again because my memory for such is very good. I have not intentionally committed wrongdoing; here or anywhere else; the retirement plan for those who get caught is not to my liking."

Inca gave the man a shallow bow of respect and turned to his brother. "Prince Quoholocet; as you are aware, I speak with anyone who will stop and listen to me, and I listen to almost anything they tell me in return. It occurs to me; since coming here I have heard different people at different times; mention some object that was once in a place has gone missing. The most common thought is it was moved somewhere else. Because this Spaniard was taken from out of others deliberately and sold; I must presume this is no accident but an act of deliberate theft. I believe our Father will be deeply interested in finding out who these people are and just how far the corruption spreads; does this thought sit well with you?"

"It sits very well; brother Cuauhtémoc. This is in line with my own experiences; I have also had things come up missing and presumed that it was only mislaid. Now I think on it, we have always had problems with things going astray, but usually they turn up elsewhere; but perhaps in the last six lunar cycles or more the problems have become more common. I think we would have figured it out on our own, but as is typical, you have put your finger on it first. Whatever I and my men can do to help, speak, and it is yours."

Inca turned to the man who waited; "It is my wish you come to the palace with us. You are not a prisoner, but an ally, and you shall be treated with courtesy. I suggest you have your guardsmen take your belongings back to your home and await you there. Once you are done at the palace, Prince Quoholocet will have some of his Royal Guardsmen escort you back to your place as a courtesy, and to make sure that you arrive safely; does this meet with your approval?"

"Yes, Great One, I like this very much; I have always wanted to see inside the palace; if only to be able to say I have."

"It shall be done then," he said, and then turned to his brother. "I just had a thought; the Healers have places within the city where they buy their herbs and other plants; if you know of such a place, I would like to go there, because there are certain florae that may help our searching very nicely."

"I have heard of these, but I don't know where any are, Inca; my apologies."

"I may speak; Great One?" the man asked courteously.

"Yes, of course," Inca replied.

"I know of one such place; it is not far from here. If it is your desire we can take a slightly different path to the palace and stop there on the way and you can see for yourself if it meets your needs."

"Yes; this is very good. I now think Father Inti must have led us to you, my friend, because you are helping uncover a hidden evil within the palace; and that can only be the doings of the Greatest One of all." He gestured to the man to lead them, and then as they started walking he turned his attention back to the Spaniard. They wound their way between ancient buildings made up of stone blocks carved out of the nearby mountain; and as they walked he talked to the Spaniard.

"You rightfully belong to me, Son of Spain, because our Emperor has given me the ships and all belongings and people. I wish you to understand I take no slaves and I am willing to give you your freedom. You may walk away this moment as a free man and no one will stop you, but I hope you will stay at least awhile, for there are many things I would ask. To begin with, exactly what is a 'bowyer,' and how is it you are the best to have lived?"

There are those who endure their jobs as a necessary evil and there are those who enjoy their labors and look forward to each working day. Then there are those who are obsessed: these eat, sleep, think and dream their fixation and Son of Spain was one of the latter. It was as if a dam broke somewhere and instead of a wall of water it was a deluge of words; the man absolutely spewed his enthusiasm about such. Cuauhtémoc only barely stopped him. *"Please, Son of Spain, I have only been speaking and understanding your language for a short time and there are many of your words I do not yet know; to start off, exactly what is a 'bowyer?'"*

"Yes, I understand, it is one who uses a bow;" and he pantomimed holding a bow and pulling back on the string and releasing an arrow.

"I comprehend as well. Now then; what makes you say you are the greatest to have lived?"

"Well, maybe not the greatest of all," he admitted with a smile; *"but one of the best to ever live. This is so because not only am I a superb bowyer; I am also skilled in the making of bows. Most people take a likely stick and carve on it until it looks like a bow, and then they string it, and use it as*

such. No; this is not the way I do these things. I make my bows in layers; some wood, some sinew, some specific glue and then they must be laced tightly together until they cure. Once this is done they may then be shaped and used; properly made, one of my bows will shoot farther and more accurately than any other bow made today; I even have ancient books on the subject . . . or I did have," and he glowered at the distant bay where the ships still floated.

"If your books and property can be found they will be returned to you. I have too many questions to ask for now but there is one thing you may be able to answer: these bows that you say you make; exactly how long can you make them?" Inca asked, because an idea came to him and his mind, as always, was not far from making better wings.

"Pardon, Patrón?

"Can they be made from here, where you stand," he turned and walked six steps away and turned back around, *"to here?"*

The Spaniard gave Inca a blank stare and then like the sun coming out from behind the clouds he broke into a huge smile. *"You speak of the ballista, my friend, what a joyous day it is for you that you should meet me for I am the world's foremost expert on the ballista."*

"What is a ballista?" he asked in Spanish and then switched into Mayan, "and why are we standing here and not walking?"

"We have arrived, Great Prince, this is the place you asked about;" the man said.

"I knew that all along, I just wanted to make sure that you were paying attention," he replied with a sly smile. Prince Quoholocet shook his head and took a slow swing at Cuauhtémoc as if he was going to swat him and they all headed for the open door.

"We shall speak of the ballista later; yes?" Son of Spain said softly.

"Yes; and in great detail," he replied, and then he turned his attention inward.

A thousand smells came out to meet him and each scent was wonderful. His grandfather had two huts back in the High Reaches village where he was raised; one smaller and one much larger; he lived in the smaller one because the larger was filled to the doorways with every kind of plant, herb, root, mushroom and the like that had ever existed in the area: this shop was the same, only more so.

"Phew; what a stench;" Son of Spain muttered and then spoke no more.

There were two Healers in the shop being waited on by two different men. As the group entered the four turned and looked, saw all the 'feathers' coming, and the Healers stepped back and the two shop men came forward and bowed deeply; "How may we serve the Greatest Mayan today?" the senior shop man said smoothly.

Inca's eyes glanced between the two men and then locked upon the second. *"You are Incan as I am,"* he said, speaking in the old tongue, *"do you understand the ancient language of our fathers?"*

"I am not allowed to speak that language in this shop," the man said stiffly and his eyes looked angry.

Prince Cuauhtémoc turned to the shopkeeper; "Why aren't we permitted to speak Incan in this shop?' he asked politely.

"The Incas are a barbaric people; they worship the Jaguar god, and not Inti as we Mayan," the shopkeeper said indignantly.

"I am Incan. My father was Incan as was my grandfather and my fathers before them; for a thousand years and more my ancestors are Incan and I have the blood of Incan Emperors in me. But all of these, with the exception of my mother and grandfather, are dead; what I am today is my doing and not the doing of the deceased.

"This one beside me is Prince Quoholocet; thought to be the next Emperor. His father and mother are Mayan, as was his grandfather and fathers before them, for a thousand years and more his ancestors are Mayan and the blood of the Greatest Mayan flows through him. Yet we two are brothers. Not because of an accident of birth but because we wish it. We only have these few things that are different; that we are of different nations, that we are not the same age and that we are of different heights. We have discovered that in spite of these few things that are not the same we have the same heart within us for we both love good food; the sight of a beautiful girl walking; the sound of birds singing and the feel of Inti's warmth upon our bodies as well as many others. We also share a common hate of evil in all its forms; from the pirates who raid and kill our people; to deception and treason; to the abomination the Sun Priests have become. We have far more in common than not; and for this reason we are brothers.

"You;" he said, turning to the Incan man to his left, "why do you stay here if you feel unwelcome; are you a slave or indentured servant?"

"No, Great One, I am a freeman and can come and go as I wish; I stay here because this one pays me well."

"Is that your only reason for staying; that he pays well?"

"No, Great One, you will not understand this but I have a great love for all the things in this room; I love the different plants and roots and herbs and I love knowing how these things can be used to heal the sick and injured: in this I share a common bond with the Great Healer up in the northern village as I am told that he too has this love."

"He does. And I do understand for the Great Healer is my grandfather and he has taught me most of what he knows." He turned his attention to the shopkeeper. "As for you, if you dislike Incan people, why do you permit this one to serve here?"

The shopkeeper looked at his employee for a long moment and then turned to Prince Inca. "This man is the best employee I have ever had. That is why I pay him so well. He is good with customers and knows my stock better than I do. If I may speak the truth, there are things within this shop I would not have if it were not for him. As it is, I feel I have the best-equipped medicinal-plant shop in the city, and perhaps even in all Maya."

Inca looked at the shopkeeper and said, "When Father Inti made men he made us all a little different that we could tell each other apart. Some he made wise and some he made fools; some are tall and some are short; some are Great Emperors and some labor in the fields of the Emperor; yet he shines his light equally on all of us because he loves us all equally. Before His great light, we are all idiots, a thing you two seem to be going out of your way to prove. You, Incan, stick your right hand out like this;" and he extended his right hand. The Incan obeyed without hesitation. "Not to me but to your employer. You, Mayan, stick your right hand out as you see the Incan do . . . yes, now each of you take hold of the other's wrist . . . yes, exactly like that.

"What you now have is the grip of friendship, or perhaps in this case, that of co-workers. When two labor together of the same mind, each is greater than he is alone because he shares the other's strength. When two labor against each other, each is less than he is alone because the other works against him and thus weakens. Look upon your hands and see that the grip cannot be broken unless both of you release; this is a symbol of unity and strength and you will be wise if you remember this thing.

"Of course, you will physically have to let go at some point; to go to the 'needed' if nothing else, not to mention scratching your, ah . . . your . . . ah . . . your nose, of course." As he spoke his right hand made vague, random motions, first behind his rump, and then his around his crotch and belly, only to scratch his nose carefully. He stopped, sniffed his finger suspiciously and muttered to himself; "Huh! I wonder where that thing's been." He crossed his arms, putting his right hand under his left armpit and looked brightly around for a few heartbeats and then looked at where his hand was; "Oh, yeah, now I remember."

Even the Spaniard was laughing. He might not understand more than a few words of Mayan but Inca's antics needed no explaining: Quoholocet reached out and took Inca by the upper arm and pulled him close. He took Inca's headdress off and handed it to the nearest guardsman "Here, hold this," he said; "I've wanted to do this ever since he landed on our roof." He got Inca in a headlock and rubbed his knuckles briskly over the top of Inca's head. The Birdman did not resist but instead used his time to give his older brother a hug.

A short time later he had his headdress back on and once again faced the two men who worked in the shop: "There are three items I wish from your place, shopkeeper, but I only know them from words my grandfather told me; and when we spoke of these things, we always spoke in Incan. Perhaps you can tell me the Mayan name for them that my own knowledge might grow."

"Yes, Great One, speak the names of what you need and if we have such I will surely know," the Incan worker said with a deep bow.

"The first one is a leaf called '*jaguar's claw*,' the second is a root called '*willbane*' and the third is a berry known as '*snowdrops*.'"

The Incan man repeated each name in Mayan and when Cuauhtémoc was done with his list the man gave him a long stare and then bowed deeply. "You are truly the grandson of the Great Healer," he said politely, "and yes; we have all three of these in stock, and like all of our wares, they are fresh within the month." He bowed deeply again and turned about and headed out on his tasks.

"Pardon, Great Prince, may one speak?" one of the Healers asked hesitantly. Cuauhtémoc looked at him and nodded. "I have a patient that complains of head pains. These plague him constantly and even the greatest herbs for such only relieve his aches for short periods of time; do you know of anything that might be of use?"

"What is this one like; is he wealthy or poor?" Inca asked, intrigued.

"He is very wealthy, Great Healer," the Healer admitted.

"How does this one eat; does he eat rich foods only or does he eat as others do?"

"He is widely known for the table he sets; only the most expensive cuts of meat may be served him and only equally rich pies and such will pass his lips."

"How are his movements; does he pass liquid and solids with ease?"

"I'm . . . not sure Great Healer; he has never discussed such with me."

"Is he lethargic in his actions; in other words, is he tired and slow?"

"Yes, to both of those, Great Healer;" the man replied.

"My grandfather, the Great Healer, told me this when I was seven; 'Many human afflictions can be traced to the emptying of the bowels and bladder. Food goes into us and food is filled with nutrition for the body. But once the body has removed these nutrients, that which is left becomes a poison and must be eliminated as soon as practical. The longer such stays within body; the worse it is for us.'" What you must do is make a light tea of *chitum* bark and see that he drinks two swallows of it every fist of the sun until his bowels run clear. He then must eat only fresh fruit and raw vegetables for five days to give his body a chance to clear itself of the buildup within. Once this has been done he may go back to a more normal meal but unless he wishes to return to the head-pains and tiredness he must now have a minimum of either two servings of fresh fruit or two servings of raw vegetables with each meal, but it is best not to have both fruits and vegetables at the same time, as the body digests each somewhat differently. Your patient should lose his head pains within a day and as long as he eats well they shall not return. This I have told you should be understood by all healers everywhere, and every healer should make sure each and every one of his patients understands this, because failure to do so brings about a poorer quality of life and an earlier death."

"I have never heard of these things, Great Healer, the merest crumb from your table is a feast to one such as me."

Cuauhtémoc looked at the healer and then at Quoholocet. "It just now comes to me that no nation can truly call itself great until they take proper care of their elderly and sick." He turned back to the two healers who were watching him with unwinking stares. "All of my days are, for the most part, taken with one thing or another but my evenings and nights are usually my own. I spoke to the healer up in the northern birdman's camp it was my wish as much of my grandfather's knowledge as possible should be shared with as many healers as feasible. Go and speak with your brother healers and if you should wish it, I will arrange for us to meet and share knowledge, perhaps one day in seven. My only condition is you also tell these things to all of your brothers as best you can, so all Maya may benefit. But the only time I will be able to do this is very late at night or early in the morning before most people are awake. If this is agreeable with you, and your brothers, please contact me at the palace. Tell the guards on duty that Prince

Cuauhtémoc has summoned you and that should get you in with no problem. Or say Prince Birdman or Prince Inca; all of the guards will know of whom you speak."

The Incan shop man brought three different containers in three different trips and laid them on the counter before Cuauhtémoc. The first looked to be dried leaves; somehow in the drying they curled in on themselves until they did vaguely look like oversized claws of sorts. The second container held dried white berries; and the third container held pale roots that were more off-white than anything else. Inca stopped talking to the others around him and began examining the contents of the three containers.

He took small samples from the containers, one at a time and tested them with his eyes and his nose and finally his tongue. He passed jaguar's claw and snowdrops without hesitation; but paused at willbane. He looked the root over carefully without actually touching it; the Incan man, seeing the Prince's motions, took a small scrap of leather and handed it to him. Inca took it with a nod and picked one of the small roots up, keeping the leather gently wrapped around it, so he didn't actually touch the root with his fingers. He sniffed it cautiously several times and then gently scratched the root with a fingernail, moving his nail upward rather than down as is usually done. He touched his nail to his tongue and immediately spit onto the floor. The Incan worker anticipated this and handed his Prince a cup with water in it; Cuauhtémoc nodded thanks and took a quick mouthful and swished it around and promptly spit that onto the floor as well. The floor was covered with loose straw and light dirt because it was not uncommon for healers to do things like this.

"All of your products are fresh as you have said, shopkeeper, and I offer my congratulations. Your willbane, while fresh, has been improperly harvested and stored; I speak this not in criticism but to share knowledge. Willbane is a root and all roots grow in the ground where it is dark and cool. This being so, roots are happiest when kept dark and cool. When dealing with willbane, this process is critical. One must harvest willbane very early in the morning when there is only just enough light to see by; a morning directly after a moonless night is best of all. The roots should be taken from the ground as swiftly as reasonable and put directly into a clay pot with a tight-fitting lid. The root must then be removed to the darkest and coolest part of a building and put up on willow racks or similar and permitted to dry completely. Once this is done, return them to a clay pot with a tight-fitting lid and put them where the temperatures are cool. Properly done, the root is good for many years without lightening, such as these roots have done. When my grandfather was teaching me of such he showed me a pot of willbane he said he had taken many years earlier and he claimed it was as good as a root recently harvested."

The two shop men bowed respectfully before him; "Thank you Great Healer; we will speak your words to those who supply us with such. These are good men who truly care about the products they sell and they will be very happy to learn the proper way of harvesting and storing such an arcane root. As I do not question you already know this; I won't bother mentioning it is a product we sell very little."

"I have never even heard of this root, Great Healer, exactly what are the uses of this?" the healer he had been talking to earlier asked.

"This root has very limited use and none of it strictly medicinal. For this reason I shall not go into it at this time. Perhaps some future date when the more needful things have been covered we shall speak of this again." The healer bowed deeply before him as one is supposed to bow before a Prince and backed away without straightening up until he was three paces away.

He selected the amount of each he wanted and the Incan who waited on him carefully wrapped each in separate packages and tied them into a single whole because the combined weight was insignificant. Prince Cuauhtémoc carried no money and no amount of reasoning on the part of anyone other than his father would persuade him to do otherwise. For him, gold was just needless weight and he did not wish to fly with needless weight. The Greatest Mayan understood this and did not insist. Prince Quoholocet also understood and he stepped forward and reached for the coin pouch that hung at his waist but the Mayan proprietor shook his head, and backed away, holding his hands up; palms outward. "No, Great One, your brother has already paid me in full and more; because he has opened my eyes to the truth and because he helped me to understand my own products better: perhaps on some other day; but not now."

Cuauhtémoc picked the package up and turned around and immediately faced a problem. He was now a Prince, and as such, could not be seen carrying anything. His brother was this way, even more so, and the guards were not supposed to be doing anything else except guard the two Princes. Before he could turn to the Spaniard, who seemed the only likely 'mule', the wealthy man gently took the package out of his hands. "Please; allow me, Great One. From what I have seen it will be an honor to do this thing."

"Is there anything you don't know, Inca?" Quoholocet asked; a thoughtful expression on his face.

Yes, many," Inca admitted; "I'd gladly tell you what, but," and he shrugged his small shoulders; "I don't know what they are."

Quoholocet looked at him for a moment, then yanked the feathers off of his head and tried to swat Cuauhtémoc with them, but the Birdman ducked, giggling; "Come back here, you, I'm going to whack you into day after tomorrow;" he said and he took another swing. The group left, still laughing while an older, dignified Prince tried his best to swat his little brother with a headdress that was shedding feathers faster than a duck in molt.

The owner of the shop looked at his employee and smiled. "Thank you for not quitting me like I deserve; you truly have been sent by Inti and I was too blind to see it."

"You are welcome. I also thank you for not sending me on my way because of my bad attitude. You know, he is a remarkable person, especially for one who is so young. I think when I go home tonight I shall tell my wife Prince Cuauhtémoc was in our shop this day. Once she has digested this I shall tell her the Birdman was also in our shop and then I shall mention that the grandson of the Great Healer of the northern village was here as well. When she asks if it was crowded I shall tell her that they are all the same boy. I will likely not get any meals for the next several days—or anything else for that matter." Both men laughed and then returned to business.

CHAPTER 17

Son of Spain was, perhaps, the only man in the entire city who could outtalk Cuauhtémoc. This became increasingly apparent as the group walked towards the distant palace. First, he told the Birdman not only was he Spanish, he was Castilian; (whatever that was). He went on to explain he was one the youngest son of a great Don (something like a Lord?) and he had been educated in Madrid (wherever that is) at a famous university (?) and not only could he speak Spanish, but also French, Portuguese and German and he could read these languages, as well as some Greek and Latin, but he was having great difficulty with the last two because he had not been able to find anyone who actually spoke or read these languages and so far, the only thing he had was a book written in French, Latin and Greek, with some cross-references.

The small group was making slow progress towards the palace. For one, Son of Spain was a passionate person and he used his hands to talk with as much as his mouth. Then again, Cuauhtémoc was careful to stop the flow of words every few sentences, so he could repeat everything to his brother and those with him, because to exclude them would be rude and he had never knowingly done a rude thing in his life.

Things got even more interesting when he started in on the *ballistae* because he was all but rabid on the subject. It turned out that ballistae were giant crossbows, which started another round of explanations,

215

since crossbows were unknown in Maya. Long before the palace was in sight Prince Cuauhtémoc became convinced the place to go first was not the palace at all but directly to the area where all of the things taken from the ships were being kept, because he was determined to get these books back to their rightful owner, if for no other reason than he wanted to learn to read them too. This was interesting knowledge and interesting knowledge was as close to a vice as he had.

They had not been down at the docks very long when Son of Spain turned abruptly and hissed at Inca: *"That one over there, the man with the feathers on his head as you have, but he only has three blue ones. Do not stare at him but he was the one who led me out from the others where I was eventually sold as a slave."*

There were several crates that had been taken from the cargo bay of one of the pirate ships; Cuauhtémoc turned to one of the crates and gestured at it. "Pretend to look at this wooden box for a moment. Son of Spain speaks the man with the three blue feathers in his headdress is the one who led him away to be sold into slavery; what do you know of him; my brother?" he asked Quoholocet softly.

"Nothing good," the Prince said. "He does his job and keeps to himself but he is not liked, and seems to have few known friends, here or anywhere else."

"He looks to be our first lead. I wish him arrested. We can say in a clear voice he is charged with being rude to the wife of a Great Lord and the Lord wishes to speak with him about it; that should throw off any listeners as to our real reason."

"That will be easily believed by everyone—wait; he walks this way."

Earlier, when he had been 'beating' his little brother, Quoholocet lost so many feathers out of his headdress, he wouldn't put it back on, and instead carried it in his hand. He was bent over the crate, as was most of everyone else, and the only man clearly seen was the wealthy man who still carried Inca's purchases. "Ah," the one with the blue feathers said as he came up, "I can easily see you are a man with a discerning eye. This crate before you has traveled all the way from far lands. Who knows what unknown treasures lie inside? I can get this for you for a very good price," he continued, all smiles.

Cuauhtémoc raised his head and stared at the man. "You wish to sell me what I already own, Blue Feathers?" he asked very quietly. Blue Feathers stopped suddenly and his smile slowly slipped away; his eyes darted around. He recognized Quoholocet, who was without feathers, and a young Prince whom he had never seen. As his eyes scanned more quickly he spotted the Spaniard standing in the group and he came to understand the guardsmen weren't hired men of the wealthy but Royal Guards. And in that moment he realized he had just walked into a trap. He turned to flee but nearly received an obsidian spear point in his belly for his troubles. A few moments later he was trussed up like a pig bound for market.

"You stand accused of offending the wife of a great Lord, Blue Feathers, and you shall be taken to face him; your fate will be decided by his mercy or lack thereof."

The speaker was the leader of this group of guards and he made sure he spoke clearly so those who stood not far away could hear him without trouble.

"He's the type, all right," one of the others said under his breath.

"It doesn't surprise me a bit," another agreed, "we won't be seeing him again."

"Thank you, Guardsman," Cuauhtémoc said softly; "I especially like how you spoke his fate will be decided by the Lord's mercy or lack thereof. This nicely explains why he shall not return; without alarming any of his brothers who may also be mixed up in this thing. Please take him to the palace and put him in a holding room, under guard, until we can rejoin you. There are several things I will need when we get there;" and he gave the Guardsman a short list. The man repeated the items to make sure he had it right and bowed deeply before his two Princes.

Prince Cuauhtémoc looked at the people nearby; he beckoned a servingman over; this one came with concern in his eyes. "You have no cause for alarm, Servingman; I only wish you to carry a package for me. Follow those guardsmen and their prisoner to the room they go to and leave this package there to wait for me. After you have done this you may return here or go wherever else you are suppose to be. I warn you not to monkey around with this package's contents because you will not like the result."

"I would never look into things that are not my concern, Great Prince, it is an unhealthy habit to get into at best;" the servingman replied.

"You are wiser than many; there are those who would do well to follow your example." The servingman bowed deeply, both as deference to his Prince, as well as acknowledging a compliment. Inca took the package from the wealthy man's hands and handed it to the servant, and the guards, prisoner and servant all headed out towards the palace which was some distance up on the hill.

"Forgive me; I have not adequately introduced myself nor have I asked about you. I am Cuauhtémoc, called Inca by many and I am a brother of Quoholocet, Imhoquotep and H'ratli as I have already spoken. What is your name and title if I may ask?"

"I am named Xertexes by my father; he spoke I am named after the Emperor of that name and I am someway related to him, but if this is so, my father never bothered to explain how. As for title, Great Prince, I have none; all I have is an almost obscene amount of money left to me by my father when he died. I was his only son and he had little other recourse."

"I understand; Xertexes. You have been a great benefit and I thank you for your help. If you have other things to do, you may leave when you wish, and you will be given Royal Guardsmen to escort you home. You did mention you wanted to see the inside of the palace; if for no other reason than to say you had. It is my pleasure to give you your choice of thing to do; leave now or stay awhile longer: what is your decision?"

"So far, this has been the most interesting day of my life. I would very much like to see more if I am not being too much trouble," Xertexes said politely.

"In that case I want to keep looking for those books and things that belong to Son of Spain because these things interest me."

The Mayan calendar did not predict any unseasonable rainstorms for some time yet; so the belongings were spread out along the beach both along the shore as well as away from the water. Because the Mayan mind was meticulous about such things, the piles were arraigned not only according to what the items were, but also from which ship they were taken. The group walked up the beach towards the north and they were respectfully greeted by the different guards who had been assigned to each pile. Well along the shore they found the pile of possessions that came from the merchant vessel that brought Son of Spain to Maya, and before long he spotted his own sea chests, pulled up along side of many other such. He started forward with cries of joy; when the guardsman in charge stepped forward. "You may look to your hearts content, but you may not touch or take anything, for these belong to The Birdman and I am charged with their safe keeping."

Quoholocet stepped forward and the guardsman glanced at him and then looked again. "Great Prince," he said, "forgive me but I didn't recognize you without your feathers;" and he bowed deeply.

Yes; feathers. Prince Quoholocet looked down at the headdress in his right hand and hesitantly put it back on his head. Most of the feathers were gone awry and many were missing entirely.

"I think his headdress was caught in a freak windstorm or something," Cuauhtémoc volunteered, "it was very strange because it came up suddenly and I felt the breeze of its passing on my back."

Quoholocet took a single look at Inca, yanked the headdress off and again tried to beat his little brother with it. Inca danced back; giggling. He turned his head slightly to where the Guardsman gaped in surprise. "He is my youngest brother and I am permitted to beat him whenever and wherever I choose;" he said. "Provided I can catch him, of course," he added as an afterthought.

The guard grinned and bowed deeply; "I am the oldest of five brothers and it is the same with me," he admitted, "and you speak truly; catching one can be a problem."

The Son of Spain went through the pile, selecting only those chests that were his, and these were taken out of the group and laid off to one side. There were two clever clasps on each trunk which kept it closed. The Spaniard easily snapped them open and reverently lifted out one loved book after another. There were five of such, plus two scrolls, none of which was familiar to the Mayan people. A few moments later he spotted a long object wrapped in an even longer soft leather case. The man picked it up and his face took on a glow that was almost holy: *"My Precious;"* he said.

It was the Spaniard's bow, and he handled it like it was a lover, a thing Inca understood. It was not uncommon for soldiers to become enamored of their weapons, whatever that weapon might be, and as a matter of fact; a great many birdmen felt that way about their wings— he certainly did.

The Birdman summoned a number of men and had all of the Spaniard's trunks and belongings sent to his room. Later on, Son of Spain could decide what to do with them, and what to do with the rest of his life, or at least what lay in the immediate future.

Once this was done, everyone headed back up to the palace, where the Emperor waited for their return.

There was a guard at the door waiting for the two Crown Princes; he led them to an inner room that was used to keep prisoners for questioning. Inside, they found the prisoner, Inca's package and all of the items he had asked for. They also found the Greatest Mayan and their two brothers; these latter looked to have not waited long.

"My Son; what have you uncovered for us now?" the Emperor asked, and held his arms out for a hug, a thing Inca wasted no time in giving.

Son of Spain had been doing most of the talking for over a fist of the sun. It was now Inca's turn and with his reputation as a talker at stake he wasted no time. He started at the moment when he heard the

Spaniard's words and carried his Father and brothers forward to where Blue Feathers walked up and unknowingly sprang a trap upon him. Inca did not waste any time during this. He laid out all of the equipment he had sent for, unwrapped the packages and set them carefully off to one side, and made sure a small fire was lit as he commanded and water was heating in the pot.

The Emperor and his three sons watched Cuauhtémoc as he carefully prepared the potion; they noticed the extreme care he used with the willbane. He carefully measured out portions of jaguar's claw and snowdrops and crushed them up and dropped them into a cup. He lifted one of the willbane roots out, wrapped it in a small piece of leather and without touching it, rubbed it across a coarse stone until a small pile of powder lay upon a piece of paper. He returned the willbane back to its package and dropped the powder into the cup with the other two ingredients and tossed the rock into the water; where it poured out on its way to the sea. He poured a small measure of boiling water into the cup and stirred it with a small stick. Once he was satisfied, he added an equal amount of cold water, and stirred it once more. When he was done, he tossed the stick, the paper and the piece of leather into the fire where the heat of the flames carried the smoke into the open air. He turned.

"Please remove our guest's bonds and gag and make him more comfortable," he said to the guards gently. "There; that's better. Now; I have made a nice potion for you. You are going to drink it all, and just to show you I am a fair person, I have decided to give you a choice. In the first, you can take the cup of your own will, and drink it all down quickly. For the second; you are surrounded by many large, powerful men, and between one and the other, you will drink the potion no matter how hard you may resist and no matter how damaged you may become in the process. But in either case; you are going to drink it. So how shall it be?"

"You're going to poison me;" Blue Feathers said defensively.

"I am not. If I wish you dead I have many ways that are quicker and more effective. This is not a poison intentionally; although I admit there have been some unfortunate side-effects that ended up that way. These are almost always traceable to improper harvesting, curing and storing of one or more of the ingredients. Your time is up. Drink it quickly and it will be over. Fight and you will lose, and you will still drink it, but I shall not be responsible for your condition afterwards."

Blue Feathers glared at the men gathered around him and then almost recklessly seized the cup and drained it in a very few swallows. He slammed the cup back down on the table: "Tastes horrible! What's in it, what's it supposed to do, anyway?"

"A fair enough question; I see no reason why you can't be told. The first ingredient is called jaguar's claws. While I don't expect you to understand; this is a hypnotic: one who is given this will obey most commands. The second is called willbane. The name explains its use; it banishes the will of those who take it. On the surface, the two seem to be the same, and yet they are not. Combined, they become a powerful regurgitant, even a light drink of this and one will spew like an erupting volcano. The third is called snowdrops. This is a pacificant. That is, it relaxes the stomach and mind and permits the former two to join into three, providing a powerful combination that puts one into a state of bliss. Soon; you will realize we here are your friends, and that you love us as no others, that there is no question we might ask that you will not answer without hesitation. How do you feel now; don't you feel happier than you have ever felt before?"

"Yes;" Blue Feathers said cheerfully for the drugs were taking effect very quickly.

"Wouldn't it be better if you were to explain why you took the Spaniard off to be sold into slavery?" At first the man spoke hesitantly, but as the drugs deepened their hold, he became freer with his information. Before long he was naming names, dates, times and places and it became obvious that petty theft; if done diligently over days, weeks and months, is not petty at all. "All of this is very interesting," Inca admitted gently, "but why is this happening; where is all of the gold going?"

"To Him;" Blue Feathers slurred; "he's going to raise an army up, an army that will overthrow this weak Emperor we have and we'll have a new Emperor, a strong Emperor, an Emperor who won't bow down before those—" And his voice blurred.

"Who did you say is going to overthrow the Greatest Mayan?" he asked urgently.

"Hezaraht, of course," Blue Feathers said. His eyes rolled into the back of his head and he began to tremble; in a moment he fell off the stool and hit the floor, twitching and jerking spasmodically—then he shuddered violently and was no more.

"The unfortunate side-effect I presume?" Prince Quoholocet asked politely.

"Yes; it has to be the willbane. My only regret is my grandfather does not live closer. If he did, I would ask him for some, because I do not question anything he has harvested. And should he refuse, I will just invite him over for a nice cup of tea;" and Inca glanced at the jaguar's claws and his eyes and face were filled with unrepentant mischief.

The room exploded in a roar of laughter; only the Spaniard was not laughing and even he had a smile on his face. *"What has just happened, my friend, what happened to the man on the floor and why is everyone laughing?"*

Cuauhtémoc had not deliberately left Son of Spain out, but with things happening so fast, he hadn't been able to take time out to translate. Since everyone else was in the throes of mirth; he used the occasion to explain what happened since they walked through the door. The two of them, surrounded by his father, brother and guardsmen and servants, talked quietly to each other. *"That one was an evil man,"* Son of Spain said. *"It seems a terrible death to wish upon anyone but I think it was for the best."*

"That one died better than he deserved," Cuauhtémoc admitted, *"I have a deep hatred for traitors, for they eat at a man's table and take his*

kindness, and repay it with deception and treason. I have no sadness for him at all but as he was dying he named names and places that will expose yet others of his kind; that is not much of a consolation but it is better than nothing."

Prince Quoholocet was all for rounding up every soldier he could lay hands on, and attacking the Sun Priests without warning, but the Greatest Mayan forbade it. "We only have the word of a dying man, and even though his words are likely true, we cannot condemn them on only this. I can see Cuauhtémoc has the best way of it. We shall pick up those named over many days, on various charges not related to petty theft, and we shall question them like this. After we have learned more and understand more we will be better prepared to properly decide what must be done. I once again find myself in your debt, my son; I can never adequately thank you for what you do for me and all my children. If you have a need, all you must do to receive it is ask," and the Greatest Mayan inclined his head toward Cuauhtémoc.

"I have no further needs, Father," Cuauhtémoc started to say and his voice broke half-way through and he finished his sentence in an entirely different octave. He stopped and covered his mouth in surprise and then laughed and all of the men in the room also laughed because all remembered going through the same thing and all understood what it meant.

"There won't be a young girl in the entire palace that will be safe now," Prince H'ratli said with a grin, and he held his arms open for a hug, which quickly spread to all of the men present, including Son of Spain.

"You mean our Birdman will no longer be safe from them," Prince Imhoquotep said, with a matching grin.

For the next several weeks Cuauhtémoc could rarely open his mouth to speak without his voice wavering over several octaves. He had never been embarrassed about anything and he wasn't about to start because of this so he just laughed it off and continued on with life as usual. Such changes in life don't actually last that long, although for many boys it seems an eternity, but by the time the month was over his voice settled into a pleasant baritone and men who resented being ordered around by a child, suddenly found they no longer minded.

Eilei and Yvette received the news with open glee. They had long since decided between them he was theirs to divide up as they saw fit: 'Now remember, he's yours Monday, Wednesday and Friday and mine on Tuesday, Thursday and Saturday and we'll each have him on alternate Sundays' seemed to be the way they felt. As for him, he went on as he had been before, although he did come to understand girls were starting to look very interesting to him in ways he had never noticed before.

Three days after the Blue Feathers incident, a messenger came for Inca to tell him his wings were repaired, and great strides were being made in the greater wings, and whenever it suited him he could come up and check on things. This met his approval, and he immediately went to the Greatest Mayan, who predictably, already knew these things were so.

Early the next morning Inca, H'ratli, Imhoquotep, Son of Spain and a respectable number of guards set out for the local aerie. On the way they stopped at the store where Inca had gotten the plants from. Since they were in the area; he wanted to explain to the Incan worker what had happened. When they entered, there were a fairly large number of healers in, none of whom the Birdman recognized. The two men who worked there knew him, and as was fitting in the presence of three Crown Princes, the pair immediately deserted their customers and came over.

Cuauhtémoc glanced around at the healers who had been suddenly abandoned. "This will only take a brief moment," he said politely, and then turned to the two who faced him. "I wish to speak of the products we picked up when I was here last, but because of the sensitivity of such, I will speak in Incan to this one and he can explain later when you have more time." The Mayan proprietor smiled, bowed, and went back to his other customers. He switched into Incan and explained what had happened to Blue Feathers and why. *This is not a thing for you to regret, my friend, I only mention it so your own understanding may grow.*" The Incan man bowed deeply and thanked him; and Inca and the rest continued on towards the aerie at the top of the knoll.

Cuauhtémoc knew the people at the aerie were aware he was coming. After all, it was they who notified him his wings were ready. What he did not know, and could not have foreseen, was the welcoming committee awaiting him.

There were a large number of birdmen and their various commanders there when he and the rest crested the hill and walked into camp. His main concern was his wings, as was typical for birdmen everywhere, and he headed that way immediately. He examined Xymatoc's wings closely, both the repaired parts as well as the rest and could not find one thing to criticize. "You have done very well," he said in thanks, "I am well pleased. I have looked carefully but even to my eyes it is difficult to tell that which was repaired from the original and I thank you."

He stood there, congratulating those who had worked on the wings as well as everyone else who might have been remotely involved. As he did, his eyes raked the people gathered in a loose group, and then raked again and then some inner tic in his mind brought his eyes back to two men who were very familiar. "Twuondan, Qualaktec!" he shouted in joy and immediately abandoned those closest to him to go charging across the area like a berserker. "My brothers, my sergeants, how did you get here? Well, I know how you got here, but how did you get here? It's great to see you again! How long shall you be here; you're not leaving right away are you? Because if you are, you are not! I am Prince Birdman and I forbid it. H'ratli, Imhoquotep, come here please; I want you to meet the two brothers who stayed."

"You know, Inca, you really shouldn't keep your emotions trapped inside like that," Prince H'ratli said dryly; "try and letting them out once in awhile. I'm sure there are those in the far corners of the city who didn't hear you at all."

Inca laughed in joy, he put an arm around each of his sergeants and led them back to where the rest still were. "These are my brothers who stayed and helped me fight the first batch of pirates in the Northern Soldier's Camp," he said. "It is my belief we could not have conquered the enemy as quickly as we did if it were not for their help. As I told you earlier, five birdmen were leaving with messages from the Lieutenant. Three left after I asked them to stay and help fight but these two stayed. Because of this thing we three were able to conquer the enemy more quickly and managed to save many Mayan lives by doing so."

He devoted the next three or four fists of the sun to working on the greater wings, those that were intended to get all of the older birdmen back into the air that wished.

Son of Spain became increasingly quiet. From what Inca had come to expect of him, no more than a very short while would pass without him having something to say, and now it had been nearly a fist without more than a few words. Something was troubling him and Inca intended to find out what.

"You seem very quiet my friend," he said when he had a few moments alone with the Spaniard, *"speak your troubles and I will be pleased to share them."*

"It is the ballista that troubles me my friend. I have spoken of it with much enthusiasm but I have sailed under a false flag." By now Inca knew what this phrase meant and he nodded his head and encouraged the man to continue. *"I have spoken of this as if I have actually seen such but it is not so. I have read many books on these things when I was in Madrid and I understand them as well as any man alive, but I have never seen an actual one, nor have I ever seen one used. I am so convinced they will be superior to our cannons I have let myself misrepresent and I am sorry."*

CHAPTER 18

"**C**onfession is good for the soul," Cuauhtémoc said softly, "*you are an honorable man. I have seen this in your eyes and in the lights around your head, otherwise I would have never permitted you to come up here because you now understand* it was not a demon that flew over the pirate ships and destroyed them but a birdman. In fact; that birdman was me."The Spaniard looked at Inca in astonishment: "Yes, this is so, and should you wish I can call Prince H'ratli and Prince Imhoquotep over here and they will speak the same for they were upon the roof and saw me do this thing.

"From my talks with you I am convinced you have much to add to help the defenses of the City of Emperors, and all of Maya as well, and this belief not only includes your beloved ballista but also that marvelous bow you have. This brings me to why you are up here. You have seen the wings and are learning to understand how they work. One of the problems that has plagued wing designers from the start is a thing I believe you hold the answer to; and you are as yet unaware of it. It is this wonderful joining of wood and sinew into a flexible bow. Come here and let me draw on the ground and see if you understand what I mean.*"

He led the Spaniard slightly off to one side where there was open earth mixed freely with sand. He picked up a convenient stick and knelt down and began to sketch on the ground, drawing a crowd while he was drawing a number of pictures. The first sketch was of a standard set of wings. This was two horizontal sticks that were not quite parallel with a number of crossing sticks that were set at angles intended to brace and strengthen the whole. *"This is how my wings now look and all of the wings that are made up in the birdman's camp where I learned how to fly,"* he said, translating as he went along.

"This next is the bones of bird's wings. The interesting thing about this is I have examined every set of wings I was able, from of a dead condor I once found to those of hummingbirds, and with very little variations, the bones are much the same, differing only in length and thickness.

"This last is what I have come to believe should be our first effort at greater wings. You will note, Son of Spain, the way the limbs form and swing outward and then are bent back one by one, can only be possible by your method of bow making. Or at least it so seems to me."

"No; it shall not be; I will not permit such foolishness to be done in my camp!"

Inca stood up and turned and faced the speaker. The man was middle-aged with grey-shot hair and an attitude. "How is that? You do understand I am Prince Birdman and I have control over all birdmen and birdmen camps all over Maya, from the far north down to the deep south."

"You ain't my Prince; all you are, is a stinkin' Incan, and you got no say-so in my camp . . . hey! 'stinkin' Incan,' that rhymes; I'm a poet!"

"I am so happy for you," Inca said politely, "seize and bind him; the Mine Masters will be so pleased with your wit." Prince Cuauhtémoc looked the rest of the people calmly. "I would have hoped by now that everyone, down to the youngest child, understands we face an enemy who has no soul or mercy. This enemy will willingly come into every town and village and kill all they come across, including small ones: this I know because I have seen it with my own eyes. It may be you would have gotten along well with the pirates," he said, looking at the now trussed-up man, "but we shall never know, because you shall be working your life away down deep in the darkest mines, and I shall be up here in the open skies busily killing every pirate who attempts to place foot on Maya. I have spoken and it is so." He stared coldly at the man, and he clapped his hands three times slowly as he had seen the Greatest Mayan do, because he now understood what the words on his headdress meant when it said "Speaks for Emperor."

The next few days slipped gracefully into history. The Greatest Mayan made good on his words, and one by one, those named by Blue Feathers were picked up and taken to back rooms where the Emperor and his sons waited. And always; Cuauhtémoc was there with his supplies of Kickapoo joy juice. Sometimes the men were picked up on false charges and sometimes they were told—when in a group of others—the Greatest Mayan had taken note of their faithful service and they were being promoted and sent to a different place where they would have greater authority and benefits. This latter seemed to go over very well with those who were told this. In either case, they were led off and drugged and their minds dredged of all the useful information that could be found, and then, invariably, the men went into convulsions and died and their bodies were quietly disposed of.

Gradually a picture of deceit and greed began to form that first started some years earlier, not long after Hezaraht had taken over as High Priest of the Sun. For awhile, it almost seemed all of the servants were involved, but Cuauhtémoc changed his questioning slightly, and started asking who was known to be faithful, and a long list of untouchables emerged; a thing that made the Emperor very happy because to a man, these were the same servants he dealt with on a daily basis, and who he trusted the most.

Those who live lives of deceit and treachery are well aware what they do is wrong and the punishment for being caught is dire indeed. This creates a sure-fire formula for paranoia, and like rats abandoning a sinking ship, these took to leaving the palace with whatever they could carry. Most were caught and they too got a drink of potion and yet more pieces were added to the puzzle.

One of the more interesting things to come to light during this particular era was Hezaraht was also having problems; all which started the day Cuauhtémoc tried to kill him with a thrown sword. Many who believed his lies, now understood the truth, and these were slipping away in the dark even faster than the deceivers were leaving the palace. That, and the offerings the priests depended upon for support from the populace in the way of food and money, had dwindled down to the merest trickle. Hezaraht, of course, blamed all of his troubles on Cuauhtémoc and for once the charge was richly deserved.

Coercing truth from the unwilling was only a small part of the Birdman's activities. He was fully occupied with the building of an aerial army and as his predictions came true; many of those who were indifferent at best when dropping message arrows suddenly became obsessed with practicing precision dropping of anything they could lay hands on. This came to a head the day Twuondan and Qualaktec got their hair cut. Cuauhtémoc's hair was still too short for experimenting; but the two sergeants were overdue for a trim, and once the Birdman and the Haircutter explained their idea, both men became rabid with the thought.

By the time Haircutter was done he created a true work of art, and the men's hair now looked like they had sprouted feathers from their heads with the dark areas providing the body, and the lightened parts forming the edges. The results were stunning, and utterly different from anything that had ever been seen, and a great many others—including great lords—were dismayed when they learned they were not permitted to wear such. Only the birdman-soldiers were allowed, and the Greatest Mayan dictated anyone else found with such a haircut would immediately be shaved bald. And in a single day, 'feather head', went from insult to compliment.

The first pair of greater wings came off the assembly line at this time with yet more not quite complete. These new wings were covered, not with animal skins, as had been used for so many generations, but sailcloth that had come from the pirate ships down in the bay, which were now being carefully refitted. Cuauhtémoc, two of his brothers, the Birdman-Commander and upper echelon gathered to see how these things were going to work out. Cuauhtémoc watched the wings grow from the first, and would have had no hesitation about picking them up and flying off with them, a thing many were betting would happen. He turned to the two men who flanked the then Birdman-Commander on that fateful day and beckoned them near. "As I spoke before, our great need is to get all the older birdmen back into the air who wish to; it is my pleasure to give you two the first sets of wings. Go, my brothers, take up your wings and fly."

The pair stared him in the eyes with tears running down their faces and then as a single man they dropped to their knees and then onto their faces. He permitted it for a few moments because he understood the need was theirs, and then he gently helped them back onto their feet. "You are wasting air, my brothers," he said with a gentle smile; "now take up your new wings and show the disbelievers just how wrong they have been all along." The two bowed again and turned and with shaking hands they lifted the wings up and ran downhill into the wind and within a short time they caught air and were climbing fast.

"Qualaktec, Twuondan, attend me please." His two sergeants, surprised at being summoned, promptly came forward. "You two are very near your weight limit for flying. In other times, you would soon have to turn your wings in and become grounded, but you two stood beside me when others left and I shall stand beside you now. I have decided the next two wings off the line shall be yours and you shall be the first birdmen to take up greater wings without ever having lost the ability to fly." Inca turned to where his brothers stood, watching, he nodded slightly and the two came and sided him. "As things progress I shall need men I can trust as no others. I do not question your bravery and dedication because you have proven yourselves in combat. Please be so kind as to remove your sergeant markers;" the two did as commanded.

Cuauhtémoc took the markers and handed them to Imhoquotep. Quoholocet stepped forward with a pair of fancy Lieutenant Headdresses in his hands. Inca took one of them and turned to Twuondan; "Bow your head slightly please." He did as he was ordered and the Birdman put them on his brother's head. He turned again to Quoholocet who handed him the second headdress; "Qualaktec, bow your head slightly, please." He also did as ordered and Cuauhtémoc put the second on the man's head.

"It is my pleasure to speak that you two are now over-Lieutenants. I have spoken at length with my brother Quoholocet who is Supreme Commander of all military forces as well as my father, the Greatest Mayan, and both have assured me I have authority to do this thing and far more. You are both from Southern Maya and it is my wish—after your new wings are made and you have become used to them— that you shall fly back down into southern Maya and stop at every birdman's camp along the way and tell them of this new enemy that has come to our shores. I have spoken with Son of Spain and he speaks that the pirate, Greenbeard, is believed to have at least one hundred ships under his command and likely more. The danger this represents to Maya cannot be overstated. You are also to be given papers to document this is so; that you may show these papers to the commanders of each soldier's camp you come to, that you may also alert them to the problem although most are already aware of it. These papers carry my stamp upon it as well as the Great Seal of the Greatest Mayan and that of Quoholocet; few will know my seal yet but all shall recognize those of the Emperor and their Supreme Commander.

"I have spoken with my Father and Brothers and we have decided I must return to the Northern Birdman's camp at least for awhile to get yet another camp set up to make greater wings. Yesterday; a group headed out northward by war-kaks, carrying half the sailcloth on hand as well as half the silk, accompanied by a generous number of Royal Guardsmen for protection. I shall be here in this area for another ten days or so and then I shall fly northward and hope to meet them somewhere along the way. There are about three more lunar cycles before the next rainy season starts and I expect to be back well before that time. But for tonight, my Father wishes to meet you because I have spoken about you favorably, and he wants you to come and have evening meal with him and the rest of us."

(Eight days later.)

Cuauhtémoc woke early as was usual for him; he got up and used the 'needed' and walked out onto his private garden area. Above him the moon goddess smiled down upon him, he reached into an alcove and pulled out one of the drawing stands and turned it around. Five days earlier, just when the waxing moon neared toward full, he started on his latest drawing. He remembered telling Quoholocet he might draw Eilei as he had done the Greatest Mayan, but somehow the drawing became so much more, much as he had done with his Father's picture. In this one, he started out with Eilei asleep on the bed, her face relaxed in slumber while a sweet dream made the corners of her mouth curl upwards. This, he finished fairly quickly, and because he had so much paper left, he started smaller pictures of her in each corner. In the upper right she was looking out at him; an impudent look on her face her parents would know well. The lower right showed her with a puzzled expression she once wore as Yvette was trying to explain one of the complex French verbs to her. The lower left was the sly smile she showed when she tricked him into helping her back into her clothes, and the upper left was the one he was just finishing and it showed the tearful face she wore when she and Yvette came to understand he must leave for at least a month; and perhaps even more. It was a labor of love, and he was already laying out a mental concept of a picture he would do of Yvette, once he returned. He sighed softly, picked up two of the finest drawing sticks and began to add detail to the sketch.

The moon was nearly set by the time he was done with the intricate details of the final picture. He stepped back and looked it over and saw it was good. It was exactly one lunar cycle to the day since he had come to The City of Emperors and in less than two days he would be leaving. He looked lovingly at his art one last time and then wiped the sticks down and put the lid back on the ink pots and put them all away. He went in and took a bath and got ready to face yet another day.

He walked out his door and turned right and headed deeper into the palace. The guards who once stood watch over him had gone on to other things. He was well within the depths of the palace and there were many tens of guards between him and any outside door and even the Greatest Mayan admitted he had no need of such.

He rounded a corner to his left and only begun to walk down a dimly-lit corridor when four Sun Priests stepped out from behind a niche in the wall. "There he is, right on schedule, just like we were told he would be;" the leader said. "You are to come with us, Birdman," the leader of the group said confidently. "The High Priest Hezaraht wishes to speak to you. Do not be alarmed, you shall not be harmed, he only wants to ask some innocent questions." As the four stepped forward, shadows played across their faces and the words "liar" seemed to appear, followed by "deceiver"; the first word was in French and the second in Spanish.

Cuauhtémoc felt no fear; only anger that these foolish little men would come into his lair and try and take him. He curled his upper lip, baring his fangs and a low growl rumbled somewhere deep within his chest, closely followed by a snarl and his right hand lashed out like stokes of lightning, fingers curled as claws. The four priests stopped; their eyes wide with astonishment. He squalled in rage and the walls echoed the sound, bouncing it down corridors and around corners and he could hear the sound of distant voices shouting and the thud of feet approaching fast.

"He is of the Jaguar god; we dare not touch him," one of the priests cried out in terror, and in an instant he went down on his face, closely followed by a second and then a third. The fourth, who was the leader, yelled at his men; "Get up, you fools, the guards come and we have no time for this."

The smells! Ah, the odors that wafted to his waiting nostrils. There was the scent of great fear as well as the unwashed and over it all was an odor that elicited impressions of the criminally insane. "Kill him now that we may find blessings of Father Inti;" the priest screeched, and he yanked his knife off his waist strap and holding it smallest finger to the hilt he advanced, his face of the demented.

Holding a knife with the smallest finger to the hilt is the way the priests were trained to hold their sacrificial knives, blades that were used on the defenseless. This is the worst possible way to hold a knife in a fight against an alert and aggressive adversary, and as he stabbed downward at Cuauhtémoc, Inca stepped lithely out of the way. The next instant the priest tried slashing sideways but the knife was still wrong in his hand and Cuauhtémoc dropped sharply to his left, his left knee bending effortlessly, and as the priest's knife hissed over his body he lashed out with his right foot and kicked the priest over the kneecap and in a blink the knee bent in the wrong direction. The priest screamed in agony and dropped his knife and it went skidding across the stone floor. Cuauhtémoc stood over the crippled priest and growled menacingly. Other humans were coming fast; these were good humans, humans that would help, and not harm. The thought came to him on some primitive level. He squalled one last time, then the spirit that had come to him left, and he was himself once again. Now all he had to do is explain what happened to the wide-eyed guards who stood staring at him in confusion.

"You," he said pointing at one of the guards at random, "go and notify the Greatest Mayan I have been attacked by Sun Priests. Make absolutely sure he understands I am not harmed in anyway whatsoever—the same cannot be said of the priests; of course."

That one bowed deeply and scurried off about his task. "Look!" one of the guards said, pointing. The priest who had said he could not attack was laying on his side, his eyes vacant and his jaw working and his hair stood out away from his scalp at an angle. As Cuauhtémoc and the guards watched, his hair turned white, starting from the roots, working its way outwards and in a very few moments it was done.

"I heard one could be so frightened his hair would turn white, but I never believed it—until now. Was that you making those sounds Prince Inca; it was you, wasn't it?" one of the guardsmen asked politely.

"Yes," he admitted, "I have mentioned many times since coming here I can make the sounds of most of the animals in the jungle; including the jaguar. In years past, my voice has been too high-pitched to do it well, although I have always been very accurate; the people in my village where I grew up said I was scary that way. Just in the last while my voice has changed; maybe that was why I sounded as I did."

"Maybe," the guard admitted, "but that doesn't explain how you looked when I first came around the corner."

"How was that?" he asked curiously.

"I'm not sure . . . something big . . . and black . . . with hair . . . and teeth, and, and claws: nothing I would want to meet in a dark hallway . . . or out in the open at midday for that matter."

Cuauhtémoc looked around, a puzzled look on his face; "This hallway is very dark with some strange shadows in it, perhaps that is what you saw. Maybe we should get some more torches lit before my father and brothers get here so they may see well." The guard looked unconvinced but he busied himself with a wood stick used for such and got more of the torches lit. As it turned out, all of the torches were kept full of oil, they just weren't always lit. Even in the day and age there was every effort being made to conserve oil.

Cuauhtémoc used the time to examine the four priests without touching them. The one whose hair turned white was distinctly Incan in heritage as were the two who lay trembling on the floor. The last priest's face was twisted in agony and he was moaning.

"Quit whining," he said unsympathetically, "you brought this on yourself. You could have stayed in the temple and behaved; but no, you just had to go where you're not wanted, and try to make trouble."

The guards used the time to search for yet more enemies but there was no sign of such and there was no trace of how these four could have gotten into the palace and past so many guards without being seen.

After awhile he heard voices coming, one of who was unquestionably the Greatest Mayan. He walked away from the priests and guards and met his Father about half-way down the hall.

"You are well; my Son?" the Emperor said and reached his arms out for a hug; Cuauhtémoc came forward and gave as good as he got. "What kind of mischief have you uncovered for us now?"

He only started to explain when he heard Quoholocet's voice echoing along the hallway. "Are you sure Inca is unharmed?" he bellowed, his voice loud with anger.

"Yes, Great Prince, the Greatest Mayan is already there and Prince Imhoquotep has also been notified and should be here soon;" the guardsman answered.

A moment later Quoholocet rounded the corner and came towards Cuauhtémoc, his black eyes flashing in fury. As he grew near his pace slowed and then he stopped for a moment. "Father Inti; what happened to *them*?" he demanded in amazement.

"As you once so nicely put it, our Birdman 'happened' to them," the Emperor said serenely.

Prince Quoholocet walked up to the four priests and looked them over. "What happened to this one's knee?" he asked "and why is that one's hair white like that and why is he chewing on his own hand?"

"He is afraid, he is very afraid," Inca started to say when he heard yet other approaching footsteps. He sighed softly and waited for Imhoquotep to arrive.

He, like his father and brother before him, looked the Sun priests over but unlike them it was more of a glance and then he turned to Cuauhtémoc and waited for the explanations to come.

Cuauhtémoc looked around, suddenly noticing that one of their number was missing. "Where's H'ratli?" he asked in surprise; "In fact, I just now realized I haven't seen him in . . . nine days; where did he go?"

"You have been so busy with other things, my son, we didn't get around to explaining that H'ratli is off on one of his tours. He is the Prince of Merchants and from time to time he must leave in one direction or another to deal with merchandise of one sort or other. He shall return when he is ready."

"Thank you, Father," he said politely with a bow. And then, since it was obvious why everyone was there, he started explaining things in the way he always did, glossing over how he perceived the priests with an almost animal mind, and in the end his father and brothers understood very well.

"What I want to know is how these priests got in here in the first place. If I find out which fool let them in that one will pay for it with his life;" Quoholocet snarled.

"I am not convinced anyone let them in. If you will remember, our sources have stated of the all guards are 'untouchables' and Hezaraht has been unable to buy even one," Cuauhtémoc said quietly. "Did any of you notice the one there with the broken knee stated I was coming right on schedule; just like they had been told that I would? It seems to me we have not yet weeded out all of the traitors in our midst.

"Oh; quit sniveling, you," he snapped at the injured priest, "I told you before this is all your own doing."

He turned to the Greatest Mayan and bowed slightly. "May I have this one, Father? I grow weary of his whining."

"Of course, my son, you have already put your mark upon him and he is yours by right of conquest."

"Thank you," he said and then turned towards the guards, "here, bring him to his knees . . . uh, make that knee; sorry." The priest screamed as his leg was twisted anew. "I told you, stop sniveling; I'm working as fast as I can. I'm a healer, you know, I understand the way of these things. Just give me a moment and I'll make your knee stop hurting completely." He moved behind the injured man and reached his right hand around the left side of the priest's face and put his left hand to the right side; he moved the man's head to the right, paused for just a heartbeat and then quickly twisted the rest of the way around. There was a muted 'crack' and the priest's limbs went into death throes and then he was gone. "Another satisfied patient . . . or not," he said looking down.

He turned to the group who were watching him with unblinking eyes. "I was not yet five when we were gathered around the fire one night and my grandfather started speaking of the place where he was raised. He spoke of this, stating it was a thing his father used on the condemned because it was so much less messy and the servants approved of not having to mop up buckets of blood. Well; there is some soiling inside the one's clothing but that would take place regardless."

"That is just plain sweet, Inca," a guardsman said and then glanced around, "I mean . . . Prince Inca."

CHAPTER 19

"Quite all right we're among friends after all. Here; take the white-haired one and I'll show you how it's done: he's trying to eat his arm now, and frankly, it's freaking me out. Yes, bring him to his knees – here, quit that, you'll give yourself a bellyache. Now stand directly behind him . . . reach around his face with your right hand, past his ear and put your fingertips on the other side of the bump just below the skull; yes, that's very good. Now, with the left hand, reach over to the right side of his face, your thumb aimed downward and wrap your fingers around his mouth; take care that he doesn't bite you; he doesn't know what he's doing. Yes; very good! Now twist to the right until you feel a point where the neck doesn't want to turn any more . . . got it? Now all that you have to do is give a quick twist further, and . . . Yes! Most excellent; you did it exactly right."

Cuauhtémoc was discussing things as calmly as if he was giving instruction on the proper way to sew a corner into sailcloth to keep it from ripping on a set of wings. Now they were down two priests; with two left.

He looked at his father and brothers. "It occurs to me, from what we have heard, Hezaraht is running low on followers. This being the case, I would presume these four are either among his most trusted men or his most expendable. I think we should give the two remaining some of the potion and see what floats to the surface. It further seems to me Hezaraht is well aware four of his people came into the palace by some unknown means and expects them to come back with or without me. When they don't return I believe he will not be pleased. Did they slip off into the night like so many of his others; have or have the four been caught? And if they've been caught, will they talk? What will they say? What will the Greatest Mayan and Crown Prince Quoholocet do? Will they attack any heartbeat or will they do something else even more unexpected? I tell you; I would not wish to be Hezaraht right now. It seems to me the best thing for us to do for the time being, is nothing, and let Hezaraht's twisted mind do our work for us."

"Once again, my Son, I find myself in your debt;" the Emperor said politely.

"No, Greatest Mayan, this is only a trifle towards the debt I and your people owe you. Since they are unable to come in person to thank you; I am trying to do it for them.

"Let us have both the dead and the living removed to the proper places before any more people are about. Perhaps, if we are careful, we can even catch the rat who has spoken my routine to the Sun Priests. It shouldn't be hard; we'll just look for the one who seems the most astonished when next he sees me." He stared toward the place the priests appeared from; "Who knows what evil lurks in the hearts of men; only the Shadow knows," and he thrust his chin towards the darkened alcove.

The guardsmen carried away the dead and directed the living toward secure rooms where they would be kept until the Emperor and his sons had time and inclinations to see what, if anything, their minds might hold of value. The Birdman turned to his Emperor and took his hand up and pressed it against his face; his Father smiled down upon him and caressed his cheek gently.

"I have a thing that I would like to show you," he told the three; "I just finished it this morning and you shall be the first to see it." He took the Greatest Mayan's hand in his right and Quoholocet's hand in his left and he led them back towards his room. The Mayan people didn't think it strange that three males would hold hands, especially when one of the three was still a child. They had no homophobia; perhaps because homo-sexuality, that particular aberration of the human psyche, was very rare in Maya.

The four, tailed by three of the Royal Guards, headed back to Cuauhtémoc's room. He led them through the room and out onto his garden area where the sun was just now sending its rays to the plants arranged in neat groups below. He gestured with his chin as was normal for him, and as he had done the lunar month before, he stepped back and let the men look and marvel.

"Is this the drawing you said you were thinking of doing for my favorite wife and me?" Quoholocet asked in a choked voice; "as always, you astound me. If it is well with you I would like to go and get her now and bring her out to see it."

"That would be nice," he admitted, "it will give me a chance to see what Eilei will look like some years from now. Speaking of whom; be sure to bring her and Yvette along as well: even they don't know that I have done this. I have discovered I enjoy doing this, and I think I may start doing more of them in the future, depending upon how much time I have. I have already thought of doing Yvette next and then perhaps in time I shall do you who are my brothers: I would like that very much.

"It's a shame that you can't do yourself," Quoholocet said thoughtfully, "that is one that we all would like to see."

"Even that may be possible," he admitted, "Son of Spain spoke to me about a thing made of glass that shows a person back at them; he called it a 'mirror.' Such a thing would be greatly loved by females. I believe as they could spend half of each day looking at them to make sure they are as beautiful as they wish."

Perhaps a fist of the sun passed by quietly; mother serving-woman and her daughters came in with his breakfast and were talking with him when a knock sounded on the door. Mother serving-woman opened the door, gasped and bowed deeply, and first Quoholocet came in closely followed by a woman who looked to be in her early forties, a woman who still held the beauty she had when she was young. This he knew for a fact, because other than the obvious differences in size and age, mother and daughter looked very much alike as they stood side by side; Yvette peeked around from behind them and waved. "Please come in," he said graciously, "I have heard so much about you and now I get to meet you in person."

She was everyone's Mother. She immediately hugged him and ran her fingers through his hair and straightened his clothing out, whether it needed or not, talking softly all the while. Quoholocet already told her Cuauhtémoc intended to marry Eilei and make her his first wife; a thing both mother and daughter approved of completely.

He endured, as sons have endured motherly affections for as long as time has been, and then he took her hand in his and kissed her fingertips very gently; this was a thing Yvette taught him recently and it was his first chance to try it out. "I have a thing to show you, Mother, or has you husband already spoke of it?" he asked politely. Both husband and wife shook their heads although the favorite wife showed surprise.

"If you will give me your hand and follow me with your eyes closed I will show you a thing that is a surprise for you." The woman gave her hand willingly and he led her carefully out into the garden and positioned her directly in front of the drawing. Quoholocet stayed back far enough to keep his daughter and the rest from giving the surprise away. "Open your eyes now," he said softly. She opened her eyes and an incredibly short time later, she was hugging him avidly, weeping all the while.

After a moment she abandoned him and rushed to her husband's side and still weeping, cuddled up to him; "Is this for us," she asked, looking up at his face, "has the Birdman done this thing for us?" Quoholocet admitted this was so. "Oh look; up there in the corner—I have seen that expression on her face a thousand times. And there she is, asleep . . . this is incredible, Quoh, how can this come to be?"

"How is it the wind can blow or the tide can come in and go out? When dealing with Inca, I have found it best to simply accept things, and be grateful."

With her mother out of the way, Eilei zeroed in on Inca, and she and Yvette sandwiched him between them and both took turns showing him with passionate kisses. It was well for everyone involved that the three were still children or there's no telling what might have happened.

It ended up as a picnic of sorts, although the Maya had no name for such, but mother serving-woman and her daughters brought more trays of food and everyone, including the Greatest Mayan and Imhoquotep and others, sat around and ate everything in reach and visited happily for this was the last full day Cuauhtémoc would be here for many weeks. The two girls refused to leave Inca for more than the few moments it took to go and bring yet more food to him or to go to the 'needed,' . . . as needed. Part of their ploy was the hope they could make him gain so much weight in the next few fists of the sun he wouldn't be able to fly tomorrow, and he would have to wait until he lost some weight, which both were determined would not happen. This ruse didn't work either; but they tried.

Later in the day Inca, as well as the Emperor and two sons, paid a visit to the remaining sun priests. He gave them some of his concoction but they learned very little; in the end, he and the rest decided that this particular batch of priests were from the 'expendable' list, rather than the 'most trusted.'

The next day dawned clear and warm as most days were. As Cuauhtémoc and the rest stood upon the rooftop he could see the winds were favorable and he expected to make good time. He took up a message package and stuck it in his net, because Prince or not, he was still a birdman and delivering messages is what birdmen do. He hugged everyone goodbye and looked around for two girls to kiss but neither were able to make it; both were inconsolable and weeping in each other's arms. This is the way of females everywhere, and especially so of the young, who tend to over-dramatize things.

"Remember my Son, wherever you go you are Maya, so walk with pride and know that Father Inti is never far from your side."

He took his father's hand in his and gently raised it to his lips and kissed the fingertips as Yvette taught him and then he tenderly turned the hand over and kissed the palm of his hand. "For later, my Father, in case you get lonesome," he said in way of explanation and gently curled the old Emperor's hand into a fist.

There was nothing left to do but leave, so he took his wings up, paused in concentration as he always did and then raced across the roof as fast as he could and jumped and promptly vanished from view. A moment later a wild k-e-e-e-r floated back to the observers and soon he caught air and then a strong uplift and before long he was little more than a distant speck in a cloudless azure sky and then even that was gone. The old man looked down at his clenched fist and opened his hand and tenderly pressed his palm against his chest directly over his heart. "You are barely out of sight, my Son, and already I miss you more than I can say." He turned toward the rising sun for it was still early, and bowed deeply, bringing his right knee to the stone beneath his feet. "Please be with him Father Inti and bring him back to us safe because I don't think this old heart of mine would care to go on beating without him." The Greatest Mayan struggled erect, since old bones can't move as fast as when they were young, then surrounded by his guards and servants he headed back into the palace, determined to make each day a busy one, so time would fly by quickly until he could see his Birdman once again.

Cuauhtémoc climbed higher and flew due north. The winds today were from the southeast and steady, the most favorable wind possible for a journey northward. As Inti gradually crept toward zenith he flew onward, buoyed aloft by steady uplifts he found over the great fields and rock outcroppings scattered all over Maya. In its own way, it was even better than uplifts in the mountains, a thing he didn't know a month earlier.

Most of the ground below was new to him because last time he had been further inland and this pleased him because he enjoyed covering new territory each and every time he went aloft. This way, should the need ever arise; he would be able to draw very accurate maps of all of the ground he covered.

Father Inti moved steadily to the west as he had been doing for endless ages and the ground flowed below his wings in a continuing panorama of beautiful jungles and wide rivers interspaced with seemingly countless villages and towns. When he first leaped from the roof of the palace he was not sure how long the flight would take. He knew it had taken Qualaktec and Twuondan three days to get to him, but they were older birdmen and almost too heavy for their wings, and they had to spend too much time in the uplifts to cover much ground.

The wildlife below was incredible in its variety. There were multi-colored birds flitting from place to place and bands of monkeys moving about; the great rivers supported their own form of life and sometimes from his view on high he could see creatures that never left water moving about their concerns. Yet more towns and villages passed below and people farming were everywhere. He kept his eyes moving about. This was not only because he was memorizing the details incase he ever needed to make a drawing of these things but also because there was beauty everywhere he looked and life in its many forms moved about below him in a grand panorama.

In the land of the Greatest Mayan the climate supported crops year around for those who wish; the winters were a little cooler than the summers and the summers a little dryer but other than that, things were much the same. It was not uncommon for people to be planting fresh crops between the stalks of plants which were almost mature; in this manner an enterprising man could get in four or five crops per year, although the winter rains could be unreasonable about such, and farmers might lose a cycle.

Father Inti was more than two fists above the mountains when he first spotted the Northern Soldier's Camp. This startled him because it was much sooner than expected. He finally decided not having to go up to the mountains and then come back down had cut out a great deal of distance, and that the lowlands had uplifts of their own he hadn't known about, being a mountain-trained birdman. This was very interesting to him and a thing he intended to discuss fully with other lowland birdmen to see if their experiences were the same.

He circled high above the landing field, getting ready to spiral down, and he screed out to let those below know he was coming in. Faces turned upward, located him and he saw several start running as if to notify the Commander he was landing. That seemed improbable to him since it would mean they knew he was coming and this was, of course, unlikely. He circled down and by the time he dragged tail he had a nice reception committee waiting for him.

"Great Prince, it's good to have you back," the men said and bowed deeply before him. Now how in thunder did they know that; he wondered. Oh yes . . . feathers . . . he was wearing them. He bowed politely; then dismounted his wings and went over to greet them in a way he was more familiar with.

In the distance he saw the camp's Commander limping his way towards him, a thing that jogged his memory. He went back to his wings and picked up the larger of two message packages as well as a wooden jar filled with a salve he made; he turned about and went to greet the Commander.

"It is good to see you again, Great Prince Inca," the Commander said and bowed deeply before him.

"That's enough with the bowing," he said with a grin, "we're among friends after all. I brought all of the messages that were due out this way; and a little something for you as well."

The officer looked at him in surprise; "A Prince carrying messages?" he asked; startled.

"Of course; I may be a Prince but I am also a birdman-soldier and I always will be for as long as I live; and even a birdman-soldier carries outgoing messages with him when he flies. If I demand this of my birdmen; I demand it of myself as well. It is good to see you again my friend; how are you doing?"

"I am doing well. We got a message from my friend, Prince Quoholocet, just three days ago; speaking you were headed out this way about this time. How was your flight? We heard you made it all the way down to the City of Emperors in only a single day; that's incredible flying."

"Well; I made it all the way back in less time than that and learned some very interesting things along the way. But before we get into anything else; I brought you a little present. As you are already aware, I am the grandson of the Great Healer, and he has taught me much of what he knows. While I was in a shop that sells medical herbs and such, I remembered a salve my grandfather used to make, to soften and ease the pains of ancient scars. This salve turned out so good that many times its use over some months would reduce or even eliminate scars altogether. This evening, after we get all of the paperwork and talk out of the way, I will apply the first time and show you the way of doing it and then you can have your wife put it on or maybe you'll be able to do it yourself."

"A Prince rubbing salve into a subordinate's leg?" the officer asked in surprise.

"Why not? I was a healer long before I became a Prince—or even a birdman for that matter," he said, "my grandfather would be deeply disappointed in me if I did else. Besides; it doesn't take long and it won't hurt me nearly as much as it will you." The Commander shot a startled look at Inca, who started laughing softly. "Got you on that one;" he said with a twinkle in his dark eyes. The Commander shook his head sadly in defeat.

They went up to the Commander's house because it was growing late and time for the evening meal. The Commander's wife met him at the door, along with most of his children, and the girl who had been so kind to him the month before was also there, but this time he was looking at her with different eyes.

They ate as they had before and filled their time with idle talk but Inca kept watching his Commander's face and the officer was aware of this fact. They sat around afterwards and shared yet more stories and all the while the Commander kept glancing at the wooden jar sitting just out of reach. As if he were reading the Birdman's mind; he turned to him. "Awhile back you said this would hurt me more than it did you; you weren't just teasing; were you?"

"No; Commander, I was not, I was trying for a little tenderness beneath my honesty. Instead of having your wife do this thing for you I think we should summon the over-healer. In fact, I have already taken the liberty of doing so; he should be here any time now. Soon you will hate me as you have never hated anyone because this is going to hurt. The only good thing I can tell you is it is only just for awhile, and each and every time you do this, the pain will be less. If you keep this up the next lunar cycle or two, your scar will be completely gone, as will all of your pain. Ah; the healers are here now; come in my brothers, you are just in time, we are just about to start."

Cuauhtémoc and the three healers who had come to his call took turns gently feeling the Commander's scar. This had been caused by the tusks of a boar some ten years earlier and was just above his left knee and extended around the side of the leg and towards the back. "Now we take some of this salve, my brothers, and we start to rub it in, gently at first. You will notice the pungent odor and feel your own fingers and hands begin to feel warm. This salve also works well on bone-aches. In fact; that is how I managed to first remember it. The Greatest Mayan has some bone-ache and I made some up for him and now he won't let the healers use anything else on him.

"As we work it in; we can feel the hardness of the scar tissue. This has come to resemble sinew, that connects muscle and bone, and it is this hardness that causes the pain because it doesn't belong here. Now, Commander, you will find that you no longer like me because I must start rubbing the scar more firmly. We cannot hurry this process; we must gradually break this scar tissue down over many weeks to allow the body a chance to remove it a little at a time. About the only good thing I can tell you right now is the pain will be less with each treatment and towards the end it will not hurt much at all. But I think you will have thrown your walking stick away long before then because this will do much good."

Perhaps a thumb of the sun passed quietly by as Cuauhtémoc and the three healers took turns; massaging the salve deep into the Commander's leg. To the officer's credit he made no sound but the expression on his face spoke volumes. "I think that will be enough for tonight. I wish you to have this done every morning before you leave for your duties and every evening before you retire for the night. That will give you a day, or a night, each for your body to carry the old scar tissue away. You may not think so but I believe your scar already feels somewhat softer than it was."

"It actually doesn't hurt as much," the Commander admitted.

"Is that because it feels better or because we have stopped rubbing?" Inca asked with a sly smile.

The Commander shook his head, then fought a brief battle with gravity, and stood up. "It just feels better, that's all that I know," he admitted. He picked up his walking stick and headed off to his sleeping quarters. As Cuauhtémoc watched him go he thought perhaps the Commander was limping a little less after all.

"This is a marvelous salve," one of the healers said. "I have several patients who complain of bone-ache, as you said, and I would like to try some of this out on them." As the healer spoke he reached hesitantly toward the wooden container.

"No, I forbid it," Cuauhtémoc said firmly. "I have created this salve for the Commander, and if it is applied properly, there should be enough to last to the end. If it is used on others as well there may not be enough. I admit this is a wonderful salve with many uses and the knowledge of it should be wide-spread throughout all Maya. In the morning - before I leave - I will be sure to teach you the way of it, and help you make some, providing you have the proper ingredients in your inventory. It is my wish the understanding of this is spread out among all healers everywhere so all people may benefit by it and not just the elite. It is growing late and we all should go to our beds and get some rest; for tomorrow will be a busy day."

As he had been treating the Commander and speaking with the healers, the Commander's daughter kept peeking out from the doorway to see what he was doing. Now her father had gone to bed, and the healers were leaving, she came out and looked up at him shyly. "You have grown taller this last time, Inca," she said.

"It's probably just the feathers," he answered with a laugh and took them from his head and put them on a nearby shelf; "There now; how does that look?"

"You look wonderful—but then; I always thought so. And I still think you have grown taller since I last saw you. I watched you working on my father, and it is in my heart to thank you for doing so, because he has suffered so much for so long."

"It has recently come to my attention Mayan girls do not know how to properly tell a boy 'thank you', but I have also found she is very willing to learn, if a boy will just give her a chance. Come closer and I will show you the way of it."

Things were moving in the direction the girl wished so she immediately obeyed. He brushed the hair away from her face and gently kissed her right cheek and then her left and then moved on to her lips. Eilei had been giving him 'kissing lessons' all along as had Yvette. He asked Yvette once how many boys she had kissed. Since she was so very good at this he thought she must have had much practice. She lowered her head and then looked up at him coyly and admitted he was the first boy she had ever kissed and then went on to explain the young girls of her world learned of these things by talking with their mothers and older sisters—and then practicing on each other whenever they got a chance. She also explained, in great detail, the things she heard her mother and older sisters say they most liked their men to do to them in caressing their faces and bodies. He followed instructions with her but they had to quit because it was making both of them breathe strangely and this was not the best thing to be happening: when they got older, yes, and definitely once they were married; but not just yet.

He had no such restraints with this girl because she was older than he and at the age where many girls were thinking of babies because that is what girls this age think of. So he used the skills he learned from Yvette and quickly discovered Mayan girls like the same things as the French. They moved off to her room, arms around each other, and spent at least part of the night learning and relearning things that had come to him from a half a world away.

CHAPTER 20

He intended to leave the next morning and head out to the Northern Birdman camp but it didn't turn out that way. He awoke early, as was normal for him, and slipped outside to walk around. He enjoyed breathing in the night air and this was especially true when the jungle was near because the scents of the jungle reminded him of home. He walked down to where Xymatoc's wings were and located the leather pouch that held his leaves and took them up and went to find a fire and some hot water.

His grandfather was still sending him leaves on a regular basis, and he was faithful to write a thank-you note to let the old man know he had gotten them, and keep him aware of things that was happening in his life. But to date, he had never gotten a reply, which made him sad because he didn't think his grandfather would ever forgive him for leaving, even though it turned out for the best.

When morning light filled the camp and people started stirring about he headed back to the Commander's home. As he entered he found the Commander and perhaps half of the healers in camp waiting for him.

"You're back!" the Commander exclaimed joyously; "we've been wondering where you got yourself off to. We are ready for my next treatment, but before we start, I want to thank you for this wonderful salve you brought me. For the first time in many years I slept the night through without waking from leg-pains. I can't begin to thank you enough for what you have done for me; speak what you wish in return, and if it is within my power to give, it is yours."

"It was not a problem. Besides; your daughter did her best last night to thank me for you; I now consider it is I who owe you: shall we begin your second treatment?"

The Commander looked at his daughter, who looked back and blushed. He laughed and nodded: "Yes; under these conditions I must again place myself at your tender mercies."

"Since there are so many healers here I think I must insist the actual application of the salve must be limited to we four who did so last night, but I believe it would be well if all the rest be given a chance to at least feel the scar tissue, so they may try and understand what is taking place." The different healers took turns carefully feeling the scar while Cuauhtémoc explained exactly what they were supposed to be looking for. He took the container out and removed the lid and permitted each healer to smell the scents coming out of it and then he put himself at the Commander's knees and once again began to massage the salve in, carefully explaining to the gathered healers what was being done and why, and what he expected the end result to be. As it was the previous night, the officer sat stoically and made not a sound, and while it may have been Inca's imagination, it didn't look to him like the Commander's face showed as much strain. Or perhaps he now knew what was to come he was better prepared.

A thumb later and no more he stopped the treatment and returned the lid to the container and set it off to one side and there was no mistaking the covetous looks many of the healers gave the container but no one asked for some. "Since so many are here I will take this time to explain to you what the ingredients are in this salve and how it is made that you may make some of your own after I leave later on today."

"Oh no, Great Healer, you must not leave today; there is so much that we need to learn at your feet; stay three days that we may understand."

"Yes," the Commander quickly agreed, it will take at least three days for my understanding of things to catch up."

"Yes, three days then," the healers decided and all nodded to each other.

Cuauhtémoc looked from the Commander to the healers and back to the Commander. "Why three days," he asked politely, "why not two days or four; is there something special about three days?"

The Commander flinched and would not meet his eyes. "Look at me Commander; why must I wait three days?"

"I knew I would not get this by you, Great Prince, but I had to try. I have been told to keep you here for at least that long but I am forbidden to explain why: please do not ask more of me I beg you."

"Do you swear by your leg that this is honorable?"

"Yes, Prince Inca, I would have refused otherwise."

"I trust you Commander; I will accept and shall not pry more. Besides," and he glanced where the Commander's daughter stared with wide eyes, "I think I can find something to occupy my time other than working on your leg and conferring with my brothers about different cures for the sick and injured."

"Thank you Great Prince. I may speak you will understand in time but until then I may not speak on it at all."

"That is not a problem. Perhaps you can tell me how it is that you knew I was coming; did a birdman bring you a message on this subject?"

"Three messages; Great Prince. You are aware messages can be sent by birdman; which is usually the fastest and surest method of sending messages. They can also be sent by runner and by war-kak. If the writer thinks the communication is important enough he will send identical messages by all three methods. To help eliminate confusion, such a writer will draw stick wings, stick running legs and a stick war-kak in the upper left corner of each message to let one such as I know it is considered important by the writer, as well as understand other identical messages are on the way by other means, to help prevent confusion."

"I was not aware of that Commander and I thank you for telling me this." He stopped and stared at the officer and cocked his head as he often did when he was thinking. "I know I said I would not pry further, and I intend to keep my word, but it just now occurs to me the only one whose authority would be greater than a Crown Prince would be a higher Crown Prince. It further comes to my attention my brother, H'ratli, has been missing from the palace for ten days now, or slightly more, and all my father and brothers had to say on the subject, was he was off on some of his 'merchant business.' Curious; is it not?" He gave the Commander and the healers the half-nod, half-bow used in such cases and turned and walked off.

"From the time I saw Inca put an arrow through an enemy's head from the air I knew he was exceptional. By the time he flew off, headed for the City of Emperors, I understood he has the most brilliant mind I've ever known. Even with these things in my favor I find I still underestimate him." The Commander shook his head in mock sorrow; then turned himself to the day's activities.

Three days passed almost too quickly, for there were still many things the healers were adamant about learning, not to mention the tears in the eyes of the Commander's daughter, but he felt that after the previous night's efforts he might have at last fathered a child. He certainly had done his share at making that come true, and from the stars in the girl's eyes, she thought so too.

Most of the camp gathered to see him off. The Commander was walking much easier now and carrying his walking stick almost as much as using it; he was a very happy man. As seemed usual in such cases his daughter did not come; probably because she didn't want to show a tear-stained face to people. He took up yet another message pouch to go along with the one he already had and after bidding everyone goodbye he took a running start at the slope and quickly caught air and in a short while he was winging his way north, towards the birdman's camp.

He was incredibly happy. Part of him would always hunger for the birdman's camp and the people who were there. The ground slipped by, but he scarcely noticed the flora and fauna below, because his mind and heart were on his destination ahead.

After flying all day to get to the City of Emperors, and then again flying most of the day to get back to the soldier's camp, the trip to the birdman's camp wasn't worth mentioning. Before long he saw the camp in the distance like jewels in a crown to his eyes. He stared hungrily as he closed in, and then circled, looking for familiar faces down below. It didn't take long for him to spot Xymatoc. He was over close to the Dispatcher's hut, talking to the Dispatcher, and standing nearby, evidently listening, was one who sprouted a great many fancy feathers from the top of his head.

"K-e-e-e-r," he screed long and loud, "k-e-e-e-r" and he swung about and headed towards Dispatcher's. This was not a landing area nor was it intended to be but he wanted to get down and give them hugs so bad he was about ready to jump from his wings and just walk down. He glided in just above stall speed, doing all things right except for his landing point. People turned and stared, and began to move around in joy at seeing him, but he kept on coming. After a few moments it became clear to even the dullest he intended to land his wings on the Dispatcher's lawn, so to speak, and people started moving outward; unsure how he hoped to do this because the area was not large enough for such. In the end, Prince H'ratli stood watching calmly, with his arms folded across his chest. Xymatoc started to run and then saw his Prince wasn't leaving so he moved back just to H'ratli's left and stood with arms crossed and waited.

He glided in, and somewhat sooner than he usually did, he dipped his left wing down and it dragged on the dirt and grass. He understood in advance ground was not unyielding like stone and he would need more distance to swing himself about and that is exactly what happened: his tail came up and his beak bit dirt and for a few heartbeats he was again flying backwards, then all movement ceased: he stuck his feet out and he was on the ground.

"That, people, is your Prince Birdman; I'd recognize that landing anywhere;" Prince H'ratli said dryly and then moved forward to give him a hug. "I'll bet you're surprised to see me here," H'ratli said after he released Inca.

"No," Inca replied, with a smile on his face.

"No?" H'ratli demanded; "who was the rat that squealed on me?"

"No one; it's logical. In the first; I hadn't seen you since just before the supplies were to leave for this camp. When I hadn't seen you for awhile and asked our father and brothers, they just said you had gone off on one of your merchandizing things, but you had not said anything to me about it before you left; not a single word. When I flew into the Soldier's camp and told them I intended to leave the next day, everyone agreed I needed to spend yet another three days there before I could leave, but no one could explain why three days was ideal but not two or four. I tried to get information out of the Commander and all he would tell me is that he couldn't tell me. And then I understood the only one who has greater authority than a Crown Prince would be a higher Crown Prince."

"I can't get anything past you Inca; I don't know why I even try."

"Since we are on these things; when are you going to tell me why you are here? There are a great many honorable men who would have been able to do this thing; why did it have to be you? — I'm not complaining or anything; you're good company."

H'ratli looked around with exaggerated motions and then looked back at Inca. "Have you notice who is not here anymore?" he asked suggestively.

Cuauhtémoc looked about and the camp seemed to be as it had always been since he had first flown in with Xymatoc over two years earlier. "Someone who is not here?" he asked, puzzled. "Some of my brothers are gone but that is normal since messages are always coming in and going out; is that what you mean?"

"No. Ever since you told our father about the one here who wished you dead; he has been determined this is not to happen. He intends no mistakes and no excuses. I am, of course, speaking of your late, unlamented Wingmaster; I took care of him right after I got here yesterday morning. Everything you ever said about him was so; I've never met a more disagreeable person or one more twisted; it was more of a mercy killing than anything else. In case you've not figured it out for yourself; you are important to a great many people, too much so, to risk a deranged one such as that."

"So this is the main reason you went many days journey out of your way; to make sure a thing was done, any one of the Royal Guardsmen could have done, and willingly?"

"Well, yes, it takes a certain touch to . . . now why are you looking at me like that?"

"Why am I looking at you like how?" he asked politely.

"You know; sometimes trying to talk with you can give a man a headache. Ahh; I'm sorry Inca, I shouldn't have said that, please forgive me."

"Forgiven and willingly so; now why don't we get to the real reason you came here. Is there something else you wished besides having Wingmaster killed and getting all of the supplies this far north?" Inca's voice was very gentle and a compassionate expression was on his face. H'ratli stared at him and his shoulders slumped in defeat.

"You know then?" he asked.

"I suspect; but that is not enough. I must hear it from your lips; what is the real reason you came out here when it would have been much easier to delegate authority to others?"

H'ratli dropped his gaze to the ground and then looked Inca in the eyes: "I want to become a birdman. I know I am much too old, and it is too late to train one such as me, but I want to try anyway. Ever since you flew out of the sun I have been enchanted with the idea. I have seen you destroy entire shiploads of pirates, as if they were insects, and fly back as if nothing exceptional had happened at all. I have seen you soar with the eagles and talk to them, and even though you say you only make the sounds they do, you talk to them none-the-less. I want to be just like you. I want to fly like you, and I know it is not possible. So just tell me I am too old and it is too late for me and I will understand and my life will go on."

"It is not too late and you shall fly. I have seen the hunger in your eyes and I have watched you conquer your fears and practice standing on one leg with your eyes closed; as I have mentioned. Before the greater wings were possible, it would have been too late, but now I have seen men your age take these greater wings and fly off; and if they can do it so can you. You will have to become a nestling. You will sleep with the nestlings and eat with the nestlings and study with the nestlings and you will go on to become a fledgling and you will learn all of the things a birdman must know to stay alive while he is in the air. Then, once these things are done, you will learn how to make wings. Not the lesser wings, of course, as they are much too small for you; but greater wings. And when you are done with these things, and when you are a birdman, and when you can fly; you will not walk back to the City of Emperors, you shall fly at my side, and you shall in time become my Wings Second because I have great need of a man of your ability to back me and side me and help me put this birdman-soldier organization together, because you would not believe the number of fools who do not understand because they cannot, or because they simply do not wish to."

H'ratli stared at Inca, his heart in his eyes, and then he bowed deeply before him and took his feathers off and handed them to his brother. "It would not be well a mere nestling be found wearing feathers so far above his lowly station in life," he said simply. But the look in his eyes spoke the words his mouth could not.

"Agreed;" Cuauhtémoc said as he took his brother's feathers and looked around. There were a great many people gathered about, people who knew him from before, and who waited patiently to be noticed; among them was the Flightmaster. "You have heard everything, Flightmaster?" he asked politely; the man bowed deeply and nodded.

"When does your next class start then?"

"It starts when you say it starts, Great Prince," Flightmaster said respectfully.

"How many nestlings do you now have, including this, your latest?"

"With nestling H'ratli included, it makes twelve, Great Prince."

"Twelve is a good number; nestling class begins tomorrow morning. Be sure you give nestling H'ratli as many beatings, as you do all your others, Flightmaster; I'm counting on you to be fair about such things."

The old man laughed softly and nodded; "I shall not give him anymore than I ever gave you; and that includes the ones you deserved but never received." Inca laughed with everyone else and then since he had not been back in camp very long he got busy greeting people and hugging everyone in sight.

Inca spent the next few days moving about the camp, talking at length with the camp healer about many things, including the salve he remembered and had given to the Commander. As it turned out, there was one ingredient the healers in the Soldier's camp lacked, and that one thing was crucial; without it, it was no more than a greasy blob. As he spoke to the healer about it the man became very interested. "Great Prince; I would not wish to build up false hopes, but from what you have described, I think I know where a fairly large patch of this might be. I remember how pungent the odor was and thinking any plant that smelled that strong should have some value in medicine, but I was never able to figure out what."

He decided to go out the next morning to examine the plants on the chance it was what he needed. This put the camp guards and huntsmen against the Royal Guards almost before he finished speaking. The camp guards and huntsmen rightfully claimed they knew the surrounding jungle as no Royal Guardsmen could ever know it, while the Royal Guards declared protecting the young Prince was their duty, and no less a person than the Great Mayan stated this to be so. He got around the dilemma with the tact he was known for. It was true the hunters and local guards knew the jungle and it was also so the Royal Guard were charged with his safekeeping; some of each would go; they were only going for some plants after all.

It seemed odd that it took nine adult men and half-grown child to go out and gather a few hands full of plants but that was exactly how it came to be—at least he was headed out into the jungles again and this was a thing he missed very much while in the great city.

The patch of plants was not far away; as the healer said. Cuauhtémoc looked the plants over, checked them for color and scent and even cautiously tasted them: they were excellent. He, the healer and several of the healer's helpers got busy and carefully dug the plants up, roots and all, for every part of this particular plant was useful; although not for the same things.

In not much more than a fist of the sun everyone was back. Not only did he have enough plants for the camp, he also had more than enough for the Soldier's Camp, a thing that would make the Commander and the healers there very happy. Bitumen was between tasks and he volunteered to take the rest of the pungent plants to the Soldier's Camp; and because he knew the way and since the day was still very early Dispatcher gave him what few outgoing messages there were, and soon the birdman was a speck on the far southern horizon, growing smaller with every passing heartbeat.

Creating greater wings became a camp obsession. There were birdmen there that were forcibly retired, and the question that filled everyone's mind was, who would get the first set made. H'ratli, nestling or not, put an end to that; by order of the Greatest Mayan; the very first set off the line belonged to Cuauhtémoc. In the end, the wings looked more like a bird than anything yet, coming upward and forward from the body at a shallow angle only to bend at the knuckle and trail backward and downward at the same shallow angle. The wings were carefully skinned with precious silk, causing some of the women in the camp to actually weep: guards had to be set not only on the supply of silk but also on any scrap left over.

They put the greater wing beside Xymatoc's old wings and compared them. Just by eye, the newer ones looked to be half again longer in the wingspan and comparably more in width and the entire length was also longer because the experts in such felt the proportion would have to be kept or the wings would be unstable. Everything looked good. Inca carved a very close scale replica out of balsa and it flew even better than the model he had made over a month ago, that had mysteriously 'blown' off the shelf where Dispatcher put, it and was 'accidentally' stepped on, although no one in camp would admit having been in the Dispatcher's hut to do so, and Dispatcher knew for a fact he had not done it.

Inca turned to Xymatoc, who with many others, was looking at the wings with lust in his eyes. "It was my intent the very first set of greater wings to be built would be yours because of the promise I made; that you would have new wings and you would fly higher and farther than ever before. I can't do that now because I cannot disobey the Greatest Mayan; even though he did not know of my promise. What I can and will do is give you right of first flight. This is only fair since I've been using your old wings now for more than a month . . . unless, of course, you don't wish to fly wings you have not personally made;" he ended slyly.

"Just don't get between me and the down slope, that's all that I have to say," Xymatoc said and his eyes looked suspiciously wet.

Cuauhtémoc bowed slightly to his older brother and waved him onward; "Please don't forget One and Two have not flown in awhile either; leave some daylight for them as well."

Xymatoc walked up to the wings and lifted them and a startled expression came over his face. "These things aren't as heavy as they look, Inca, why's that?"

There is less actual wood in these because of how the ribs are formed and silk is very light. Now I've actually seen how these things come to be I think sailcloth will do as well; perhaps we'll make the next set of wings that way unless you specifically want silk."

"Anything—I don't care—please; may I go now?"

"You are wasting air, my brother, take up wings and fly;" he said.

Xymatoc lifted the wings and paused, focusing his mind, and then he ran furiously down slope and caught air and within heartbeats he was climbing at an amazing rate; these wings *wanted* to fly and if there wasn't a birdman handy they seemed willing to chance it on their own. Xymatoc banked left and swung around the camp, still climbing; he leveled off and headed north, starting to follow his old route, as if by habit.

It wasn't long and Xymatoc leaned to his left and the wings responded perfectly. He leaned forward and they dropped into a shallow dive; he leaned back and they lifted as if carried aloft by a higher power; he circled and dipped and did figure eights in the air; all was smoother and easier than he could ever remember. These wings were made by a birdman, for birdmen, and not created by those who could only do what their fathers had done; and the difference was incredible: long before he returned to camp he was a believer. Even as he glided in—reluctantly—the wings carried him as carefully as a mother carrying her child, and when he finally dragged tail to land, the wings set down as if they too were ready and he only had a quick step or two and it was done: he stood with the main spine of the wings between his legs and wept in joy.

Xymatoc was the focus of a great many eyes. He walked up to Prince Inca and then bending at his knees he went onto his face before him. He held this pose for just a few heartbeats and stood up again. "When you promised over two years ago you would give me wings that were better than those I had; you did not say you would give me the first of such made. I have flown these and have found them to be superior in every possible way to anything I have ever flown and I say you have fulfilled your vow to me because I know you will give me mine whenever it pleases you and my heart now soars with the eagles in joy." He again bowed deeply to Inca and then with eyes filled with tears he held out his arms for a hug, a thing he knew his little brother was willing to give, and it was so.

The birdman known as 'One' was the next one aloft and he did as his friend before him, flying in circles and banks and dipping and rising as birds and birdmen do. In time he also came back to land; not because he had his fill but because he knew other birdmen had been grounded for far too long still waited for their turn.

'Two' followed 'One' and then several other older birdmen came out of retirement long enough to at least try the wings out, but these were men who had been on the ground too long, and deep down inside they only wanted to say they had tried it, they didn't actually want wings to start flying again. In each and every case the flyers pronounced the newer wings to be the best they had ever flown.

It wasn't until every retired birdman in camp who wished, had flown at least once, that Cuauhtémoc tried his new wings out. As was typical of him he went not to the slope where all the rest jumped from but in the opposite direction. While H'ratli and a host of others looked on he took a quick run and a leap and promptly vanished over the edge of the cliff, wings and all.

CHAPTER 21

This time was different. Before he fell a fourth the distance of his original wings—which were still in the wings shed, awaiting his attention—he felt pressure building and as he leaned back the wings took off with him and he felt himself squirt up into the air at a speed which rivaled the time he flew through fire. He soared high above, and he thought with these wings he really could get a thousand tall trees into the air, but it was getting late and there were still many things down in camp that needed to be done. So after he flew long enough to get a solid feel of what he now had, he swung back around and approached the landing area, coming in slower and more smoothly than he had ever done in his entire life. He landed into the wind as is usual for birdmen everywhere and when it came time to set down he leaned back slightly, not even enough to drag tail and the wings slowed and then seemed to hover above the ground for a heartbeat or two and he stuck his feet out and the wings settled to the ground with him.

He looked at the men gathered around him and spoke. "It is my opinion this new wings design is the best that has ever been made. From this day forward we must also make the lesser wings built in this form. This way, our newer birdmen will never know what it is like to fly the older model, a model that should have been replaced many decades ago. I am The Birdman; I have spoken and it is so." He clapped his hands three times as the Emperor did and that was the end of it.

H'ratli had never been so happy. He was a kid again; surrounded by kids who were somehow about half his size and all were listening intently to the words Flight-master was telling them. As he listened; he came to appreciate there was a great deal more to this than just jumping on a set of wings and flying. He spent his days learning the ways of flight and his evening surrounded by young boys as they earnestly discussed the day's lessons, trying to remember everything they had been taught that day. His nights were spent on a pallet that was almost too small for him, covered by a llama skin that was defiantly not large enough – from the moment he learned he was to become a nestling, he refused even the smallest favor because of his age, size or rank.

The boys were unsure at first because he was so much larger than them and they knew he was still a Prince, headdress or not, but as time slipped away they forgot these things; and in the end he was just another boy trying to understand all that was laid out before them. By now, all had heard tales of The Birdman, and all were determined not to fail, no matter what.

Time slipped by, as time has a habit of doing, whether it is desired by humans or not. H'ratli graduated from nestling class, and for the first time in all the years the birdman's camp had been, so did all the others.

Fledgling class was far more involved because it also included survival techniques to be used in the off-chance a birdman was brought down by one thing or another and lived; this was shaky at best but better prepared for than not.

Wingmaster had his hands full with all of the new things that were happening. This was a new Master, as the former had been tossed off the cliff on the orders of Prince H'ratli, and the two men who were so devoted to the deceased, decided on their own it was time for them to leave. Now; with a somewhat older, more mature outlook on things, Cuauhtémoc came to realize the pair had, in their own underhanded way, also prevented any improvements in wing design.

The time finally came when H'ratli graduated from fledgling class and could at last call himself a birdman. He and eleven young boys stood stiffly erect as Prince Inca handed out birdman feathers to each new graduate and this too was a new record because for the first time ever there was a one hundred percent graduating class without any of the boys falling by the wayside. Perhaps it was just a coincidence; perhaps it was because an adult was taking the class with the others; encouraging the youngsters to try harder. In any case, H'ratli received his feathers like the rest, and cried the same as they did; it was an intensely happy moment for everyone in camp.

Two now had his own set of wings as did Xymatoc and One; all three opted for sailcloth coverings on their wings and while they admitted these did not slip through the air with the smooth ease that silk did, they were so much better than anything they had ever flown, no one was complaining; in fact, it was a difficult thing to find a frown anywhere in camp.

Excluding the women; of course. Which was an oddity in itself because none of them had never actually seen silk, other than that which was on Cuauhtémoc's wings, and only a few had ever touched the fabric. No; the main reason was, they understood women in foreign lands wore this thing, and if other women in other lands wore it then they should also be able to wear it—such is female logic.

Nearly forty days had come and gone since the day Cuauhtémoc took the message package from Dispatcher's hands and flew off on Two's old route. Now that Two had new wings to fly he was once again ready to service his old pathway as before. Prince Cuauhtémoc was remembering a village well to the north, where a comely young girl waited his return, not to mention a young boy who well might be a birdman himself some day if the wind should blow the right direction. It was in his heart to make sure it did so because he clearly saw the look in the child's face and knew the boy at least deserved a chance.

Two had his message pouch in hand and headed out to where his new wings waited him and discovered that his Prince also waited with his original wings beside the new. "It is in my heart to fly beside you my brother at least part of the way for I find there is some unfinished business awaiting me in a village north of here. For that long we shall fly wing to wing; after that you are on your own."

The pair left from the down slope as was usual for birdmen because Inca did not want Two to think that he had to jump from the cliff with him. Doubly so, since the wings were new to him, and he had not yet flown them long enough to get to know them with the sixth-sense that birdmen get when they at last become one with their wings. They flew north in a ragged, zigzag pattern, dropping message arrows and occasionally landing to leave off or pick up yet other messages. The village that had once tried to keep him was off to his right and he drifted that way to see what had become of the place.

"I don't go to that village, brother; there is nothing but bad news down there;" Two called out as they approached the village.

"So I found out for myself; the fat fool thought he was going to pen me until someone brought him tribute;" Inca yelled back as they grew near the village. As they flew over they could see several decomposing remains that looked to have once been human. There was nothing within the village except animals that were either eating the dead or what remained of the corn crop: other than these, the village appeared to be deserted.

"I suspect the villagers finally had enough of their chief and killed him and his guards and then fled into the jungle, perhaps afraid of being punished," Inca called out; Two nodded and they again headed north towards the next village on the list.

Not long before Inti set himself behind the western mountains they once again saw the village where he spent the night with the pretty girl; each gave cry to their calls and they spiraled gracefully down towards the ground and the friendly people who waited.

Cuauhtémoc removed his headdress before he had taken wing, mostly, because he didn't want to frighten the people in this village. As he and Two landed he saw the pretty girl and her brother, both moving cautiously towards him, because both wanted to greet him; each for their own reasons.

He held his arms out to receive the boy first, giving him a quick hug and tousling his head in a friendly, familiar way and then turned to the young girl who stood only a few steps away, surrounded by others like her as well as the rest of the village. "It is good to see you again," he said politely, "will you serve me yet again this night?"

She blushed as before and looked shyly up at him. "If it pleases you, birdman, I shall serve you this evening as I did when you were here last. Why did it take you so long to return? I had hoped to see you again before this."

"There is a story to this; a story about The Birdman and How He Came to Fly. Perhaps if it pleases everyone here I will speak this story tonight while we eat, but before that can be, I would like some hot water that I might make the tea I like."

The pretty girl bowed and turned to get the hot water as she had before. He turned to get his leaves but Two stepped before him and bowed very deeply. "If it pleases you, Great Prince, I will be glad to get your leaves for you as well as your Royal Headdress; if this is your wish." Cuauhtémoc stared at him for a moment and then gave a single nod of his head. He looked about and most of the people in the village had stopped whatever they were doing and were staring at him.

"This is also part of the Ballad of The Birdman; be patient awhile longer and you will come to understand;" he said kindly.

Two brought both the headdress and the pouch of tea leaves to him. He took the pouch and let Two fit the headdress upon him. Once these things were done he approached the fire and swirling about as was usual for him he sat down. The small child who had fallen asleep in his lap before, kept staring at him, trying to remember where she had seen him; somehow, his sitting in that exact place jogged her memory – it was the nice one who had held her once before—and if he had done it then, why not now? Such is a child's logic and that is how it ended up, with the tiny tot sitting crosswise on his lap while they all ate, and he began his story.

"This is The Ballad of The Birdman and How He Came to Fly. It is also a story about this village, and the people in this village, because it is a story of all villages and all people who live in Maya; as well as people who live far away in distant lands that lay beyond the great waters."

He began his story, speaking of himself in the third person, because it felt less like bragging and more like giving a report on events and places. He started when The Birdman left the village of the pretty girl, and moved downward, leaving messages as birdmen have always done. He got them to the bay with the three great ships in it and how The Birdman saw the villain kill the small one, one not much older than the tot cuddled against him in his lap. He spoke of the wrath of The Birdman and how he killed the villain with an arrow through the eye.

Then he continued on through his experiences at the Northern Soldier's Camp; and how The Birdman had been sent on to the great city where the Emperor lives. He dwelt on the kindness of the Greatest Mayan and his three Sons; and the ships that came into the bay and how The Birdman recognized them as the same ones who had murdered innocent villagers; and how The Birdman was again filled with fury and flew out with a goatskin filled with oil, and in the end, destroyed all three pirate ships and how he returned to the Greatest Mayan with one wingtip on fire and almost out of height.

He told of the Greatest Mayan's kindness and generosity, and how in the end he made The Birdman a Crown Prince, that he might be better able to organize an army of birdmen who would be trained and equipped to be ready when the pirates once again came to murder innocent villagers, because the Greatest Mayan in his wisdom understood as the villagers protect their Emperor, a wise Emperor also does all he can to protect his villagers: only in unity against a common foe could the Mayan people survive such a calloused and heartless enemy.

Next; he spoke of how the Mayan soldiers rescued an innocent child from the defeated pirates, and how Hezaraht, the High Priest of the Sun, came to the Greatest Mayan and demanded the child so he could kill her on his alter; and how The Birdman, in his great wrath, threw a sword half-way across the throne room in an effort to kill the High Priest and how Hezaraht fled in terror. He spoke the Greatest Mayan that same day declared no child would ever again be taken from their villages and their homes to be killed on an altar by a heartless and deranged clergy who were supposed to be helping the people instead of preying upon the weak and innocent.

Cuauhtémoc told this story so people would be warned of the enemy and understand the Emperor was doing all in his power to keep them safe. He also intended the mother of the young boy would come to see being a birdman was a very good thing and there could be great honor involved. In this way, perhaps her own heart would perceive her son might be leaving her, but if this became so, he was moving toward greater things; because if one birdman could ascend so high as Inca, then other birdmen could also climb. He also wanted her to understand the power of the Sun Priests to harm children was no more because the Greatest Mayan forbade it forever. He wanted her to realize the sister she lost so long ago was finally avenged. In this part he succeeded because he saw the look in her eyes which said it was so.

The small one once again fell asleep in his lap, her face against his belly and her first two fingers in her mouth. He raised her up to his face and gently kissed her forehead. "This is a thing I learned from the young girl who came to us from across the sea; the same girl Hezaraht thought to kill and I fought to save. It is called a 'kiss' and is used by their people to show affection and love for each other. I have come to learn I like it." He kissed the tiny tot once more and then held her up so her mother could come and claim her. Time had grown late and many children were already drifted off to sleep but the young girl who served him the last time sat very close to him on his left and the boy who wanted to be a birdman leaned against his right side. He reached his arms out and hugged both to him and smiled.

Two had been staring at Inca throughout his tale with an indecipherable expression on his face. He stood and bowed deeply before him. "Thank you for telling us this story, Great Prince, I promise to do all I can to spread this tale to every village and town; that everyone can hear of your deeds, and understand when they see the birdmen of Maya in their skies, they may sleep well because they know they are safe."

It turned out the girl who had been so aggressive to him the last time he was through, was a favorite of Two; perhaps which was why she had been so forceful. Or perhaps she was just that way and Two found this to his liking. It is so it takes all kinds to make a world; and time and place have very little to do with anything.

The boy who laid up against him all through the dinner and story time got up and rubbed his eyes for it was well past his usual bedtime; he walked up to his mother and looked up into her face. "I shall be a birdman when I grow up, Mother," he announced.

His mother looked down at her son fondly and nodded as she gently caressed his face and ran her fingers through his hair as mothers have done to their children for ages. "Yes, my son, I know; and I now know you will be as safe with The Birdman as you are in my own arms; but I also know my arms will miss you very much. Perhaps once in a while you will be able to take time out from your duties to fly back here and visit and make your father and me even prouder of you than we already are."

He put his arm around the pretty girl as she led him toward the empty hut where a bed was already laid out, but even as he walked with her, part of his mind was back with the mother and her son. The child *could* return whenever he wished—and so could he.

This was a thing that had never occurred to him before: he *could* return to his own village; it really wasn't that far from where he was in fact. He intended to stay at least three more days in this village because he promised the girl he would try and give her a child and he regarded all promises as vows before Father Inti and therefore a thing that could not be broken. But he now understood he could take part of that time and go see his mother and grandfather, and with this understanding, came the quiet resolve within that led to certainty.

He did his best to put stars into the eyes of the pretty girl as he had with the Commander's daughter. He thought he must be getting better at this, because by the time they were done, he was pretty sure he had seen a few stars of his own: they cuddled up and went to sleep.

He awoke somewhere in the early pre-dawn as was usual for him and he got up and used the needed and then went to get another cup of the brew he favored. While he was in the middle of this the girl's father approached and bowed deeply before him.

"You have again honored my family, Great Prince, I can never thank you enough and I can never repay you. My woman has mourned the loss of her sister; even though it has been many years since she was taken. For the first time last night she was at peace with both this and that our son will soon leave us and become a birdman. Before you came yesterday she was set against it and would hear nothing else, but now she is of a different mind, and almost seems to be a different woman; this is more wonderful than I can say and all I can do is thank you." Again the man bowed deeply before him; paying respect that was due.

Cuauhtémoc nodded at the man in the way that a Prince does and then spoke. "I also have thanks to give you and your family. Before your woman took your son to bed she told him he could fly back here and visit when he had the time and wished to. When I left my own village over two years back my grandfather was set against it and would hear of nothing else, but the eagles came for me and the birdman and I left and I have not heard a word from him since, even though I send messages to him faithfully. With her words I came to understand I, too, can return to my home village for it is not that far from here.

"I intended to stay here for at least three more days in an effort to keep my promise to your daughter, but now I believe when my brother leaves today I shall also leave, and go and face my grandfather and beg his forgiveness. If he refuses at least I will know I tried. After I have done these things I shall return for yet another three days so your daughter may have a chance to carry my seed within her as she wishes."

Cuauhtémoc spent the rest of the night telling the night guards of how life was in the Soldier's camp as well as the City of Emperors. In time, darkness gave way before light, and then Inti once again peeked above the distant waters and it was day once again.

Two and his girl for the night came out of their hut, followed by his own girl not long after. As she had done the last time she paused, rubbed the sleep out of her eyes, and then she came quickly over to him and raised her lips for a kiss, which he willingly gave her. They parted; only to discover every eye in the village was upon them.

"This is a different kind of kiss; as I spoke that the foreign girl showed me. I have found that the French, as they are called, have many different kinds of such. There is a light kiss to each cheek"—he moved the pretty girl's face and demonstrated—"and also a light kiss to the lips," and again he demonstrated with his very willing partner. "Then there is a very serious kind of kiss; watch closely and we shall show you." He guided her arms around his neck, held her in a gentle but firm embrace and kissed her with all the skill he had been able to learn over the last few weeks. Yvette would have been proud of him—also insanely jealous it wasn't she. By the time the two came up for air she clung limply to his body, unable to stand on her own, and from the expression on her face she was ready to drag him back to the hut then and there.

"Which brings up another thing; men, if you do this thing correctly to your woman, you must remember to not step away suddenly because she will lose every bone in her body and she needs a few moments to grow new ones." He smiled down on the girl in his arms and once again gave her a light kiss on her lips and then gently moved away—she did indeed look to be wobbly in the knees.

For the next fist of the sun or so there was very little activity within the village that did not have something to do with kissing and the learning thereof; Cuauhtémoc looked at Two and his girl and grinned.

"Neither rain nor snow nor gloom of night will stay these couriers from their appointed rounds. A beautiful girl on the other hand—" and he smiled with a roguish glitter in his eyes.

He was the first to kick off and climb into the blue sky. Two and his girl vanished not long after they had first started practicing kissing and that was true of most of the younger couples. He could see that in six or seven lunar cycles the big tummy syndrome would be sweeping the village in wholesale numbers and he laughed at the thought.

Almost as soon as he started climbing his mind focused anew on the thing that lay before him; he had no idea what he would do if his grandfather did not forgive him. He would have to move on to other things, but for a boy who never felt fear, there was an uncertainty that tried vainly to gnaw at his innards.

Perhaps a fist of the sun slipped by; it was not yet quite midday when his village first came into view and he gazed upon it like a love-starved swain looking upon the woman he cherished. He circled the village twice, spiraling ever downward before he uttered his cry; "K-e-e-e-r" he screed down toward the ground, "k-e-e-e-r," and he swung around on his final approach. At first only a few people glanced skyward because most thought that it was just another eagle passing overhead but then someone spotted a 'descending eagle' of a different kind: "Cuauhtémoc, it's Cuauhtémoc, everybody come quickly; Cuauhtémoc has returned."

The village people became kinetic, with everyone running frantically, yelling at everyone else. First he saw his mother pop out of her hut, scanning the skies in frantic sweeps, closely followed by his grandfather who moved only slightly slower than his much younger daughter. He glided in as silent as a falling leaf and then dragged tail and he was down. He stepped away from his wings and two men came up and grabbed the wings; for all such had loops dangling from each wing so people could fasten the wings to solid objects to keep them from accidentally being blown away.

He walked forward and faced his grandfather. "I have come to beg your forgiveness, Grandfather," he began; but the old man would have none of it.

"*You*? Beg *my* forgiveness? It is I who should be down on my belly and my face before you, begging *your* forgiveness," he exclaimed incredulously.

This was not going the way he pictured it in his mind. In his thoughts he had come to his grandfather, begging his forgiveness and his grandfather had given it in the end, but only after chastising him for his disobedience: nowhere in his imaginings had he ever thought of something like this.

"My forgiveness; what have you ever done against me?" he asked, confused.

"What have I not done? I tried to make you stay, even when I knew Inti had called you through his servants, the eagles. When you flew off into the skies with the birdman, you were so angry you would not even turn around, or wave goodbye and I knew you would never forgive me because my errors were so terrible against you."

"Grandfather; when I flew off with Xymatoc I was not yet ten. The last thing Xymatoc said to me when he put me on the wings was to hold still—you know how I am when someone in authority tells me to do something."

"Yes," his grandfather said, wiping tears off his face; "you are the most obedient child I have ever known. And when you decide to hold still; only the dead can be more still than you. Your words give my heart wings, Temmo, I shall always be grateful and I shall never again come between you and the will of Father Inti; a thing I knew better than, but tried anyway."

"There is so much that I want to tell you Grandfather, but before I can do that, there is a thing I want to show you." He walked over to where his wings were now anchored to several small trees and a large rock; no vagrant breeze would carry these wings off. He bent over and carefully took his headdress out and still bent over he checked the feathers to make sure none of them had become too crooked. Once convinced all was well, he put them on and faced everyone. They all stared for a long moment and then bowed deeply before him.

"My child; what are these feathers you wear?" his grandfather asked.

"Read the banding, Grandfather, see if you can say what is written there."

His grandfather was taller than he and had to bend to read the banding; "I see the word for Prince and there is a half-sun above it: this means 'Crown Prince' does it not?" Cuauhtémoc nodded. "Next to that is a descending eagle with a feather falling away; I have seen this before and I have no trouble reading it, it means you, it means Cuauhtémoc." Again he nodded his head. "The next is the sigil of the Emperor and close behind it is a mouth. This banding announces you are 'Crown Prince Cuauhtémoc, Emperor's Voice;'" and the village as a whole bowed deeply before him as they would to the Greatest Mayan himself.

CHAPTER 22

Inca looked his grandfather in his eyes and then reached up and took the headdress from his own head and put it upon his grandfather's head. "You have always been my Crown Prince, Grandfather," he said quietly and bowed deeply before him.

His grandfather bowed slightly in return and then removed the headdress and put it back where it belonged. "And you have always been my Crown Prince, Temmo," he said. "Let us put the past behind us and start anew for a brighter tomorrow . . . and I am sure that there is quite a story behind the feathers you wear and I believe we all would very much like to hear it. You couldn't possibly know this, Temmo, but right now you remind me of my father more than I can say. I obviously could have not known him at your age but I believe he must have looked exactly like you; the resemblance is uncanny."

"You speak of Texaquahotyl then?" he asked politely.

His grandfather stopped in mid-step and gaped at him; "How could you possibly know that name?" he demanded in disbelief.

"You told me;" he answered quietly.

There is very little privacy in a village where none of the huts have doors; the closest anyone can come by such is to politely ignore anyone who looked to need some privacy. So while Cuauhtémoc and his grandfather were discussing things, the rest of the villagers went back to their normal routines, keeping a polite distance and trying not to listen in on other people's words, yet still be close enough to be called in case of need.

"I remember everything. I had not yet learned to walk. Mother had dropped me off with you. You were sitting cross-legged and I was between your knees: I was holding on to your fingers, trying to walk. I remember how hard it was for me because my legs would not do what I wished.

"As I stood so, my hands raised up, holding onto your fingers because I could not yet stay erect, you looked down upon me and said; 'Ah, my little Cuauhtémoc. You must stand straight and tall for you are the descendant of the great Emperor Texaquahotyl. Yes, I know you do not understand, but I am the youngest of his seven legitimate sons and I know this to be true; you must grow up to be a man and become the greatest healer of all for you must cure . . . .' At this point mother returned for me and you picked me up and handed me to her. I was much too young to understand any of this, but as I have already said, I remember everything."

His grandfather stared at him in open amazement. "How can you remember that, Temmo? You were not yet eleven months old; I am sure of this because you were walking by the time your eleventh month was upon you."

"I remember but I don't know how or why; I just do. What must I cure; Grandfather? I have thought on this many times and have even spoken of it to those I trust but I never understood who or what: do you recall; do you know?"

His grandfather stared him in the eyes and slowly nodded; "You must grow up to be a man and become the greatest healer of all for you must cure *the illness of nations.*

"Natomis, please come here," his grandfather said. His mother immediately quit what she was doing and came over. His grandfather turned to him; "Please tell your mother what we have been speaking of."

Cuauhtémoc understood his grandfather did not want him to give a word by word of everything that had been said since he landed so he repeated what had just happened.

She listened thoughtfully and when he was done she nodded her head; "It is as the great Mayan calendar predicted; a child will be born of great abilities and he will heal nations. We have always presumed the healing was of the physical self, of the body, but somehow we forgot there are also healings of the mind as well as of the spirit; and we should not have overlooked that healings can be of all three. If we look at it in that way it would explain the strong spike that takes place in the third quadrant of the fourth phase of the great outer circle. I admit I never was able to understand how this would affect our child here: viewed from a concept of triple-heal, it makes more sense. I think I must go back to the second inner circle and see how it relates to both the least as well as the greatest circle." She bowed before both males and turned and headed towards her hut.

His grandfather turned to him and said, "Your mother has the best understanding of the great Mayan calendar of anyone I have ever known. If she had lived back in the court of my father she would have been a priestess, if not high priestess, for her understanding approaches that of seeress; she is in so many ways wasted in a small village such as this."

"You both are, grandfather," Inca said. "Your works is known among healers all over the Mayan world; your abilities are legendary in their scope. I think at times a frog will not wish to leave the pond he is in because he is the biggest frog in that pond and fears to go to a greater pond. I think perhaps that is why Father Inti brought me out of this village; that I may grow to my full potential in the largest pond of all.

"I am almost out of the leaves you have been sending me all along; do you have any more? I would very much like a drink of brew that is picked fresh and not from leaves that are many tens of days old."

"Yes, Temmo, I have some I was going to send by the next birdman who stopped by. I must admit the birdman who took you away and never returned was the best birdman we've ever had; did he not return because he also thought I was angry?"

"No; Grandfather. The day Xymatoc took me from here was the day he had grown too heavy to reach the highest villages and it was his last flight until very recently. We have now started making greater wings, so the older and heavier birdmen who wish, can once again fly the skies of Maya. If it is your desire, as well as Xymatoc's, I will speak to Dispatcher to see if he may again serve your village as well as others."

"That would please many; including me. Speak these words to me, my child, how long will you be able to stay before you must again leave us on Father Inti's service?"

"The rest of today and all of tonight but before Father Inti drops below the mountains tomorrow I must again be back in a village not far from here. From there I must return to the birdman's camp and in time back to the City of Emperors; but we shall get in as much visiting as we can in that time; this I vow."

They went into the healer's hut where the healer had a large pouch filled with freshly picked, dried and crushed leaves. His grandfather handed the sack to him, and gestured toward a mat, that he might sit down. Cuauhtémoc did as he always did; he walked up to it, spun smoothly around and settled down as elegantly as a bird on a limb.

"I have always missed the graceful ways you have, Temmo; that, among so many other things. I was writing in my notes when I heard people speaking you had returned. I'm afraid I made a mess of my sheet in my haste. I remember leaving my notes out where you would be sure to see them, but even then your heart was on flight, and you would have nothing to do with them." His grandfather looked at him and a sad expression came over his face.

When was this; Grandfather?" Inca asked politely.

"Right after your eighth birthday; I felt introducing you to these any earlier would be too soon for your mind to grasp."

"I remember that very clearly; Grandfather. The reason I showed no interest when I was eight, was because I had already looked at, examined, and memorized every one of your notes I could lay my hands on, before I turned four."

Cuauhtémoc reached out and took the ruined note and turned it upside down where the page was still fresh, and carefully keeping his hands out of the ink at what was now the bottom, he began to write. He took one of the pages he memorized when he was small and began to carefully trace the images that seemed to float on the page before him, only to vanish one by one as he applied ink from the writing stick to paper. He did this for some long moments and when he thought he had enough down to make his point clear he laid the ink and writing stick down and handed the still-wet page to his grandfather.

His grandfather started scanning the paper, his eyes moving from symbol to symbol; at first he smiled and then he chuckled and in the end he laughed in delight. "From the day you were born, you amazed me, Temmo; from the moment of your birth you have always left me a step or so behind, and now I look upon this you just wrote, I see you are consistent; you are still ahead of me. Come, my child, and see what I mean. Tell me; do you know what these words mean?"

"No; Grandfather. I have asked several healers since leaving here, but none could read them, so I must believe these are written in Incan and not Mayan."

"That is so, and not only Incan, but the written language of the Royal Court which is, or was, understood by very few. And I can tell these are specifically from my notes because not only do I remember writing them, I have a unique way of making some of my words; I like putting small flourishes here and there because I think it looks more beautiful; and you have duplicated these little marks perfectly. Come and sit beside me and I will read these to you so you may understand; there are only a few hundred such words normally used. Considering your memory, we should be able to cover most of these in the next fist of the sun or so, and then I must release you to the village and your little sister, Xochitl, who I see keeps peeking through the doorway to see if you have yet noticed she still lives."

Cuauhtémoc looked up and saw a small face peeking in from the edge of the doorway. "Xochitl; it is you. I kept seeing you but I thought, no, my sister is not as tall as that girl . . . and you have grown so beautiful!" It was all the encouragement the child needed and she squirted through the doorway and crawled into her brother's lap; once her favorite place to sit. He cuddled her up to him and then turned to his grandfather: "I am ready whenever you are."

Xochitl settled down in her big brother's lap. Normally, she was as full of energy as any other almost nine year old, but she contented herself with quietly waiting while occasionally reaching up and touching the feather headdress that Cuauhtémoc wore. He watched and listened as his grandfather read first one note after another, tracing from one pictograph to another and before long he was reading aloud with his grandfather. By the time they were done he understood most of the symbols and was at a point where he could interpret the ones he didn't know. As the healer at the birdman's camp once supposed, all of these were his grandfather's medical notes, and while they would have been dry reading to anyone not interested in medicine and healing, to him they were fascinating because these were yet other facets of plants and how they were used.

This led him to relate how the things he remembered helped others over the more than two years he had been gone, and as he spoke them one by one, he understood they were many. His grandfather listened with growing pride in his grandson and he came to see the very things he thought to do with the child before him; the child had gone out and done in ways he could have never foreseen.

The evening hours were spent in feasting and visiting and he spent much of this time telling his family and friends all of the things he had done, from the time he left, on through to his return; he painted his picture with a broad brush, leaving out all the minor detail and covering only the greater—to him at least—including his graduation from fledgling; his two years as a birdman; his seeing the pirate ship and witnessing the death of a child and his reaction; quickly touching upon his stay at the soldier's camp and ultimately relating much of what happened to him after he landed on the rooftop of the Emperor's palace, nearly colliding with his Emperor, and ending up with his meeting with the Sun's High Priest and how he very nearly killed him. This last went over very well because the people in his village were all Incan and none of them believed in sacrificing children.

The hour had grown late; he hugged everyone in the village at least twice; including some who were much too young to remember him at all and most had gone to their own beds. In the end only he and his grandfather sat around the fire while he had yet another cup of his favorite brew. He usually only took one or two a day because he wanted to carefully ration out what he had, but here there was more than enough, and he was working on his seventh cup since landing and he wasn't remotely sleepy.

"You really enjoy your drink; don't you Temmo?" his grandfather asked softly.

"Yes; and somehow it always tastes best when I am here with you. Do you know I recall the very first time you ever gave it to me?" He described what he remembered of his grandfather when he had given him a few drops from the end of a hollow reed and what his mother and grandfather had said: his grandfather looked at him.

"My child, you were not more than a few fists of the sun out of your mother's belly when that took place, yet your memory is clearer than mine, because until you spoke of it I had forgotten all about it."

"What are these leaves called, Grandfather, is this something that you can speak?"

"I would be glad to speak these words to you, Temmo, but I have none to say. I came upon this place while on another errand. I don't know what the leaves are called."

"Temmo's leaves;" he said with a sly grin.

"From now on that is how they shall be called, as ordered by our Crown Prince," his grandfather said with a twinkle in his own eyes. "If it pleases you I will take you to this place tonight if you are not too tired. It is three days past the full of the moon but there is still good light to see by if we stay to the cleared pathways."

Cuauhtémoc finished his last cup with a few quick swallows and rinsed the cup out in the stream and placed it upside down on a stick rack used for that purpose; "I am ready to go when you are, Grandfather," he said politely.

Ever since the incident with the first batch of pirates, he had never gone anywhere without a bow and some arrows, and now he had one of the first bows crafted by Son of Spain, it was even more true; he took his bow, a quiver of arrows and a knife; his grandfather did the same as well as taking a net to gather leaves in. By now everyone was in bed asleep with the exception of the night guards.

"Temmo and I will be gone for a few fists," the Healer told two of the guards, "we shall be back when we have returned." The guard bowed politely to the Healer and more deeply to his Prince and then grandfather and grandson eased out into to the night of the jungle, moving vaguely north.

They followed faint trails dimly lit by the moon's light filtered through trees that towered on either side. They had gone no more than a thumb's distance when the trail opened up into a moonlit glen and in the middle of this glen a jaguar stood, staring at them, its hackles raised and tail stiff upright; signaling an attack.

"No, I forbid it," he told the jaguar, *"we mean you no harm and you shall not harm us. Go your way, for you are already fed, and you have cubs waiting your return."* The great carnivore stared at them and her tail slowly lowered. She seemed to pause in thought. A soft kind of snarl came from her and in his mind came the impression — *'no attack; no fangs, no claws'* and then she calmly walked by them. As she passed Inca she brushed his leg with her flank and flicked him lightly with her tail and then she vanished down the gloomy trail the two humans had just trod.

Inca looked up at his grandfather who was staring at him, his face indecipherable. "You remind me so very much of my father; Temmo.

I have never spoken to you of him for my own reasons but I think I should now tell you, not only was he truly a great Emperor and greatly loved by his people, he was also the Chief Jaguar Priest."

"Texaquahotyl was of the jaguars? That is of the Lord of Darkness; they killed innocents, they killed children," he said; aghast.

"You are both right and wrong," his grandfather said gently. "Father was the Chief of the Jaguar Priests, but he worshiped Viracocha, The Uncreated Creator. He never offered innocents to the jaguars and he never offered children. Just the opposite, he loved all children and he was very good with them and all children trusted him—you are most like my father when you hold a child close. Most of the wars he started with the Mayan people were because the Mayans do, or rather did, offer human sacrifices. You also strongly remind me of him when you speak to the jaguars—what did you say to that cat?"

"You didn't hear my words to her?" he asked; puzzled.

"I heard you growling and snarling at her and I heard her snarl back and then she calmed down and walked past us without concern, and as she passed, she brushed against you and flicked you with her tail; why would she do that—and how do you know she was female?"

"The eternal female;" he said laughing as he looked up into his grandfather's face. "She has cubs in her den and no interest in a male, not to mention the whole interspecies- thing, but she just had to flirt. As for knowing she was female, I could smell she was and I could smell the odor of her milk as well as the sweet meaty scent of her breath so I knew she had freshly eaten, " Then he repeated what he thought he said in Incan at the beginning.

His grandfather listened intently and then nodded his head when he was done. "It is as I said, you remind me of my father so very much; he would have been proud of you if he could have seen you, Temmo—and perhaps he has, and is. We Inca also believe in the spirit world and in good spirits and bad and we also believe if a man has been good in this world of flesh and blood he will go on to live in the world of spirits as a good spirit: he may have even been here as you talked to that jaguar.

"You seem to think that Father offered the innocent and children up to the jaguars but I have sworn to you this is not so. But he did offer humans up and tied them to trees and sprinkled them with goat's blood and left them for the jaguars. If he did not offer up the innocent and children; can you guess who he did offer?"

Cuauhtémoc paused; a puzzled expression on his face and then that expression gave way to delight. "His enemies; he would have offered his enemies up to the jaguars."

"Yes," his grandfather said, nodding his head with exaggerated solemnity; "as you have seen for yourself in the form of Hezaraht; a powerful ruler, or any wealthy one for that matter, will have those - who in their conceit - will imagine they are the better choice and who will do or say any underhanded thing to take away that which is rightfully others. My father was no different; a great many others thought that they would be a better Emperor. All of these he caught he fed to the jaguars; it was the best of all possible solutions; he got rid of his enemies and the jaguars got fed.

"Do you see that tree to my right, the one with the misshapen bole which is west of us?" Inca glanced at the tree his grandfather mentioned, and then looked up at his grandfather, and nodded. "Remember this opening and this tree, as I know you will, from here we travel west; it is not far but because the trail we are now on is well traveled I have made every effort to hide this for several reasons."

The pair worked their way west. If there was a marked trail, Cuauhtémoc couldn't see it, but he memorized trees and directions and that they were working steadily towards a large outcropping of basaltic rock. They, in time, worked their way through a narrow crack which led to the interior of what once was in eons past a vent of a volcano. It was somewhat oblong and perhaps one hundred double-paces by eighty; the soil was made up of a black loam which smelled faintly of sulfur. The area was mostly covered with plants with large silvery leaves; but in one corner there was a small patch of plants with very dark green leaves he recognized immediately. He walked over and carefully pinched a leaf and brought his fingers to his nose and inhaled deeply.

He turned to his grandfather; "Did you know you once sent me an entire leaf and until that time I didn't even know what they looked like?"

"You got it then?" his grandfather asked, pleased. "I picked it fresh and stuck it in with some crushed dried leaves and sent them off to you; I always wondered if you got it whole and what you did with it."

"I drew a picture of it and gave the drawing to several of the healers in the palace with a request to see if they could find the like but they never did. You spoke to Mother you had been unable to grow it anywhere else so I didn't expect them to find any."

"That is so; for years I tried to plant these in other places, and while they would grow, they were not the same. I even tried carrying out some of this soil for the plants to grow in but it just doesn't grow properly any place but here."

"What of these other plants; what are their uses?"

"None. I have tried ever test I could think of but for all intents they are no more than weeds."

"If they are of no use and you need more room to grow more plants why don't we uproot some of these weeds and plant Temmo's leaves in their place?"

Grandfather stared at Cuauhtémoc for a long moment and then turned and walked away. He took three or four steps, stopped, turned and walked back. "I have been coming here since before your mother was born, before her mother was born and before her mother's mother was born; for over a hundred and fifty years I have been coming here, struggling to get enough leaves out of this little spot, and in all of that time I never once thought of the obvious. Can you explain why to me; Cuauhtémoc?"

"Sure, it's easy, brilliant minds are so used to brilliant thoughts they sometimes miss the mundane;" he smiled slyly up at his grandfather.

He looked down on his grandson and nodded thoughtfully. "I see; now explain how it is you are here three heartbeats and you figure it out."

"Oh, well, I'm just not as smart as you are so I can see—" Cuauhtémoc jumped quickly out of the way to keep from being swatted by his grandfather.

"Come back here you impudent pup; I'm going to give you the beating you've always deserved; starting with your first breath."

"Yes, Grandfather," he said and moved his feet slightly closer because he was now standing about as near as he could get. His grandfather shook his head and gave him a hug.

The first plant Cuauhtémoc pulled broke off just above the ground as did the second. By the time he started on the third plant he held his hands touching both plant and dirt and slowly stood up, pulling directly in line with the plant's growth. At first resentfully, and finally with a rush, the plant came up roots and all; it was shallowly rooted but the roots spread nearly as wide as the leaves themselves.

"How did you do that, Temmo? I keep breaking mine off." He carefully showed how he had done it; his grandfather gave a soft grunt and tried it on his plant: slow and easy turned out to be the way and after that they had no further problems.

Perhaps a fist of the moon later they had opened an area that doubled the original plot and planted it with seeds the healer had put away in a ceramic jar in years past. The pair looked up on their work with satisfaction and then each picked up a single pulled plant and tucking it in their waistbands they took their bows and arrows at ready and headed back to camp. They returned not long before the moon set for the night. Each nodded to the other and they went to their respective beds. Inca returned to the same bed he had slept in most of his life. The straw was new and the llama skin cover had been well aired out, but other than that, it was the same as it had always been. He crawled in and was almost asleep when there was a small stirring in the darkness and in the next moment Xochitl crawled in with him. This too was normal; the first six years of her life she had always slept with him, excluding her infancy when she was too small; they cuddled up as children do and he was asleep before he knew it.

It was full daylight when he awoke. His little sister had already slipped out bed, which surprised him, because he was a light sleeper. By the time he got up, had breakfast and had gotten all of his goodbyes said, the sun was high overhead. Xochitl clung to him like a human burr, determined to keep him there with her no matter what it took, but when he suggested they could both fly off to his next village she quickly let go because she had a dread of high places and the thought of being that far up in the air did not set well with her at all. She consoled herself by getting into a game with some of her friends and being a child, soon put Cuauhtémoc to the back of her mind where she could take him out, dust him off and admire him whenever she wished; which was good.

CHAPTER 23

Time and tide await no man; and this is as true of birdmen as anyone else. By the time six weeks elapsed, H'ratli had passed his birdman's test and had flown everyday for more than ten days. His skill and confidence grew so much he was ready to take his wings and head south with Inca. The pair set out from the regular slope since Cuauhtémoc didn't want to push his brother faster than he was ready. It was not a long flight and with H'ratli just off his right wingtip they soared over the soldier's camp landing field. Inca screed his wild cry while H'ratli hooted softly like an owl. H'ratli wanted to be an eagle as his brother but the frequency and volume were beyond his reach and he could make a fairly good owl.

They spent the night with the Commander who was not the same man he was. He had thrown his walking stick as far out over the water as he was able and by the time Inca and H'ratli were fully on the ground he came down the path almost skipping in his joy. Inca examined the Commander's leg and was amazed at how little of the scar was left. He had no trouble believing well before the two months he had given the man were up; all of the scar would be gone. And better than that from the healer's viewpoint, the plants Bitumen brought them weeks earlier, blended in with the salve perfectly and there were a great many whose bone-aches were things of the past.

The next morning Inca and H'ratli kicked off in their greater wings and both wings, clad with silk, slipped through the air very smoothly. Long before Inti was even thinking of going to bed for the night they saw the Palace of the Emperors in the distance. H'ratli followed Inca's lead perfectly and no sooner did Inca drag-tail on the rooftop than H'ratli landed behind him. His father, brothers, and assorted guards and servants took one look and bowed deeply.

For the first time ever, H'ratli out-talked both Inca and Son of Spain combined, and almost every subject had something to do with flying or learning to fly. He might forget to put his headdress on or even not wear his clothes but he never was caught without his birdman's feather cluster set above his right shoulder: his wives insisted he even wore them to bed—they said they tickled.

Inca was attacked not long after arriving back at the palace. He was walking towards his room when two feminine shrieks echoed off the hallways and Eilei and Yvette tackled him in tandem, giving him a one-two assault that would have made a Packers fan grin—under the circumstances he didn't mind.

(Three years passed.)

The Mayan people didn't have weekends off and while they did have different holidays celebrating one event or other these were not allowed to interfere with the business of living.

Son of Spain made good on his brag about *ballistae,* which proved to be every bit as good as the man claimed, plus they had the advantage of being well within reach of the Mayan's current technology and Inca, working hand in hand with his brother Quoholocet, put up points all around the edge of the great bay, spacing them with the precision the Mayan mind was known for. Once all of the bugs were worked out of the system there was no place out in the bay one of the ballistae could not reach. The heavy shafts the ballistae threw had considerable weight and anything the heavy bolts hit, went down, and stayed down.

Cuauhtémoc kept busy organizing and training his birdmen into an armed force to be reckoned with, and by the time three years were up, there was no large village, town or city that did not have at least a few of the 'feather-heads' wandering around, ready in case of need.

Inca also made strides in the weapons that were dropped. The new 'greater wings' could safely carry much heavier loads and he had his men trained in precision dropping of these things. They had nets of rocks like he used up in the soldier's camp on his first attack; and skins of oil that could be dropped with devastating results. He even combined the two, filling a goatskin up with basaltic rocks, and then topping it off with oil. This was almost too destructive because the oil-soaked rocks would catch fire and ricochet all over the place, creating unbelievable destruction among the enemy, and by now it was understood total immolation was a thing of last resort because if a pirate ship could be seized relatively intact; there were almost always things that were valuable either as products or as weapons against other enemies. Arrows could be dropped from height and deliver an entirely different message than otherwise, and quite recently, a way had been found to take large hollow canes and fill them with black powder with feathers on one end to make them fall true and these would explode on contact: Prince Cuauhtémoc was very pleased.

On the opposite side of the world in the northern hemisphere there was a man who was not pleased at all. He was called Greenbeard and at the age of 44 he sat atop a pile of wealth he and his men had plundered from half of Europe. His people had told him of a land far away where gold was so plentiful the buildings were made up of the metal and the streets paved with gold ingots and the gutters were littered with emeralds, rubies, diamonds and other gems which glittered in the sunlight like pretty pebbles. The name of this far-away land was Maya and even though he sat upon enough wealth to last him a thousand years it was not enough: he wanted it all—such is the way of greed.

He knew exactly where this fabulous land was because some of his captains had seized merchant vessels that had come from there and the ship's logs showed the exact latitude and longitude of this incredibly wealthy city. He intended to go there and confiscate it all. Perhaps he would even move his headquarters into the palace—after he killed the present occupants; of course.

He planned this raid over a period of two years. By the time the fifteenth of March was upon him he had a sizable fleet of almost thirty ships, and all were well-equipped for a long ocean voyage, and all were armed to the teeth. The weather was fair for days; he boarded his own private ship and gave orders to drop sail and Greenbeard's version of an armada left the safety of his home port and sailed southwest towards a distant land he had only heard of from the lips of others.

March is called the 'windy month' for a good reason. For awhile it looked like he would have fair weather all the way and then a tropical depression formed ahead of him and he and his ships sailed into a baby hurricane being born: this was not good. Several of his ships were just overloaded with weapons and gunpowder and sank. Others were blown a point further south than they were supposed to be sailing and by the time the storm passed, Greenbeard was down to twenty ships.

Along the way he had several brushes with England's Royal Navy, for these seamen were always on the lookout for those who sailed under the Jolly Rogers, and even though the pirates fought back and outnumbered their foe, the British Man o' Wars had the larger guns and the greater range and more of his ships were damaged in one way or another; these were left to fend for themselves because Greenbeard cared for no one but himself. This cost him yet more boats. By the time he struck the coast far to the north in the Incan lands he was down to thirteen ships. Sailors, be they pirate or merchant or other tended to be superstitious, and the number thirteen was considered bad luck but the captains of the pirate ships were more afraid of their leader than a silly number so they joined him and headed south, well away from the shoreline to avoid any hidden underwater reefs and the like.

They were not hidden from Mayan eyes which by now understood what the black and white flags meant and as soon as the ships were spotted sailing south the birdmen-soldiers were notified; these took up their message arrows and wings and flew. The message arrows the birdmen-soldiers carried were created for this specific purpose. The upper part of the arrow was bright red signifying blood or danger, with white feathers tips dipped in ink, giving the black and white of a pirate's flag. The lowest part was painted blue which indicated the attack would come from the ocean, and the middle section wore different color-stripes which was assigned to places up and down the coast. Anyone who understood the code could pick up such an arrow, and knowing about how long it would take a birdman-soldier to fly the distance from his home base, could give a very close estimate on how near the pirates were and if they were coming from the north or the south. Well before Greenbeard was anywhere near the City of Emperors, The Birdman had one such arrow in his hands, and knew very closely how much time he had left – which was more than enough.

The Mayan people believed to live close to nature was to live close to Father Inti and so the city and the area that surrounded the waters of the bay were left in as natural a state as possible and the Mayans set most of their great ballistae in the shade of these trees which protected the weapons as well as gave natural camouflage.

At the moment he was standing up on the roof of the palace. Of late; drum messages took the place of flags or gestures because they could carry over longer distances. He nodded his head at the drummer: "three sets of 'Alert!'" he said. 'Alert' was a series of three quick drumbeats, three slow and then three quick beats again; a single set meant that 'this is a drill; everyone man your weapons and get ready.' In the manner of birdman signals, three of any message sent, meant the message was very important: in this case it meant 'this is not a drill but the real thing, get ready to fight'. Down below, people scurried about, preparing to play whichever part in this they had been assigned.

Cuauhtémoc and H'ratli and the rest of his primary attack team met on the rooftops of the palace and nearby buildings. When he first talked with Son of Spain about the ballistae, he was thinking both of the leading edges of wings and their ribs as well as something that would propel a birdman off the rooftops with enough speed they didn't have to dive off as he was used to. The ballistae proved far too violent and powerful for this but he found what he wanted in what the shipmen called 'block and tackle.' This was a pulley yoked together with yet another of the same on the other end. A rope ran between them continuously, creating a small distance raised with great power from a large distance moved with very little strength. He turned this around and currently had polished teak boards atop many of the nearby buildings with wings and people and weaponry waiting.

A fist of the sun passed quietly and then another; this gave what few merchant ships that were in the harbor chance to weigh anchor and catch the current out of the bay and sail yet further south because neither the merchant ships nor their captains or crew wanted to be in the middle of a fight; and the Mayan didn't want it either.

Everyone was in their places and ready when the first pirate ship cleared the jungle's growth, followed by a second, and then a third and before they were done; thirteen of the craft floated into the bay and dropped anchor. Along the shore in both directions people stopped and stared, and then pointing fearfully, they ran into houses that lined the beach. So far, this was exactly as Greenbeard expected; he sent his men by boat with instructions to demand immediate and total surrender or face sudden death.

The commanding officer spoke Spanish, which by now was a second language, because so many of the merchant's were of Spanish origin. He listened to the pirate's demands and then politely told him to go back to his own ship and sail out of the bay and back to wherever he had come from; do this and his own life would be spared.

The pirate received the news exactly as expected. He drew his sword and did his best to kill the commander but the commander dropped to the ground while yelling "Attack;" in Mayan. A brief heartbeat later, archers stepped from behind every drying rack in the area, and before the pirates on the shore and in the long boats could adjust to the change, all were sprouting feathers.

Greenbeard half-expected this and had even hoped for it because it gave him a good excuse to spill some blood. He and his men saw the people scamper into nearby huts; these, then, were the logical targets to start with and the cannoneers cut loose with barrages that set sticks and mud flying because that's all the huts were. What the enemy had not seen was the people had continued out the back and dropped into low areas where they scampered away long since and were now well out of range.

Son of Spain watched avidly. He already picked out his target, the Captain of the closest ship. As the cannons fired away at empty facades created for this sole purpose he drew 'My Precious' full back and released his first arrow. His bow was all he said it was and he was every bit as good a bowyer as he claimed and the only reason he didn't kill his intended target was that the man took several steps away at the last eye blink and the shaft hissed through the space he had just left and completely penetrated the pirate who had the misfortune of standing behind him—so much for preliminaries.

Now the ballistae cut loose, and the shafts, each as long as a tall man and the diameter of his wrist, shot across the distance and wiped out anything it happened to hit. A solid strike on a mast was almost guaranteed to shatter it and the cabin walls of a captain's quarters were no match on either entering or leaving the scene. One enterprising ballistero even managed to send one of his oversized bolts directly down the muzzle of a cannon just an instant before the cannoneer discharged his weapon: the result was interesting—for the ballistero; the canoneer didn't think anything because the explosion instantly killed him and those standing nearby. All of this was just the warm-up; the main act was about to start.

Up on the roof of the palace Cuauhtémoc took his place on his wings; the wings were properly loaded with two young goatskins filled with rocks and oil and his drop tubes were filled with two hands of the exploding arrows—any of which he could drop one at a time or all at once, whatever his need. His wings sat on a long teak ramp that hung out over the outer walls and several strong men held onto ropes and waited his signal. He gripped tightly and nodded his head; the men pulled on the ropes and the reverse leverage gave him a long strong thrust outward and by the time he cleared the edge of the teak plank he was already catching air and climbing fast in spite of his load. The men behind him immediately pulled the platform he had been on back to its starting place and Wings Second H'ratli took his place. A few heartbeats later and he was also in the air and climbing quickly. From the pirates view, had they bothered to look, it must have seemed that every single rooftop in the city suddenly sprouted great winged creatures launching themselves.

The final act - by definition - is the last, and for the pirates below, final was what it was all about. Cuauhtémoc always thought the best way to kill a snake was to cut its head off and before he was launched from the rooftop he picked his target; it was the largest and most gaudy ship around and therefore most likely the one the leader of the pack was on. As he flew over the ship from prow to stern he saw an ornately-dressed man below with a violently green beard. He dropped a row of five of his exploding arrows, or 'fire-eggs,' as he liked to call them. The moment the last egg was away he banked left and as he looked under his left arm he saw the first fire-egg strike. This had not landed near the one with the violently green beard but it didn't matter because there were a number of smaller black powder barrels nearby and the first egg landed close enough to one that when it detonated it set the barrels off. Greenbeard wasn't that far away and the blast picked him up and threw him perhaps six or seven good steps and slammed him into the wall of a nearby cabin. He stood for less than a heartbeat and then toppled over, either dead or unconscious, Inca didn't care which;

he was out of action and that was all that mattered. Straight ahead of him was yet another ship. He, speaking with Quoholocet and H'ratli earlier, had determined that at least a few of the ships would have to be torched; to get the attention of the others if nothing else, and he privately decided to attack either the seediest-looking or the most aggressive, and this particular ship filled both criteria.

He banked right and lined himself on his next target. Over the past three years he had flown over this bay countless times and by now he knew the winds about as well as anyone could. He also experimented with a number of men he trusted and had them fire different guns and such up into the air. Not at him but near enough to him he could see just how high the musket balls would climb before they dropped back to earth. He'd even gotten Son of Spain to launch a number of his arrows into the air and the Spaniard could consistently put his arrows higher and faster than any rifleman could hope to duplicate. He remembered this height and trained all of his birdmen to attack from this elevation; thinking this would lessen his losses by a useful amount.

He was slightly higher than this when he dropped his first goatskin sack of oil and rocks. He gauged the drop as carefully as possible and his reward was seeing the sack strike a mast and shatter, spewing oil and rocks all over the place and in a matter of a few heartbeats no one on the ship was fighting anything but fires which were already out of control. He laughed maniacally and then shrieked and gibbered as he had before and as before the pirates below went insane with terror. As he watched, one of the pirates took a heavy chain that looked to be two or three time his height in length and wrapped the chain around his body, forming a sort of X across his chest. Once he was content, he jumped off the ship and splashed down into the water, followed by a stream of bubbles a few moments later. "What a nice man," Inca said, "how thoughtful of him; if we could just train the rest to be like him this world would be a better place."

All during his attacks he kept a careful eye on his birdmen. The ballisteros quit launching their shafts the moment the birdmen attacked;

this was considered necessary to avoid one of the great bolts hitting a birdman by mistake. H'ratli proved to be a natural at this, and all through his testing phase, he had always placed at the top of his peers and this was no different; Cuauhtémoc saw his brother make several determined attacks on first one ship and then another and in every case he connected and did his part in spreading destruction and panic among the enemy ranks. By now all of the birdmen were shrieking and gibbering and the pirates below had taken about all that they could. Cuauhtémoc made another pass over a ship that didn't look too badly damaged and dropped both his oil and his last five fire-eggs at the same time: the effect was quite exciting and very interesting from his point of view.

"Throw down your weapons and surrender," he yelled in Spanish to the pirates down below and then yelled the same thing in Portuguese and French, just in case. Evidently not all of the pirates were ready to quit because as he flew over the ships, yelling the same thing over and over, one of the men raised a musket and took a shot at him. He was lower now and within range but the man made the same mistake others had; he shot at where The Birdman was and not where he would be when the musket ball got there. He didn't have a chance to learn from his error because H'ratli flew above and slightly behind his leader and as he saw the pirate take aim he made a pass and dropped a fire-egg. The only way H'ratli could have come closer would have been to put it directly down the pirate's gun barrel; there was an explosion and that particular one was no more.

It has been said it's not over until the fat lady sings but by now even she had left, exiting stage right. Three of the pirate ships were well on their way towards total immolation with scattered fires on several more. Not one ship was unscathed and now all were unseaworthy in one way or another. One by one, those who were able ran a white flag of some kind up their main mast, and all threw down their weapons. Prince Birdman was lower than he liked but nowhere as low as the last time he fought pirates. He swung around and flew over the burning ships and even with silk skin on his wings he didn't worry about anything catching fire because the fire was only very warm at this height and not baking; he and his brothers circled like hawks, watching Mayan soldiers in war-kaks launch themselves from shore, and swarm over the remaining pirate ships, killing all who offered even token resistance.

From the time the pirates entered the bay and dropped anchor until the last ship surrendered was not much more than a fist of the sun; if any. The Greatest Mayan had a very comfortable view of the entire thing. By now an awning had been set up near the entryway and a number of cushioned chairs and settees all the way from France were set out with a matching table, silverware with crystal drinking glasses and a decanter with some of the French wine the old man had come to favor. He cheered like any elderly baseball fan at the World Series and there was no question of which side he rooted for: the home team—of course.

There was more than enough room on the roof for his servants and guardsmen as well as a generous number of women who served the royalty in one way or another but the two faces who could be depended upon being in the middle of anything concerning the Birdman were missing: Eilei was in her quarters being miserable and Yvette was doing her utmost to console her best friend; but to no avail.

Eilei's entire problem was she was to be married within three days and Inca, the boy she adored with every molecule in her body, had done nothing to save her. He could go out and fight pirates by the handfuls and kill them by many handfuls but could he spare a few moments to drop a hundred or so fire-eggs on the home she would soon have to call hers . . . Nooo! Yvette tried in vain to assure her friend there was no way Inca would abandon her to another boy, and even as they spoke he was undoubtedly working out some ploy to deliver her out of durance vile, but Eilei would have none of it. Yvette, abruptly having her fill of Eilei's theatrics, exploded in an eruption of French invectives, because she always resorted to her native language when vexed beyond her limits and she stormed out of the room; making Eilei cry even harder because now even her best friend had deserted her.

Yvette headed towards the rooftops in hopes the fresh air would clear her head. She hadn't seen Inca for some time now and that in itself was odd; perhaps he actually was working on some devise to save Eilei from a boy she had never met and now loathed with a passion seldom found in the heart of a young maiden. As she raced up the last few steps she heard a distant rumble that sounded all too familiar; she stepped out onto a crowded rooftop and saw three pillars of black smoke rising up into the sky from where she knew the bay was. With her heart suddenly hammering inside of her in fear she walked towards the edge and looked down upon a scene of carnage as she had never dreamed of. There were pirate ships scattered all over the bay; for the ship's Captains had been careful to anchor their ships in such a way they would not be hitting each other with stray cannon fire. Three of these ships were in full blaze with two more thinking about it and everywhere she looked, Mayan soldiers were swarming over the ships that were not on fire like ants on dead carcasses. Overhead, the birdmen of Maya circled and swooped, making sure there was no further trouble from this particular band of brigands.

"Yvette; please, my child, one side or the other." She recognized the voice immediately as the Greatest Mayan; she turned and bowed deeply and then moving toward him she went down on her knees.

"Please forgive me Greatest Mayan," she said; "what is happening out here?"

"What is happening, is your friend, Cuauhtémoc," he said with a twinkle in his eyes; "come child, sit beside me and see yet another facet of the one you love. We here who know him are used to seeing him as the sweet-natured boy who cannot seem to do enough for us; but this is another side of him. You saw a bit of this three years back when Hezaraht thought to take you off to his vile domain. Now you are seeing the rest; that of a destroyer, one who does not understand the meaning of the word 'defeat,' except when it applies to his enemies.

While he is unfailingly polite and kind to we who are his friends; he is truly a demon of destruction to those who would attack us. Tell me, child, can you pick out which set of wings is his?"

The question was rhetorical. Not long after he returned from the birdman's camp with H'ratli, he got with some artists who were good with paints and dyes. When they were done with his wings, he had the leading edges made up in a yellow-gold dye that lit up like the sun when light came through it, and reds, greens and blues streaked from front to back; it was almost like watching a rainbow fly by. Not long after, all the birdmen wanted something similar done to their wings, but Prince Birdman forbade it, saying only birdman-soldiers could have the special haircut and only birdman-soldiers could have any kind of design painted or dyed onto the wings or bodies of their wings. He softened the blow by reminding all there was no limit to the number of birdman-soldiers and all birdmen could turn into such if they wanted to become proficient enough. This latter was to encourage any slackers who hung back to pick up the pace because deep inside, he intended *all* birdmen in Maya would eventually become birdmen-soldiers: the benefits of this were obvious.

CHAPTER 24

"Yes, I see him," Yvette admitted, "he's so beautiful, don't you think?" The Emperor sitting beside her didn't know if she was speaking of the birdman or his wings but in either case he agreed.

In time Inca was satisfied that the soldiers in the war-kaks had everything under control, and he screed three times, long and loud to get the attention of all of his birdmen. He swung his arm in a great circle over his head twice and gestured towards the city with a sweep of his hand; this was the signal for everyone to head back to their base, wherever it might be. He was surrounded by hoots and caws and squawks of every imaginable kind of bird, and the birdmen dispersed, their job done for now.

With all of his weapons and extra weight dropped, his wings were on the light side so he came towards the rooftop moving slowly and set down on the roof with the gentle ease of a dragonfly landing on a twig: he was down.

Men rushed forward and grabbed his wings and carried them off to one side because H'ratli was not far behind. The Prince was heavier and landed faster but with nearly the grace and precision of his leader; for one who had once been afraid of heights, he turned into a superb birdman, one whose accuracy rivaled Cuauhtémoc, a fact Cuauhtémoc both noted and gladly admitted. The two birdmen, safely on the rooftop, stopped and stared at each other and then of a single mind both tucked their thumbs into their armpits and flapping their elbows madly they began to circle left, squawking loudly, causing everyone within sight and hearing to break out laughing.

Cuauhtémoc greeted the Greatest Mayan with a deep bow and then moved in for a hug. He was now fifteen and had grown so much he could look the old man eye to eye. This didn't slow him down in the least when it came to hugs; he was as affectionate as he had always been; a thing the old Emperor hoped would always be.

He moved through the crowded rooftop, greeting everyone and being congratulated by all, but the entire time he was looking for two faces that seemed to be missing and then he saw one of them standing slightly behind the Greatest Mayan. "Yvette," he said and held his arms out; she needed no second invitation and she came quickly and willingly into his arms. He held her close and exchanged a quick kiss. "Where's Eilei?" he asked, mildly surprised to see the one and not the other because since the very first night they had almost always been a team.

"Can we talk?" she asked quietly.

"Sure; why not? But not just yet; let me get some of these loose ends tied off and then we can speak of anything you wish." She nodded, feeling she had at least made some headway for her sister, who was still down below; feeling miserable.

He made his report to Quoholocet and Imhoquotep, telling his two brothers things he notice while flying over the ships out in the harbor, and especially the pirate with the flamboyant green beard. Yvette, holding his left hand, gasped.

"My God; if that is the same Greenbeard who is the leader of the pirates, you have struck a powerful blow against them. Every king in Europe has a price on his head; and on the heads of all of his Captains;" Yvette said in liquid French.

"Yes, my heart, those are my thoughts exactly. But please remember not everyone here understands French and it is considered rude to close others out except in rare cases."

"Yes, of course, please forgive me;" she said in very good Mayan and then repeated what she said about Greenbeard and the price on his head.

"What are your thoughts on this; my son?" the Greatest Mayan asked politely.

"First we must make sure that it actually is the same Greenbeard that is wanted by all of the Crowns of Europe; there should be log books and other papers in his cabin to tell the truth of it. If it turns out to be so; then I believe that we should make every effort to send the heads to the King of Spain, or France and let them decide what to do with them. Since it will be a long voyage, we can take one of the powder kegs which have been emptied and fill it with heads and salt; that should take care of things until whichever king gets our little present. We can send a note along speaking that the Greatest Mayan has heard the king wishes these heads; so he has decided to send them to him. And then we shall mention if they have more pirates they can spare, please send them along as soon as possible, because The Birdman found these to be quite tasty and is now squawking for more." He nodded his head and pure mischief twinkled in his eyes.

Everyone, including Yvette, burst out laughing at Inca's suggestion but he wasn't done. "We will send this note with all the fancy flourishes and seals that the Kings over there like. If they get the heads and letter as intended they will understand their problem has been at least partially solved. And if somehow one pirate or another intercepts the heads and letter and reads it; the letter will perhaps give him second thoughts about approaching our shores with evil intent."

There was a prolonged silence as everyone digested this last thought and then there was a Clap! . . . Clap! . . . Clap! and the Greatest Mayan made it official. "You never stop thinking, do you Inca?" H'ratli asked; an expression of approval on his face.

He looked at his father and brothers and everyone else who was staring at him and shrugged his shoulders; "I don't start out to do things like this but sometimes I will get started down one road and find a detour that I end up liking even better."

People down on the edge of the bay started bringing prisoners and their belongings in: several years earlier when Maya first started to become known to the merchants of the world, the Greatest Mayan had a fairly large number of buildings made on the shore, up away from the water; these were intended for storage for both incoming and outgoing merchandise. Several of these were not in use at the moment and all weapons, gun powders and such were stored in one of these buildings and anything else of value was stored in yet another. It was now late fall, and at any time the rains could start in a more serious way than so far, and with the heavy rains, high winds often came and even as sheltered as the bay was by the jungle growing around it, it could still get some serious buffeting from time to time.

Cuauhtémoc turned to Yvette and smiled; touching her face tenderly. Her ancestors were one of the blueblood families of France and their bloodline happened to be quite tall by European standards. Still, the top of Yvette's head did not quite reach his chin, and he was still growing and would likely keep doing so for at least another three or four years: he would be very tall when he got his growth done. He lifted her chin and gently kissed her lips. "Now then, my heart, what did you wish to speak of?"

For a moment his nearness and gentle touch made her forget what she wanted but then Eilei's tear-stained face came to mind and she started explaining everything. He listened to her until she ran out of words; others in the area, sensing the two needed to be left alone, worked around them and ignored what was happening. "If you would just tell her what you have planned, maybe she would understand and not be so miserable," Yvette ended up.

He pulled her to him and gave her an affectionate hug and then gently held her back. "I have no plans, Yvette; beyond I intend to make both of you my wives. I have spoken to Father Inti, also called Viracocha and Les Bon Dieu, and have explained my heart to Him and I now await His decision. Sometimes I think we mortals make too many plans, setting things exactly so in our minds, as we labor for a specific goal. I also believe that Viracocha opens doors that we may walk through and reach our desires but the doors He opens are not always the ones we expect. If we spend all of our time watching the one door that we think is good; we often miss yet other doors which leads us to the same thing, but in a much better way; or sometimes, to a better thing entirely. I trust Father Inti and try my best to serve him in everyway I can, and wait on whatever His will may be. I don't know how this thing can possibly happen but I know it shall become so. Other than this I have just told you; I have no plans."

The next two days passed in relative quiet. All the lower ranking pirates were stripped naked, killed and their bodies rowed out beyond the bay, and dumped into the great waters beyond in what had now become the usual way of doing things. Those who looked to be of higher rank were herded off into escape-proof buildings and fed and guarded day and night until Prince Birdman told the guards what was to become of them. For the time being, Prince Birdman had his hands full with not only figuring out whose heads had to be sent where, but also, exactly who these people were. One thing was determined the same day the pirates attacked: the log book and journals of the pirate called Greenbeard was found and brought to The Birdman and since they were written in Spanish, he could easily read them. The pirate was a flamboyant egotist and Inca had absolutely no problem in determining this was indeed the one they believed.

Grief has a number of stages including Denial, Anger and Acceptance. Eilei managed to work her way through the first two in record time and fell prey to the last. She understood Inca, who she was now furious with, did not intend to lift a finger to save her because of something that had to do with honor and keeping his oath—but what about his oath to her? Eilei was suffering from teen-age angst, and at fourteen, she was old enough.

The next day the Lord Herdsman was due at midday to come and examine his prize and take her back to his own place so the wedding between Eilei and his son could take place according to plan. Cuauhtémoc looked up at Inti, hanging a fingernail's thickness above the distant mountain. He bowed to the sun; even though he now understood it was just a sun and not a god as he once supposed. "Father Viracocha," he said, "look upon my heart and see it is the same now as it was three years ago when I first asked about Eilei. I know you are busy with ordering the universe, which is now believed to be even larger than we thought, so I won't take up any more of your valuable time, other than to say whatever your will is I shall obey. But I must admit before you if she goes to that other, my arms and heart will miss her overmuch, and I thank you for listening to me now." He bowed deeply, touching his right knee to the ground and then stood up and went back into his room to read yet more in Greenbeard's ships' log and private journal.

The journal and logbook Greenbeard kept was mostly a list of all the places he had plundered as well as the people he had either personally killed or had killed; he either didn't always know the names of his victims or else they weren't important enough to him to write them down. In any case, it was a journal of death, and as Cuauhtémoc skimmed through the pages he wondered how a man's mind could become so calloused and evil, he could not only commit these crimes, but also brag about them endlessly in the pages of the ledgers he wrote. Inca knew without question any ruler in any land would seize such information and use it to both condemn the man as well as give justifiable reason to execute the notorious pirate.

He went to bed about his usual time and promptly fell asleep: he dreamed. Somehow, he was high in the air, overlooking a beautiful home that sprawled out with many pens filled with animals that teemed in the hundreds. He looked around and Eilei stood just to his right and Yvette was on his left; both women were older, perhaps in their late teens or early twenties and both were in the final stages of pregnancy and he knew both unborn were his. He awoke. It was early in the day of a moonless night and the darkness was only broken by faint reflections from the starry sky and oil lamps flickering feebly in the distance.

He got up; the dream fresh in his mind. He had taken a Spanish pistol off one of the pirates. The gun was unloaded because he didn't think much of guns as weapons; but he had been shown a trick he found to be very useful. He took a healthy pinch of black powder from a container and put it into a dish with some flammables, cocked the pistol and pressed the trigger; the hammer fell and sparks showered into the black powder which instantly flared up, catching the rest on fire. He took a small stick and let it blaze up and used the burning stick to light several candles.

The home with all of the pens was familiar to him because he had flown over it some days before, but at the time it was no more than another beautiful home, laid out to carefully blend in with the landscape. The home was a ranch of sorts, situated next to one of the arms that fed the river which flowed through the city, and there were pens that held many animals. Now, because of the dream, he knew who owned this home and he understood where his door was. He put a fresh piece of paper on one of the tripods and began to draw what he saw in his dream.

The tools he had to work with now were far superior to those of three years back. Much of Europe was in unrest, and because of this a great many of the intelligentsia moved to the City of Emperors, and because the climate, both physical and political appealed to them, they stayed. By now a small university had sprung up with the blessings of the Greatest Mayan, and just in the last year, even more scholars were flocking to what was rapidly becoming a new world center. In the process of these things he found and purchased an incredible array of pens; charcoals; brushes; paints in oil-base as well as water and many other artist supplies which made him very happy. He took up some of these and by the flickering light of three candles he began to draw the home and surroundings of his dream.

Time moved by on swift wings as it always did when he was fully occupied. By the time he was done he had a very nice picture that combined the best parts of his dream with those of the actual scene he had noticed when he'd flown over it some ten days in the past. He looked at his finished drawing and decided it was in many ways the best he had done yet, because this was the first serious work he ever made that was in color, instead of just black and white: the trees were green, the trunks were brown, the water was blue and other things in the picture were very close to what he had seen. He cleaned his pens and brushes and made sure that every jar had its proper lid tightly fitted; he climbed into the water and took a leisurely bath, got dressed and made ready to face both the day and the one who only thought he was taking Eilei away for his son.

"Um, Inca, I suppose you know Lord Herdsman is here for Eilei;" Prince Quoholocet said hesitantly. He watched Cuauhtémoc's face carefully; trying vainly to detect even the slightest trace of uncertainty.

"Yes; I know. I have spoken to Father Viracocha and he has opened my eyes to the door he has provided me," Cuauhtémoc said confidently, his oldest brother gave a sigh of relief and his face cleared of worry.

Cuauhtémoc disliked the Lord the moment he set eyes upon him. The man was too arrogant by half, and reminded him strongly of the Commander's brother, the one he abused so badly: he hoped this would not have to go quite that far.

Quoholocet; Imhoquotep; H'ratli; Cuauhtémoc and the seated Emperor met in the middle of a great hall. Eilei stood off to one side, flanked by Yvette on one side, and her mother on the other. She was not long from her tears and her face was puffy and her eyes red; she was nowhere near the beautiful maiden she usually was.

"Quoholocet, Imhoquotep, H'ratli; we're all here to hand your daughter over I see," the Lord Herdsman said tersely with only a token glance at the seated Emperor and his sons who stood directly before him.

"One moment," Cuauhtémoc said, breaking in; "how is it you speak to three Crown Princes in equals' speech, without honorific, or even a proper bow?"

"Who are you?" the Lord Herdsman asked in surprise.

"I am Crown Prince Cuauhtémoc, thought to be fourth in line for the Crown of Maya. I am also The Birdman, Prince of all birdmen, and birdman camps the length and depth of Maya. The thirteen pirate ships out in the bay were destroyed by my hand and by my command and I demand again; who are you to address Four Crown Princes as equals, without so much as an honorific, or even the most casual bow!" By now Cuauhtémoc was staring at the Lord with a look of cold anger.

"Forgive me Great Prince," he said to Cuauhtémoc, and then repeated it to his three brothers.

"Why have you not properly greeted our Greatest Mayan then?" he asked only slightly more civilly. The Lord Herdsman bowed deeply before his Emperor who nodded calmly back. He looked at Inca, and was already regretting coming here today, he would grab the girl and run; but when he faced her his stomach gave a lurch.

"What is wrong with that girl?" he demanded, and then remembering he had only just been taken to task, he respectfully added; "I mean, Great Prince, what is the matter with her face?"

Quoholocet looked at Inca. He looked calmly back at his brother and then nodded politely. "She has spent the last three days weeping, Lord Herdsman," Inca said; as he turned to face the Lord Herdsman. "Her problem is simple; she was given to your son five years ago when she was nine; but since then she has grown up and has fallen in love with someone else; in fact, she has fallen in love with me, and I with her. I now ask you to release my brother from his vow, because he will not break it otherwise, and it is in my heart to marry her: what are your words?"

The Lord Herdsman looked around and saw everyone was watching him. This young prince had only recently taken him to task; now was his chance to withhold some-thing from him he obviously wanted: "No; absolutely not; the wedding shall take place as planned."

"That is your final decision?"

"Yes; absolutely!"

"Wings Second; attend me please."

H'ratli loved being called 'Wings Second,' and he instantly responded, "Yes; Prince Birdman."

"You will remember three days ago about this time of day when thirteen pirate ships sailed into our harbor. We now know they intended to kill most of us and enslave the rest and take what is rightfully ours away from us. You will also remember how our birdmen-soldiers, working with ground forces, destroyed them in no more than a fist of the sun. While circling overhead I distinctly saw one of the men in your flight drop his entire load of fire-eggs out in the bay, well away from the fighting. The only reason I can think for this is he was afraid to attack and afraid of going back and landing with a full load; what is your opinion on this?"

As he spoke about dropping the eggs out into the bay Cuauhtémoc drew a half-circle in the air and then dropped his hand, palm-down, about half way. Among birdman signs, this meant that the previous message was a mistake, and to ignore it. H'ratli saw the motion and duplicated it; "He dropped his eggs in the bay and did not attack?" he asked cautiously.

"Yes, exactly," Inca said; again making the half-circle and hand-drop. "It was in my heart to have him beaten. And then I thought I would have his head shaved and his wings taken away, but all that the first would do is teach him fear of me, and since Maya needs all of the birdman-soldiers it can get, the second is also out.

"What I have decided is our birdmen need more practice with live eggs. How many do we have now, a hundred or so; do you know?" He made a small movement spiraling upward with his hand which meant 'more' and then extended his thumb and first finger and then an eye blink later added his middle finger.

"Oh, much more than that, Prince Birdman; perhaps two hundred or even three hundred;" H'ratli said, guessing what his brother wanted, and he guessed right.

"That many!" Cuauhtémoc said; obviously pleased. "This is what I wish to have done then. On one of my flights over the city, checking things out and making sure that all is well, as is part of my duties; I spotted a place off to the southwest. It is located next to one of the arms that feed our main river and a smaller stream forms a vee. There is a very nice ranch of sorts there; they seem to have a great many llamas in pens and a great field out towards a cleft in the mountain where an old tree sits half-dead. What I have decided is; we will start arming our birdmen with live eggs as well as the practice eggs that we have used all along. The tree is very distinctive and our birdmen will have no trouble picking it out; we shall stage attacks on this tree at different times of the day since we can't depend upon the enemy giving us advanced warning—"

"No, that cannot be, that is my place and I forbid it;" the Herdsman said with considerable heat until Cuauhtémoc fixed him with icy fury in his eyes.

"How *dare* you break into a private conversation between two Crown Princes; where did you learn your manners; in a bordello?" Cuauhtémoc snapped in rage.

"Greatest Mayan," the Lord Herdsman protested, but the Emperor was staring at him coldly.

"My Son Cuauhtémoc has my every confidence and if he says he must attack your alpacas then he must attack them—and I must say he is correct, you must have learned your manners in a bored hello, although I admit that I don't quite follow this."

Cuauhtémoc gave his father the benefit of his biggest smile and the look that he sent him was pure love. "I will explain everything as soon as I can, Father," he said; bowing deeply; the Emperor nodded his head and his expression was that of a doting father watching a favored child.

Yvette covered her mouth with a hand, fighting off the giggles and Eilei's expression oscillated between hope and despair. Eilei's mother watched things with wary eyes but she was beginning to smile and nod to herself.

"Forgive me, Greatest Mayan, forgive me Great Princes;" Lord Herdsman said; bowing deeply to each in turn, "I may be wrong-headed at times but even I can see when I have met my match: Prince Quoholocet; I release you from your oath." The Herdsman's shoulders slumped in defeat. "I have heard tales of your abilities in combat and I now know that they are true;" he said, speaking to Cuauhtémoc, "if you wish this girl for your wife I will not stand in your way. If the truth be told—and I mean no offense, Prince Quoholocet—my son does not wish to marry your daughter anyway; he's madly in love with the daughter of one of my servants: she's not even of blood. Please, I beg of you, do not drop your terrible weapons anywhere near my flocks, for my herds of alpacas are my one true vanity, and it would destroy me if they were harmed."

Cuauhtémoc nodded his head at the Herdsman, "It shall be as you say," he replied and then he turned to a nearby servant and beckoned him over. The servant bowed, approached, and listened intently as Cuauhtémoc spoke softly in his ear. He bowed deeply again and then backed up several paces before straightening up, and nudging another one to follow, they both walked out of the room.

Wildly conflicting emotions flitted across Eilei's face, and her mother stood nodding her head with a look of relief in her eyes; Yvette positively beamed at him and his Father and Brothers were staring at him as understanding came to them.

"I still believe that we need more practice with live eggs," he said thoughtfully, "but now that I think of it, very first pirate ship I burned to the water line and floated out of the bay, only to get caught in the eddy and circle for fists of the sun and finally wash up on shore, would be much better. It's closer, and being the remains of a ship, is more near what we need for a target anyway." He turned to H'ratli; "Actually, I'm surprised you didn't think of it," he said with just a hint of accusation in his voice.

"Forgive me, Prince Birdman, I just wasn't thinking;" H'ratli said apologetically.

"Quite all right Wings Second; you are so very much a great birdman and friend that this is a very small thing indeed." He bowed politely to H'ratli who returned it.

He turned to Eilei who was staring at him, her eyes wide with emotion. "It appears we shall be married after all," he said. She looked at him and started to rush forward but he held up his hand, stopping her before she was well begun. "I want you to go back to your own place now and see if you can find your pretty face, the face I so adore looking at, because I must say I don't like the one you now wear—go now," and he pointed.

"Yes, Inca, yes; I'll go and find my pretty face," she said, and quickly turned and left. Eilei's mother stared at The Birdman in amazement and Yvette covered her mouth with both hands to stifle giggles. "You too, my heart," he told her and waved her on; she curtsied in the supple manner she had, then scooted down the hallway, her progress marked by a string of feminine giggles with a distinct French flavor.

He shook his head and turned to the others in the room; "Girls are the strangest creatures; when they get into one of their moods they either need to be loved or spanked, and it doesn't seem to matter to them which, just as long it is something . . . how odd."

CHAPTER 25

"My son would never have been able to handle her like you do, Birdman. I mean no disrespect to my offspring but it is the truth. If I may ask; you wouldn't have actually, um, gone ahead with what you said you were going to do; you were just trying to shake me up; isn't that right?"

"It has long been my practice to learn all about a potential enemy that I can; or anyone else that I may have to face in any form of fighting; and that includes learning all about you and your love for your home and your alpacas. If you had taken my heart from me I would have most certainly taken yours; by the time I and my birdmen were done dropping fire eggs on your herds you would have not had even one left alive. I admit I am not a gracious loser; in fact, failure is not an option with me no matter who I face.

"On a much happier note I wish to tell you I have seen your place from the air several times as I have flown around the city and I can say with conviction yours is one of the loveliest. Because I know you are unable to fly I have taken the liberty of drawing your place up. I intended to use it as a training guide for my birdmen if you failed me, but since you were so quick to see reason, it shall be my great pleasure to gift it to you." He turned to the two servants who were just coming into the room, carrying the drawing between them, the back to the Herdsman as Cuauhtémoc instructed them. They turned it around at

The Birdman's nod and the Herdsman saw his own home and fields as it looked from the air for the first time: the Lord Herdsman looked at him and tears began to form.

"I have been told I make a very dangerous enemy, Lord Herdsman, but I like to believe I make a better friend." He held his hand out and the man looked at it. He was originally from the southern part of Maya and knew very well what the gesture meant. At first cautiously and then with greater confidence he took Cuauhtémoc by the wrist and gripped firmly.

"I see that everything I have ever heard about you is true, and you may count me among your most devoted admirers," the Lord Herdsman said.

"I am pleased to hear you say that, Lord Herdsman, because I have always believed a man cannot have too many friends or too few enemies. Please feel free to take this painting to your own home and set it up wherever you will. My only caution is the paints I used are water based: this means they dry quickly; but they will not tolerate water being splashed upon them."

"Thank you Prince Birdman. Even I can see this all worked out for the best for everyone. If I may, I would like to leave now, and take this home with me."

Cuauhtémoc bowed slightly and two of the Herdsman's servants carefully picked up the picture and carried it toward the exit while their Lord followed them like a nervous hen watching her brood.

Within a very few heartbeats he was surrounded by his three brothers. "I almost began to wonder if just this once you would be unable to do as you claimed but not only were you able to make our Lord Herdsman change his mind—and he is notoriously

hard-headed about such things—you managed to let him leave a very happy man: my feathers are off to you, my brother," Quoholocet said and took his headdress from his head and bowed politely.

"So—when is this marriage supposed to take place?" Imhoquotep asked.

"I'm not sure," Inca admitted. "In my home village, when a man and a woman decide to be a couple, she will move into his hut with him or some such thing and they are considered mated. The opposite is also true, if they decide that they no longer like each other, one or the other will move out; this last thing does not happen very often but it has been known to."

"You villagers have all the luck," Quoholocet admitted in admiration.

"What are your wishes, Father?" he asked politely, "there is one thing I must insist; no matter which girl I marry first, the other will have her feelings hurt, and she will feel resentment: the only way I can see to avoid this is to marry both at the same time; then they can be mad at me instead of each other."

"Both at once?" Quoholocet demanded in disbelief.

"Sure; I'm up to it;" he glanced below his navel and then lifted his eyes back up at his oldest brother. "Yeah;" he said and his eyes darted first left and then right and back again in quick movements. This was a thing he learned from Son of Spain nearly three years earlier and the beauty of it was; it was useful in many situations, and those who saw it, immediately understood. Everyone burst out laughing and the Greatest Mayan held his arms out for a hug which Inca promptly gave him.

Once he got the loose ends tied up with his father and brothers—he was a Crown Prince and there was no way he was going to get off with moving in with two girls: there was going to be a ceremony and a feast and that was the end of the discussion—he headed back to his own room, only to be waylaid by his wives-to-be.

"When are we to be married, Inca; how soon can we be wed? I think after we have been married for six months or so you should be able to marry Yvette," Eilei said brightly, earning a venomous glare from her best friend.

"I have been speaking with the Greatest Mayan and your father about this, and they have decided it will be in three or four days, and I shall be the first to tell you two the best part; I shall be marrying you both at the same time."

"What? No! We don't want to be married at the same time;" both girls insisted as one. Cuauhtémoc not only expected this reaction; he was counting on it.

"Why not?" he demanded: "Yvette; I remember you telling me the young girls of France learn of such things by listening to their mothers and older sisters and then practice on each other: it seems to me, Eilei, that you learned how to kiss very well, very quickly and I am now wondering what else you two have been practicing. Being male and your future husband this is very interesting to me, perhaps you would like to—"

"What? No! We haven't been doing anything;" the two said, speaking as one.

"Hm . . . why are you holding your hands behind you; what are you hiding?"

"We're not hiding anything," the two said, again speaking with a single voice.

"I wonder now," he said and moved around behind them; their hands immediately went to their fronts: he reached down and caressed both bottoms with a possessive touch.

"Eilei; Yvette; Prince Inca; what is going on here?" Mother serving-woman, Kymeninie and another girl whose name he didn't yet know were standing with trays of food, staring at the three in surprise. The new girl had taken Zypolitc's place because she and Inca's guardsman had decided to make their lives combined and at the moment she was in the final stages of the big tummy syndrome and unable to carry much else.

"I am checking these two girls over to make sure they have nothing hidden upon them, Mother serving-woman," Inca said matter-of-factly.

"Hidden? The way those two girls are dressed they couldn't hide a copper coin between them. Besides; what are you doing here anyway, Eilei, you are supposed to be down meeting Lord Herdsman; this is the day you are to marry his son; how could you forget that?"

"You have a good point Mother serving-woman; these two girls couldn't possibly have anything hidden on them. And for your information, Eilei is not going to marry the Lord Herdsman's son; both girls are going to marry me at the same time. I have waited three years for this; and my patience is worn thin. If they don't stop pushing their fronts out at me; something unseemly is going to take place right here in the middle of the hallway." He gave the girl's bottoms a final stroke which they liked very much, if they were cats, both would be purring.

The three older women broke out in laughter and both girls started to giggle; everyone knew that Inca was teasing but there always was an uncertainty factor. "There is quite a story behind this, Mother serving-woman, perhaps you and your helpers would like to come into my room and we six shall eat together while I tell the tale to you. This way, when you return to the kitchens you may tell one or two of the other workers, providing you wish to do so." He grinned good-naturedly at them and they laughed all the more because he was well aware he was frequently the topic of gossip.

Prince Cuauhtémoc kept very busy the next three days; not that he was usually idle. Greenbeard regained consciousness but he was now profoundly deaf and utterly dazed. The exploding powder barrels had either robbed his mind of reason or the impact with the wall behind him; in any case he was useless for information and Cuauhtémoc beheaded him and had his body rowed out of the bay and left for the sharks; which by now should be getting fat on the likes of him.

The rest of the pirates who were still alive were interrogated one by one. In each case the pirate was given a drink of Cuauhtémoc's concoction and before long each spilled his guts; naming names, dates, places and victims. It was not a happy time but Cuauhtémoc listened intently and he had people from other lands who were good at writing, and such information was compiled into English, Spanish, Portuguese and French, all to be bound up into four packages to be spent to the respective kings because most of this was taking place in their waters and The Birdman did not question the kings of these nations could make good use of the information.

The Mayan understood mummification since they used this process on their dead Emperors and other notables. As each pirate leader was drained of useable data they were taken out, still under the influence of drugs, since Cuauhtémoc had long since gotten properly-harvested willbane, and their heads were removed from their bodies and mummified in preparation for the long ocean voyage back to the lands of their birth.

The fourth day arrived and Prince Cuauhtémoc dressed up in his finest clothes and feathers and headed towards the throne room. The Mayan people did not have much in the way of ceremony for a wedding; there was no 'dearly beloveds' going on. Generally, the woman would walk out of one doorway and the man out of a different doorway, the two would convene before whoever was witnessing the event: the pair would meet, bow before the witness and then leave together through yet a third door. The Maya people were very practical about things; getting married was nice and all of that, but there was food waiting on tables, and food once cold, was not as tasty: with a French girl involved who had different ideas; it was not going to be that easy.

Someone would have to give her away. Cuauhtémoc thought H'ratli might work for a substitute father, providing he didn't change his mind and decide to keep her for himself. Both girls were nervous wrecks by the time it was over but that was just pre-wedding jitters. Prince Cuauhtémoc thought the entire thing silly and the people in his own village had the right of it but because both girls were so wrapped up in it, he smiled, nodded his head and went along with things as males have since the dawn of time: weddings were definitely dreamed up by a woman; somewhere; somewhen.

What finally took place was Cuauhtémoc walked through the open door that led to the throne room, past the sword in the door and towards the throne. About halfway up, a white quartz circle, two steps in width had been inlaid into the grey stone floor; this was the place from where Inca had thrown the sword. The Emperor was so enamored of the deed he had Cuauhtémoc retrace his steps of that day. Considering his memory, he placed the spot where he'd thrown the sword within a thumb's width of where he had stood, and the Greatest Mayan put his stone masons to work; it actually looked very nice and even those who had not heard the story thought it attractive; what they thought of a sword sticking out of a door was a different thing entirely.

Eilei, her hand on Quoholocet's arm and sided by Yvette whose hand was on H'ratli's arm, followed him up the way. Prince Inca stopped before his father and bowed very deeply. The Greatest Mayan nodded at his son. Once this was done the two girls on the arms of their fathers came up and one girl was left on either side of him and both fathers bowed before the Emperor, and left, their duty done.

The Greatest Mayan sat on his throne, wearing his Royal robes and held the scythe and scepter in the proper hands but without the gold sun-mask. "My son; are you sure you want to take these two girls for your wives?" he asked softly.

"Yes, Father, I do;" he replied.

"It shall be as you wish; they are yours. By Mayan lore a man must never beat his wife with a switch larger than his smallest finger. I offer you this advice; never use one smaller. You may, um, what am I supposed to say next Imhoquotep?" the Emperor asked his son who stood immediately to his right.

"That he may now kiss the brides, Father," Imhoquotep said respectfully.

"You may now kiss them both," the Emperor said, with a smile on his wizen face.

Cuauhtémoc looked up at his father and noticed anew how truly old he was looking; and his mind and hearing was not what it was even a year ago; but with the old man's words a solution to his dilemma popped into his mind. He turned to his wives who were already moving into position for their very first kiss from their new husband. "Do you remember when you two were first in the water together, how you had your faces pressed against each other?"

The two looked at him blankly;

"Here, bring your faces to together . . . yes, just a little more, let the corners of your lips touch . . . turn just a bit more . . ." and then he leaned forward and kissed both of his new brides at the same time in what turned out to be a three-way kiss. For a moment neither girl understood and then in the same instant both did and the kiss became fairly long and approached torrid. "I think that shall be enough for now or we're going to embarrass ourselves before everyone."

The Greatest Mayan clapped his hands together slowly three times and spoke; "You and your wives are now married, and I can see you have again taken an impossible situation and solved it in a way that is obvious, once it has been seen; go my Son and enjoy your feast; I find that I have other things I must attend so I will offer my congratulations now." Cuauhtémoc left his wives and walked up to his Emperor and as he had done many times in the past he knelt before him and cupping his left foot in his hands he pressed his face against the Greatest Mayan's arch.

He rose with the effortless ease he had and bowed deeply to his Emperor. "The happiest years of my life have been here with you and my brothers and I look in my heart and find I lack the words to say how much it has pleased me: thank you Greatest Mayan, thank you, Father." He bowed deeply again and without straightening up he backed up several paces before he stood erect and turned and took his wives, one under each arm and walked towards the food, chatting happily with them.

The Emperor looked first at one son to his left and then the one on his right; "Does he know; does Cuauhtémoc suspect anything?" he asked anxiously.

"He . . . doesn't seem to Father," H'ratli said hesitantly, but deep in his heart he knew better because he had never been able to get anything past Inca . . . ever!

The newlyweds walked out the doors and made a right and down to the dining area where the staff had laid out a banquet fit for a king, or in this case, a Prince who had just become married. They walked into the dining area and were immediately mobbed by well-wishers who remembered Cuauhtémoc was a Prince and deserving of certain respect. Eilei beamed and waved at everyone but Yvette was more subdued. "Why wouldn't the Emperor come with us; what could be so important to keep him away?"

"Ssh! I'll explain later;" he hissed at her; and Eilei who heard the question and turned to hear the answer.

The three mixed with Lords and their wives and others who wished the newlyweds well but were more interested in eating at the Emperor's expense. No one actually expected the three to stay around until the last dog was hung so when they made their excuses and left, the rest exchanged knowing smirks, and went back to the business of stuffing their faces.

The three returned through the throne room but by now it was empty except for the occasional servant wandering through; he had his arms around his wives and pulled their heads close in what looked to be a fond embrace. "It has now been ten days since I've seen the Greatest Mayan doing anything but sitting, and eleven days ago when I did see him on his feet, Imhoquotep and H'ratli were on either side, holding him up as he walked. I don't know exactly how old he is now but he must be close to eighty. My personal diagnosis as the grandson of the Great Healer is he is languishing—he is becoming increasingly frail—but he is trying to hide it from me because he doesn't want me to worry; what with everything else that is going on. I must tell you this with all sincerity; when he passes on into the spirit world, you two must be strong for me, because when that sad day arrives I will have no strength of my own." His wives looked on his face and they could see tears coursing down his cheeks and his lips tremble: both hugged him and kissed him and tried their best to be strong for him then and there.

They reached his room and opened the door and stepped inside. While they were getting married and feasting, servants were busy rearranging his room. The place was decked out with what looked to be hundreds of flowers of every sort, and an equal number of feathers, some in clumps and others lying around singly. The pallet he usually slept on was gone and a larger pallet that looked able to sleep ten comfortably lay in its place and it was tidily covered with an enormous alpaca wool covering with a small note written in Mayan—not pictographs but the new writing—saying it was a gift from Lord Herdsman, and scattered everywhere were small gifts and arrangements; some of which unquestionably came from his birdmen. As they stared about the room they started to laugh and as they laughed, the door, which was counterweighted to close on its own, quietly shut and what happened afterwards behind closed doors was nobody's business but their own.

Fall weather slowly gave way to winter. As close to the equator as Maya was, all this meant was it rained more often, and it was more often windy and what passed locally for cold. In time that gave way to the approaching spring and within five weeks, his sixteenth birthday. Normally, turning sixteen was a joyous occasion for any teenager, any place and any time but Cuauhtémoc was increasingly sad. The Greatest Mayan had stopped pretending and now it was understood throughout the palace if not the entire city that his days were dwindling down.

Cuauhtémoc made sure he stopped in to visit his Father at least once every day and sometimes more often. What seemed to make the old man the happiest was hearing his son tell tales of attacking pirates. Inca had stone workers come in and bore holes in the stone ceiling at specific spots and eye-bolts carefully fastened so there was no possible way they could come loose. He then attached pulleys to the bolts and had strong ropes attached to the four corners of the dying emperor's bed. When four burly guardsmen pulled on the ropes just so, the bed would rise up off the floor, and could be swung about in fairly generous arcs. He would push and pull the bed about while telling the Emperor stories; making believe that he, the Emperor, was diving and swooping about and this pleased the old man in ways that were incredible.

The sad day came when a servant came rushing up to Prince Cuauhtémoc and whispered frantically in his ear, Cuauhtémoc immediately dismissed the people he was talking to and turned and left; hurrying as fast as he could to his father's side.

"Where is he? Where is Cuauhtémoc? You said he was coming;" a querulous voice demanded from his father's room. He stopped on the very edge of the doorway and tears began to form. He threw his head back; "K-e-e-e-r!" the wild, sweet sound echoed and re-echoed throughout the room.

"Cuauhtémoc, is that you, Son?" the failing Emperor asked eagerly.

"Yes, Father, the pirates have come! They have followed two merchant ships into our bay; we must fly!" He looked at the four muscular guardsmen who stood with ropes in hand and nodded, they pulled as one and the Emperor, bed and all came up off the floor knee-high on Inca. "We must act quickly, Father, or the pirates will kill innocents again: but what can we use for a weapon?"

"Oil," the Emperor said; a broad smile on his wrinkled face.

"Yes, the very thing; thank you Greatest Mayan, you have once again helped the fight against evil; oil it is—we must fly!" He pushed the bed to one side and back again and the old man laughed in joy. "Be ready to dive, Father, we must hit the rear mast with the goatskin of oil; are you ready to drop?"

"Yes, drop," the old man said; the men on the ropes lifted the foot of the bed upwards while others lowered the head; Cuauhtémoc moved the bed in a twisting motion and the Emperor laughed in delight.

The guards moved with practiced ease and the bed rose and fell and twisted and skewed about and somewhere along the way the Emperor's voice became still. Cuauhtémoc stopped the bed from moving and gestured to lower it to the floor; he looked upon the face of the Greatest Mayan but the Emperor's eyes were open and unfocused and Cuauhtémoc knew his Father was now on a different kind of flight, the kind that has no landing point in the physical realm. He gently drew his hand across the dead man's face, closing his eyes, and then he knelt beside the bed and took the dead hand in his and kissed the palm again and again, saying the kisses were to tide him through his journey into eternity. He put the Emperor's hand on his stomach because the Mayan believed there was great power there; he bowed his head and wept. "How shall your people survive without your love and wisdom to guide them; how shall I survive?"

He rose with tears in his eyes and turned to face his brothers; the three of them stood several paces away from the foot of their father's bed with Quoholocet forming the apex of a triangle; they stared at him and they also had tears in their eyes. Of course; the Greatest Mayan was their father before he became Inca's. Quoholocet held his arms out and Cuauhtémoc fled into his brother's embrace and wept bitter tears on his shoulder. He was almost as tall as his brothers now and they surrounded him and held him while his eyes flowed like rivers.

He had always known that the Emperor must die. Because of that, he had been prepared, but now the time had come he was defenseless. In time the worst was over and he backed away from his brothers and bowed deeply before Quoholocet, who was the oldest. "I have always obeyed the wishes of our father, and now that he is no more, I shall obey yours." He bowed very deeply again, almost bringing his right knee to the floor.

"He doesn't know; does he?" Prince Quoholocet asked quietly.

"Not a clue, and usually he's quite sharp about things," Imhoquotep admitted.

"Well; personally, I've never gotten anything past him," H'ratli injected; "and Father Inti knows I've tried."

"I guess if we must, we must," Quoholocet declared; speaking to his two brothers.

"Yes; let's," Imhoquotep added.

"Quick now, while he's still in shock, if we're fast we'll get him before he bolts for the door;" H'ratli said: "Here, Inca, hold this please;" and he handed him the gold scythe; Inca looked down at his hand blankly. "No; the other hand my brother, always remember the scythe goes in the left hand, it is the scepter that is held by the right." As H'ratli spoke Imhoquotep put the gold scepter in his right. Quoholocet circled Inca and put the Royal cloak upon his shoulders while he stared around in confusion.

"If we're quick enough, we'll get this done before he wakes up," H'ratli said; then Quoholocet put the Headdress of the Greatest Mayan on his head; it had been altered to his size and it fit perfectly.

"It is we who shall obey you, our brother," Quoholocet said and all three bowed deeply before him. "Actually, we've pretty much been doing that since the day you flew into our lives . . . or did you know that already?"

"I can't be Emperor;" Cuauhtémoc said as understanding came to him; "I'm only fourth at best, and besides, I'm not even blood."

Prince Quoholocet stared at Inca sternly. "It is the final will of our father that you shall replace him as our Emperor and it is the will of the three of us as well. You have always obeyed the Greatest Mayan; do you intend to disobey him now?" The room held a fairly large number of guards and servants as well as the Royal Healer who was inching his way to the door: he now stood, staring, with a look of utter horror on his face.

"I spoke an oath to Father Inti and swore I would obey the Greatest Mayan until I die. I cannot disobey him, not even in death, for Father Inti reminds me of my vow;" he said and he turned and bowed deeply to the still form on the bed.

CHAPTER 26

The door swung open and three of the Sun Priests swept into the room. In the last year or so silk became more common, and from the looks of these three, the Sun Priests had been able to get more than their fair share. The three located Quoholocet and from that moment they ignored everyone else. "We heard of your great loss, Prince Quoholocet, and we priests share your sorrow. We Priests will, of course, support you as our new Emperor and will crown you with all due ceremony. Even as we speak our brothers are combing the countryside seeking only the very best chil—

"What's this? No; you shall not be our Emperor; we forbid it!" The speaker for the group saw Cuauhtémoc standing, studying them like a cat watching a rat, and the speaker reached out to yank the Royal Headdress off of Cuauhtémoc's head, not unlike the Commander's brother had tried some four years earlier. The results were predictable and very similar; as the priest reached towards Cuauhtémoc, he stabbed forward with the scepter lightly, and struck the man in the solar plexus; the spot directly under the sternum of the chest. The priest's air whooshed out of suddenly limp lips and he sagged down to his knees.

"Cute, very cute, I understand completely. I despise it; but I do understand. You 'confirm' the crown upon the wearer, thereby leaving the impression you have the authority to do so. And if you have the power to 'confirm' the crown, that by implication, gives you the right to take it away. The very first time the Emperor speaks in a way you disapprove of; you threaten him with this very thing—very cute indeed."

The new Greatest Mayan looked about the room. The Royal Healer was watching things with growing dread and just now started inching his way towards the door once again. "You; guardsmen," Cuauhtémoc snapped, gesturing with his left hand which still held the gold scythe; "you shall not let anyone leave this room until I tell you otherwise: fail me in this and your lives are forfeit. Do you understand?"

"Yes, Greatest Mayan," the guardsmen said and presented their spears; from the grim looks on their faces, anyone who managed to get out the door would have to do it through them, because they were determined it would not be around.

"I have yet other patients who wait on me, Greatest Mayan, they will sicken and die if I do not get back to them soon;" the healer protested.

Cuauhtémoc stared at the healer; "Liar!" he said; "you only had one patient to care for and he is dead." As the words left his mouth thoughts popped into his head, and as each arose from within, the expression on his face grew darker: he stood and glanced about.

"Well, we can see that we've come at a bad time," one of the priests said.

"Shut up;" he snapped; "no one in this room is to speak until I say otherwise." He looked over and saw an apprehensive expression on his brother's faces. "None of these commands apply to Crown Princes, of course," he added and a look of relief came over them.

Impressions swept through his mind one after another and he liked none of them. He looked around his father's bedroom. It was huge even by Mayan standards and furnished with the most beautiful furniture, rugs and other things as befitted the Emperor of a large and incredibly wealthy empire. As he looked around his eyes kept coming back to the old man lying so still upon his bed. His eyes did not want to look there because it reminded him of his recent loss; a loss he was not yet beginning to heal up from—but *why* must he look there? Instead of fighting it; he walked over and started looking around carefully. His father lay still. Nearby, was a nightstand of sorts with a few objects on it for the Emperor's use, including a goblet made of thinly-hammered gold. He switched the scepter to his left hand, with the scythe, reached out and picked the goblet up; it was still half-full of the wine his father favored in his last years—that couldn't be it; could it? He raised the cup to his nose and sniffed the contents carefully and in a blink he knew what was wrong from the beginning. He sensed it earlier but his mind was unable to put a name to it. He raised the goblet to his mouth and took a careful taste, rolled the liquid around in his mouth and spit it out onto the floor. He turned and stared at the Royal Healer who was sweating in fear.

"It is known as *takalak* and it is a flower found in the mountain regions. Takalak is a well-regarded pain reliever because it doesn't cloud the mind when given in standard dosages; about enough powdered flower to cover a thumbnail's area in the palm of one's hand, wouldn't you say, Healer?" His words were very courteous but the man's expression became even more frightened. "Yes; I thought you'd agree; about a thumbnail's worth in a cup and most pains will be gone for many fists of the sun. The thing that puzzles me is; I've never heard my father complain of pains." He turned and stared at his three brothers who were watching him with unwavering intent. "What of you, have you ever heard our father complain of pains, my brothers?"

"Never," Quoholocet said promptly, "but then; Father rarely ever complained about anything."

"As the Royal Healer, I was privy to—"

Cuauhtémoc swung around to face the man and his expression was that of a carnivore about to pounce. "What part of 'shut up' do you not understand?" he snapped and his eyes seemed to shoot sparks.

He turned to his brothers and his look was that of love. "I have never disobeyed our father in anything and I have never disobeyed you who are my brothers and I am not about to start now. But I find that I have something to do, so if you will be so kind," and he held out the scythe and scepter. As these were taken from his hands he shed the feathered cloak and headdress and stood as he was before was crowned Emperor.

"Yes, takalak is a marvelous plant. A single thumb's nail on the palm of one's hand will relieve almost any pain for many hours; two such dosages will eliminate all known pains. **Ten** such dosages would put the healthiest man into a deep sleep and ten such dosages, given to an old man who is weak, would unquestionably stop his heart . . . don't you agree?" he said, turning to the healer. He again took the cup in his hand; now he threw the contents forcibly into the face of the man and his eyes were brittle: he held the cup in his right hand and stared at it.

He had a powerful, rangy body and had just recently started what would turn out to be his final growth spurt and his fingers were quite long. His hand wrapped around the cup and his knuckles turned white and in a few brief heartbeats he crushed the goblet in on itself—gold is a soft metal and it was hammered thin, but still—. "No one shall ever drink out of this cup again," he said and dropped it to clang metallically onto the stone floor; he had just destroyed his father's favorite cup but under the circumstances it hardly seemed important. He turned and stared thoughtfully at his three brothers.

"My only question now is; did our father actually drink of this cup? This is a thing that must be resolved before I know what to do with 'that one;'" and he indicated the disgraced healer with a thrust of his jaw.

He walked over to where the dead monarch lay. He bowed deeply before the body. "Please forgive me Father for what I am about to do." He bent over and tried to smell the old man's breath, but without breathing, it proved impossible. He placed the heel of his left hand on the middle of his father's chest, moving his father's hand out of the way for it was almost over his heart. He pressed down vigorously and then tried to get a quick sniff in but it didn't work. He repeated this several times, finally pushing down very hard with both hands in quick succession but to no avail. "Again, forgive me Father," he said respectfully and he pinched his father's nose shut and pulling his jaw down he put his lips against those of his father and blew several times, trying to get a scent; the last time he took the deepest breath yet and exhaled it all into his father's lungs. This time when he sniffed quickly he caught the faint but familiar smell he sought. "Takalak;" he said; "most definitely."

He turned and stared thoughtfully at his three brothers who were glaring at the disgraced one.

"You will remember a few years back when we first discovered just how many spies and thieves Hezaraht had been able to infiltrate into the palace. You will also recall the 'untouchable' list we were able to learn of. As you no doubt remember, 'that one'—and he did a chin-jut at the healer—was most definitely on the 'untouchable' list. It now seems somewhere along the way Hezaraht found 'that one's' price. Or was able to otherwise threaten him . . . or whatever.

Cuauhtémoc turned to the three priests. "What I now wish to know is exactly how you three got into the palace when all of my guards have strict orders to not admit any of your kind, and since I'm on the subject, how did you know the Greatest Mayan was dead? He left this world less than a thumb before you arrived and it would have been impossible for a messenger to have notified you and still give you time to get here. You; you shall answer my question," and he indicated his choice by pointing at him with his left forefinger.

"The Sun Priests have a power that you cannot imagine—" the spokesman for the group started to say, and then Cuauhtémoc took a few quick steps and buried the instep of his right foot between the priest's legs. The man groaned in agony and doubled up and lay on the floor in a fetal position.

"Power that!" He said calmly; "you are very stupid. I was not speaking to you; I made it very clear you were not to speak; and you spoke anyway. And the only power that you priests have I cannot imagine is the power to do evil.

"Brothers, attend me—you as well, Captain. I know I am growing older, and perhaps my memory is not as sharp as it once was, but did I not command Hezaraht and his priests to never enter this palace again?

I also seem to remember speaking that I would spare Hezaraht's life only as long as he left the children and the Greatest Mayan alone. Now; I learn Hezaraht has evidently not only taken it upon himself to start rounding up children for yet another bloodbath, he has conspired to murder our father and presumed he would place the throne of Maya under his direct control. I find this intolerable: what are your thoughts?"

"From the look on your face, I would say the same as yours," Quoholocet said with a bow; like his brothers his face was dark with anger. The Greatest Mayan looked around and every face there—excluding priests and healer of course—also showed anger.

"Then it is settled. Captain; nearly four years back I took your sword without asking because I was in a hurry; this time I shall ask politely for the use of your blade."

"It is my pleasure, Greatest Mayan," he said and promptly drew his sword from his sheath and presented it to Cuauhtémoc, the flat of the blade laying on the palms of his bare hands, the hilt to Inca's right. He gripped the hilt and waited for the Captain to remove his hands from the sharp edges of the blade: he turned.

The healer had long since been tied to a chair and a rag stuffed into his mouth because in his fear, he wouldn't stop trying to escape, and he wouldn't stop lying to protect himself. He saw Cuauhtémoc approaching him with a naked blade in hand and he began to bounce up and down in the chair like a puppet controlled by a spastic hand. But the Emperor was not interested in the terrified man. He walked up to several cane chairs sitting off to one side; he chose one that looked to be the worst of the batch and attacked it with the sword. In a few careful strokes he reduced the chair to a pile of pieces and splinters. He returned the sword back to the Captain in the same manner as it was handed to him; "Thank you Captain; that will do nicely."

He beckoned one of the guards over and he started picking up splinters, showing them to the guard as he did so. "Do you see the size of these, guardsman, do you believe you can find more of this size for me; perhaps even make more if I need them?"

"Yes, Greatest Mayan, I can easily do this thing for you."

"Most excellent;" he said and patted the guard on the shoulder fondly; he turned with the few splinters he kept.

"This is an amazing thing Viracocha has done. When I was seven, my father walked out into the jungles to hunt, and never returned. Not long afterwards a man wandered in from a different direction with a sliver of cane up under his fingernail; a splinter that looked very much like this in fact;" and he held one up for all to see.

"Now this is where it gets interesting. My grandfather gave him a double potion of takalak to ease his pain—in fact; it is the takalak given to our father which reminded me of this entire thing. I won't bore you with the details because they do not apply. What does matter was the agony I saw on the man's face. He begged my grandfather to cut his finger off but grandfather refused—and that is also a different story. The thing I want to stress is the suffering I saw in that one's eyes. Being young and curious about such things I always wondered if pain is cumulative, that is, does it grow with each additional dose? Or does it reach a threshold and from there on not hurt so very much?"

He turned to the three priests and stared at them. "Now; one of you lucky ones shall get the chance to tell me if this is so. This is the rules of the game: I shall ask a question—not you though, because you've already had some pain, and it gives you unfair advantage. I shall ask a question. If I do not like the answer, in other words if I believe you are lying to me, I shall insert one of these slivers under one of your fingernails. Once we have run out of fingers, we will start in on the toes, and if that still doesn't work we will find yet other places on your body to experiment on;" and he gave a thoughtful look at the priest's crotches. "On the other hand; if I like your answer, in other words, if I think that you speak the truth; then I will not put the splinter anywhere.

"Let me see—yes, I think you will do nicely to start with," and he chose the priest who looked the most frightened.

He held the sliver of his choice in his right hand and reached out with his left and took the priest's right hand in his. Two Royal Guardsmen closed in on his victim and he chose a finger at random; it turned out to be the middle finger.

"Please don't hurt me Greatest Mayan;" the Sun Priest wailed in fear, "this is all the doing of Hezaraht. He bribed the Healer with the offer of all the gold that five strong men can carry and even showed him the gold in our vaults. He was to gradually weaken the Emperor over several weeks, but either the Emperor was stronger than the Healer believed, or else the Emperor didn't take the entire potion he should. When weeks turned into months, Hezaraht informed the Healer it must be done soon, and he finally spoke it must be done today, by this time, and the Healer said he would do it and Hezaraht ordered us to come here and see if it was done, and if it were so we were to confirm Quoholocet as Emperor and then we were to discover it was a murder and we were to attack and kill the Healer in outrage unless the guards beat us to it andpleasedon'thurtme GreatestMayanbecaus eI'mafraidofpain."

Cuauhtémoc stared at the terrified priest interestedly. He glanced over to where his brothers stood; "Did you three get all of that, especially the last where he was speaking so fast?" The three nodded their heads; they also had very intrigued looks on their faces.

"What of you, Healer, did you understand all of that? Especially the part where these three had orders to 'discover' you murdered the Greatest Mayan and then kill you? You did catch that; didn't you? I can see it in your eyes. As you have just learned, crawl into bed with a serpent, and you shall surely get bitten."

He turned his attention back to the priest. "I like you; you know I really do. Just for that I'm not going to stick a sliver into you this time. "My next question is: how did you three get into the palace? And kindly do not try to lie to me and tell me of the great powers the Sun Priests have, and how you can walk through walls and things like that, because I will most definitely not like that answer."

"Seek, seek, secret pas, pas, passage wa, wa, way."

"Secret passageway?" Cuauhtémoc asked politely; the priest nodded his head so furiously it looked as though it might fly off his shoulders at any moment.

"I'm starting to like you more all the time, priest, you keep up the good work and you just might discover you are still alive when the dust settles." He turned to his brothers: "Quoholocet, as Commander of the Palace Guards, I would be very pleased if you would round up every available man you can. I want double guards on every external entryway; the rest are to arm them-selves with whatever weapon they can lay hands on and report back here as quickly as possible. And by the way; if you should see Son of Spain wandering around, lonely and bored, do invite him and his Precious to come along. I think it is about time we go and remind Hezaraht of my vow, since not only has he managed to not leave the children alone, he has also managed to not keep his hands off our father."

"By your command, Greatest Mayan," Quoholocet said with a deep bow and immediately turned to the Captain of the Guards: "Do you understand what your orders are; Captain?" he demanded.

"Yes; Prince Quoholocet. Yes; Greatest Mayan." The captain of the royal guards turned towards the door and stopped. The door guards had been commanded to not let anyone through, and as they saw their orders, it included princes and captains. They glanced at Cuauhtémoc; unsure of what to do.

"A little less than four years ago, not long after the first three pirate ships made the error of sailing into our bay, my brothers, my father and I discovered Hezaraht had managed to infiltrate the palace by buying many people—some whom had worked here for years. In the process of weeding the traitors out we uncovered an extensive list of those who could not be bought—a list of untouchables. It is my pleasure to speak every single guard in the palace was found on the untouchable list and not all of the Sun Priest's blandishments or bribes could touch even one of you or your brothers. I would like to give you the honor you all deserve;" and he bowed deeply to the guardsmen with his hands on each shoulder. He held this position for just a moment and then straightened back up. "You who stand guard at the Emperor's door so faithfully may now permit all to enter or leave at their need and you may return to your regular duties."

The guards did as they were commanded by their emperor. But now each man stood a little straighter, and held his head a little higher, and the captain of the guards as well as the three princes also bowed to them and then everyone headed out to obey the commands the Greatest Mayan gave them.

Inca's brothers, H'ratli and Imhoquotep, stayed at his side because there was nothing else that they could do at the moment. "That thing you just did, Inca, is only one of many reasons why I like you so much; you never miss a chance to give a man a pat on the back when he's earned one," H'ratli said.

"I admit that a pat on the back is not as dramatic as a kick in the crotch, but from where I stand, it's more appreciated by the one who receives it." Both men nodded their heads but neither laughed—there were too many grim things going on to find much humor in anything at the moment.

Inca looked around; several servants stood back, waiting orders, including the one who had been sent to him originally and who had proved to be very devoted to his father. He turned to him. "It appears things are about to get interesting. Perhaps this would be a good time for you to dress me."

"Yes, Greatest Mayan," the servant said. Dressing him was more involved than returning the things to him he held before. The servants moved in on him and in short order they had him stripped nude and then dressed him from the floor up. Everything was made to Royal standards and everything fit perfectly: this was obviously planned well in advance. By the time soldiers and guardsmen started filtering in; he was dressed as the Emperor from the skin out, and looked every inch the Ruler of a great and powerful nation. Son of Spain walked in with Quoholocet and both stopped and stared in wonder.

"*Patrón;*" the Spaniard said in his own tongue, "*what is happening, and why are you dressed this way?*"

"*My father, the emperor, is dead; killed by his own healer at the order of Hezaraht. We are going to pay a visit to Hezaraht to remind him I promised to kill him if he didn't leave the children alone and didn't keep his hands off of my father;*" he said in Spanish and then switched back to Mayan. "You are invited to come along with your Precious if you so desire and you have my permission to call me '*Patrón*' as long as you wish."

"Yes, *Patrón*; yes, Greatest Mayan; I have always been yours to command: speak and it shall be done;" and Son of Spain bowed deeply before him as befitting his rank.

By now the room was getting crowded with heavily-armed men; he looked toward the priest who had decided to be helpful. "What I now require of you is to take us to this secret entrance and show us how to enter it. You will then lead us to the way which leads to Hezaraht; if there is more than one passage. If you obey my commands, and serve me well this day, I promise before Father Viracocha you shall not be killed or harmed; what is your decision?"

"I obey; Greatest Mayan. I never did truly wish to serve the Sun Priests but I was useful to them and because I have the heart of a coward they were able to make me obey. I think that is why Hezaraht trusts me as much as he does; because I am terrified of him. But now I have found one who scares me even more."

There was in the man's eyes that which showed Inca he was speaking the absolute truth and he vowed deep within no matter what occurred; this one would not be harmed if he could prevent it because a man cannot help what he is born.

They headed out of the door in a long string of men, lead by their Emperor and the three Sun Priests; the spokesperson for the group had not spoken since Inca kicked him. This man did not serve Hezaraht out of fear, but because of love for power, wealth and the suffering of the weak and innocent. As such, he knew he was a dead man walking, and his mind was already withdrawing into himself as the inevitability of his death loomed ever closer.

Someone brought a great many oil-fired torches and these were passed out to every fifth man and were then lit. The priest led them down first one corridor and then a second and they ended up in the same hallway where the four priests had attacked Cuauhtémoc nearly four years back. He stopped and turned into the shallow shadowed area Inca had noticed and commented on. He went to the bare wall, stood upon one stone, moved his left foot to a second stone, pressed his left hand against a brick in the wall and the entire wall swung quietly inward: a long series of narrow stairs led downward into a narrow dank tunnel that led towards the south.

They walked under the streets of the city, headed in the direction of the Great Pyramid and the domain of the Sun Priests, lead by one who found someone who frightened him more than Hezaraht ever would. In time they came to a fork in the tunnel; one led upward straight ahead and the second turned upward to the right. "This is where the path splits, Greatest Mayan. The one straight ahead leads to the commons room where most of the other priests are except when they are above. The right leads to the place where our guardsmen are; but I must tell you that most of the guards have left us. Hezaraht refuses to pay what he promised them and always leaves them months behind in their pay so they will not leave without their gold, but nearly all have left anyway, for many reasons. There is yet a third set of stairs that leads to the left and these stairs go directly to Hezaraht's personal quarters. The entryway is hidden, but once he brought a group of priests out this way, and I saw how the thing is done; what is your desire?"

Cuauhtémoc turned to those who clustered close around him and also heard the priest's words. "Quoholocet; I want you to take a group of guardsmen straight ahead. Captain; you are to take a second group to the right. This priest and I will take this hidden entryway to the left. I want you to stand here," he said, picking out the guard who was closest; you are to send the next five guards after me; the following five after Quoholocet and the third five after the Captain, and keep repeating this over and over until we run out of guards. If we wait at the respective doors until we have enough men, the shock of seeing us entering without warning will no doubt do most of the work for us; I have spoken and it is so."

He waited until he had at least ten guards waiting on him and then he nodded to the helpful priest; "I am ready; do what you must to get us in." The priest stepped on and pushed a combination of stones as before and again a door slid quietly aside. There was a long set of stairs leading upwards to a cloth curtain and he could hear Hezaraht say—

CHAPTER 27

"**N**ow then my pretties; once we get you up on the roof I will be cutting your hearts out one by one. Yes, I know it will no doubt hurt, but only for awhile; and then you will find oblivion." There were the sounds of children crying and whimpering in terror. Cuauhtémoc took the helpful priest by the arm gently and whispered quietly in his ear; the man listened, nodded and grinned.

He walked through the curtain, stopping Hezaraht in mid-gloat.

"What are you doing here?" the High Priest screeched in fury; "you will suffer a thousand deaths before you die for this outrage!"

"I have brought The Birdman, just as you have always wanted," the priest replied without a trace of fear in his face and Cuauhtémoc swept the curtain aside and stepped into the room, followed by one Royal Guardsman after another.

"Surprised to see me, Hezzie old boy?" he asked, trying to put a British accent into Mayan words: it worked; after a fashion. The High Priest stared at Cuauhtémoc, dressed as the Greatest Mayan, and suddenly understood his plan had failed and his time was done. He turned to flee but Cuauhtémoc was waiting for that exact moment, and as the terrified man started to run, he flipped the gold scepter lazily at him. It swapped ends twice and struck flat in the middle of the man's back with the larger and heavier end cracking him on the base of his skull. Hezaraht went down into a limp pile and twitched feebly.

"Bind him, but don't hurt him otherwise, because he is mine."

He looked around. There were many children within a fairly large room. With the exception of the deposed priest; there had been no other adults. Evidently, when Hezaraht terrorized children, he wasn't brave enough to do it in front of witnesses.

"Great One; are you truly The Birdman?" one boy about nine asked, looking up at him solemnly.

Cuauhtémoc looked down at the child and then removed his headdress; revealing the feathered-looking haircut he had worn for nearly four years now. "Yes," he said, "I am The Birdman."

The boy looked at the other children and said, "It's all right, we don't have to be afraid anymore. My Da says; 'there's no need to fear when The Birdman is near.'"

He felt tears start to run down his face. Without actually looking, he handed his headdress to the priest, and dropped to one knee and took the child in his arms and hugged him close. Within a few heartbeats all of the children ringed him and he was doing his best to hold and love them all. Once he got the young ones calmed down and allayed their fears he turned to the guardsmen who stood next to him. "It is my wish all of these are taken back to the palace by the way we came and given to the serving-women that they may be cleaned up and fed, and once these things are done, we will make every effort at returning each of them back to their rightful place."

"Yes, Greatest Mayan," the guard said and his eyes looked suspiciously damp.

The Priest handed the headdress back to Cuauhtémoc and looked into his eyes. "I don't think I'm afraid of you anymore, Greatest Mayan, but I still want to serve in any way I can. How is this possible?" he asked with a confused expression on his face.

"It is always better to serve because of love than fear or hate; perhaps you are starting to learn this." He took his headdress and put it back on his head. The guards bound Hezaraht and lifted him to his feet; the twisted little man seemed dazed, his mind unable to make the sudden adjustment. He turned to the priest at his side. "I wish you to show me the ways to where the other priests and guards are and then take me to the great pyramid because Hezaraht and I have unfinished business there."

"It shall be as you command, Greatest Mayan," the priest said; and it was.

It was a bloodless coup so far. The priests surrendered in fear at the unexpected arrival of Royal Guardsmen and their Emperor and Crown Princes; the Sun's Guards surrendered in disgust because they had no reason to fight; they weren't being paid as agreed and they had come to understand they'd been deceived all along.

In time, all of the priests that could be found and their guards as well as all of Cuauhtémoc's people, were gathered on top of the great pyramid. There was a gong there and the Emperor's pet priest went over and beat out the signal that was meant to draw the attention of the people. At the sound, men and women started gathering, as they had been doing for all of their lives and the lives of all of their ancestors: they stood and gaped upwards because instead of the twisted form of the Sun's High Priest, the Greatest Mayan stood at the top of the steps and looked down upon them.

"Come closer, my children, come closer; you shall not be harmed. I am Cuauhtémoc, also called The Birdman, and I am now your Emperor. I have sworn a vow before Father Inti to destroy the Sun Priests because they murder the innocent in His Name and I find this intolerable. Come closer, so you may see with your own eyes and hear with your own ears, that the Sun Priests are no more."

The people moved in closer and murmured among themselves: "Can this be true? Can this actually be happening at last?"

His guards brought Hezaraht forward; they placed his headdress upon him so the people would recognize him even at a distance. The guards pushed him to his knees, facing the crowd of people who were growing larger with every passing moment. "You will recall, Hezaraht, I commanded you to not touch the children anymore and to leave the Greatest Mayan alone. I told you specifically if you obeyed, I would spare your life, but if you disobeyed then it would be your blood which flowed down the steps of the pyramid, followed by your grotesque head: you do remember do you not?" There was no reply because the High Priest was so gone in terror he could not speak.

He turned to the cowardly priest and beckoned him over and handed the gold scepter and scythe to him. "I have a job for you to do. I want you to line all of these priests up in order of rank and I want you to hold these things for me so all will under-stand you act under my authority." The priest took the items and held them as he was shown and bowed deeply. He turned to the Captain of the Royal Guards who stood nearby along with his brothers and Son of Spain. "I find I must again ask for the use of your sword, Captain," he said politely. The Captain bowed deeply and since he already held his sword in his hand he laid it on the palms as he did before and held it out. Cuauhtémoc did not take it by the hilt, but placed his hands beside that of his officer and raised the sword and turned and held the blade up to the sun, as an offering.

He lifted his face to the sun and spoke: "Behold, Father Inti; see that I obey you and keep my vow to you; even as you keep your vows to all." He bowed deeply and touched his right knee to the stone of the pyramid and held it there for a moment and then stood erect. "Bend that one over so I may fulfill my promise to Father Viracocha," he said. He stood just to the right of the terrified man and focused himself. Inside his mind he saw the sword's descent through the Sun Priest's neck and a moment later he did it: the High Priest's blood jetted from the stump of his neck, spraying blood down the pyramid's steps and his ugly head rolled down afterwards one step at a time.

He turned to the Captain and gently placed the point of the sword onto the stone roof and held it in place with a single finger on the hilt. "I will yet have more use for this Captain, but for now, please take care of it for me." He turned and took a spear from a nearby soldier and walked down the steps where the head came to rest; he thrust the spear through the open mouth hard enough the point came out the back of the head: he turned to the nearest citizen.

"I have a task for you," he said. "It is my wish you carry this head throughout the northern part of the city and show it to everyone you meet, and I want you to speak the Sun Priests are no more. They have lied and deceived their Emperor, they have lied and deceived their Great Princes, and they have lied and deceived the people of Maya; but no more. Is this a thing that you can do?"

"It is already done, Greatest Mayan," the man said and bowed deeply; placing his hands on opposite shoulders. Even as the man worked his way through the gathering crowd he held Hezaraht's head aloft and was already speaking the words his Emperor had said.

By the time Cuauhtémoc was done, eight heads bobbed about in eight different directions, while their owner's bodies were stripped nude and rowed out of the bay to join the pirates who preceded them.

He turned to the altar that was stained with the blood of innocents. "It is my will this stone be broken up into many pieces. No piece shall be greater than my fist and no piece smaller than my thumb. When this is done, I want these pieces carried throughout Maya and a piece given to every city and every town and every village no matter how small, and in every case these people are to be told the same thing. The Sun's Priests are no more and they shall never again take children away to be murdered by a demented group, who were intended to serve the people, not prey upon them." He bent down and picked up one of the sacrificial knives and used the point to draw a square about the size of his hand on the eastern-most corner. "I want this piece to be taken out first and brought to me, that I may see it is being done, and then I intend to send it to my grandfather that he may also know it has been done."

He looked at the remaining priests and sun-guards and regarded them calmly. "I am now aware the lies and deceit of Hezaraht was not limited to the palace and populace and that many of you were also lied to and deceived. It is my wish you take chisels and hammers and break this altar up as I have spoken. If you are faithful to do these things, you shall have earned my forgiveness, and you will be permitted to leave this place and take up jobs wherever you wish and you shall not carry any other shame: this is my command;" he raised his hands and clapped three times and it was so.

He made his way back to the palace, surrounded by his brothers, Son of Spain, the guards and the once-cowardly priest who seemed to have gone through a magical trans-formation and was no longer a priest or afraid. They climbed the stairs and exited into the hallway and headed back towards the chambers where the Emperor laid awaiting entombment. They just rounded the first right turn when the one who served the Emperor so faithfully for the last few years, rushed up to him, frantic.

"Please; you must come immediately; he has been demanding to know where you are and when you are returning and he's driving me crazy with his words."

"Who is?" Inca asked, puzzled.

"The Greatest Mayan . . . I mean the Emperor . . . that is . . . your Father!"

"My Father is dead!" he said bluntly, displeased at the servant's words.

"No! That is what I am trying to speak. Within heartbeats after you left, he sat up in bed and spewed like a geyser, and ever since he's been demanding to know—"

The servant was abruptly talking to Inca's back. Somehow, the Greatest Mayan squirted out from under his robe and headdress, and these joined the scythe and scepter and sandals on the floor in a heap because Inca was no longer wearing them. For just a moment they could see him as he rounded a corner and then he was out of view.

The servant raised his hand because he was the one who liked to explain things, but Prince H'ratli touched the servant's shoulder, stopping him before he began. "Don't bother trying to catch him," he said, "once he gets into one of these moods it can't be done. Father Inti knows I've tried but it's not possible." The servant and the ex-priest picked up the items their Emperor shed and at a far more reasonable rate they followed him into the Emperor's bedroom.

They found him on his knees beside his father's bed, laughing and crying and holding and kissing his father's hand, all but incoherent in his excitement. "—but Father, don't you see, I'll make a terrible Emperor; I no sooner took over for you and I had a tantrum and look what happened!"

"Yes, let's do," Prince Quoholocet said. He was standing just inside the doorway, leaning against the wall with his arms folded across his chest, while he watched his youngest brother and father as they talked. "You were Emperor no more than a few breaths when you discovered that the death—pardon me, presumed death—was not of age as the rest of us believed but a deliberate attempt at murder. Soon after that, you not only discovered who the culprits were but developed a plan for punishing the guilty that not only eliminated the Sun Priests, who we've been trying to get rid of for decades, but managed to save—how many children was it?"

Cuauhtémoc thought for a moment; "Eleven," he said.

"Eleven children then; and you see how easily you came up with the proper number? None of us could have done that without going and finding the children and counting noses. You even managed to turn one of the priests upon his own brethren; creating a valuable ally in the process."

"Well; sure; anything sounds good when you put it like that," he said and wiped his tear-streaked face with the heel of his hand, but he was smiling as he did so.

"Then it is settled," the old man said, "I shall have my servants move me out of your room today and then you can—"

"No, Father, this room is yours and shall remain so until you leave us forever."

"It is my wish—" the old Emperor said with a battle-gleam in his eyes.

"No! I forbid it! I am now the Greatest Mayan and I have spoken and it is so." He clapped his hands three times and the old Emperor laid his head back into his pillow and laughed softly.

He turned to the three Princes. "You see my Sons; if Cuauhtémoc will not back down before me he will not back down before anyone. Father Inti was right when he guided him into our lives four years back and I shall never speak otherwise."

It was decided. The aged Emperor would stay in his own room, surrounded by familiar things and servants, until Father Inti decided to call him into his starry world once and for all. Cuauhtémoc visited with his father and brothers and introduced his father to the priest who was no longer so. Inca offered the man a job in the palace as one of his personal servants and he all but fell over himself in his eagerness to accept. Many fists later he left and headed back to his own room, his thoughts on the day's events, and the surprising outcome. He walked through the door and was promptly mobbed by his wives and the Mother serving-woman and her daughters because they had been waiting most of the day for his return. "What happened; Inca?" his wives began and then realized he wore the headdress and apparel of the Greatest Mayan.

"First things first," he said, "I am very hungry; go and get some trays of food and bring them back and then I will tell you everything." While the serving-women obeyed, he spent the time cuddling his wives, but he refused to tell them anything until the women returned, with what seemed to be half of the kitchen's staff. He invited them in, moved everyone out into the garden area, and over the next fist of the sun, told them everything; from the death of their Emperor to discovering he was still alive.

The three brothers decided Cuauhtémoc had done enough for one day so they made sure he was left alone with his wives. The three did all the usual things young marrieds do and by the time night had fallen he was on his back, in his bed, with two beautiful young girls cuddled up against him, their arms formed an X across his chest and their legs were intertwined with his. Tomorrow he would be sixteen: he slept.

He found himself on a beautiful beach with white sand spread as far as the eyes can see and nowhere was there spot or blemish or hideous red streak and the ocean's water was peaceful and calm. As he stood, the sun left its position and moved before him, and once again he looked upon the form of Viracocha.

"Greatest One," he said, bending his right knee to the sand, "I have done what I said I would and have kept my vow to the best of my ability."

"Yes, my child, and now I have come to keep my vow to you. Speak what your heart desires, and if it is within my power to give, it shall be yours."

"I have no further needs, Greatest One, because you have filled me to overflowing with your love and kindness; how could I think to ask for more?"

"There is nothing your heart wants; Cuauhtémoc?"

He looked up into the face of his God; he could not see anymore than the outline of his face but he could see his eyes and saw the kindness and love that was within. "I could use a hug, Great Viracocha," he admitted shyly.

Being hugged by the Uncreated Creator is like no other hug has ever been or can ever be and his face shone like the stars forever afterwards. Those who loved him and were pure in heart only saw a greater beauty; but those whose heart's held evil would scream and throw their arms over their eyes and try to flee in terror. This made cleaning the remaining driftwood out of the palace incredibly easy.

Still not . . .
The End
Continued in;
CUAUHTÉMOC: Descendant of the Jaguar

9 781990 695957